Praise for Evangeline Anderson's
Wishful Thinking

"Ms Anderson has created a fast paced story with intriguing characters who engage the reader from the start.... I will be waiting for the next installment of The Swann Sisters Chronicles."

~ *Teresa, Fallen Angel Reviews*

"The really wonderful thing is that even though this book is laugh-out-loud hilarious, it doesn't lack one bit of the erotic heat Ms. Anderson's fans have come to expect...WISHFUL THINKING is a sweet and funny erotic romance that will alternately have you in stitches and squirming in your seat. I cannot wait for the next edition of this magical series!"

~ *Wild on Books*

Look for these titles by
Evangeline Anderson

Now Available:

The Swann Sisters Chronicles
Wishful Thinking *(Book 1)*

Coming Soon:

Str8te Boys

The Swann Sisters Chronicles
Be Careful What You Wish For *(Book 2)*

Wishful Thinking

Evangeline Anderson

A SAMHAIN PUBLISHING, LTD. publication.

Samhain Publishing, Ltd.
577 Mulberry Street, Suite 1520
Macon, GA 31201
www.samhainpublishing.com

Wishful Thinking
Copyright © 2009 by Anderson, Evangeline
Print ISBN 978-1-60504-409-5
Digital ISBN: 978-1-60504-242-8

Editing by Angela James
Cover by Natalie Winters

First Samhain Publishing, Ltd. electronic publication: November 2008
First Samhain Publishing, Ltd. print publication: September 2009

Dedication

To Eve—I couldn't have made it through this year without
you.

Love, Sis

Chapter One

How do you ditch your fairy godmother?

Philomena Zara Swann wished she knew. She was turning twenty-five the next day and her two younger sisters had thoughtfully decided to take her to a pre-birthday strategy session at The Garden of Eatin', a trendy south Tampa bistro that specialized in vegetarian cuisine. They were seated outside despite the late June heat, under a large green umbrella that cast just enough shade to keep the early afternoon sun at bay.

"So, are you ready for your birthday? Got a wish all picked out?" Cass wrinkled her perfect button nose and her vivid violet eyes sparkled with mischief.

"Oh, God, I've been wracking my brain for days and I still have zilch. I just hope you guys can help." Phil dropped into a chair across from her sisters with a groan. The idea of making a wish for her twenty-fifth birthday was more than just silly talk. In her family, it was serious business. When you had an actual fairy godmother to grant your birthday wishes, you'd better be prepared with something good to wish for. Or at least something that wouldn't screw up your life forever.

Phil looked down at the field-greens-and-strawberry salad her sisters had ordered for her and hoped they could come up with something. Sunday was half over and she would be in no shape to think of a suitable wish while she was busy at work tomorrow.

"Remember that time you wished that all your Barbie's clothes would fit you?" Rory, the youngest of the three flipped her long red hair over one shoulder. Its brilliant ruby color clashed with her orange T-shirt but since there was also dog and cat hair on her jeans from volunteering at the local animal shelter, it didn't really matter.

"Hush, you're not even old enough to remember that. You were only four when I made that wish." Phil frowned at her little sister and reached up to make sure a sudden gust of wind hadn't disarranged her own hair, gathered at the nape of her neck in a severe bun. It was a long waterfall of platinum blond when she let it down, but she almost never did.

"Yeah, but I've heard about it often enough." Rory, whose real name was Aurora Tatiana, laughed, her green eyes glowing with glee.

"Yup, Phil thought it would be cool to wear Barbi's tutu and live in the big pink dream house Nana bought her." Cass, short for Cassandra Esmeralda, pushed her tangle of dark curls away from her lily white forehead. As usual, she was dressed from head to toe in black, which emphasized her dramatic coloring. "She just didn't think about the fact that being twelve inches high for the rest of her days might put a serious crimp in her social life."

It was typical of their fairy godmother's magic that instead of enlarging the Barbie clothes to fit Phil, it had shrunk her down to the size of a plastic bimbo doll instead. Magic tended to be very exact and their godmother was lazy with her application of it, probably because she resented having three fairy goddaughters with hardly a drop of real fairy blood in their veins.

Their great grandfather had been a full blooded fairy who fell in love with a human woman and then his daughter, the girls' Nana, had fallen in love with a human man and further diluted the family's magical blood. By the time their mother, who was only one fourth fairy, had also married a pure human with no fairy or fae blood, there was no getting the bloodline back to full strength. And at this point, being only one-eighth fairy, Phil and her sisters wouldn't even be allowed into the Realm of the Fae, where the full-blooded fairies and other magical creatures lived, to find a fairy husband. Not that any of them wanted to.

As far as Phil was concerned, nothing good had ever come of their dubious heritage. She had often thought being one-eighth fairy was like barely belonging to any other minority group—you might get some of the perks but you were bound to get all of the hassles as well.

"Anyway, she reversed the magic," she mumbled, looking up at the sunny sky which showed signs of clouding over. If it got much darker, her eyes wouldn't match the pale blue blouse she had on anymore which would be a shame.

Eyes that match the sky above
Hair like gold, the sunbeams love
Lips that shame the reddest rose
Beauty will grace her wherever she goes

Those were the words spoken over her at birth by her fairy godmother. The spell had shaped her appearance and in some ways, her entire life. Not that she had asked to have eyes that changed with the weather and lips so red she had to wear neutral lipstick to hide their true color, Phil thought resentfully. Her hair was long and silky but too light in her opinion. Also it had a tendency to sparkle, as though the sun was shining on it whether she was outside or not. Their fairy godmother's magic hid the more obvious aspects of itself fairly well—for instance, no one without fairy or fae blood in their veins was able to notice that her eyes changed colors—but Phil kept her sparkly hair up as much as possible just in case.

Her sisters had received similar gifts at birth—Cass's verse had gone:

Skin as pale as fallen snow
Eyes like dewy violets glow
Hair as black as coal at night
She'll always walk in Beauty's light

Of course, having snow white skin, bright purple eyes and hair as black as coal meant Cass looked permanently Goth. But since she was an artist and the dramatic one in the family, it didn't seem to bother her. In fact, she consistently dressed all in black to play up her pale skin and vivid eyes although Phil didn't know how she could stand to wear it in the middle of the summer. Despite being the middle sister, she probably had the strongest personality of the three of them, including a quick temper that matched her artistic nature. She was both a painter and a sculptor and her work was just beginning to sell at some of the smaller galleries around town, much to Cass's relief. She hated the various menial jobs she had to work in order to get enough money for her raw materials.

Rory, the youngest sister at nineteen, had gotten a verse

too.

> *Hair from purest rubies spun*
> *Eyes like emeralds in the sun*
> *A voice like songbirds in the spring*
> *Beauty to her form shall cling*

All in all Phil thought her baby sister looked the most normal of the three. Her bright red hair and green eyes were striking without crossing the line into bizarre. Of course, if she tried to sing, all that came out was a warbling, cheeping sound since their fairy godmother's magic was extremely literal. So joining the chorus was definitely out. Luckily Rory, who was in her first year of college, wanted to be a veterinarian.

Despite their physical differences, they were very close—so much so that Phil really didn't feel the need for any girlfriends outside her own family. But no one would ever guess the three of them were even remotely related—let alone sisters. She often wondered what they all might have looked like without their fairy godmother's early interference. Would they all have frizzy brown hair and blue eyes?

"The FG only reversed that Barbie wish after I bitched at her," Cass said, breaking Phil's train of thought. She picked up a grape and popped it in her mouth. Phil knew the Garden of Eatin's vegetarian menu wasn't her standard fare since she was a confirmed carnivore but according to Cass, the fruit plate was better than a fake-tasting "veggie burger".

"It's a good thing I was there to make her change it, too," she continued, wrinkling her nose at a piece of pineapple. "She's so damn lazy, never wants to change anything for us little half-breeds."

"More like eighth-breeds," Rory put in with a sigh. "I wish we had enough fairy blood to do some magic of our own."

"Well, we don't," Cass said. "Not even Nana has enough to do real magic—not that she'll ever give up."

Their grandmother was half fairy which was just enough to make her flighty and eccentric but not enough to give her any control over what little power she possessed. Their father had run off not long after Rory was born and their mother had been killed in a car accident, so Nana had raised the three of them. Phil was eight, Cass was six, and Rory was barely two when they came to live with their sweet but erratic Nana in her big lavender house on States Street.

"Oh, no," Phil muttered, biting her lip. "Don't tell me she's at it again." Nana seemed to attract trouble the way honey draws flies.

"With a vengeance." Cass speared the unoffending pineapple on the end of her fork. "She's into the Craft now—didn't Rory tell you?"

"No." Phil stared accusingly at her youngest sister. "Why didn't you call me? Everyone knows fairy magic and witchcraft don't mix! They're like oil and water."

Cass snorted indelicately. "More like mixing nitro and glycerin. Stand back and wait for the explosion."

"That's not the point," Phil said. "The point is, what if Nana gets herself into trouble again? And why didn't you one of you tell me?"

"I tried to call you but you never answer your cell," Rory complained. "You're always either at work or off entertaining Christian's important clients. Or maybe you were busy planning the wedding of the year. Have you set a date yet?"

Phil sighed and went back to picking at her salad. "Not yet. Christian says he needs time to get settled in with his new firm before he takes time off for a wedding." In the past year she'd begun to wonder if her fiancé was ever going to set a date but she wished her sisters wouldn't start in about it.

"And before *that*, he needed to finish law school," Cass said, frowning. "And before *that*—" She broke off, shaking her head. "What you need to wish for this year is a spine, Phil. Make that man commit."

"Leave Phil alone," Rory said. "She can't help it the FG made her meek as a sheep."

"The phrase is 'A lamb's mild nature, sweet and kind'," Phil cut in, deciding she didn't need rescuing:

"A lamb's mild nature, sweet and kind,

Forgiveness she will ever find

Within her heart so full of love

As gentle as the cooing dove

Which doesn't mean I'm spineless—it just means I'm easy going."

"You are *not* easy going." Cass pointed her fork in Phil's

13

direction. "In fact, you're one of the most uptight people I know, Phil. But you let people walk all over you."

"No, I don't," Phil protested. She had always resented the fact that their fairy godmother had decided to tamper with her personality as well as her outward appearance, but it didn't make her a doormat. "Just because I don't grab life by the throat and choke it like you doesn't mean I don't enjoy myself. I'm just a little more...well..."

"Repressed," Cass finished for her.

"I was about to say reserved." Phil patted the corners of her mouth with her napkin and arched an eyebrow at her younger sister.

"Too bad you can't just wish Christian would pop the question for your birthday," Rory said with a sigh.

"You know the rules," Phil pointed out. "The wish can't permanently affect anyone but the wisher, you can't wish for more wishes, and the magic keeps you from telling anyone outside the family about it directly, no matter what the result." That last one was especially tough. Phil had often wished she could explain the dire consequences of a backfired wish but it didn't do any good to try. No one without at least a drop of fairy or fae blood in their veins could hear what she was trying to say when she attempted to explain about the magic. It sounded like buzzing or humming to them or else it slipped their attention and they changed the subject and started talking about something else entirely.

"Speaking of rules and regulations, what is your straight-laced fiancé doing for your birthday this year?" Cass asked, signaling the waiter for more wine. "Maybe removing the stick from his ass so you two can have some fun for once? Now *that* would be a reason to celebrate."

Phil flushed. "I don't know what he's doing yet. It's a surprise."

"Like last year? 'Surprise, I forgot?'" Cass made a face as the waiter filled her glass with more Chablis.

"He didn't forget," Rory protested. "He sent the most beautiful bouquet of pink roses with one perfect red rose bud in the middle. It was so *romantic.*"

"Christian didn't send those," Cass said flatly. "Josh did."

"Oh, I just assumed it was Christian. But Josh? Josh the

cute guy from your office, Josh?" Rory lost interest in her sweet potato fry and looked up. "I saw that picture you two took together at your last office Christmas party—he's hot. Those big brown eyes and that sweet smile. Mmm." She smiled dreamily.

"I saw that picture too," Cass remarked. "Rory's right. And I thought I saw some muscle definition too. He may be your office computer nerd but I bet he's hiding a Brad Pitt body under those baggy business clothes, Phil."

"He's my best friend." Phil looked down and twisted the diamond engagement ring Christian had given her four years before around her finger. "I mean, I don't notice things like that any more than he notices me...that way. He sent the roses because he knew I was feeling down, that's all. Josh is thoughtful like that."

"Well, it was still a romantic gesture," Rory insisted.

"No, it was a gesture of friendship," Phil said firmly. "That's what pink roses mean—*friendship*. Anyway, he didn't even pick them out. He just called the order in because he could tell I was feeling bad. Besides, Christian made up for forgetting my birthday. You should have seen how bad he felt—I mean, he almost cried and that's saying a lot for him." She gestured with her fork, trying to make her sisters understand. Christian and Cass had hated each other almost from the start. As for Rory, she was too hung up on the picture she'd seen of Josh to appreciate Christian's finer qualities—not that Phil could always remember them herself, especially in the past year when things with her fiancé seemed to be going all wrong.

"Almost cried, huh?" Cass asked dryly. "My, my, that certainly doesn't sound like Mister By-the-Book Unemotional Attorney to me."

"Well, it's *true*," Phil protested. "He took me out to an expensive restaurant even though we really couldn't afford it. *And* he bought me the most beautiful dress and he even got the size right."

"Oh—he got it right because he called and asked me and Nana," Rory put in. "But you're right, Phil. It was a sweet gesture."

"He had to call and ask? He never said..." Phil frowned determinedly. "Look, the point is that whether you want to see it or not, Christian is handsome and intelligent and—"

15

"And close minded and boring," Cass interrupted. "But hey, I'm not the one who's going to marry him. Of course at the rate you're going, you won't be either, Phil."

"Enough." Phil held up a hand. "We're not here to discuss my wedding even though Christian and I *are* planning to set a date very soon. We're here to plan a strategy for my birthday wish. I need your help, guys. Twenty-five is a big one and you know birthdays that end in odd numbers are especially bad. The magic gets stronger somehow and when the person who's waving the wand doesn't care about the consequences..."

"Disaster," Cass said and Rory nodded sympathetically.

"Exactly," Phil said, pointing at Cass with her fork. "Just look what happened to you on your fifteenth birthday."

"Oh, wasn't that the year you wished for porno titties?" Rory asked in a voice loud enough that the senior citizens at the next table glared at them.

"Shout it next time, why don't you?" Cass hissed. "And no, I did *not* wish for 'porno titties'."

"What she wished for was to have breasts exactly as big as Christy Seaton's." Phil felt a smile creeping over the corners of her mouth. "She was a girl in my class—couple years ahead of Cass, and she always had the cutest boyfriends for...ah, some pretty obvious reasons. The only problem was, the FG thought Cass had asked for breasts as big as Trixie Teetons, the adult film star." She grinned. "Boy, was that a mess."

Cass sighed. "Yeah, I looked like a toothpick with two cantaloupes. Had to go around like that for a whole week too, until the FG finally agreed to take it back."

"You'd think she'd realize that a fifteen year old doesn't want a double G bra size." Rory shuddered and glanced down at her own chest.

"It's not so much that she doesn't realize, it's that she doesn't *care*," Cass said. "We're not full-blooded and we don't have wings or carry wands. We can't fly or do magic or disappear into puffs of pretty pink smoke. We're nothing but a pain in her sparkly ass that she has to deal with three times a year. And to her way of thinking, that's three times a year too many."

"So why doesn't she just leave us alone?" Rory demanded. "I've had enough of her gifts, anyway. Who wants to sounds like a bird when they try to sing?" She opened her mouth to demonstrate and let loose with a nightingale warble that made the waitress passing by stare. Cass kicked her under the table and she shut up abruptly.

"We've been over this time and again. Anyone with even a drop of fairy blood gets assigned a fairy godmother—kind of like being assigned an attorney in court if you can't afford one. The Fairy Council would have her wand if she stopped at least *pretending* to keep an eye on us," Phil said grimly. "So we're as stuck with her as she is with us. The FG is here to stay so I need to decide on a wish."

It was surprisingly hard to keep coming up with wishes that wouldn't backfire and ruin your life, as they had all discovered the hard way. Rory had once wished to be able to talk to dogs, and had been turned into a Schnauzer—not at all what she'd had in mind. Phil and Cass had an awful time hiding the disaster from their excitable Nana. They'd had to use their allowances to buy their baby sister dog food until their fairy godmother had finally bothered to show up and reverse her badly cast magic. And that was one of the *lesser* birthday wish disasters Phil could remember.

"What about a good parking spot everywhere you go?" Rory suggested.

"Did it." Cass raised a hand. "That was what I wished last year. We never go shopping without each other so that would be a wasted wish. Speaking of which, when are we going to go look for a new bathing suit for your office beach party, Phil? You know your old one is a write off because Nana accidentally bleached it."

"Can't be tomorrow because Christian probably has something planned for my birthday." Phil coughed self-consciously and her sisters let it pass. "And I can't do it Tuesday either. Maybe Wednesday since the pre-Fourth of July beach party is on Thursday." She took a sip of wine. "Now, come on—back to the wishes."

"Wish that your tea will always be hot, no matter how long you let it sit," Rory suggested.

"I did that my freshman year of college during finals when I was taking a summer semester. I didn't want to have to keep getting up to steep a fresh pot while I was studying," Phil said.

It had been one of her better wishes, actually. One of the few she didn't regret and hadn't had to beg their fairy godmother to reverse. Simple wishes worked the best, they had found. The more complicated a wish got, the more room for disaster there was.

"Well, what about—?"

"Excuse me, ladies." Their waiter, a nice-looking young man with a neatly clipped mustache and dark hair, was standing at Phil's elbow with a covered tray. He leaned toward her confidentially and she nearly groaned when he half lifted the lid and she saw what was on it.

"I heard you talking about a birthday and thought the lady might want dessert," he said, smiling at her politely. "Compliments of the house, of course."

"Of course," Phil said weakly, knowing there was no point in protesting.

"Ooo, what is it?" Rory, who had an insatiable sweet tooth, leaned over to look at the tray.

"What do you think it is?" Cass demanded. "It's what it always is."

"Oh." Rory looked disappointed and both sisters said in unison, "Éclair."

"Well...yes." The waiter lifted the tray completely, looking faintly surprised. He deposited the cold dish with its chocolaty, creamy treat in front of Phil, who tried to suppress a shudder at the sight.

She had made an ill thought-out birthday wish at the age of eight that she could have an éclair every day for the rest of her life. And ever since, no matter where she was or what she was doing, at some point before the clock struck midnight and the new day began, someone offered her an éclair. It might be a waiter, a family member or even a complete stranger on the street, but come what may, she got her éclair even though she had long since become thoroughly sick of them.

Once she had locked herself in the bathroom for the entire day and refused to come out, trying to avoid the gooey desert. It hadn't worked—the magic had compelled Cass to go to the bakery and use her allowance to buy one, even though she very much didn't want to. She had shoved it under the bathroom door complaining bitterly about people who didn't face up to the consequences of their wishes. Phil had never tried to hide from her daily éclair again.

Thanks goodness, she thought, looking down at the chocolate and cream confection, that she hadn't wished that she could actually *eat* an éclair every day of her life or she would have had to become bulimic by now. As soon as the waiter left she shoved the plate towards Rory who dug in philosophically. Chocolate was chocolate, as far as her little sister was concerned.

She glanced at her watch and saw that their pre-birthday planning session was almost over and she still hadn't gotten any good wish ideas. She had to think of something good, something small, something that wouldn't change her life forever...

Suddenly a muffled rendition of "Pachelbel's Canon" began to resound from inside her sensible black purse.

"Hey, Phil, your purse is ringing," Cass said smugly. Her own phone rang the X-men theme and Rory's changed according to who was calling her. Phil dug the cell out of her purse and glanced at the number.

"It's Christian. I'd better go."

"Honestly, before I'd let a man order me around like that..." Cass grumbled. Rory just shrugged, her mouth full of éclair.

"He's not ordering me—we have plans. And if you hadn't spent the whole strategy session dishing, *I'd* have a plan too," Phil groused. Her magically induced mild temperament insured that she never completely lost her cool, but she came closest with her annoying younger sister.

"Whatever. You better get the phone before Christian has a coronary. You know how he gets when he has to wait for anything," Cass said, raising an eyebrow at her.

Phil flipped open the phone.

"Hey, babe." Christian's voice filled her ear. "Look, I don't like to rush you when you're with your sisters but you know we have a big night planned tonight."

"Hi, hon." Phil suppressed a small sigh. She had gotten upset with her sisters for saying that she was always out "entertaining" her fiancé's important clients but it was the truth. Sometimes she wished that things could go back to the way they'd been before Christian graduated law school and got his job as a hotshot attorney. As crazy as it sounded, she kind of missed the nights when they just sat home and ate sandwiches together because they couldn't afford anything else. At least then they'd had time to talk—to really connect. In the past year since Christian had been working so hard all day and entertaining clients all evening, she felt like she hardly knew him anymore.

Phil pushed her disloyal thought to the back of her mind and tried to sound happy. "So who are we entertaining tonight? And where are we going?" she asked brightly.

"We're taking out Heidi and George Ghent. And I made reservations for four at Berns." He laughed and Phil winced. Berns was one of the most expensive and exclusive steak houses in Tampa. The restaurant had dry aged steaks and a wine list that was supposedly unequaled anywhere in the country. "Couldn't have afforded *that* this time last year, huh, Philly-babe?" Christian continued. "Gotta love that expense account. But as my senior partner says, the client is always right and that's where Ghent wanted to go. This could be a very important account for us."

"Sounds...wonderful," Phil said, hoping he couldn't hear the hesitation in her voice. It seemed like *every* client represented an important account but she had never dreamed that Christian would spend as much time wining and dining prospective clients as practicing law. Certainly that wasn't what she hoped to do when she got through law school herself. Phil intended to be a civil rights attorney and stand up for people whose rights were being trampled on. Somehow she didn't think most of her clients would be bigwigs who demanded to be taken to the most expensive restaurants in town.

"...so you need to get back here if you're gonna have time to get gorgeous for tonight." Christian's voice continued in her ear and Phil realized she had spaced out, daydreaming of her own future legal career.

"Oh, yeah?" she said, hoping he hadn't noticed her momentary lapse of concentration.

"Yeah," Christian said, apparently unaware that she had tuned him out. "I know how long it takes you ladies to get ready and don't say I'm being a sexist pig, either, Phil. You know it takes you twice as long as me to look ravishing."

"But I'm always *ravishing*," Phil reminded him. It was an old joke between them and Christian usually replied with a naughty come-on about exactly how much he wanted to "ravish" her.

But this time he just said, "Uh-huh. Look, babe, I got a few more things to take care of on my end. Will I see you soon?"

"You bet," Phil said, feeling deflated. But then, she couldn't expect him to remember every old joke they'd ever shared, could she? "I'm leaving right now," she told him. "See you soon. Love you."

"You too, babe. See ya."

"Bye." She closed the phone and stood up to gather her things. "I have to go."

Rory swallowed her mouthful of éclair hastily. "But we haven't thought of the perfect wish yet. You have to be careful, Phil! Don't forget the year you wished to always have on pretty shoes and then those spike heeled pumps were stuck on your feet for two weeks."

Cass snorted. "Yeah—pretty they were. Comfortable? Not so much."

Phil winced. "Don't remind me. It's a wonder I don't have fallen arches from *that* little wish fiasco." She leaned over and brushed a light kiss across her youngest sister's cheek. "But don't worry about me—I'll think of something."

"You better," Cass said grimly. "And you better have it ready by six fifteen tomorrow night—the exact time you were born. Or the FG will choose for you and you know what her choices are like." Sadly, they all did. One didn't have to look any farther than their dramatic hair and eyes, Rory's songbird voice and Phil's mild temperament to know that their fairy godmother was either completely out of touch with reality, or else watching way too much Disney Channel.

"Look, just keep an eye on Nana for me and call me if she gets into trouble," she said, bending to kiss Cass on the cheek as well. "And don't worry about me, all right? I'll be okay."

But she couldn't help feeling the tension sitting in her stomach like a cold éclair. Her birthday was coming and she was completely unprepared.

Chapter Two

"Guess what the flavor of the month is."

The voice on the other end of her cell phone perked Phil up considerably. She'd been moping on the sofa ever since they'd gotten home from the night out with Christian's clients at Berns. Or at least that was what Christian had called it—Phil called it feeling blue. And she couldn't help it—not considering the way her night had turned out. Especially when she'd been feeling so good at the beginning of the evening.

Even though their dinner company had been less than pleasant (Mister Ghent was a boor who liked to brag about his investments and Mrs. Ghent was a snob whose main conversation consisted of how hard it was to find a good maid service that wouldn't chip her Waterford crystal) Phil had still managed to have a good time.

On the ride home she'd snuggled up next to her fiancé, feeling the effects of the ungodly expensive vintage the client had ordered from Berns' famous wine list like a warm tingling in her veins. Champagne tended to make her silly and what Cass would call horny. Phil chose to think of it as amorous and since she couldn't remember the last time she and Christian had made love, it seemed like a good thing. But her fiancé hadn't felt the same way.

"Stop it, Phil. Can't you see I'm trying to drive?" he'd demanded when she nibbled his ear.

Since they were practically the only car on the back road he had chosen to take, it didn't seem like a big deal to Phil. "Come on, Christian," she'd murmured in her sexiest voice. "Loosen up. What's the worst that could happen?"

"We could get pulled over and I'd get a DUI," he'd growled irritably. "How would that look on my record? My career would go straight in the toilet, all because you couldn't keep your hands to yourself until we got home."

"Sorry." Phil had slid back to her side of the car with a sigh. Why was it lately that every time she wanted to make love Christian put her off? He was always too busy or preoccupied with work to have time for them. It made Phil feel sad and cut off from him, like there was a distance between them she couldn't bridge no matter how hard she tried—not that she would admit as much to Cass or Rory. In fact, she wouldn't have been admitting it to herself if she hadn't had several glasses of bubbly fizzing around inside her. Well, she told herself, maybe he was just concerned with his driving and he'd be in a better mood once they got back to their apartment.

Only he hadn't been. With barely a look at Phil, he'd brushed by her the moment she opened the door and went straight for the spare bedroom he'd designated as his study the day they moved in.

"Sorry Philly-Babe, lots of work to do," he'd thrown over his shoulder when she protested.

And that was how she'd wound up sitting on the couch, painting her toenails and feeling blue and neglected. Was it her imagination or were things just not right between her and Christian anymore? He seemed so preoccupied lately. Of course Phil knew he was doing demanding work but still, it seemed like he could have found *some* time to be with her. Well, maybe he was busy planning something big for her birthday. In which case she would gladly forgive him for tonight. She decided to put the whole thing out of her mind and concentrate on something else.

She knew she ought to be trying to think of a wish but her mind was still fuzzy from the champagne and she didn't feel like wracking her brains at the moment. Surely she would think of something before her birthday moment rolled around. Wouldn't she?

And that was when her phone rang, pulling her out of her blues.

"Guess the flavor," the familiar voice urged. "C'mon, Swann. It's one of your favorites."

"Uh...chocolate fudge mocha?" she guessed.

"Nope but warm. As warm as ice cream gets, anyway." Josh, her best friend from work chuckled. His deep voice warmed her, even across the phone.

"Peanut butter ripple," Phil said, putting down the bottle of nail polish and getting into it. This was a game she and Josh played every week when the flavors at I Scream, U Scream, one of their favorite hang-outs changed. It was supposed to be the flavor of the month but in actuality, it changed more often than that. Which was as good excuse as any to eat ice cream in Phil's opinion.

"Wrong again and cold, Swann. Really cold." Josh still sounded amused.

"Okay, something with chocolate then." Phil closed her eyes, trying to concentrate. The champagne buzz was wearing off now and she was feeling more like herself. "Uh, don't tell me. It's not...it can't be..."

"Love Potion Number Nine!" Josh finished for her. "Your favorite. Wanna get some? I can be there in five minutes to pick you up."

"Oh, I don't know, Josh..." Phil glanced at her watch to look at the time. "It's really late and besides, I don't know how Christian would feel if I left now."

"I'm sorry, Swann." His voice was subdued. "Am I uh, interrupting some kind of pre-birthday celebration? Were you two about to paint the town red?"

"Huh? Oh, no." Phil blushed even though she knew he couldn't see her. "Not unless painting my toenails red counts."

"Red toenails? Wow, hot stuff coming through. I better let you go then." Josh sounded like he was about to hang up but suddenly Phil didn't want him to.

"No, wait." She stood up, walking carefully on her heels so she wouldn't smudge her pedicure. "Let me just tell Christian I'm going out for a few minutes. I could use some Love Potion Number Nine right now." *In more than one way,* she told herself as she hobbled to the study door. But she pushed the thought aside. Her fiancé was just busy and preoccupied with work. Things would be better soon, she was sure. Just as soon as he got really settled in his job he wouldn't have to work so hard and they would get close again.

"Christian," she said as she opened the door. "Josh and I are going to go grab a snack from I Scream. You want anything?"

He was on the cell phone with someone and he turned to give her an irritated look. "Hang on a minute," he told whoever was on the other end. Then he frowned at Phil. "Now, what?"

She repeated herself adding, "They have Love Potion Number Nine right now. You want some?"

"No, babe. Go have fun and don't worry about me."

"Okay." She smiled at him. "Guess I'll see you later then."

"Yeah. Hey, don't wait up for me when you get back. I'm liable to be working on this stuff half the night." He indicated the stacks of paper he had strewn over his desk and ran a hand through his dark blond hair.

"Oh," Phil said in a small voice. "I thought...thought maybe you'd want to get to bed a little earlier tonight."

"Can't. Sorry, babe—too much work." Christian went back to his conversation, obviously not taking her hint, and Phil sighed. So much for a night of passionate love-making. Well, there was still chocolate ice cream with her best friend to look forward to. Now she was twice as glad Josh had called.

"So we're on?" Josh asked when she closed the door and brought the phone back to her ear.

"Oh, did you hear that?" Phil felt her cheeks growing red. She hoped Josh hadn't heard her ask Christian if he was coming to bed early. It was bad enough to be turned down by her fiancé, she didn't need an audience for her shame.

"Some of it," Josh said tactfully. "Just enough to know we're going. I'll be there in five—is that enough time for your toes to dry?"

"I'll go barefoot and we can just go through the drive through," Phil told him. "Meet you in front of the building, okay?"

"Sure. Bye." Josh hung up and she ran to get changed. Shimmying out of her evening dress and into a pair of jean shorts and a T-shirt without smearing her polish was a trick but Phil still managed to be waiting on the sidewalk when he arrived. The cement was still warm from the summer sun and she could feel it baking up through the soles of her feet when she hopped into his little hybrid.

"Looking good, Swann." He smiled at her as she buckled her seat belt. Josh Bowman was ridiculously tall with broad shoulders to match and shaggy thick brown hair that always looked in need of a haircut. He had big brown eyes and a charmingly lopsided grin with one crooked tooth right in front— not the classical features like Davis Miles, the hottest guy at her office, or sandy blond hair and piercing blue eyes like Christian, but there was something about his mismatched features that just seemed to work. Which was, doubtless, what had prompted Rory to call him "hot" after seeing his picture. Of course, Phil never thought of him as anything but a friend, but the open, easy way he talked and his warm laughter had drawn her to him from the start.

"In this?" Phil looked down at her plain blue T-shirt and shorts. "I'm hardly dressed for the opera at the moment."

"No, your hair. He gestured at her. "I almost never get to see you with your hair down."

"Oh." Phil put a hand to her long blond hair self-consciously but Josh was already talking about something else.

"So let me see the new sexy red toenails," he demanded as he pulled out of her apartment parking lot.

"Josh..." Phil laughed at him.

"No, seriously, let me see them." He patted the dash. "Put 'em up here."

Christian would have died if she'd dared to put her bare feet on the dashboard of his Lexus but Josh was easygoing enough that Phil didn't hesitate.

"There, happy?" she asked, propping her bare feet on the dashboard and wiggling her toes at him.

"More than happy. What hot little piggies." Josh made a lustful face at her toes and pretended to swerve as he leaned forward to look. "And tomorrow at work I'm the only one who'll know what's under those sensible black shoes of yours."

Phil giggled. "Didn't know you had such a foot fetish, Bowman."

"Oh, yeah, I'm big into foot porn," he said with a straight face. "And I have all these websites book marked, you know, like Kiss My Foot and Toe Bondage."

"And The Foot Forum," she said, getting into the game.

He nodded. "Oh, yeah—that's one of my favorites. And I have a subscription to *Penthouse Foot Letters.* Except all the letters seem to start, 'You're not going to believe this but it's true—the other night I was working late at the shoe store when this incredibly hot blonde with corns walked in and asked me for a foot massage. The next thing I knew she had chocolate syrup between every toe and whipped cream up to her ankles...'"

Phil was cracking up by this time. "Eww! Josh, you're too much. And why would anyone have chocolate syrup and whipped cream at a shoe store?"

He grinned at her. "I don't know—maybe the guy was going to make a banana split later. Shoe store employees like ice cream too, you know. Speaking of which, here we are. You want one scoop or two?"

Phil sat up, surprised that the drive had gone so quickly. Josh was already pulling into the drive through of I Scream, U Scream, ready to place their order.

"Uh, better just make it one," she said. "We were at Berns tonight and you know how rich the food is there."

"Entertaining more clients?" Josh knew all about the situation with Christian's job. Phil found him easy to talk to and not as quick to criticize as Cass and Rory usually were.

"Always." She sighed as he placed their order. I Scream was unusually quiet and they were able to pull through and get their order in a matter of minutes.

"You wanna eat it here or take it home?" Josh asked, passing her a plastic spoon and the little paper cup of ultra-premium ice cream.

Phil thought about sitting alone on the couch at home while Christian worked into the night. "Let's park," she decided, digging her spoon into the gooey chocolate lump in her cup. Love Potion Number Nine was basically frozen fudge dotted with tiny little chocolate cups filled with raspberry sauce. It was decadent and sinful but after the night she'd just suffered through, Phil figured she deserved it.

"You got it." Josh pulled into an empty space across from the small pink ice cream shop. "You're sure Christian won't mind me keeping you out late?"

"Huh? Oh, no." Phil shrugged. "Christian's not the jealous

type." It was true that at first she'd felt a little funny about doing the date-type things with Josh that she was used to do with her fiancé. But Cass and Rory weren't always available and Christian was busy working all the time lately. Also he genuinely didn't seem to mind. 'Go on and have fun, don't worry about me,' he always told Phil, so she did. It was easy to have fun with her best friend—Josh could always make her laugh even when she was blue.

"He's a little too trusting if you ask me," Josh said, putting the car into park and digging into his ice cream. "I mean, how does he know I don't have you out here sucking your sexy toes?"

"Josh!" Phil nudged him with an elbow and laughed. "He knows he can trust me because you and I are just friends."

"Friends with a foot fetish," Josh reminded her gravely. "For all your fiancé knows I could be licking chocolate sauce off your instep this minute."

"Enough already." Phil gave him a mock glare. "Is the only reason you got me out here to talk dirty?"

"Dirty?" He leaned over and looked at her feet. "I don't know, Swann. They look pretty clean to me." Phil pretended to hit him and he ducked. "All right, all right, I did have ulterior motives. I have something for you—kind of a pre-birthday gift."

Phil sat up in the seat, ice cream forgotten. "Josh, you shouldn't have."

"Sure I should." He smiled easily. "Besides, it's not any real big thing. I just burned you a CD. Here." He reached in front of her to open the glove box and Phil couldn't help noticing the warmth of his muscular arm against her side. He fumbled for a minute and then pulled out a flat green plastic case. "Here it is; I knew I stuck it in there somewhere. For you, my lady." He handed it to Phil with a flourish and she opened it excitedly. She loved getting little presents and loved Josh for knowing that about her. At least once a month he gave her some little trinket he'd found in a flea market or specialty store that he knew she'd like. It was never anything big—just little, thoughtful gifts that let her know Josh was thinking of her.

"Oh, the soundtrack from *Wicked!*" she exclaimed, looking at the CD. He'd even gone to the trouble of making a label for it with the original soundtrack's logo. "Thank you, Josh. I've been wanting this for ages." Ever since Rory had raved about seeing the touring production of the hit musical for her music appreciation class last semester, Phil had been longing to go herself. There was no point in asking Christian, though. Even if they could afford the tickets, and she was sure they couldn't, he wouldn't have been caught dead at a musical.

"It's coming to the performing arts center next year, you know," Josh said, smiling at her delighted reaction.

Phil sighed. "I know but there's no way Christian will take me. He doesn't do musicals."

"Tell you what, I'll go with you if you want when it comes to town."

"You wouldn't mind?" Phil looked at him doubtfully. "I mean, Christian says musicals are for girls and gay guys."

"Well I'm neither one of those." Josh laughed. "But hey, good music is good music. I was listening to it after I downloaded it for you and I kinda liked it."

"It *would* be a lot of fun," Phil said wistfully. "I can't remember the last time I got dressed up to go anywhere but out with one of Christian's clients. Well, at least it'll just be the two of us tomorrow."

"To celebrate, right." Josh looked thoughtful as he scooped up the last of his Love Potion Number Nine. "Well, I guess we better get back since tomorrow's Monday."

Phil groaned as she put down the CD and picked up her cup of rapidly melting ice cream. "Don't remind me!"

"Just another day in paradise, Swann," Josh said cheerfully, starting the engine. "Just think, if we didn't both work at beautiful BB&D, we might never have met. And then who would take you out for ice cream and beg to lick chocolate off your toes?"

"No one," Phil admitted, laughing. The answer ought to have been Christian, she knew. But her fiancé never seemed to have time for the simple pleasures in life, like going out for ice cream or having a little fun that didn't involve the almighty expense account. Not for the first time, she wished that her birthday wish could change another person's life besides her own. She was sure if she was very careful and worded it properly, the wish could make a difference in her relationship with her fiancé. Maybe she ought to wish she would be more visible to Christian. But then, her fairy godmother's magic would probably make her grow a horn in the middle of her forehead or turn her purple. That would certainly make her visible all right and not in a good way. No, it was no good wishing for anything to do with Christian. She would have to deal with her fiancé on her own.

"You're awfully quiet. What are you thinking of?" Josh's voice surprised her and she looked up to see that they were already outside her apartment building.

"Oh, nothing. Just spacing out," Phil lied, wishing she could tell him the truth. Somehow she had a feeling that if she could get anyone to understand about her fairy godmother's magic, it would be Josh. But that was crazy—he would just hear a buzzing sound or change the subject like everyone else without fairy blood.

"Are you sure?" Josh looked concerned. "Seriously, Phil, you know if you want to talk about something..."

"I know." Phil smiled at him. Not even her sisters picked up on her moods as quickly as Josh. He seemed to have some invisible radar tuned just to her and he always knew when she was unhappy or upset about something.

"Guess I better get going." She sighed and fumbled for the door latch. "Here, give me your ice cream cup and I'll throw it away."

Josh did as she asked, stacking his small paper cup neatly with hers. "You want me to walk you up?"

"No, I'll be fine." In their old apartment complex she would have said yes in an instant—it was spooky at night and not in the best part of town. But now that she and Christian lived someplace halfway decent, she had no excuse for Josh to see her to her door although she knew he would have if she'd asked.

"Well, see you tomorrow then." He smiled at her and Phil returned the smile warmly. She was so lucky to have such a great friend, especially now when she and Christian were going through kind of a rough time. Well, not really a rough time per se, she backpedaled hastily. They were just...getting settled. And once Christian got really established at his new law office, she knew things would go back to normal. In the meantime, she had more immediate problems to worry about—like what she was going to wish for when the FG appeared.

"See you tomorrow," she told Josh as she shut the door. She saw him wave as he put his little hybrid car in gear and she waved back, her hands full of empty ice cream cups and the *Wicked* CD.

As she walked up the steps to her apartment, she dragged her mind away from her best friend and her fiancé and wondered what she could wish for that wouldn't mess up her life completely.

Chapter Three

The quiet beeping of her alarm clock woke her and Phil pulled on her robe and slippers and climbed out of bed quickly to go make the coffee. Christian liked hot black coffee and the morning paper as soon as he woke up or he was cranky the whole day. He always said it was the only way to start things off right. Phil had been making sure his mornings went smoothly for almost five years now—four of which they had been engaged.

Phil had met her fiancé in college where they were both pre-law and they moved in together very quickly. Christian was the only serious boyfriend she'd ever had and when he'd pointed out that it made more sense for one of them to go to law school at a time, to avoid taking too many loans, she had reluctantly agreed. Phil had gotten a degree as a paralegal instead but she still planned to go back and attend law school herself after the wedding. If there ever *was* a wedding.

She squashed that negative thought and tiptoed to the front door to get the paper. They had recently moved into a much nicer apartment building than the one they had been able to afford before Christian passed the bar and got a job with the leading corporate law firm in the city. What Phil liked most about the apartment was that the paper boy actually delivered right to the door. In the old building, she'd had to go down three flights and across a walkway filled with sharp gravel to get the morning news. Here, all she had to do was reach outside her own front door.

Phil opened the door and reached...but no paper met her grasping hand. Wrapping her purple bathrobe (a gift from Cass) more tightly around her shoulders, she looked at her watch. Seven exactly and the paper was always delivered at six fifteen on the dot—Christian had made sure of that when they signed the lease. Phil ground her teeth together. She knew exactly where her missing paper had gone. Sighing, she stepped to the door across from hers and rapped lightly on its glossy brown wood.

She could hear a set of shuffling steps on the other side and then the sound of innumerable locks and bolts being thrown. The door cracked open to show one beady black eye and Mrs. Tessenbacker, her neighbor, was peering out at her.

"Yes?" she said suspiciously, before she caught sight of Phil. "Oh, good morning, Philomena!" she warbled, a wide grin creasing her cheeks. The improbably white dentures in her wrinkled face made her look like an ancient crocodile. And ancient *cheap* crocodile, Phil thought resentfully.

"Mrs. Tessenbacker," she said, trying to smile. "Did you happen to see our paper this morning? You know how Christian likes to read it every morning before work."

"Hmm." The old lady wrinkled her forehead even more and tapped her cheek with one crooked finger as though lost in thought. Phil repressed the urge to tap her foot on the floor at the Oscar-worthy performance. It was all a formality and they both knew it.

"It's supposed to be here at six fifteen," she reminded her neighbor tightly. *And I know you took it!* Of course, she couldn't make the accusation out loud. Thanks again, fairy godmother.

"Oh, of course," Mrs. Tessenbacker said. "I remember now—I was running low on potty paper for my little Doodle-bug so I borrowed it. I didn't think you'd mind."

Phil suppressed a groan. Doodle-bug was the name of Mrs. Tessenbacker's bad-tempered Yorkshire terrier that barked half the night and peed on everything in sight. Phil could see why her neighbor needed newspaper—if she owned an animal like Doodle-bug she would've been tempted to paper every surface in her entire apartment. But it wasn't like the old lady couldn't afford her own. Phil regularly saw her walking Doodle-bug on a long leather leash with a diamond studded collar. But her elderly neighbor was too cheap to buy her own paper and had been stealing Phil's at least twice a week ever since she figured out that Phil wouldn't make a fuss.

"I hope it's not a problem." The old lady gave her another

crocodile grin.

Phil took a deep breath. Once, just once she wanted to be able to tell her thieving neighbor that she *did* mind. That she didn't buy the paper for some spoiled bundle of ratty fur to use as a toilet. In fact, she didn't buy the paper for herself at all— she bought it for Christian and now he was going to be in a bad mood all day because he didn't have it. Was it too much to ask that her fiancé be in a good mood on her birthday, she wondered. Was it?

Out loud, she said, "Did you at least save the sports section, Mrs. Tessenbacker? If I could just have that..."

"Well now, let me see." The old lady disappeared again and returned with a wrinkled section of newspaper that was damp on one corner. "Here you are," she said proudly, as though she were doing Phil a favor. "Doodle-bug only made wee-wee on part of it. He's such a little scamp."

As though in answer to her words there was a sharp, yipping bark and a ball of dirty brown and gray fur came rushing from between Mrs. Tessenbacker's ankles. Doodle-bug glared up at Phil, his miniature body quivering with the high pitched growl that rumbled up his tiny throat. Then, before Phil could step back, he hiked his hind leg and liberally sprayed the purple fuzzy slippers that went with her robe before retreating.

"Oh my." Mrs. Tessenbacker looked like she was trying to hold back a giggle. "That naughty boy! He certainly makes it known when he doesn't like someone."

Phil bit the inside of her cheek with frustration. *I'd like to show him what I think of him too—preferably with my foot!* "Goodbye Mrs. Tessenbacker," she said stiffly. With as much dignity as she could muster, she squished back across the hall with the damp paper held out at arm's length. It was already turning out to be a fabulous birthday so far and she still hadn't thought of a good wish.

Once inside she took a quick shower and dried the paper with the blow dryer. She believed honesty was important in a relationship but in this case what her fiancé didn't know wouldn't hurt him.

Christian staggered sleepily into the kitchen, which Phil had painted pale green with a daisy border, just as she was pouring his coffee. "Morning, sleepyhead." Phil smiled at him and folded the sports section neatly, trying not to touch the slightly yellow part. "Nice day, isn't it?"

"Morning, babe." Christian yawned hugely and rubbed a hand through his hair until it stood up in a dark blond halo around his head before plopping down at the table. He had big blue eyes to go with his blond hair and a natural tan that never seemed to fade even in winter. His classically handsome features made other women stare when they were out together, which always made Phil proud that he had chosen her. Now he looked sleepy and rumpled but still devastatingly handsome as he mumbled, "Nice my ass. Just another Monday, huh?"

"Uh-huh." Phil tried not to let her hopes drop too much. Maybe he really had remembered it was her birthday and he was just leading her on. Sometimes Christian liked to tease her that way. "You know," she said, giving him a tentative smile. "If you have time later on tonight I'd really like to talk to you. About plans for the wedding—Cass and Rory and my nana all want to know when we're setting a date."

"Aw, c'mon." Christian frowned. "Don't hit me with that first thing in the morning, okay? I know you want to set a date and I promise we'll do it soon. But we need to save enough money so that you can have that nice big wedding you deserve."

"I don't know, Christian." Phil looked down at her bare feet. "Lately I've been thinking that a big wedding isn't so important to me. We could even run off to Vegas if you want to."

"Look, Phil, can we talk about this later?" Christian was beginning to look annoyed. "You know I want to get married as much as you do. Hell, we've been waiting four years to do it. But just...not now. Okay?"

Phil sighed and bit her lip. Her fiancé always seemed to have some excuse for not talking about the future they had planned together.

Christian must have seen her expression because he put down his coffee and reached out an arm to pull her close and gave her a squeeze. "Aw, don't look like that, babe. You know how much you mean to me and that I want to spend the rest of my life with you. Don't you?"

Phil nodded. "I know. It just seems like you're always too busy to talk about the details."

Christian grimaced. "It's this damn job—has me tied in

knots day and night. But I promise we'll talk about it soon, okay? You know how I feel about you—right?" It was an old joke between them and Phil answered automatically.

"The same way I feel about you. Hate your guts, you jerk."

"That's right. Hate you so much I can't stand to be without you." Christian laughed and dug his fingers into her side, just below her ribs. Phil yelped and jumped away.

"Christian! You know I hate to be tickled."

He grinned at her charmingly and picked up the mug of coffee and the paper. "Why do you think I do it, Philly-babe? Seriously, I promise we'll talk about plans for the wedding and all that crap later, okay?"

When Christian had decided he didn't want to discuss something, there was no point in trying. Pasting a smile on her face Phil said, "All right, I guess we can talk about it later just as well. So—did you sleep well?"

"Well as can be expected with so much on my mind. Got a big day today."

Phil felt her heart leap. He *had* been teasing her earlier! This year he really had remembered! "So, you have something special planned for tonight?" she asked, trying to sound casual.

"Sure do, babe. And you better be ready at seven sharp 'cause we're going out."

"Really?" Phil nearly did a little happy dance right there in the kitchen. She knew Christian wasn't a sentimental kind of guy—he'd warned her he wasn't when they first started dating. So when he *did* go out of his way to make a gesture like this, it meant that much more to her.

"Really." Christian shook out the paper and sniffed the air suspiciously. "Hey, what's that smell?"

"Nothing," Phil said hastily. "I spilled some coffee on the burner and it smoked up some. So can you tell me where we're going?" She couldn't keep the excitement out of her voice.

Christian sniffed the air again, shrugged and took a sip of coffee. "Sure, we're going out to Ivarone's with the Vances—new clients of mine. Remember I told you about them? He's into foreign imports and she collects some kind of art. Thought maybe you could schmooze 'em a little since that wacky sister of yours thinks she's an artist." He laughed and took another sip of coffee.

"New clients?" Phil felt her heart drop. *Please don't tell me you forgot again!* she thought desperately. "But...but Christian, don't you remember what day this is?"

"Sure I do." He shook out the paper so he could read the date at the top of the wrinkled page. "It's...Monday, June thirtieth. Looks like a beautiful day." He slurped down the last of his coffee, belched and stood up to kiss her on the cheek. "Gotta go, babe, I'm running late. If you're gone by the time I get out of the shower, have a good day. And don't forget to be ready by seven tonight. Can't keep the Vances waiting."

He brushed past her, leaving Phil feeling like someone had poked a hole in her heart and let all the good feelings out, like air leaking out of a balloon.

Chapter Four

The drive to work was uneventful although Phil found, when she pulled in to the parking garage for Brummel, Brummel, & Dickson, that someone had parked in her assigned space. The sleek red Mercedes seemed to mock her smaller, shabbier, pale blue Volkswagen bug. Phil had been working at BB&D for almost four years and she knew exactly who the Mercedes belonged to—Alison, the office flirt who used her charms shamelessly to get anything she wanted. Alison had her own assigned space, but it was toward the back of the lot and she didn't like to walk. How she could afford such an expensive car on her salary, which was supposedly the same as Phil's, was a subject of ongoing office speculation. Sighing, Phil found a spot in the back and walked slowly towards the elevator.

"Hey, lady! Hey, lady! You wanna buy a pencil?"

Phil winced as she passed the kid, who looked to be fourteen or fifteen, wearing large, dark sunglasses and jingling a cup of change and pencils. He was short for his age and only the dark fuzz of hair on his upper lips gave it away. There wasn't supposed to be any solicitation on the BB&D premises but somehow the little blind pencil boy never got caught. Honestly, Phil wasn't even all that sure he was blind, or even sight impaired. She was fairly certain she'd seen him or someone who looked exactly like him riding away on his bike one day, sunglasses tucked in his back pocket, as soon as all the employees had gone into the building. But still, every day he made her feel guilty and every day she bought a pencil she didn't want for a dollar she would have preferred to spend at lunch.

She'd told Cass and Rory about it and they had laughed at

her, and called it 'the not-so-blind-pencil-boy diet". Phil supposed she could see the humor in it but somehow today she just didn't feel like being taken for a ride.

"Please, lady, don't you wanna buy a pencil?" the boy begged, tilting his head appealingly. Sighing, Phil reached into her pocket. Why should today be any different?

BB&D was located at the top of the Continental Bank Tower, a large silver building that rose forty-seven stories to loom over downtown Tampa. Phil stepped into the elevator and pressed the button for her floor, trying not to see the defeated look on her face in the mirrored walls of the elevator. She stepped out onto the plush maroon carpet that complimented the pale pink walls of the office.

One of the senior partners had hired a color expert to remodel the entire space a few years back who had claimed that soft pastels on the walls were both soothing and invigorating—supposedly making people more focused on their work. In Phil's opinion, the "expert" had probably just had about fifty gallons of pale pink paint to use up because she felt neither soothed nor invigorated when she hit the doors of BB&D. Instead, she felt like she was stuck inside the middle of a giant seashell and she couldn't get out. But maybe that feeling had less to do with the color scheme and more to do with her job.

Once at her cubicle, she stuffed the useless pencil in her desk drawer along with about a hundred others and put her purse on the shelf. A look at the calendar told her that Atwood Dickson Junior, her boss, had a big day in court this afternoon and she was willing to bet he wasn't half done with the files she'd sent him home with that weekend. Just another day in paradise.

"Phil? Hello, Earth to Philomena. Come in Philomena." It was Kelli, the paralegal who sat in the cubicle beside Phil's, practically shouting in her ear.

Phil suppressed another sigh. If she had been quicker, she might have missed Kelli this morning since her coworker was almost always late. Now she would have to listen to the bizarre details of Kelli's social life until she managed to get away.

"Good morning, Kelli." She attempted to smile. "How was your weekend?" It was the wrong thing to say.

"Oh. My. God." Kelli widened her eyes dramatically, her

long black hair swirling around her narrow hips. Phil often thought her coworker looked like what might happen if an evil scientist had taken a shrinking ray to Cher and miniaturized her. "So you know how all those bad things were happening to me last week? I mean, how my car was broken into and that tree in my yard fell over and James broke up with me for like, absolutely no reason whatsoever at all?"

"Mmm-hmm." Phil nodded, glancing longingly at her stack of paperwork. Kelli was harmless, but she sprayed the details of her personal life like a leaky garden hose and kept talking even when Phil was trying to work. *Especially* when Phil was trying to work.

"So, anyway, I was like—this can't be right. Bad luck comes in threes. So I had my cards done this weekend. I had a, um, reading?" Kelli had an annoying habit of turning every other sentence into a question. Phil nodded again, wishing that for once in her life she could tell Kelli to shut up.

"So the lady who did my cards? She's from Puerto Rico and she's a priestess of Santeria or something like that. Anyway, she said..."

Phil kept nodding, stacking the files she needed to take to her boss's office and letting Kelli's high, annoying voice pour over her. If she tried to leave in the middle of the story, her coworker's feelings would be hurt, but she really needed to get going. How would Kelli like it if Phil started bitching about how her own day had started? *Hey Kelli,* she imagined herself saying. *This morning my next-door neighbor stole my paper, her dog peed on my slippers and my fiancé forgot my birthday— again. How's that for the trifecta of bad luck?*

"I had kind of a rough time this morning, too," she said, when her coworker seemed to have reached a break in her narrative. "You wouldn't believe what happened to me."

"Oh, yeah?" Kelli's eyes glazed at once. "Well, maybe you should have your cards done. It's like the Puerto Rican priestess told me, she said, 'Kelli, you are under a curse.' Just like that! Can you imagine? So then I was like, 'No way—I can't be.' And she was like..."

Phil let it wash over her again, unsurprised that her conversational gambit had failed. In her experience, Kelli was only interested in Kelli. Phil was doomed to hear the details of her coworker's life forever. She wished again that she could tell her to just *shut up.* But there was no way to say that without starting a huge fight so she put up with it—as always.

Finally Kelli seemed to be winding down. Phil nodded rapidly and started edging out of her cubicle. With a "That is such a shame, Kelli. You'll have to tell me all about it later," she escaped and went about her morning duties with a sigh of relief.

Someday she would be the one sitting in the corner office ordering files, Phil reminded herself. Someday she would be the one making partner—not the one making coffee. Dickson liked it with four creams and five sugars and he always made the same joke when she brought it to him—"I like my women like I like my coffee—hot and sweet."

Just as she was about to leave the break room, the coffee in one hand and the files in the other, Alison Tanner wandered in. Per usual, she was dressed as though someone had asked her to star in a porno movie about a naughty secretary who gets spanked over her boss's desk. A white silk blouse open to the third button showed plenty of cleavage and a hint of her lacy white bra and her black pencil skirt was short enough that if she sat down, no doubt the matching panties would be revealed. Black spike heels at least four inches high completed the look and gave Alison a slithering walk that seemed to hypnotize almost every man in the office.

"Why, good morning, Philomena," she purred. "My, aren't we looking, ah *professional* today." She raked poison green eyes up and down Phil's frame, turning the compliment into an insult.

Her nasty-nice tone made Phil want to smooth her hands self-consciously over her own sensible navy blue skirt and the tight bun of hair at the nape of her neck. Since her hands were full, she resisted the urge.

"Good morning, Alison." She tried to keep her voice level. "I, uh, happened to noticed that your car is parked in my spot."

"Oh, my—is it?" Alison raised an eyebrow, managing to make her tone sincere despite the mocking look on her face. "I am just *so* sorry, hon. I just seem to keep on forgetting and parking in the wrong spot. Silly me."

"Mmm-hmm." *How stupid do you think I am? You've been*

41

parking in my spot for months and you expect me to believe it's an accident? Phil seethed, knowing that nothing she could say would change Alison's behavior.

"Not to change the subject, but what are you wearing to the beach party on Thursday?" Alison continued. "I've got a naughty little bikini all picked out. But you know..." She gave Phil another critical look. "I'm thinking maybe you should go with a one piece. Maybe the kind that has the little skirt attached. Those are just so cute and they hide so many *flaws*." She smiled as though she honestly wanted to give helpful advice.

Before Phil could figure out how to reply, a voice interrupted them. "Morning, you two." It was Davis Miles, one of the attorneys who worked at BB&D. He hadn't made partner yet but the office buzz was that he was on the fast track.

As always, when she saw him, Phil couldn't help wondering what he might look like with his shirt off. She knew she would never cheat on Christian but Miles was hands down the most handsome man she'd ever seen. He looked like he'd just stepped out of the pages of GQ with his dark hair and eyes and crisp, hand-tailored suits. He had broad shoulders and teeth so white they belonged in a toothpaste ad. But even so, there was something about him—a professional distance, perhaps. Miles never talked about his personal life and was never anything but polite when she spoke to him. Considering that she had to work closely with both Kelli and Alison, Phil appreciated that quality immensely.

"Morning, Mister Miles." She nodded at him politely. But before the words were out of her mouth, Alison brushed past her, knocking against her arm and slopping hot coffee down the front of her white blouse.

"Ow!" Phil gasped as the hot liquid soaked her blouse and scalded her skin. Alison paid no attention. At least, not to Phil.

"Davis," the other woman purred, linking her arm with his and giving him her most seductive look. "You bad boy—why didn't you call me this weekend? I waited and waited by the phone."

"Well, I..." Davis Miles looked uncomfortable, but men tended to be sucked into Alison's orbit like cosmic debris into a black hole. Phil had yet to see one escape.

"Now, no excuses. I want to know every little thing you did this weekend. And are you all ready for the beach party this Thursday? I was just telling what's-her-name here about the naughty little pink bikini I'm going to wear. I mean, it's practically *see-through*. So now tell me—what are *you* going to be wearing, Davis? I hope it'll be something to show off all those muscles I see bulging under that expensive suit of yours..."

They walked out of the break room arm in arm, leaving Phil to stare down at the brown stain on the front of her blouse. She wanted to scream. Instead, she put down the half-full coffee mug and the stack of files and ran to the break-room sink to try and get the coffee off before it set permanently. The result was a see-through patch on her shirt right over her left breast which left her feeling more exposed than if she were wearing Alison's "naughty little pink bikini". She wouldn't have minded so much if she wasn't just about to go to her boss's office but... There was no point thinking about it. Better just get it over with.

"Good morning, Mister Dickson," Phil tried to sound businesslike as she sat the coffee and the stack of files and paperwork down on his desk.

"Morning, Philomena, sweetheart. Aren't you pretty today?" Atwood Dickson was short, squat, and balding with piggy little eyes the color of mud. He always had coffee breath and his fingernails were never very clean. He was also the son of the senior partner of the same name. Everyone at BB&D, including him, was certain he was going to make partner regardless of his performance. Accordingly he slacked off as much as possible and Phil knew for a fact that he was looking at internet porn on his computer most of the time he was supposed to be working.

"Did you get through the Jackson file this weekend?" she asked, ignoring his remark.

"Aw, hell—who could get through all that mess?" He kicked back in his chair, his feet on the desk, his gut bulging up from his too-tight suit pants.

Phil wanted to say that *he* had better get through that mess if he wanted to avoid looking like an ass in court that day but she controlled herself. "You have a big day in court today," she reminded him, going to look for the file in question. Doubtless it was at the bottom of his briefcase, untouched, and she would have to go through it and point out the salient points to him herself.

"I've got all kinds of big things, if you know what I mean, darlin'. 'Specially now I see we're havin' a wet T-shirt contest this morning." Dickson leered at her see-through blouse and Phil felt a red blush creeping up her face.

"I spilled some of your coffee on myself." She nodded at the mug still sitting untouched on his desk.

Dickson took a sip from the mug, his greedy little eyes never leaving her chest. "Mmm, I like my coffee like I like my women—hot and sweet." He laughed at his own joke the same way he did every morning.

Phil bent the corners of her mouth into an approximation of a smile and continued to dig through his briefcase until she found the Jackson file. She would have complained to HR, except that another member of the Dickson family worked there—Atwood's cousin, Herbert.

Sometimes she wondered why she cared. When she'd first started the job, she and Christian had needed the money to survive. Her fiancé had been dead set against them taking out any more loans than they had to, which was the main reason she'd put off going to law school herself. But now with Christian making more money maybe she could afford to quit. Then she got practical—they were saving for the wedding and being suddenly unemployed would put a serious crimp in her plans.

Besides, she needed this job as a recommendation for whatever law school she ended up attending. Atwood Dickson Senior, her boss's father and one of the senior partners, had even promised to write her a letter when the time came. Phil knew the letter would probably talk about her excellent work habits but in her opinion, there was no higher praise than the fact that she was willing to put up with his pig of a son.

Phil sighed to herself. She'd tried a few times over the years to let her fiancé know what she put up with at work, but his response was always the same.

"Look, babe," he'd say in his most reasonable voice. "I know you have it tough but I do, too. School is killing me right now and I just need you to be strong and hang in there a little while longer. I promise as soon as I get out and start my career with a good firm we'll get married and you can ditch that crappy job and go back to school yourself. Okay?"

Right. Only he'd been out of law school almost a year and

here she was, still working at BB&D and getting nowhere fast. Phil wondered if she ought to wish for career advancement when her fairy godmother appeared that evening. But then again, who knew what the FG considered advancement? She might find herself the highest paid hooker on Seventh Avenue if she wasn't careful. No, she'd learned the hard way that fairy magic wasn't the answer to bettering her life. But what was?

"Hey, sweetheart, what about that file?" Dickson's voice broke into her inner monologue and Phil brought the Jackson file to his desk. "Good girl!" He swatted her behind and Phil had to bite the inside of her cheek to keep from slapping him. *Jerk! Asshole!*

"Mister Dickson, can we please get down to business here?"

"Well, now, we can do that. Why didn't you just *say* you wanted to give me the business?" He gave her a leering grin and Phil felt the skin between her shoulder blades start to crawl. God, what she wouldn't give to be able to tell him off! Instead, she gritted her teeth and opened the file. It was going to be a long morning.

Chapter Five

Phil shut the door of Dickson's office and trudged down the hallway to the break room where the first aid kit was kept. She'd managed to get a nasty paper cut from one of the files she'd been going over with her boss but it turned out to be a good thing. Dickson couldn't stand the sight of blood so she was able to shave a few minutes off her time with him and go in search of a Band-Aid.

"Swann!" The familiar voice was like a ray of sunshine warming her. Phil turned to see Josh behind her in the narrow hall leading away from Dickson's office.

"Bowman." She tried to smile but the corners of her mouth just didn't want to turn up. Phil knew her smile's failure to launch was just aftermath of spending the morning with her lecherous boss. It was like treading water in a pool filled with slime—she always felt exhausted and in need of a hot shower when she finally got out of his office.

"Hey, you got a minute? It's almost lunch time." Today he had on a dark green shirt with the top two buttons undone and his tie was pulled adorably askew so that she could see the natural tan of his broad chest.

"Sure, I guess I could take my lunch now," she said as he fell into step beside her. "So what have you been doing all day? Defragging the computers? Keeping us safe from evil viruses?"

Josh grinned and nudged her gently with one elbow. "Nah. Trying to install a new application for the file directory that Dickhead Senior thinks will make you guys more productive." He shrugged. "Fair warning though—it won't. I think it's gonna make your life hell. But don't worry—after about a week it's going to crash and burn and you'll be back to a system that works."

Josh was the IT guy and a good one at that. Phil often wondered why he stayed in such a dead end job when he could have moved anywhere in the country and probably made a lot more money in the process. Although the senior partners at BB&D didn't know it, he saved them hundreds of thousands of dollars each year by keeping the office computer systems running smoothly and personally vetting all the new software they purchased. If an expensive new application turned out to be a complete bust, it would either crash or be declared "incompatible" after a week or so, much to the relief of the secretaries and paralegals who actually had to deal with it.

"Crap." She sighed. "Why do they keep doing this to us?"

"Haven't you heard, Swann? Progress." Josh furrowed his brow and made his voice deep and pompous, doing a flawless imitation of Dickson Senior.

His expression was so comical that Phil put a hand to her mouth to stifle a giggle, forgetting the paper cut until she rubbed the wounded pad of her finger against her cheek. "Ow!" She pulled back at once and looked up at Josh. "Do I have blood on my face?"

"Yup, looks like war paint. What did you do to your finger?" He took her hand gently in both of his and examined it.

"It's just a paper cut. I was going to the break room for a Band-Aid."

"Well, it just so happens that's exactly where I wanted to take you. Come on." Without relinquishing her hand, Josh led her to the break room, which was thankfully empty of the slithery Alison and any of her man-prey.

He sat her at the small table, which was just about big enough for two, and began rummaging in the cabinets for the first aid kit. "So, are you going to the beach party Thursday?" he asked, bringing the kit to the table and pulling out hydrogen peroxide and a piece of gauze.

Phil sighed. "Of course—how could I miss it? If it's anything like last year I'm sure it'll be very, ah, *entertaining.*"

"Meaning we get to see Dickhead Junior in a banana hammock again, I take it." Josh grinned.

"Ugh!" Phil made a face. "*Please*, Josh."

He laughed, a deep rumbly sound that Phil had always

liked. "What a sight—definitely a morale booster, I'd say. And isn't that the point of the office beach day? I mean, getting to see your coworkers in their bathing suits is *so* much more rewarding that getting say, a raise or a bonus." He began arranging the first aid items in front of him. The little white gauze squares looked tiny in his large hands.

"Absolutely. Seeing all the senior partners and their hairy, sunburned backs is better than a bonus in my book any day." She reached for the gauze but Josh pulled it away.

"Uh-uh-uh, Swann. The doctor is in. Just sit still and let me do my thing."

"Oh, I didn't realize you held an advanced degree in finger bandage-ology." She gave up and relinquished her finger.

"There's a lot you don't know about me, Swann." Josh's brow furrowed as he worked on her finger and he spoke with the distracted air of someone concentrating deeply on the task before them. One thing Phil liked about her best friend was the way he gave his complete attention to whatever he was interested in. When she talked to him, she always got the feeling that he was focusing on what she had to say, not just waiting for his own turn to talk—the opposite of coworkers like Kelli.

"So speaking of coworkers in their bathing suits, you should have heard Alison describing her 'tiny naughty bikini' to Davis Miles this morning," Phil said, trying to distract herself from the sting of the peroxide. If it had been up to her, she would have rinsed the cut finger in the sink and slapped a bandage on it. But typical of Josh, he was treating the whole process like a complicated and delicate surgical procedure.

"Uh-huh. And what are *you* going to be wearing?" He glanced up at her and grinned, taking the innuendo out of his words. "Something that will leave us all buzzing for days with its daring cut? A fashion statement to end all fashion statements?"

Phil frowned. "Only if you promise to stay between me and Dickson Junior at all times—I don't need to see that bright yellow Speedo pointed in my direction. I get enough of that at work."

Josh's chocolate brown eyes darkened, making his friendly face stern. He had a very strong jaw and a dark five o'clock shadow despite the fact that it was only noon. For a moment, he almost looked frightening. "Is he giving you a hard time, Phil?"

There was steel in his voice instead of laughter and Phil was reminded of what a really big guy he was. All joking aside, if he wanted to, Josh could probably break her nasty boss over one knee like a dry stick. But she didn't want to be the cause of her best friend losing his job or committing felony assault so she just shrugged uneasily.

"You know—no more than usual."

Josh looked like he was going to say something else, but then he shook his head. He deepened his voice and squared his shoulders. "You want I should break his kneecaps for ya, doll?" he asked, the teasing back in his tone.

"Dork." Phil slapped his shoulder with the hand he wasn't doctoring. She was relieved that Josh wasn't making a big deal. He was good about knowing when she just needed to vent. "He's just hard to take on a Monday, that's all. Especially—" She broke off, shaking her head. She had too much pride to mention how badly her birthday was going so far. It would sound like she was begging for sympathy or presents or both.

But Josh wasn't about to let her get away with it. "Especially what? Come on, Phil, give."

"Well..." When they first became friends, Phil had been shy about talking to Josh about her fiancé. But he was such a good listener that she had gradually loosened up until nothing was really off limits for discussion but her and Christian's sex life.

"Come on," Josh prodded again. "You know I'm not going to stop until you tell me."

"It's just that, well, this morning when I woke up I was hoping that Christian...well, you know how last year—"

"Wait a minute—did he forget your birthday *again*?" Josh interrupted her halting confession, one side of his full mouth pulled down in a frown of disapproval.

Phil nodded her head miserably. "Uh-huh. I tried to give him a hint and for a minute I thought he really had remembered. But..." She shrugged.

"But he didn't," Josh finished for her again. "Damn it, Phil, you know I usually try to just act as a sounding board and not get involved with this kind of thing. But forgetting your birthday *two* years in a row is not good."

Phil sighed. "I know. It's just...he never used to forget. Before he got this job he had more time for me—more time for *us*. I mean, I know he's busy working and trying to make a name for himself at his new firm but it just...well, it *hurts*, Josh."

"Of course it does," Josh said softly. He stopped bandaging her finger for a moment to rub one large warm hand over her forearm soothingly. "So did you say anything to him about it? Remind him?"

"Uh-uh. He was in such a hurry to get to work and besides, it's not like he could do anything about it at this point even if I reminded him. He already made plans for us to go out with some clients of his to Ivarone's."

"So he should cancel the plans," Josh said, the steel coming back into his voice.

"He can't cancel—it's part of his job." Phil hated that she was constantly having to defend her fiancé. *Please understand,* she wanted to say. *Christian is really a sweet guy. He's just been distracted lately.* Lately, right. Like for the entire last year. She looked down at the table.

"Since when is his job more important than you?" Still holding the finger he was bandaging in one hand he reached across the table and lifted her chin with the other. "Phil, do you want me to give you a guy's perspective on this?"

With his warm, gentle fingers under her chin she couldn't help meeting his eyes. "I guess."

"He's acting like a jerk," Josh told her. "He doesn't realize how lucky he is to have a girl like you but if he isn't careful he's going to find out—by losing you."

"Just because he forgot my birthday once or twice doesn't mean I'm going to leave him!" Phil pulled away from her best friend's gentle touch, feeling slightly panicky. She'd been with Christian for five years and the thought of being back on the market, looking for someone else to spend her life with, made her feel nauseous. There were a lot more frogs than princes out there to hear Cass, who had considerably more dating experience than Phil, tell it.

"So you're just going to hang around and let him treat you like that indefinitely?" Josh's voice was soft. "Why, Phil? What are you afraid of?"

"I'm not afraid of anything," she lied, looking down again. "But you have to understand about Christian—he's a good guy. It's just that he's been busy with work. And...and I know he's going to feel terrible when I remind him about my birthday. But that's no reason to leave him. I mean, it's not like he suddenly turned into Dickson or anything."

She heard Josh sigh and looked up at him questioningly. But he only gave her what looked like a forced smile. "Speaking of which, it sounds to me like it's time ol' Dick Junior caught another virus. I have just the one in mind, too."

"Josh!" Phil laughed, relieved that they were back on safe territory. Their mutual dislike of her boss was something they could both agree on. In fact, it was the way they had become friends in the first place. Josh had found her crying in the supply closet after a particularly bad day at work near the end of her third week at the law firm. He hadn't said much, but the next day someone had 'hacked' the BB&D website and Dickson Junior's head had somehow been pasted on the voluptuous nude body of the Playmate of the Year. Dickson had ranted and raved and Josh had made all the right noises about correcting the problem but somehow it had still taken an entire week to get it fixed.

Ever since that first time, whenever her boss was giving her an especially hard time, something happened to his computer. Phil thought it was surprising that he hadn't caught on yet. But Josh was so good at looking sincere and explaining how he was trying hard to fix whatever was wrong, it apparently never penetrated Dickson's thick skull that his PC was being sabotaged.

"I think you'll live now." Josh had finally finished bandaging her finger but he continued to hold her hand, as though admiring his work.

"Thanks, Josh." She smiled at him and he held her gaze for a minute before releasing her hand and jumping up.

"Okay, and now that the first aid segment of our show is done, I have something for you. Close your eyes. Now, I mean it—don't look."

Phil laughed and did as he said. She heard him rummaging around in the cabinets and refrigerator and then he was behind her. "You're peeking, aren't you? Are you peeking?"

"No, honestly!" Phil protested. She could smell something sweet and thought she knew what it was. This day just wasn't getting any better.

Josh put one large, warm hand over her eyes anyway. "Keep 'em closed," he directed sternly and Phil heard the clattering of a china plate on the table before her.

"Now?" she asked, blinking grimly behind his fingers.

"No...now!" He uncovered her eyes, revealing a miniature cheesecake topped with fresh fruit. There was a single candle stuck into one of the strawberries on top.

"Oh, Josh—it's gorgeous." Phil clapped her hands in delight. One of the things she loved about Josh was that for the entire time they had been friends, he had never once been the bearer of her wish-induced éclair. And she was so glad he wasn't now. It would have spoiled things somehow, although of course she would have eaten it to avoid hurting his feelings.

"You like? Cheesecake is your favorite, isn't it?"

"It is." She looked at the beautiful little confection with delight, then looked up at her best friend. "I just thought—for some reason I thought it was an éclair."

"No way." He made a face. "You hate those things. Anytime anyone gives you one, you ditch it as fast as possible."

"I sure do," she agreed fervently. She was surprised that Josh had noticed her aversion to the daily dessert, though. Her fairy godmother's magic flew under the radar of most non-fairy folk. "You shouldn't have done this after you already burned me that CD."

"Please." Josh arched an eyebrow at her. "Can't you tell the difference between a pre-birthday present and a birthday present? They're in two entirely different categories, Swann."

Phil laughed at his mock serious tone. "All right then. You want to share this with me?" she asked, motioning to the cheesecake. "There's no way I can eat it all."

"Well, since you twisted my arm..." Josh grabbed a spare fork. "But first you have to blow out your candle and make a wish."

"*Oh.*" Phil bit her lip, feeling like a cold hand had squeezed her heart. Her wish! Zero hour was only six hours away and she still hadn't thought of anything good to wish for. Her day had been so horrible up until Josh had met her in the hallway that she had almost forgotten about it.

"What's the matter?" Josh was looking at her with concern. "You look sick all of a sudden—did I say something wrong?"

"No. I...no." Phil tried to smile. She still had time. She would think of something. "Why don't you blow it out for me?"

"But then your birthday wish won't come true," Josh protested.

"Oh, trust me. It'll come true." Phil shook her head. "You go on—blow it out and make your own wish."

"You got it, Swann." Josh shrugged and puffed out the candle. "Now take the first bite—it's only fair since it's your birthday cheesecake."

"Thanks." Phil scooped out a generous spoonful and tasted it. "Mmm, this is wonderful, Josh!" She licked the back of the spoon and went in for another bite. "But what did you wish for?"

He took a bite himself. "Mm-mm, can't tell you. If I tell it won't come true."

Phil sighed, wishing that was really the way it worked. Wishing that she didn't have the added burden of her birthday wish on top of all the crap she was going through at work and home. Too bad she couldn't just wish the wishes away, but that was another rule that couldn't be broken. No wishing for more wishes and no wishing for no wishes.

"You look deep in thought—that's the second time in two days. Better be careful or it's going to get to be a habit." Josh licked his fork and Phil was surprised to see that they had nearly finished the cheesecake. She took half of the last bite, leaving half for him.

"Just thinking about tonight," she murmured. She half expected her friend to say something but Josh seemed to decide to leave their earlier topic of conversation alone.

"Oops." He looked down at his watch and ran a hand through his thick brown hair. "My lunch is almost over."

"Mine too, I guess." Phil was grateful that her boss was going to be in court all afternoon and she wouldn't have to put up with anything more annoying than Kelli's chatter. "Thanks again for the cheesecake, Josh." She got up from the table and started to take the plate to the sink but he stopped her.

"Uh-uh, birthday girl. Allow me." He put the plate in the sink and ceremoniously poured a huge dollop of green dish liquid on it, making Phil giggle.

"That's enough to wash a whole sink full of dishes," she pointed out.

"Well, Supersize Bowman is what they call me. I think you can guess why, *sweetheart.*" Josh wiggled his eyebrows at her and did a little bump and grind with his hips, imitating her boss.

Phil laughed out loud. "Josh, you are *bad.* I need to get back to work. "

He grinned. "I have to get back, too. I have a very special virus to work on, as I recall. Hold on." He put a hand on her arm to stop her from leaving the break room.

"What?"

"You're still wearing your war paint." Josh grabbed a paper towel and wet it. "Hold still," he directed, leaning down to cup her chin in one hand.

Phil submitted quietly, a little surprised by how much she enjoyed his touch. Then she pushed the thought away—she *was* engaged and she didn't think of her friend that way. Of course there was that one time she'd had that really embarrassing dream about him... Okay, better not go there, either. Phil tried to clear her mind of any inappropriate thoughts. Josh was too important to her to mess up their friendship with sexual tension.

"Thanks," she said when he had wiped the small smudge of dried blood off her cheek.

"Any time—can't have you going on the war path even if Dickhead Junior deserves it." Josh smiled, an expression that lit his whole face. Then he shrugged, his broad shoulders rolling under the dark green shirt. "Well, I'd better get back."

"Wait a minute." Following an impulse she couldn't explain, Phil reached up and put her arms around her best friend's neck, even though he was so tall that it was a stretch.

Josh stood frozen for a second, like a statue in her arms, and then he wrapped his own arms around her carefully, as though he were afraid he might break her. "What's this for?" he asked, his breath warm against the side of her neck.

"For just being you. And for remembering my birthday. Twice." *When some people can't even remember once.* She planted a kiss on his slightly scratchy cheek. "Thank you, Josh. You have no idea how much it means to me." She started to withdraw but his arms were still around her waist and Phil found herself noticing how good he smelled. Spicy and warm and masculine. She wondered what kind of cologne he was wearing or if it was just him. She could feel the entire length of his body pressed against hers now, the hard, warm wall of his chest felt good against her and his arms wrapped so tightly around her were strong and sturdy, giving her a sense of security. Suddenly she wished the hug could go on forever.

"Maybe I *do* know," he murmured softly in her ear. "Phil, for a long time, I—"

"Well, isn't *this* a cozy scene."

They both looked up to see Alison standing in the doorway, one hip cocked to the side and a sardonic expression on her sharp, fox-like features. "Why don't you two love birds get a room?" she purred.

Phil disentangled herself and jumped back. "I was giving Josh a hug for remembering my birthday," she babbled, feeling strangely guilty.

"Oh, it's your birthday?" Alison gave her a smile as real as a three-dollar bill. "Well happy birthday, hon. How old are you now? Thirty-five?"

"She's about five years younger than you, I think Alison," Josh said mildly. "So I guess that makes you forty?" Alison frowned but before she could come up with a reply, he nodded at both of them. "Hasta la vista, ladies. I've got to go fight for truth, justice and the American way. Or at least make sure the server doesn't crash."

Phil watched as he walked down the hall, whistling carelessly. She couldn't shake the feeling that he had been about to say something before Alison walked in. But she still had piles of work at her desk—and a wish to think up before six fifteen that night.

Chapter Six

"We have a crisis of epic proportions on our hands." Cass's usually sardonic voice sounded panicked.

"What are you talking about?" Phil spun the steering wheel and stared at her cell phone as though her sister's face might suddenly appear to clarify the situation.

"It's Nana—remember, the woman who raised us?" Her younger sister's voice was sharp and Phil wished she could shout back. Instead she took a deep breath and blew it out.

"Tell me all about it. What happened?" She turned a corner too fast and nearly ran a light.

"I don't have much time right now. Are you anywhere near the house?"

Phil knew her sister meant the big Victorian mansion at the crest of States Street where all three of them had grown up and where Cass and Rory continued to live with their grandmother. Nana was a sweet, excitable lady with delusions of grandeur where her half-fairy status was concerned. With her modest inheritance, she hadn't had to work, and had turned toward magic as a full-time hobby. The only problem was, she didn't have enough fairy blood to do any kind of magic very well and she was constantly getting into trouble. Phil thought she might be the only granddaughter she knew of that had bailed her grandmother out of jail. Twice.

"Rory has my car but she's on the way. We all need to go together. We need the power of blood behind us." Cass's voice on the other end of the cell phone pulled Phil back from her musings.

"Go where?" she asked, with rising apprehension. Though

they didn't have much fairy blood in their veins, having all three sisters together did increase their ability to deal with magical situations. "Is Nana in the lock-up again?"

"No but she will be if we don't get down there. Just hurry up!" Honestly, for a younger sister, Cass was unbearably bossy and sometimes Phil ached to tell her so. Like right now.

"But I'm supposed to go out with Christian at seven. And I still haven't even thought of a wish!" she protested. But she was already taking the left that would take her to States Street. Even without her sister's bossing she knew she would always come to her nana's rescue. Despite her eccentricities, her grandmother had done the best she could to raise three little girls on her own.

"We'll think about it on the way."

"On the way *where*?" Phil demanded, exasperated.

"The bowling alley," Cass said and clicked off abruptly.

By the time she got to the big lavender mansion at the top of the hill, Cass and Rory were both waiting out front. Cass was dressed all in black, tapping her foot on the sidewalk. Rory was dressed more conventionally in jeans and a T-shirt, twisting one long lock of her brilliant red hair around her finger nervously. Phil barely had time to pull up to the curb before they were piling into her ancient bug.

"Hurry up," Cass directed as she settled into the passenger seat with Rory in the back. "We have to get to Splitsville"

"Splitsville?" Phil raised an eyebrow at her sister.

"It's that new bowling alley down by USF," Rory supplied. "You know, the one on Fowler?"

"I think so." Phil started driving in the general direction of the bowling alley, glancing at her watch nervously. She had left work late and it was five thirty now. In exactly forty-five minutes her fairy godmother would appear and demand to know her wish. If Phil didn't have it on the tip of her tongue, she'd be saddled with whatever the bad-tempered fairy thought up herself. She might get "fingernails as strong as diamonds" and never be able to file them again. Or something much worse.

"What is Nana doing at a bowling alley, anyway?" she asked, trying to push the worry out of her mind and not succeeding very well. "Has she joined a league?"

Cass snorted. "And risk chipping a nail? I don't think so.

She's down there trying out her new love potion."

"Love potion?" Phil nearly ran a stop sign. "Are you serious? Fairies don't make potions."

"No, but witches do. Remember we told you she was dabbling in the Craft?" Rory wrinkled her nose. "You should smell the inside of the house—it's awful! Like dill pickles and cat pee."

"I told her it wouldn't work." Cass drummed her fingernails on the bug's dashboard. "Can't you make this thing go any faster?"

"This *thing* is the same age I am so cut it a break," Phil said, making the turn onto Fowler.

"See, that's what I don't understand," Cass said. "You and Christian lived hand to mouth all those years and now that he's got a new job you'd think things would be different."

"Things *are* different," Phil protested. "We're living in a much nicer apartment now."

"Yeah, but you're still driving this hunk of junk and still working that crappy job with the boss that likes to play grab-ass with you. I thought you going to quit and go back to school."

"I *am*," Phil said, grimly hanging on to her temper. Why did her sister always have to make everything sound so hopeless? "I'm going back to school after the wedding."

"Oh, did you set a date then?" Rory leaned forward.

"Look, can we please for once not talk about my life?" Phil took a deep breath. "Just tell me what's going on with Nana."

"She told me she was lonely," Rory said. "She said that all of us were growing up and when we left home there would be no one to keep her company."

"So why didn't she sign up with a dating service?" Phil asked. "We live in Florida—there's plenty of them that cater to senior citizens."

"That's not Nana's way and you know it." Cass crossed her arms over her chest, her wild black curls bouncing with the gesture. "She told Rory and me that she wanted to be able to 'pick and choose' whatever that means."

"So she decided to try her potion in a bowling alley?" Phil frowned.

Rory shrugged. "She seemed to think it was a good place to pick up men."

"You know how she's always had a thing for blue collar type guys," Cass put in. "Remember the way she always flirted with repair men? We're probably lucky she didn't decide to try it out down at some construction site."

Phil had a brief mental image of her sweet little nana tottering around in her impractically high heels in a hardhat zone and thanked her stars she hadn't. "Well how do you know she's in trouble?" she asked. "Did the bowling alley call and say she was making a disturbance?" It wouldn't be the first time they had received such a call about their nana. Up ahead she could see a huge neon bowling pin and the word *Splitsville* in red cursive script across the top.

"No, Nana called herself," Cass said. "She was a little hysterical—but that's normal for her. What worried me was she kept saying that she thought she'd gotten the potion wrong somehow."

"She called me too," Rory said darkly. "And I heard all these guys in the background. It sounded like a football game or something the way they were cheering and chanting. I just hope she's all right."

"Me too." Phil felt a quick stab of panic as she pulled into the Splitsville parking lot. "Let's go get her."

The three of them nearly ran to the entrance of the bowling alley. As soon as she pushed open the front door, Phil caught a whiff of what must be the potion her grandmother had been working on. As Rory had said, it smelled like strong Kosher pickles mixed with ammonia. She wrinkled her nose and pressed forward into the dark interior.

The bowling alley was dimly lit and under the strong odor of the potion, Phil could smell fried food and stale beer. She scanned the identical lanes for her nana's plump form but they were all empty. Where was everyone? And where was her nana?

"There!" Rory was pointing to the far corner of the building. It was a big bowling alley but as soon as she saw the crowd gathered at the far end, Phil wondered how she could've missed it. They ran toward the disturbance, and as they got closer, she could hear the rumble of male voices over the click of the pin machines at the end of each lane. And over all of the confusion she could hear her grandmother speaking.

"Boys, please. Now this isn't what I had in mind at all!" declared the prim, slightly breathless voice Phil knew so well.

"Nana," she gasped, wishing she had removed the heels she'd worn to work. They really weren't meant for running and her arches were already aching. The smell of dill pickles and cat urine was overwhelming at this end of the building and she nearly choked as she called for her grandmother again. "Nana!"

"Oh, girls! I'm so glad you came but there was no need to rush. I have the situation under control now." Nana was about seventy-five although the fairy blood in her veins acted to make her look and feel at least twenty-five years younger. Phil couldn't remember a time when her grandmother had looked any different from now. Her long silver-gray hair was piled atop her head in an old-fashioned Gibson girl do and her plump, matronly figure was swathed in a matching lime green pants suit that might have been fashionable in the mid-nineteen-seventies.

Nana was in the middle of a crowd but she looked perfectly in her element as she reached for a bowling ball, surprising Cass, who murmured, "I can't believe she's actually bowling."

"But look who she's bowling with," Rory said.

"Look, hold it like this," one of the men in the crowd surrounding her was instructing their grandmother. But he wasn't exactly a man—not quite, anyway. In fact, none of the crowd that had gathered around Nana were men. Phil's eye was caught by a large banner hanging on the wall caught her eye. *Welcome Eagle Scouts of Tampa/St. Petersburg Annual Bowlathon.* That was when it hit her—not a single one of the guys milling around her grandmother was a day over eighteen and some looked as young as fifteen. The group of admirers Nana had gathered was entirely made up of teenage boys.

"Holy crap!" Cass spoke out of the side of her mouth. "Nana's having herself a Mrs. Robinson moment."

"She sure is," Phil whispered back, relieved that the situation seemed harmless enough.

"I can't believe we rushed all the way over here for this," Rory complained, flipping her long red hair over one shoulder. "If Nana wanted to be a den mother she could have just volunteered instead of dragging us all over town saying she got her potion wrong."

"Look again," Phil told her youngest sister. "I think those Eagle Scouts think that Nana has a slightly more than uh *motherly* interest in them."

"Now, get your hips in line and swing from the shoulder," they heard the boy teaching Nana to hold the ball saying as he positioned his hands on either side of Nana's waist.

"Oh my God!" Cass looked scandalized. "Look at him hitting on her! It's indecent!"

"Chill, Cass, he's just teaching her how to bowl." Rory sighed. "Ya know, I haven't been bowling myself in a long time. Think we could rent some shoes?"

Phil turned to tell her that they didn't have time for an impromptu game when she came face to face with a balding, middle aged man who had a confused look on his face.

"Hello, ladies," he said politely. "You wouldn't happen to know who that attractive older woman over there is, would you?"

"As a matter of fact, she's our grandmother," Cass answered before Phil could speak up.

"And we're sorry if she's caused any trouble," Phil put in quickly.

"Oh, no trouble, really." The man tried to smile. "It's just that we were in the middle of a league championship when she walked in and suddenly all my scouts lost interest in the game."

"They did?" Rory asked with very little surprise. "What happened?"

The balding man who must be the Scout Master frowned. "Well, they all left their lanes and started milling around her. I thought they'd get tired of talking to her and want to get back to the game eventually. But it's been almost forty-five minutes and, well..." He shrugged helplessly, indicating the Eagle Scouts who continued to vie for Nana's attention. Another boy was trying to take over the bowling lesson at this point and the first boy was giving him a hostile stare. From the other side of the lane several more scouts had approached Nana and Phil thought she heard one of them asking for her grandmother's phone number.

"I'm so sorry," Phil said. "She, uh, tends to be a little, um, disruptive at times. But she doesn't mean anything by it."

"Well, I can understand the attraction," the Scout Master said. "I mean, for her age, your grandmother is certainly a very attractive woman. Between you and me, I'm a happily married man. But if I wasn't..." He took in a deep breath and looked at Nana longingly. "I mean, she really is a knock out. And her perfume is *amazing*. In fact, the more I smell it, the better she looks." He took another deep breath and looked confused. "Does that make sense?" He wandered away without waiting for an answer, drifting towards Nana like an iron filing drawn by a magnet.

Phil could see where this was headed and apparently so could Cass.

"That potion she made is attracting the teenagers because they're all just bundles of hormones at that age," she muttered to Phil. "But she almost got it right. If she would have tweaked it just a little bit..."

"It would have attracted anything male in the vicinity," Phil whispered back. "And apparently the longer someone is exposed to it..."

"Someone with a Y chromosome, anyway."

"The stronger it gets," Rory said, joining in the conversation. "I don't think that Scout Master was all that interested in her at first but like he said, she's been here forty-five minutes and now look at him."

They all did, watching as the Scout Master pushed past the boys that were milling around Nana and took her hand with awkward gallantry.

"It took longer to work on him because he's older but now..." Phil shook her head. "Just look at that! He's actually *kissing* her hand."

"Okay, that's enough." Cass squared her shoulders. "She's going to cause a riot in a minute and the last thing we need is a Boy Scout jamboree right here in the middle of the bowling alley. Come on." She grabbed both Phil and Rory by the hands and Phil felt the familiar tingle of power run through her fingertips and up into her arms. Then Cass dragged them through the crowd of boys to where the starry-eyed Scout Master was still smooching Nana's hand.

"Your charm escaped me at first, dear lady," he was murmuring. "But now I see that you are a woman of surpassing beauty." His bald head gleamed in the dim overhead lighting as he leaned over her hand.

"Hey, Scout Master Jenkins, do you mind?" the boy who had been teaching Nana to bowl protested. "I was gonna ask if the hot granny lady here wanted to go to Prom with me. How 'bout it, huh?" he asked Nana over the Scout Master's shoulder, grinning to expose a silver mouthful of braces. "I'll get a limo to pick you up in and everything. It'll be *hot.*"

"Hey—the hot granny lady is going to my prom with *me!*" growled another boy, puffing out his narrow chest. He had a bad case of adolescent acne but he was taller than the first boy and the Scout Master both by about a head and a half, Phil saw. Things were about to get out of control.

"That's enough, boys. The hot granny lad' is coming with us." Cass, Phil, and Rory were still holding hands as they surrounded their grandmother, forcing the Scout Master to relinquish her hand. The power of their blood wasn't much alone, but they were stronger together. Strong enough, hopefully, to rescue Nana from her magically induced predicament.

Hand in hand they shepherded their grandmother through the crowd of milling boys, Cass leading the way. A few of the boys looked to be almost Rory's age but even though her baby sister was very pretty, not a single one of them glanced her way. They were all focused intently on Nana.

"Oh, my, girls—did you see that?" Their grandmother put a plump hand to her heaving bosom, and widened her eyes dramatically. "I'm so close to a breakthrough. I must have just gotten the ratios a bit wrong."

"You certainly got *something* wrong," Phil agreed, using her free hand to hold her nose. Their grandmother absolutely reeked.

"Nana, we tried to warn you not to get mixed up in the Craft," Cass said reprovingly as the girls continued to lead their grandmother though the crowd like a phalanx of bodyguards.

"Yeah, Nana. You know fairies can't do witchcraft," Rory said, patting their grandmother's arm.

"Well now, that's just an old wives' tale!" Nana exclaimed, her jewel-green eyes sparkling with defiance. "I just wanted to attract a man and if I hadn't used just a little too much hemlock... Oh, do we have to go now?" She looked around as they reached the edge of the milling crowd of teenage boys. "Goodbye, boys," she trilled, fluttering her hand flirtatiously. "It was nice to meet you all. I'm sorry I have to leave."

There was some discontented grumbling and one of the boys yelled, "Hey, where are you taking her? Bring her back!"

"Quick," Phil whispered to Rory. "Do you have any perfume on you?"

"Perfume?" Rory looked confused.

"To cover the scent," Cass hissed, catching on. "It's that awful potion that's egging them on—it smells like ass!"

"Uh..." Rory fumbled in the pocket of her jeans with her free hand. "I have some breath spray—sparkling mint."

"That'll do." Phil grabbed the tiny cylinder from her sister's hand and began spraying left and right. As the strong scent of the breath spray began to cover the stink of the potion, the Eagle Scouts and their Scout Master fell back, looking confused.

"What the hell?" The boy with braces who had asked Nana out to his prom shook his head like a dog trying to get rid of a flea. "What happened?"

"You asked my grandmother to go to the prom with you." Cass grinned at him, a wicked twinkle in her violet eyes.

"Shut *up!*" The Eagle Scout eyed Nana doubtfully. "I did not."

"You most certainly did, young man." Nana frowned at him. "And to think I was almost considering it. But I'm afraid my answer will have to be a resounding *no."* She lifted her head and marched proudly through the crowd, reminding Phil of a queen going into exile.

Phil only wished that this experience would teach her grandmother a lesson. But if she knew her nana, it would only make her try harder the next time. If Nana decided she wanted a man, then by God, she would get one. Even if he was fifty years too young for her.

Chapter Seven

"I really have to get moving," Phil said pointedly. "Christian is taking me out and I have to get home, get showered and dressed, and be ready by seven."

"Uh-huh." Cass was still sitting in the front seat of the VW bug, which now smelled like dill pickles, cat pee, and minty fresh breath spray. The ride from Splitsville back to the big lavender mansion on States Street had been nearly unbearable, even with the windows wide open. Rory had already taken their grandmother inside, presumably to get a hot shower, but Cass hadn't budged from the front seat.

"Well?" Phil motioned that Cass should get out.

"You asked me to help you think up a wish," her younger sister reminded her. "Unless you thought of one back there during bowling for hormones?"

"Oh my God!" In all the excitement, Phil had completely forgotten about her birthday wish. She glanced at her watch and saw that it was six ten. Five minutes. Just five minutes to decide on a wish that wouldn't ruin her life.

"Calm down," Cass said, putting a hand on her arm. "There's still plenty of time. You'll make your wish and be home in time for your birthday dinner."

"It's not a birthday dinner," Phil said, without thinking about it. "We're going out with some of his clients again— probably so he can use the expense account."

"What?" Cass immediately bubbled up with all the indignation that Phil couldn't seem to express. "You're kidding me? He forgot again?"

"Yes, he forgot," Phil muttered, wishing Cass didn't always

have to make everything so dramatic. "But I'll remind him later and he'll take me out some other time, I'm sure."

"Some other time isn't good enough, Phil." Cass's pale cheeks were red with anger. "That jerk! He hasn't treated you right from the first. Making you ditch law school to put him through first. And now he won't marry you. And you just sit there and take it. Why don't you say something? Anything? Do you want to be a doormat forever?"

"No, all right?" Phil burst out. It was a controlled shout, but a shout nonetheless. "I'm tired of taking everything everyone dishes out and never saying anything about it." Images of Mrs. Tessenbacker and the nasty little Doodle-bug flitted across her mind. "I'm tired of being taken advantage of," she said, remembering the not-so-blind pencil boy. "I'm tired of listening to what everyone else has to say and never getting to speak my mind. And most of all I'm tired of putting up with self-absorbed jerks who think they're God's gift." This last was directed at the leering image of her boss she could see in her head. But Christian came to mind as well. Was it so difficult to remember her birthday once a year?

Cass looked taken aback. "Well, er, good for your, Phil," she began, but Phil wasn't done.

"You want to hear a wish?" This was as close to yelling as Phil had ever gotten. "I'll tell you what I wish—I'm tired of keeping everything I think and feel all bottled up inside me all the time. I wish I could really speak my mind. *That's* what I wish."

"Done," a bored voice with a haughty British accent declared in her ear.

"What?" Phil looked around wildly and saw that Cass was no longer alone in the front seat of the bug. Sitting on her lap was a tall, thin, blond woman who looked to be in her mid-forties. Which meant that in fairy years she was probably well over a thousand. She was wearing a pale pink designer suit and fashionable mauve slingbacks that looked suspiciously like Jimmy Choos, if they had Jimmy Choos in the Realm of the Fae, Phil thought, feeling dazed. Sprouting from her fairy godmother's back was a large, glittery pair of pearlescent wings that didn't look like they ought to be able to fit into the tiny confines of the bug.

"I said done. It's done. Your pathetic little wish is granted," her fairy godmother elaborated.

"But...I..." Phil felt the tingling rush throughout her body—the sign that a wish had been granted and that her life was already changed in some, as yet undefined way. Rory always said having a wish granted felt like your entire body was made of Pop Rocks and someone had dipped you in a Diet Coke. There was no mistaking the feeling.

"Ah, articulate as ever, I see," the FG said. She waved her glittering silver wand, nearly taking out Phil's eye, and a long thin pink cigarette appeared. She pressed the end of the wand to her cigarette to light it and began to puff large clouds of noxious pink smoke in Phil's direction.

"Hey, there's no smoking in my car," Phil protested, choking on the pink smoke rings her fairy godmother was blowing. The tingling sensation was beginning to fade but she was afraid her troubles were just beginning.

"And get your bony ass off my lap!" Cass spoke up, glaring around her godmother's shimmering mother-of-pearl wings.

"Honestly, the lack of gratitude in this smelly little vehicle is appalling," the FG sniffed, not moving a muscle. "Do I or do I not come here year after year after year and grant your stupid little wishes? And the things you wish for—hot coffee, pretty shoes, good parking spaces. It's sad what a lack of imagination you half-breeds have."

"You know, the only reason we make such mundane wishes is because your magic sucks. Either you don't know how to use it or you don't care. I can't even count the number of times you've screwed up my life and my sisters' lives." Phil shut her mouth with a snap, unable to believe the words had actually come out of her lips. Cass was staring at her like she'd just stepped off a flying saucer. Their fairy godmother looked very offended.

"Oh my God, I didn't mean..." Phil put a hand to her mouth, shaking her head.

"You most certainly did, you little upstart." The FG waggled her wand at Phil and sniffed. "You know, this is the reason I gave you the gift of a lamb-like temperament when you were a child. You always were such a mouthy, bothersome little thing."

Phil felt a red rage growing inside her and this time, instead of bottling it up, she let it come right out her mouth. "You mean you cast that spell on me just to shut me up?" she demanded. "Don't you know that you changed the whole course of my life? Without your 'lamb-like temperament' I'd probably be out of law school right now and starting my own practice. Instead I'm stuck in a dead end job with a boss that ought to be the poster boy for sexual harassment. *And* I'm living with a fiancé who won't commit to a wedding date. Hell, he can't even remember my birthday."

"As to that," the fairy godmother snapped. "I wish I could forget it myself! Have fun speaking your mind, my dear. And don't come crying to me if you don't like it." With a puff of acrid pink smoke, she disappeared, leaving Phil and Cass to choke and gasp until the noxious vapor faded, leaving only the scent of singed rose petals behind.

"Oh my God, Phil!" Cass's violet eyes were as wide as dinner plates. "Did you really just tell the FG off?"

"I guess I did. I...I can't believe it." Phil peered anxiously in her rearview mirror as though expecting to see someone else. But her familiar high cheekbones and blond hair, along with eyes that were now a deep twilight blue (since the sun was beginning to set) were all that greeted her.

"Wow, that was amazing!" Cass gushed. "You go, girl! You need to go home and tell that stupid Christian off for forgetting your birthday for the umpty-millionth time."

Phil looked at her sister. Cass might be right about Christian, but that didn't mean that Phil had to put up with listening to it. Not any longer.

"You know, I'm tired of hearing how stupid you think the life choices I made are," she said, not even bothering to try and hold back. "I know you don't like Christian and you think I'm an idiot for putting off law school. I know you think I should find a new job and you hate my car. But guess what, Cass? I am *sick* of hearing about it. So how about you put a cork in it for once and let me go home before my insensitive asshole of a fiancé blows his stack because I made him late to dinner with his new clients?"

Cass just sat there, her jaw hanging open. Her eyes couldn't have been any wider if Phil had just turned into a peacock and crapped in her lap.

"Oh. My. God." Her voice was low and hoarse. "Do you realize what you wished for, Phil? Just what I told you to wish for—a spine! This is amazing! This is fabulous! This is—"

"This is it," Phil finished for her. "I mean it, Cass. I'm glad you're happy for me but I need to go. Now."

She left her younger sister still flabbergasted outside the big lavender house and put the bug in gear. It was getting late and there was no way she could make a seven o'clock dinner appointment, but Phil didn't care. She had never felt so free.

Chapter Eight

"Today is actually my twenty-fifth birthday." Phil kept her voice light and conversational but she still saw Christian wince out of the corner of her eye. Oh, yeah, he had definitely forgotten. But she would bet her last nickel he'd try to save face in front of his new clients, Minnie and Michael Vance.

"Yup, she's twenty-five today." Her fiancé put his arm around her shoulders and grinned across the table at the Vances. Minnie was wearing a slimming off the shoulder black gown and Michael was dressed in a charcoal gray suit. Phil herself was wearing a shimmery blue sheath that Christian had bought her as an I'm-sorry-I-forgot-your-birthday present the year before. She had been certain that seeing her wear the gown would jog his memory but it became more and more clear as the night went on that he had completely forgotten...again.

Throughout the meal Phil had been speaking her mind as she never had before, even going so far as to send back her steak for being too rare even though she *never* sent anything back. She knew Christian was wondering what the hell was going on with her but she was enjoying herself too much to stop. And the Vances seemed to enjoy her witty conversation. She didn't know them very well, so telling them exactly what she thought seemed easy and impersonal. She found she liked feeling like the life of the party, instead of being a shy wallflower in Christian's golden shadow.

"Twenty-five years old," Christian repeated again, as though he couldn't think of anything else to say.

"The last five have been the longest," Phil continued, still in the same conversational tone of voice. "That's how long I've been with Christian. Let me ask you something, Minnie. Can I call you Minnie?" Mrs. Vance seemed flustered but she nodded just the same. "Thank you, Minnie," Phil said. "What I want to ask is this—what would you do if Mister Vance there forgot your birthday?"

"Well..." Minnie Vance gave her husband a sidelong look. "I think somebody would be sleeping on the couch for a while. We ladies like to have our special dates remembered, don't we, Philomena?"

"Please, call me Phil." Phil smiled at her and had another sip of wine. She'd gone through almost an entire bottle all by herself but she didn't feel the least bit drunk. In fact, she felt marvelous.

"Phil!" Christian protested. "Babe, don't be that way. You know I didn't forget."

"Oh really?" Phil arched an eyebrow at him and took another sedate sip of her wine. "Well, you see, Christian, that's actually more insulting than if you *did* forget it. Minnie and Michael seem like wonderful people, but do you really want me to think that you *planned* to entertain them on my birthday? I mean, honestly, Minnie," she said, turning to Mrs. Vance again. "Do you think it's appropriate? Not that I haven't enjoyed meeting you both." The last statement was absolutely true. The Vances seemed like people she wouldn't mind hanging out with more often. Just not on her birthday.

Minnie looked uncomfortable. "Er, well..." she began.

"Excuse us." Christian was up and out of his chair, one hand wrapped tightly around Phil's upper arm. Before she could protest, he had dragged her away from the dinner table and into the dark hallway that led to the expensive Italian restaurant's bathrooms.

"Okay, what the *hell* do you think you're doing?" he demanded as soon as they were alone.

"You're hurting me." She looked down at his fingers, which had gone white at the knuckles.

"Well you're *killing* me," he snarled, not loosening his grip. "All night long you've been dominating the conversation. What gives, Phil? Did you forget this is a business dinner?"

"I'm speaking my mind for once in my life," she shot back. "Any you know what, Christian? It feels great. It feels great to be able to say what I want instead of hiding in your shadow, hoping you'll throw me a crumb once in a while."

"What the hell are you on tonight? I think you need to lay off the wine." He sounded bewildered.

"I'm not *on* anything. But there are some things I'd like to discuss. Just a few minor details like our wedding and when I get to go back to school. You never seem to have time when we're alone, so I'm discussing them now. Here. On my birthday, which you forgot. Again." She looked down at her arm again. "I'm going to have a bruise there tomorrow if you don't stop."

Christian loosened his grip and ran a hand through his hair. "Look, babe..." He looked suddenly defeated. "I admit it—I forgot your birthday. And damn it, I am *so* sorry. I just got...I got so caught up in my new job and in trying to land the Vances as a client that I let myself get carried away."

Phil rubbed her upper arm. But she felt something inside her begin to melt a little. This was the Christian she had fallen in love with in the first place. The sweet, stammering man who declared his love for her on their second date. The man who had once climbed into a bull's pasture to gather wildflowers for her. (He had barely escaped the charging bull with only a hole in his pants to show for the adventure.) The man she'd been living and planning and hoping with for the last five years. Could it be that the man she loved had simply been buried under the stress of a new job and the need to excel in his chosen profession?

"Christian," she said at last, while he looked at her hopefully. "I just need you to know that your forgetting my birthday again hurt me. A lot."

"I understand that. I do." He nodded, a look of sincerity stamped on his handsome features.

"And there are some things I really need to talk to you about. I feel like you keep ducking me. I want to talk about the wedding. And I want to talk about when I can go back to school. My job is a nightmare and if it wasn't for...well, anyway, it's really bad. I supported you all the way through law school and I feel like right now, I could use some support too."

"Philly-babe," Christian put an arm around her shoulders. "You'll get all the support you need—I promise. But for right now, can we please just go back to the table before I blow it? It's not gonna be good for either one of us if I end up in the unemployment line tomorrow. You know?"

"All right." Phil nodded reluctantly. "But I want to talk about the issues we've been avoiding. And I want to talk about them soon."

"Let's make a date for a breakfast meeting tomorrow morning." Christian smiled at her. "We'll talk over coffee. How's that?"

"That's fine. That'll be just fine." For the first time in their relationship, Phil felt like she had gotten, if not the upper hand, at least an equal footing with her fiancé. It was a very satisfying feeling.

"Okay then. Let's go back and let the Vances know we're not crazy people." He gave her the same brilliantly white smile that had dazzled her in the first place. "And maybe there will be a little birthday surprise sometime tonight after all. What do you say?"

"I say that sounds great." Phil gave him an impulsive kiss on the cheek, then wiped off the smudge of neutral lipstick she'd left behind.

"That's my girl. C'mon, babe. Let's knock 'em dead." He led her back to the table where the Vances were looking at them a little uneasily. Phil dropped all talk of her birthday and Christian was so charming that the whole table was soon laughing and having a wonderful time again, all the earlier awkwardness forgotten. At one point, Christian excused himself and she saw him talking to the head waiter, who nodded stiffly while money exchanged hands. She and Minnie Vance exchanged a girlish, knowing look and the older woman whispered to her, "Have to train them right, don't we my dear?" Phil just winked and smiled back, reveling in the feeling of being the center of attention.

Cass had been right, Phil thought as, at the end of the meal, a waiter appeared with a covered silver tray. This speaking her mind thing had been the best thing that she possibly could have wished for. Why she hadn't wished for it years ago was beyond her.

"For the birthday girl," Christian called loudly as the waiter bent at the waist to present her with the tray. But all her good feelings disappeared when the waiter raised the lid and showed what was beneath. A large, gooey éclair was sitting in the middle of the tray with a small, tasteful white candle stuck into its chocolaty top.

"Oh..." Phil felt like someone had punched her in the stomach. For a moment she was sure she was going to be sick.

"I ordered it especially for you," Christian said proudly, oblivious to her nausea. "It's her favorite," he told the Vances, nodding at the tray. "She has to have one every day. You oughta see the way she goes through them."

"My goodness." Minnie Vance smiled at her enviously. "And you so nice and slender, Philomena. I'm sure I just don't know where you put them."

The nausea had eased its hold on her stomach and Phil wanted to say something polite. But when she opened her mouth, what came out was, "In the trash, mostly."

"Ha—she's such a kidder." Christian was giving her a warning look. "She loves éclairs, don't you, babe? Go ahead—dig in."

Once again Phil wanted to say something to save face. She liked the Vances now, especially Minnie, and she had no wish to embarrass herself or Christian in front of them. But once more when she opened her mouth, the little white lie wouldn't come out.

"I hate éclairs," she heard herself saying. "I've hated them for years. And if you really knew me, Christian, you'd know that."

Her mouth wanted to say more, but Phil didn't dare let it. Instead, she got up and ran to the women's room to hide.

Once safely inside, she splashed cool water on her face, heedless of the fact that her makeup was coming off and her natural deep red lip color could be seen. She stared in the mirror at the girl with eyes so blue they were almost black and wondered what the hell was happening to her. Why couldn't she lie when she needed to? Speaking her mind was one thing but this...

Phil blotted her face with paper towels from the dispenser. She had a bad feeling about what had just happened but she tried to push it down. Maybe it was the wine talking. After all, she hardly ever drank more than a glass or two and tonight she'd had over half a bottle. That had to be it. She'd gotten a little tipsy and the effects of her new wish were still settling in. Fairy magic and alcohol didn't mix. Surely tomorrow when the wine wore off she'd have better control of herself. Probably she'd have a terrible hangover too, but that was all right. As long as things went back to normal, she wouldn't mind having the worst head ache in the world.

It was another half hour before Christian came to get her, after seeing the Vances out to their car. She could tell by the stony look in his eyes that he was not happy but thankfully he didn't ask her any direct questions and she was able to keep her silence.

It was a long, cold ride home, with Phil trying to apologize but no words coming out. And by the time they got to the apartment, Phil no longer even wanted to apologize. Maybe her sisters and Josh were right. Maybe it was time she and Christian took a break from each other. The idea of being out on her own again after five long years was scary, but Phil was beginning to think that it wasn't half as scary as the idea of living the rest of her life with a man who didn't really know her.

"Phil..." Her fiancé broke into her thoughts just as they stepped into the dark, silent apartment. "I don't know what the hell all that was about. But—"

"Christian, I think we ought to take a break," Phil said, even though she would have liked to have a little more time to think about things first. "I feel like you don't really know me. And how can you love somebody you don't know? Maybe...maybe I should just pack some things and move back to my nana's."

"What?" Christian's look went from angry to shocked. "All this because I ordered you an éclair? Come on, Phil—you had too much wine and you're talking crazy."

"No, I'm not." Phil sat on the pale blue couch they'd gotten secondhand when they first moved in together and reached up to turn on the lamp they'd found at a garage sale. "I think I'm talking perfect sense for the first time in years. I don't think you care, anymore, Christian. And why should I stay with someone who doesn't care about me?"

"But Philly-babe, you're wrong. I *do* care." Christian sat on the couch beside her and took her hand in both of his. His palms were slightly clammy with sweat. She resisted the urge to draw her hand away because he looked so upset.

"I...I just don't know if I can believe that anymore," she told him. "Honestly, Christian, you don't seem to know anything about me. Or if you do know, you conveniently forget it."

"Okay, okay." He held up his hands in a 'don't shoot' gesture. "I know I forgot your birthday. And then I ordered something you hate for dessert without knowing it. But, Phil, that's no reason to break up. You're tired and upset right now." He put an arm around her and pulled her to him. "I want you to do me a favor, okay?"

"That depends on what it is," Phil said tersely.

"I want you to sleep on all this, and before you go to bed tonight, I want you to remember all the good times we've had together. Remember our first apartment? How the AC was always breaking so we'd have to take cold showers and go to bed soaking wet or we couldn't sleep? Or how about our second Christmas together when we were so poor we went down to the Dollar store and bought each other five presents because ten dollars was all we could spare?"

"And you got me that little glass bunny and the tail broke off. But then you glued it back on again—upside down." Phil smiled despite herself.

"And you got me that god-awful designer imposters cologne that smelled like skunk spray." Christian grinned at her. "Hard times but good times too, babe. Do you want to throw all that away just because things have been a little rough lately?"

"Well..." Phil wanted to hold on to her anger, but she could feel it slipping away. Maybe Christian was right. Maybe she was overreacting.

"Of course you don't," Christian said, interpreting her silence. "Now come on, let's go to bed and sleep on this and we'll have that conference in the morning over coffee, just like I promised you. Okay?"

Phil sighed. "Well, okay." Maybe thing would look different in the morning.

Chapter Nine

The beeping of her alarm clock woke her as usual and Phil wondered if the previous night had been a bad dream. Speaking her mind, sending back her steak, telling Christian that she hated éclairs in front of his new clients and then trying to break up with him—none of those things was remotely like her. Wish or no wish, it must have been all the wine she'd consumed. She did have a slight headache, too—proof that her limit was closer to one glass of wine than an entire bottle.

She tiptoed to the kitchen and started the coffee. Hopefully Christian would wake up in a better mood if she had everything laid out for him just the way he liked it. After all, he had promised to have a breakfast meeting with her about the issues he'd been avoiding. But she'd give him time to have coffee and read the paper first—the paper!

Phil ran to the apartment's front door and reached for the paper—just as Mrs. Tessenbacker was reaching for it, too. They came up at the same time, both of them holding one end of the morning news.

"Oh, good morning, Philomena." Mrs. Tessenbacker gave her a crocodile smile but didn't let go of the paper. Around her ankles, Doodle-bug yipped crazily.

"Good morning, Mrs. Tessenbacker," Phil said evenly. "I believe this is my paper." She took a firmer grip on the contested item.

"Well, yes, dear. But is just so happens that Doodle-bug is short on potty paper this morning. And I just thought—"

"You just thought you'd come across the hall and steal my paper like you always do?"

"Honestly, I was only going to borrow it. You never seemed to mind so—"

"Well, I *do* mind." Phil glared at the older lady. "This is *my* paper and I pay for it. I do *not* pay to have you steal it for your nasty little dog to pee on."

"Well!" Mrs. Tessenbacker drew herself up and let go of the paper. "I have never in all my days..."

Phil felt a thrill of victory. Now would have been the perfect time to simply say, "Goodbye, Mrs. Tessenbacker," and go back inside her apartment. She had won the battle and she would be willing to bet that her elderly neighbor would never steal her paper again. But she had a lot more on her mind—and to her horror, it began to come out of her mouth.

"Your dog stinks." She looked down at Doodle-bug, who was growling at her, his brown and gray hackles raised and his tiny yellow teeth bared.

"Excuse me?" Mrs. Tessenbacker's eyes widened further.

"That's right—I can smell him all up and down this hallway," Phil's mouth continued, voicing thoughts she'd had many times but never expected to put into words. "And you're cheap," she continued. "I see you walking your mangy mutt up and down the street on a diamond studded collar but you can't even buy your own paper."

"I...I..." For once Mrs. Tessenbacker seemed to be at a loss for words. Doodle-bug wasn't, however. He trotted over to Phil and started to hike his leg. Phil took a quick step back.

"The next time your dog pees on my foot I'm going to put it up his ass," she heard herself saying. "If you can't train your animal better than that you don't deserve to have one."

"Oh!" Mrs. Tessenbacker reached down with surprising speed for someone her age and snatched the bundle of fur into her arms. "Come on, Doodle-bug. Let's get away from her!" She retreated into her apartment and slammed the door, leaving Phil to sag against the wall, the morning paper forgotten in her hand.

Maybe it hadn't just been the wine, after all.

Chapter Ten

Phil waited in silence as Christian scanned the morning news, this time sans dog pee, and sipped his hot black coffee. So far she hadn't felt compelled to say anything to him but then, he hadn't said anything to her either. Also, she was standing at the far end of the kitchen, leaning against the counter with her arms crossed over her chest. She wasn't sure, but she thought maybe the compulsion to speak her mind was stronger when she was close to someone.

At last Christian looked up from his coffee. "How's your head this morning?"

"It aches a little," Phil said cautiously.

He nodded, as though he'd expected nothing less. "All that wine you drank last night, I'm not surprised. From now on I think we better limit you to one glass. Or maybe you should just stick to water."

He was only saying exactly what she'd been thinking earlier, but Phil still felt herself bristling at his condescending tone.

"Oh, so I guess you think I made a fool of myself last night." She uncrossed her arms and stepped towards him.

Christian gave a short bark of a laugh. "You could say that. Getting so upset over a stupid pastry you wanted to end our relationship. I've never seen you act that way before, Phil. What the hell got into you? Besides an entire bottle of wine, I mean."

"I...I can't exactly tell you." Phil frowned, unable as always to talk about her fairy godmother. The wish didn't apply to *everything* on her mind, it seemed—the magic was still protecting itself from non-fae outsiders. "But I do know that whatever got into me is here to stay, Christian. I'm sorry about last night but I still want to talk about the issues you promised me we'd discuss."

"I'm surprised you remembered after all your crazy talk." He put down his coffee mug with a thunk.

Phil clenched her fists. "You were just putting me off, weren't you? Reminding me of our 'good times'. Saying whatever you thought I wanted to hear and assuming I'd forget all about it in the morning."

"C'mon, babe, be fair." Christian looked uncomfortable. "You know that's not true. You wanna talk about the wedding? Fine, we'll talk about it."

"Yes, I *do* want to talk about it." Phil tried to keep her voice even. "Last night you kept me from leaving by reminding me of everything we've shared in the past. But now I want to talk about our future."

"The wedding." Christian shook his head. "I wanted to save more money and do it right. But if you want to get married so badly then fine—we'll go to a justice of the peace today if that'll make you happy."

"But will it make *you* happy?" She slid into the seat across from him, looking earnestly into his face. "It doesn't sound like it would. We used to talk about the day we could afford a nice wedding—used to wish for it and dream for it. But you haven't mentioned it in months—not since you got this new job."

Christian didn't meet her eyes. "Well, damn it, babe—the job is demanding. I've got my boss on my back all the time and I'm trying to make a name for myself and land new clients. Like the Vances." He shot her an accusing glare before looking back into his coffee cup. "In fact, I have an important meeting this morning I'm gonna be late for if I don't hurry."

Phil frowned as he started to get up. "Wait a minute—I know for a fact your office doesn't open until nine and you promised me we'd talk about this."

"Oh yeah? Well *you* promised *me* that you wouldn't act the fool again in front of the Vances last night," he shot back.

Phil felt hot tears filling her eyes but she blinked them back. "Christian, lately I feel undervalued by you. In fact, I think I've always felt that way." The wish started to work its magic, and the words came in a rush. "I feel like you always come first in this relationship, like you don't give a damn any more about my needs and feelings."

Christian ran both hands through his hair. "I don't have time for this!" he growled. "You want to get married—I told you we would, any damn time you want. What else do you want from me?"

"I want to talk about going back to school," Phil said quietly. "Remember the plan, Christian? I put you through law school and then you were supposed to put *me* through."

He sighed and sank down in his chair. "Yeah, I remember. But look, babe." His tone became softer. "I've been giving that some thought. I mean, why should you have to go back to school now that I can support us?"

Phil couldn't believe her ears. "Excuse me? Why should I *have* to go back to school? Did it ever occur to you that I *want* to go back?"

Christian sighed. "Yeah, but do you really think it's necessary? I mean, I know you want to quit your crappy job and that's fine with me. Just let me get another raise or two under my belt and you can leave BB&D and never look back. But law school is expensive. And why should you go back when it would be so much easier for you to stay home and start a family? I mean, we both want kids and it would be nice for me to come home every day to a home cooked meal. You could kick back and relax—just take it easy—take care of the house, maybe take those tennis lessons you always wanted..." He trailed off. "Babe?"

Phil took a deep breath. "So this is your answer, Christian? Instead of holding up your end of the bargain, you want me to give up everything I've been waiting for ever since we met? I've put my dreams on hold for the last four years for you and this is what I get?"

"Hey, hey, hey..." He put up both hands. "Come on now, let's get real here, babe. You always talk about wanting to be a civil rights attorney but let's lay the facts on the table. I know you, Phil, and you wouldn't be any good in a court room situation. You'd let the other side bully you and you couldn't stand up to the judge. Hell—you'd lose just about every case you tried. Why should I waste money on getting you a degree in something you wouldn't be any damn good at? It's a bad idea all the way around."

Phil felt like he'd taken her heart in his hand and twisted it. "Is...is that really what you think of me?" she asked, hoping her voice wouldn't break. "Is that really how you see me, Christian?"

Her fiancé looked taken aback. "Hell, I'm just stating the facts, Phil. I don't want to hurt your feelings but you'd make a lousy lawyer and you and I both know it."

"I don't know any such thing. How *could* I know unless I try? This is my dream, Christian. My heart that you're trampling on. Can't you see that?"

"Shit! Phil, could you stop it with the melodrama?" Christian rolled his eyes. "I don't understand you sometimes. Here I am, offering you the chance to kick back and take it easy for the rest of your life while I take care of everything and you're acting like I stomped your pet puppy dog."

Suddenly her pain turned to anger—a red rage so blinding that Phil wanted to hurt him the way he had hurt her. "May I remind you," she asked, through gritted teeth. "That I turned down an acceptance from *Stanford* to put you through school? May I further remind you that you went to State because you couldn't get into any place else?"

Her fiancé's face darkened. "That was a low blow, Phil."

"Oh, and telling me my dream is a ridiculous fantasy because I'd be no good at it *isn't?*" she shouted. She was trembling with rage and yet she felt cold inside. The wish had her completely in its grip and she couldn't stop talking. But the words were true, every last one of them.

"And you know what, Christian?" she continued. "That isn't even what bothers me the most. It's what a selfish bastard you've become. We had a deal. But you're living your dream. So why should you care if I ever get mine, right?"

He shook his head in disgust. "I can't talk to you about this right now. If you're not willing to face facts I can't help you." He got up from the table and tossed his half-empty mug in the sink. Coffee splattered up over the wall behind the sink and there was a sharp cracking sound as the mug shattered.

"I don't know why I should be surprised," Phil yelled. "It's not like this is the only part of our life you're selfish in. I haven't had an orgasm with you in the past three years!" Then she clapped a hand over her mouth. The fact that their sex life wasn't that great was something she hadn't even allowed herself to *think* about. Was her subconscious getting into the act now, too?

Christian took a deep breath and turned back to face her. For a moment she thought he was going to hit her. He had never struck her the entire time they had been together but a part of her almost welcomed it. *Come on, do it!* S*how your true colors, you bastard. Cass was right about you all along. All of them were right! I'm just sorry I wasted so much time defending you.* She opened her mouth to say it, but Christian stopped her by taking both her shoulders in his hands.

"Phil," he said softly, holding her gaze with his. "I'm sorry if what I told you hurt you but I wouldn't have said it if I didn't care." He was breathing hard but the anger was gone from his eyes. They were calm and blue and utterly serious. "And deep down in your heart, you know I'm right. Phil..." He shook her gently for emphasis. "Wedding, yes. Kids and a family— absolutely. But law school..." He furrowed his brow. "I'm sorry, Philly-babe, but you have to trust me on this. I've been there and done that and I know better. I care about you—I care enough to tell you that you just don't have what it takes. Do you understand?"

"No." Phil felt numb and all the hot rage inside her suddenly turned to ice. "No, I don't understand, Christian. I don't think I understand anything anymore."

"That's why you have to trust me," he said. "To take care of you. To look out for your best interests. I'm only telling you this because I want to spare you the pain of finding it out on your own the hard way." He gave her a swift kiss on the cheek. "Look, I know you want to talk about this but I really have to go or I'm going to miss this early meeting. Okay?"

"Okay," Phil said numbly. She literally had nothing else to say.

"Good." Christian smiled at her. "I'm glad we understand each other. See ya later, babe." He headed for the shower, leaving Phil to sink down at the table, clutching her throbbing temples with both hands.

Chapter Eleven

She would have been happy to call in sick, but Phil had a performance review with Dickson Junior that afternoon and ditching it would have meant automatic termination.

Christian had run out of the house after the fastest shower in history, leaving her to get dressed in dismal silence. Phil dragged through her morning routine, knowing she was running late and unable to make herself care. She had never had a fight like that with her fiancé before. Had never let him know what she really thought and felt, as pathetic as it sounded. But worse than hearing her own feelings voiced out loud had been hearing his. Did he really think so little of her? Did he really expect her just to roll over and forget her dreams because he said so? Phil supposed he probably did. After all, she'd been pretty much going along with everything Christian said for years. It must have been an ugly shock for him to find out she had a mind of her own.

The worst thing though, was the little voice in the back of her head that told her he might be right. Christian had voiced every doubt she had ever had about herself and somehow made it a reality. *What if I would make a lousy lawyer? What if everything I've ever wanted is just a stupid pipedream?*

A part of her knew she could succeed at whatever she turned her hand to as long as she tried hard enough. But the other part... *I'm just trying to spare you pain,* he'd said. But the most painful thing was knowing what he thought if her.

Phil was cold all over. She felt like she ought to be crying, but she hadn't shed a tear. It was as though she had cut herself deeply with a knife and was stuck in that split second between the initial slice and the instant the wound starts to bleed.

She was also beginning to rethink her wish. Maybe it would be wise to call the fairy godmother and ask her to reverse what she had done. Good luck on that one, Phil snorted to herself. She remembered the FG's nasty tone when she'd said, *"Have fun speaking your mind, my dear. And don't come crying to me if you don't like it."* Still, as pissed off as her fairy godmother had been, she supposed she could always beg...

But something in Phil revolted against the idea. It was true her latest birthday wish had had some unexpected consequences. She had said and done some things she certainly wouldn't have dreamed of doing and saying before. But if she hadn't made the wish, she never would have found out what Christian really thought of her. What she was still trying to figure out was how she really felt about him. How she'd been feeling for the past year if she was honest with herself.

When she pulled into the BB&D parking area, Alison's bright red Mercedes was parked in her space, as usual. Phil looked at it grimly for a moment, revving her engine and wishing that she had a big-ass SUV instead of her grimy little bug so she could knock her coworker's expensive car into next week. What was she turning into? She had to get control of herself. She took a deep breath and drove past her spot.

Also as usual, Phil had to park far in the back. She was trudging up to the elevators when she saw a thin shape slip around one of the concrete pillars of the garage. It was the "blind" pencil boy and he was riding an expensive-looking bike. Phil kept her head down and pretended not to notice. Out of the corner of her eye, she saw him dismount quickly and hide the bike behind a concrete pillar. Then he moved into position, pulling on his sunglasses and grabbing his pencil cup. Clearly he had seen her and just as clearly he thought she was too distracted to have noticed him setting up his act.

"Lady? Hey, lady?" It was the same as every other morning, with the boy jingling his cup in her face as she tried to get past him to the elevators. "Hey! Don't you wanna buy a pencil?"

"No," Phil said, and tried to move past him.

"C'mon, lady," he whined, blocking her path. "You always buy a pencil. Don't you want one today? Only a dollar."

"I know how much they are," Phil said stopping to look at him. "I've been buying a pencil a day from you for the last three years. But you know what? I'm not going to do it anymore."

"Why not, lady? C'mon," he wheedled. "If you don't wanna pencil, just give me a dollar."

"I will not." Phil felt the magic well up in her again. "I've given you enough money to pay for a semester of college and I've got so many pencils I could open my own stationary store." She looked him up and down. His clothes looked new and his sneakers had to have cost more than three pairs of her own shoes. Being a blind pencil boy was apparently big business. "Let me ask you something. What do you do with all the money you collect?"

The pencil boy got an uneasy look on his face. "Uh, I don't know. Buy stuff," he mumbled.

"What stuff?"

He frowned. "I don't know—stuff I need. My parents don't give me enough allowance."

"Uh-huh." Phil nodded. "And do you know what I'd like to buy with the money I've been giving you for pencils? *Lunch.* Do you know that for the last three years while I've been giving you my lunch money I've also been trying to put my ungrateful bastard of a fiancé through law school? And why? Because he promised he'd put me through when he was done. But today I found out that he has no intention of living up to his end of the bargain because he thinks I would make a crappy lawyer." Phil took a deep breath and tried to get back on topic. "The point is, you're not getting one more dime from me."

The pencil boy stared at her for a moment before shaking his head. "Holy shit, lady—you're crazy."

"I may be crazy but I'm not stupid." Phil snatched the dark sunglasses off his face and watched his eyes widen in disbelief. She folded them neatly and dropped them on the concrete, where she crunched them beneath the heel of her sensible black work pump. Then she folded her arms calmly and smiled at him. "Did you see that?" she asked the dumbfounded pencil boy.

"Uh...yeah." His eyes wouldn't leave the shattered fragments of black plastic beneath her heel.

"Exactly," Phil said.

He looked up at her. "I can't believe you, lady. Those were Oakleys!"

"Well then you're just going to have to go sell pencils somewhere else to buy some new ones," Phil said coolly. "Or you could try getting a real job. You're what—fifteen?"

"Sixteen," he answered sullenly.

"So go find a job at Burger King or Subway if you want extra money. Try being a sandwich artist instead of a con artist for a while. Now get out of here—I never want to see you on these premises again."

The boy gave her one last wide-eyed look and then ran behind the pillar to grab his bike. He yelled something over his shoulder as he pedaled away that Phil didn't quite catch. But somehow she didn't think it was "have a nice day".

Phil stepped from the elevator into the office with her head down. *Godohgodohgod.* She had told off the little blind pencil boy. Not only that, she had broken his glasses. What was next? She didn't know if she should feel panicked or pleased. The strange mixture of emotions churning in her gut were making her feel slightly nauseous. She had to get through the workday without any major episodes. Her plan was to stay as far away from her coworkers as possible and try to keep her mouth shut.

"Good morning, Philomena." A kindly voice in her ear startled Phil so much she almost jumped. She looked up to see Caroline Sanders, the head of the filing department smiling at her through her bright pink lipstick.

Caroline was a sweet old soul who had worked for BB&D for about a hundred years but she had peculiar ideas about makeup. She liked to wear bright colors and she liked to wear a lot of them. Consequently, her cheeks were always two hot pink spots and her mouth was a bright slash in her wrinkled little face. The strangest thing about her makeup though, was her eyebrows. At some time in the far distant past, she must have plucked them all out, so now she had to draw them in with an eyeliner pencil.

But Caroline wasn't content to draw her brows in with brown or black or even auburn to match the color of her hair (which was obviously dyed). Instead, she chose colors that matched whatever she happened to be wearing that day. So if she was wearing blue, she drew herself blue eyebrows. If she wore a green dress, her eyebrows were sure to match. Today, Phil noticed, her coworker was wearing a deep purple wrap dress with tiny pink daisies printed all over it. And true to form, arching purple eyebrows had been drawn in above her faded blue eyes.

"Good morning, Caroline," Phil said, her gaze drawn inevitably up to the purple arches. *Why does she do that?* she thought for the hundredth time. And then, to her horror, she found herself asking it. "Why do you do that?"

"Do what, Philomena, dear?" Caroline asked, a puzzled smile creasing her wrinkled cheeks.

"Why do you...why do you..." Phil fought the urge with all her might. *There was an old woman who lived in a shoe,* she recited silently, trying to take her mind off her coworkers bizarre makeup job. *She had so many colored eyebrows, she didn't know what to do. No—that's not right!* Phil bit her lip desperately. She liked Caroline and didn't want to hurt her feelings. Damn this stupid wish!

"Dear? Are you quite all right?" Caroline put an arthritic hand on her arm, frowning worriedly. "You look a little ill."

"I'm not ill. I just wanted to know why...why..." Phil bit the inside of her cheek until she tasted blood. *Old Mother Eyebrow went to the cupboard to get her poor dog a bone. But when she got there, the eyebrow was bare, and so the poor eyebrow got none.*

"What dear? You want to know why...?" Caroline raised her amazing purple eyebrows and leaned forward to catch the end of the question. Suddenly Phil realized there was no helping it—the words were going to come out of her mouth whether she wanted them to or not.

"I want to know why you match your eyebrows to the color of your dress every day," she said, all in one quick, miserable rush. Then she put her head down and waited to see if Caroline was angry or hurt or what. So she was surprised to hear an ancient, tinkling laugh, like a rusty music box. She looked up to see Caroline smiling.

"Is that all, dear?" She patted Phil on the arm. "Well I do it for the same reason some people like to make sure their shirt and socks go together—I like to match." She gave Phil a naughty grin and leaned in to whisper, "I'll tell you a little secret too—I like to match *everywhere.* I found the prettiest purple bra and panty set at Victoria's Secret so I'm pretty in purple all over today." She nudged the speechless Phil with one elbow, nodded, and sashayed off down the long, maroon carpeted hall humming to herself.

Phil was nearly weak with relief. Although finding out that her coworker's underwear matched her eyebrows was a little too much information. Still, at least she hadn't done any lasting harm with her stupid, wish-induced question.

"Oh. My. God. Philomena, were you just talking to Caroline?" The voice in her ear made Phil jump for the second time that day. She turned to see Kelli standing in front of her with her arms crossed over the pumpkin orange blouse she was wearing. Caroline wasn't the only one who liked bright colors.

"Yes," she said. "I was."

"Did I hear you asking her about her weird eyebrows?" Kelli asked, raising her own eyebrows, which thankfully matched her hair.

"I don't know, Kelli," Phil snapped. *"Did* you hear me ask her?"

"Uh...I guess." Kelli seemed taken aback by her snappish tone of voice but she recovered quickly. "Anyway, I think it's about time somebody said something to her, you know? I mean, with all that makeup on, she looks like a clown. Have I ever told you how I feel about clowns?"

"No, you haven't. And to be perfectly honest, I'm not especially interested to hear your views on them now." She dropped her purse at her desk, turned and stalked away from the gaping Kelli before her coworker could say one more word. And more importantly, before she could start thinking about how much she disliked Kelli and begin speaking her mind again.

She breathed a sigh of relief when the break room was free. If only everyone would just stay away from her she might get through the rest of the day. She was fixing herself a cup of hot tea and planning how to handle her performance review later that afternoon, when she heard someone behind her.

Phil turned apprehensively, but to her relief it was only Davis Miles, the handsome lawyer that Alison was always hitting on. Thank goodness she had never had any desire to tell him off. She was safe.

"Morning, Mister Miles," she said, adding some sweetener

to her hot cinnamon tea and keeping her head down.

"Good morning, Ms. Swann." He nodded gravely at her, showing the restraint she found so admirable in him. Phil watched him from the corner of her eye as he poured himself a mug of coffee. With his dark hair and eyes, she had always thought he looked like the hero on the cover of a romance novel. To her horror, her mouth opened suddenly and the thought came rolling off her tongue.

"You know, Mister Miles, with your dark good looks, I've always thought you looked like one of those handsome, well-hung hunks from the cover of a bodice ripper romance novel," Phil heard herself say. Oh God! Did she have to say it quite like *that*? She watched as Davis Miles turned around, a small frown creasing his perfect forehead.

"Uh, thank you, Ms. Swann," he said carefully.

"I've always wanted to see you with your shirt off," Phil continued, much to her own horror and, most likely, to Miles', as well. "You look like you work out. I've always kind of wondered what you look like naked."

Oh no! She slapped a hand over her mouth. Fighting with her fiancé and shouting at the pencil boy was nothing compared to this—nothing at *all*. Phil wanted to sink through the floor.

"I'm sorry..." Davis Miles was staring at her, his coffee mug halfway to his lips. "Did...did you just say you wanted to see me naked? I mean, that's what I thought you said but..."

"I did say that, but I didn't mean it," Phil gabbled. "I mean, I did mean it or I wouldn't have said it but I didn't mean to say it. I'm so sorry," she finished miserably, "I can't help it—I can't stop saying what I think."

Miles was still giving her a strange look. "Did, uh, did Alison put you up to this? Because this whole, um, this whole *naked* thing sounds like something she would say."

"What whole naked thing?"

Phil tried to stifle a groan as she turned to see her slinky coworker sliding up behind her. An old saying of her nana's popped into her head—speak of the devil and he will appear. Or in this case, she. She couldn't help wondering how much of the humiliating exchange Alison had heard.

"Nothing, Alison," she said hastily. "Nothing at all."

"Oh, I think there's *something* going on in here, Philomena," Alison purred. Today she was wearing a low-cut poison green blouse that matched her eyes perfectly and her skirt, as always, was positively indecent. "I heard my name and the word 'naked' in the same breath," she continued, batting her lashes at Davis Miles. "I hope you're not giving Davis here a bad impression of me."

"Why would I bother when you're doing such a good job of it yourself?" Phil said. The wish was in full command of her now. She couldn't even stop her mouth long enough to try and think of a nursery rhyme to distract her awful thoughts.

Alison stopped making eyes at Miles and turned, giving her full attention to Phil for the first time. "*What* did you say?"

"I said," Phil continued, unable to stop herself, "That you dress like a slut. And you act like one too." *Oh, God! This is getting worse and worse!*

Alison put a hand on her hip, her green eyes flashing. "Are you calling me a slut?"

Phil shrugged. "If the size seven fuck-me pump fits—wear it, hon." Behind her, Davis Miles snorted laughter, which he quickly turned into a cough.

Alison's eyes narrowed. "How *dare* you talk to me like that, you drab little bitch?"

Phil stood up straighter and stared her coworker in the eye. "I'm only saying what everyone else in the office is thinking. Why don't you have some respect for yourself, Alison? There's more to you than just your tits and ass—at least I hope there is. So why don't you act like it? Button your blouse, pull down your skirt and try doing some work for a change, instead of sleeping your way to the middle."

"Well, I...I..." Alison stuttered.

"And another thing," Phil snapped, pointing a finger at her coworker's considerable cleavage. "You car is parked in my spot for the twentieth time this month. If it happens again, I can't be responsible for my actions."

"Are...are you threatening me?" Alison put a hand to her heaving bosom, her narrow, fox-like face flushed with anger.

"No," Phil said coolly. "Just your car. Good morning." She brushed past Alison and Davis, her mug of tea clutched in her hand and her heart thumping in her ears. So much for avoiding everyone and not having any more confrontations.

"Philomena, I want to talk to you."

Not Kelli again! She must have been lying in wait for Phil outside the break room.

"Now is really not a good time," Phil said truthfully, quickening her step. "Honestly, Kelli, I really need some alone time right now."

"Well I want to talk about the way you bit my head off earlier." Kelli's strident voice was no doubt reaching everyone in the office.

Phil turned abruptly, slopping hot tea over her hand and onto the maroon rug. Carefully, she placed the mug on a nearby desk and crossed her arms over her chest. "All right," she said grimly. "Let's talk. But I warn you, you might not like what you hear."

"I..." Kelli looked nonplussed. "Well, I just wanted to say you didn't have to yell at me like that. I was just coming up to tell you how late you were this morning. In fact," She brightened as she spoke. "You know, I was late the other day, but I had a totally good excuse. See, I was stuck in traffic because there was this major accident. And I was all thinking, 'God, Kelli, why does this kind of stuff always happen to you?' So the woman next to me in traffic, she was like eating some hash browns or something—I don't know. Anyway, she was all staring at me, like I had the plague or something. So I roll down my window and I go, 'Do I know you?' And she goes—"

"Enough!" Phil had her hands clenched so tightly she could feel her nails biting into her palms, but it was no use.

"What?" Kelli looked at her in confusion.

"Every day." Phil raised a finger, advancing on her coworker. "Every day I come in here and I have to hear about your life. It might be different if you ever asked about my day or wanted to talk about anyone else but yourself. But no, Kelli, it's always you, you, *you*. Did it ever once occur to you that I don't want to hear every tiny little detail of your existence? Have you stopped once to consider the fact that you just might *not* be the center of the universe as we know it?"

"I...I..." Finally Kelli was at a loss for words. But Phil wasn't.

"Kelli," she said, staring her mouthy coworker in the face.

"I've been wanting to say this for years. *Shut. Up.*" She turned and stalked away from her cubicle, leaving Kelli in silence for the first time since they had started working together.

This wish was appalling and exhilarating at the same time. But Phil knew there were sure to be repercussions. Big ones. At the same time she couldn't regret telling her coworker off. Was she turning into a bad person? Or was she finally standing up for herself? Or both?

Still, Phil realized she had an even bigger problem. The wish she had made was no longer distinguishing between things she actually *wanted* to say, down in the dark depths of her subconscious, and things she was simply thinking about and had no desire to voice out loud. Everything that popped into her mind came straight out her mouth. She was literally speaking her mind.

There was only one thing to do—she had to get her fairy godmother to reverse this wish.

Chapter Twelve

"Fairy Godmother? *Fairy Godmother!*" Phil hissed, under her breath. She was huddled in the last stall at the end of the row in the ladies room trying unsuccessfully to make contact with the pink-winged bringer of doom who had screwed her yet again. Otherwise known as her fairy godmother. In fact, she'd been hiding out in the bathroom trying for most of the morning with zero success.

Part of the problem was that fairies didn't carry cell phones. In fact, they didn't communicate through any ordinary means. And, other than on birthdays, they could be extraordinarily hard to get hold of, or at least, Phil's was. In theory, all she had to do in order to contact her fairy godmother was pull on her right earlobe three times and whisper the words, "Fairy Godmother, please come for my need is dire." In actuality, Phil had been yanking until her earlobe felt like it was going to come off with no results.

It wasn't like she'd expected to get hold of the FG on the first try, she thought bitterly, stopping for a moment to give her red, swollen earlobe a rest. After all, every other time she and her sisters had been forced to ask to have a wish repealed, they had had to call repeatedly before she bothered to show. But Phil couldn't ever remember feeling so frantic before. This wasn't just a pair of pretty but painful shoes stuck on her feet—this was her life! She and her run-away mouth were systematically screwing up everything.

So far this morning she had: one—called her elderly neighbor cheap and threatened to put her foot up her dog's ass, two—had a harrowing moment of truth with the man she loved (well, was reasonably sure she loved, anyway), three—yelled at the little blind pencil boy and broken his glasses (okay, so he wasn't blind and he wasn't that little, but still!), four—she'd asked one coworker a rude question, told another to shut up, called a third slut, and told a fourth she wanted to see him naked. All in all it was the worst day of her life, hands down. And it wasn't over. In fact, until she contacted her fairy godmother, it would *never* be over.

Phil did regret that she might lose the will to stand up for herself. Then again, if she worded things correctly, she might not. The wish she'd made to speak her mind had canceled out her fairy godmother's earlier "gift" of being mild mannered. So unless the FG specifically regifted her with the lamb-like temperament, maybe she could stop thinking out loud and still keep her newfound sense of self worth. Despite everything that had happened to her, Phil knew she didn't want to go back to being a spineless dishrag who listened to her coworkers' complaints and her sisters' criticism without saying a word in her own defense. She didn't want to meekly accept whatever hand life dealt her. And most of all, she didn't want to go back to letting Christian run her life.

She rubbed her temples again, then grabbed her right earlobe and yanked as hard as she could. "Fairy Godmother come to me for my need is dire!"

"I don't care *what* kind of intestinal difficulties you're having, Philomena. You'd better get your ass out here and get to your performance review or Dickson is going to fire you. Not that I'd mind." Alison's snarky voice bounced off the pink tiled walls to Phil's ears.

Phil winced. The performance review! It was something she'd been dreading for months but in the confusion of the morning, she'd forgotten all about it. Of all days to have it! She should just go home now and consider herself unemployed.

Phil was many things, but she wasn't a quitter. And she might need this job if she suddenly found herself...well, if things didn't improve between her and Christian. Not to mention how the lack of a good reference from BB&D would look if—no, *when* she went to law school. Too bad she couldn't claim to be suddenly ill but at BB&D there was no excuse good enough to miss a review. There was no help for it, she would have to go to the review.

She stood up and banged open the stall door to see her

coworker leaning against the row of sinks with her arms crossed over her chest and a smirk on her face. On the plus side, Alison *had* buttoned her blouse and her breasts were no longer threatening to overflow. And when Phil walked up to her she actually flinched a little.

"Better get to that review, hon," Alison sneered. "You don't want to keep Dickson waiting too long or he may decide to fire you. If he hasn't already."

Phil lifted her chin. "You know, you really are a bitch," she said. Then she turned and headed out of the ladies room. Time to face the music.

Chapter Thirteen

"Come in, Philomena, sweetheart. I hear you've been a *naughty* girl today." Atwood Dickson's booming voice made her wince as Phil walked into his office. Her boss was sitting at his desk with a leering grin stamped on his ape-like features. Apparently the office rumor mill had been working overtime while she sat in the bathroom and uselessly called her fairy godmother.

"Mister Dickson, I don't know what you've heard," Phil began, trying to stand well back from his desk. "But I—"

"Oh I heard all *kinds* of things, sweetheart." He grinned at her unpleasantly and came toward her around the side of his desk. "But what interested me the most was what I heard you said to Davis Miles. Now is it true that you asked him to strip so you could see him naked?"

"Well, I..." Phil backed away from him, trying to keep her mind blank. Nursery rhymes hadn't helped earlier but maybe if she didn't think any words at all, she wouldn't *say* anything. *La, la, la, la, la,* she thought frantically.

"And is it further true that you wanted to take him in the storage closet and, uh, show him a good time?" Dickson waggled his eyebrows at her and she saw with disgust that he had big flakes of dandruff in them.

"What? No!" she protested, backing further away. He must have been drinking coffee all day because his breath was horrible. Immediately she wanted to tell him so. *La, la, la!*

"Well, honestly, I didn't hear *that*." Dickson laughed and Phil sagged in relief. He had been making a joke. A horrible joke but a joke nonetheless.

"Well, I'm glad you didn't—"

"But that's how it could *sound* on your performance review," Dickson interrupted.

"What?" Phil blinked.

"Yes, that would be a shame, *wouldn't* it sweetheart?" Dickson had her backed into a corner now, blowing his horrible coffee breath in her face and leering like a horny bear. "You see, up until today, I was going to give you a perfect review same as every other year and send you on your way. But you..." He shook his head. "You had to go and screw that up, didn't you, Philomena? I've had three separate complaints against you today not to mention that someone saw you out in the parking lot abusing a sight impaired pencil salesman."

"But...but he's not really sight impaired," Phil protested, wondering who had been watching her smash the pencil boy's glasses.

Dickson gave her an unpleasant smile. "Doesn't matter, sweetheart. What matters is what I put on your review."

"But what...how..."

"This is how it's going to work," Dickson said, leaning against the wall so that she was trapped between his arm and the corner. "Either I can give you a poor review and you can have an attitude adjustment session with HR tomorrow. Or..." He leaned closer and whispered, "Or you can give me a reason why I shouldn't."

Finally Phil's confused thoughts began to come together. "Mister Dickson," she said, staring him in the eye. "Are you propositioning me?"

He laughed, a troll-like chuckle that made her skin crawl. "Oh, I wouldn't call it that, Philomena, sweetheart. Let's just say I'm giving you a chance to get a better review—a fresh start, so to speak."

"I see," she said coldly. "And all I have to do is sleep with you to get it."

"Take it or leave it. Do you want this job or not, sweetheart? You have to admit, I've got you between a rock and a hard place. A *very* hard place." Dickson laughed and shrugged, his fat shoulders bunching under his ill-fitting suit jacket. Beneath the armpits Phil could see large sweat rings.

"You're a pig," she said clearly.

"What?" It was Dickson's turn to look shocked.

"You're a pig and you make me sick. Just the thought of your hands on me—of your disgusting, hairy body anywhere near me—turns my stomach." Phil ducked out from under his arm and faced her boss, her hands clenched at her sides.

"What did you say?" He stared at her.

"You think I like coming to work every day, putting up with your stupid, sexist remarks and the way you're always trying to grab my ass?" Phil demanded. She poked a finger in his face. "Well I don't. I put up with it because I need this job—but I don't need any job badly enough to sleep with *you.*"

"Why, you little..." Dickson's muddy eyes narrowed to slits. But Phil wasn't done yet.

"Not only are you a bad boss, you're a horrible attorney," she continued relentlessly. "I always feel so sorry for your clients. Because you'd rather sit here and watch porn on your computer and whack off than prepare for your court dates."

Dickson's face began to get red. "I didn't...I never..." he blustered.

"Don't deny it—the whole office knows it. Everyone knows what a disgusting, lazy, smelly, sexist pig you are." She wrinkled her nose. "That's right, I said *smelly.* You have horrible breath and your fingernails are always grimy. It's disgusting."

"Ms. Swann!" Dickson roared, retreating to the formality of her last name.

"I'd sooner sleep with a diseased billy goat than let you get anywhere near me." Phil's hand was on the knob of the office door, but still her mouth wouldn't quit. "So bring on the HR review. I'll be happy to tell them anything they want to know. And I don't care if the head of HR *is* your cousin. Because I'll tell him to fuck off, too!"

She left the office, slamming the door behind her. So much for her performance review. So much for her job. So much for her life.

The icy cold layer that had been covering her emotions ever since her fight with Christian that morning suddenly seemed to melt. She put a hand over her mouth and ran for the elevator.

Chapter Fourteen

"Swann? Hey, Swann?"

Phil looked up from the patch of asphalt next to her Volkswagen to see her best friend running towards her. Even in her distressed state, she couldn't help noticing that he moved very gracefully for such a tall guy. She was also relieved to see that Josh was carrying several bags in one hand and one of them was her purse. She'd been in such a hurry to get out of the BB&D building that she'd completely forgotten about it. So for the last fifteen minutes she'd been pacing beside her car in the hot parking garage, trying to work up the nerve to go back for it. But after that scene with Dickson she hadn't felt able to face any of her coworkers again. Not today, anyway.

"Hi, Bowman," she said listlessly as he jogged up to her and handed her the purse.

"Thought you might need that." He smiled at her but there was a concerned look in his deep brown eyes. "Hey, Swann, you wanna tell me what's going on? I heard through the grapevine that you yelled at Kelli and Alison, and some of the other paralegals were saying that you told Dickhead Junior where he could put it during your review."

"I didn't *yell* at them," Phil mumbled, looking at her feet. "I told Kelli to shut up and called Alison a slut. Oh, and I think I threatened to trash Alison's car if she parked in my spot one more time."

Josh broke into surprised laughter and raked a hand through his thick brown hair. He was wearing a dark blue shirt with the sleeves rolled up, exposing a few inches of tan skin on his wrists. "Damn, Swann! And the thing about Dick Junior?"

Phil sighed. "That's true too. He..." She peeked up at Josh, but glanced away quickly. "He told me that I'd had three complaints filed against me and hinted that if I was willing to...to sleep with him..." She was unable to go on. "I'm sorry, it makes me nauseous just thinking about it."

"That asshole." Josh's voice deepened and she thought she could see his biceps flexing beneath the blue shirt. Suddenly he seemed twice as large. "I'm going to give him more than a virus this time," he growled. His brown eyes were flat and cold and Phil thought if Dickson Junior could see him at that moment he would run away with his tail between his legs.

"No, Josh—don't." Phil put out a hand to stop him. "Don't go all alpha male on me. Bad enough I got my own self fired. I don't want you to lose your job too."

"Phil, don't you know the only reason I stay in this job is—" Josh broke off, shaking his head.

"What?" Phil looked at him, a feeling of unease plucking at her frayed nerves. "Josh, are you trying to tell me something? You're not...you wouldn't stay here just because...because of me, would you?" It sounded so ridiculous leaving her mouth that she wanted to unsay it at once. They were best friends, but of course Josh wouldn't stick around in a dead end job for her—that was well above and beyond the call of friendship. Wasn't it?

Josh looked at her for a long moment, his full mouth still tight with anger and his deep brown eyes full of indecision. At last he let out a breath and she was relieved to see his fists unclench. "Now why would I hang around this dump just for you, Swann?" he asked, trying to grin. "I mean, you're a great friend and all that, but you have to know I'm sticking with BB&D for all the intangible benefits—like seeing my coworkers in their oh-so-fashionable swimwear at the beach party."

"Of course." Phil laughed uneasily. She had a feeling that a very awkward scene had narrowly been averted and she didn't know whether to feel relieved or disappointed. "Too bad you'll have to watch the parade of bathing beauties without me this year."

Josh looked surprised. "Oh—you're not fired. No way can you get out of here that easily. I mean, you have to go to an HR review tomorrow, but you didn't lose your job."

"Yet," Phil said morosely. "Dickson's cousin is the head of the BB&D Human Resources department. That's one reason I never complained about him before."

"Doesn't matter." Josh frowned. "Go in there and tell it like it is, tomorrow. You think you're the first person to make a complaint against Dickhead Junior? They're a law firm, Swann. They know you could sue and what it could do to their rep. Doesn't matter how inbred the damn BB&D staff is, they'll have to take you seriously."

"You think so?" Phil lifted her head, feeling a glimmer of hope.

"Sure I do," Josh said gently, giving her a more genuine grin. "You'll probably have to answer for telling off Kelli and Alison too, but what the hell—they had it coming." He cleared his throat with a low rumble. "There was, um, I mean, I did hear one more thing though...about, uh, what's his name? The dark-haired lawyer that Alison's always hitting on?"

"Oh." Phil felt miserable all over again. "Davis Miles."

"Yeah, uh..." Josh sounded uncomfortable. "Now this is crazy, but you know how office gossip is. I heard that you, uh, asked him to, uh, to take off his clothes."

"No, I didn't," Phil protested. "I only said I wondered what he looked like naked." She could feel her cheeks burning with shame. "And it wasn't because I really wanted to see him, uh, you know, naked. It was just...haven't you ever looked at a pretty girl and thought that she'd look good without her clothes?"

Josh coughed into his hand. "Uh, sure, Swann," he said, looking uncomfortable. "But ya know, I try not to tell her, I mean, them to their faces. That's usually the kind of thought you want to keep to yourself."

"Well that's just it. It's, well...it's really hard to explain." Phil crossed her arms over her chest and looked up at him, wondering how much about her bungled wish the FG's magic would let her tell. She would have to phrase things carefully or Josh wouldn't hear anything but a buzzing sound.

"Try." Josh frowned slightly. "I'm listening." And, as always, Phil got the feeling that he really was. It gave her hope that she might be able to find a way to make him understand.

"See, lately I have this...this thing where everything I'm

thinking seems to come right out my mouth," she said hesitantly.

"Go on." Josh motioned for her to continue.

"No matter how insulting or inappropriate it is—it just pops right out," Phil said. He was getting it! She could tell by the look on his face. What a relief to be able to explain to someone. "It's almost like having Tourettes Syndrome. I can't stop it, I just—" She broke off, her eyes widening as a new thought occurred to her.

Josh was her best friend—the one person in the world she didn't want to drive away. Up until now she'd been so preoccupied with the office debacle that she hadn't had any embarrassing thoughts to reveal. But what if she thought and then said something so awful he never wanted to talk to her again? At this point she didn't know *what* might come out of her mouth. Phil froze, her mouth still open.

"What? What is it?" Josh leaned forward, one large hand out as though to take her arm.

Phil backed away from him. "Look, Josh, no offense but I have to go. I can't... I don't want to say..." *Please don't let me say anything to hurt him! Please don't let me say anything that will ruin our friendship!*

"What?" You don't want to say what?" He followed as Phil backed away, her sensible black pumps scraping against the concrete of the parking area.

"Josh, please!" Phil was feeling desperate now. *Mary had a little lamb, little lamb, little lamb. Mary had a little lamb whose fleece was white as snow.* "Please," she said urgently. "Just go! I've told off or offended everyone in my life today. I don't...I don't want to drive you away, too."

"Is that all? You think you can get rid of me by telling me to fuck off like you did Dickhead Junior?"

"I didn't say I wanted to tell you to...to do that," Phil said. *Mary had a little lamb, little lamb, little lamb...* "I just, I don't know *what* I might say. And I don't want to hurt you. I don't want to lose your friendship. Please, Josh!" She had backed all the way around her car now and she was leaning on the bug's passenger side door, clutching her purse and looking up at him appealingly. If only he would leave her alone before she said something that would damage their friendship irreparably.

"Phil, don't you know nothing you could say would make me want to stop being your friend?" Josh stopped in front of her and crossed his arms over his broad chest. There was amusement but also concern in his deep brown eyes. Phil could see herself reflected in their depths, looking like a frightened rabbit. "Okay," he said, "Come on, hit me with your best shot."

"What?" Phil was still trying to keep the nursery rhyme lodged in her brain but it was breaking up. *Mary had a little...a little...a tall, sexy coworker. No, that isn't right!*

"You heard me." He had a serious look on his good-natured face now. "Give it to me with both barrels. I want you to say whatever comes to mind about me and I promise not to be offended. Nothing off limits, just go ahead and get it over with."

"Josh, please don't make me." Phil felt like she was going to cry. *Mary had a little lamb* was dissolving into a senseless blur of syllables. Soon her traitorous thoughts would begin leaking out.

"I can take it," he said. "You want to tell me I'm a pig or that I need to shut up or—"

"You smell really good," Phil heard herself say as the wish took over. "And I love your laugh—it's all deep and rumbly and it makes me feel warm just to hear it. And when we talk, I always feel like you care about what I have to say."

"I do." He gave her that charming, lopsided grin that had drawn her to him from the start. "That's all you got? Gotta tell you, Swann, so far I'm not impressed."

"I like the way you touch me," she went on, helpless. "You're always so gentle and your hands are so big and warm..." Oh God, this was *so* inappropriate. She was probably making him horribly uncomfortable.

Josh had an odd look on his face, but all he said was, "Go on."

"I...I think that's all," Phil said with relief. But then a little voice in the back of her brain spoke up. *The dream? What about the dream?* But that was *definitely* out of bounds—far past the invisible barriers Phil had always kept between herself and her friend.

"I had this dream about you once," she heard herself say. "About us, actually."

He cleared his throat. "Do, uh, do you want to tell me about it?"

"*No*," Phil moaned. "But...but I can't help it. I...I..." She bit her lip, but it was no good. "I was sitting in a chair, in my dream, I mean. And you came up behind me and reached around and started stroking me...my..." She gestured helplessly to her chest. She could feel herself sweating beneath her white silk blouse.

"Okay, so I was uh, touching your breasts?" Josh raised an eyebrow and cleared his throat.

Phil nodded. *I'm embarrassing him, and humiliating myself. He doesn't want to cross the line either!* And yet she couldn't stop. "And then we were suddenly in...in bed. You know how that goes with dreams where suddenly you're someplace different than you were a minute before?"

"Uh-huh."

"So we were in bed, uh, naked and...and...And you were kissing me. We...were kissing each other." Phil felt like her face might set fire to her blouse. What would Josh think of her when she was done? "We...you...were touching me again. All... all over." Phil swallowed. "And your hands felt just like they do in real life—big and warm and gentle. And I was...I was..." She felt like she might strangle on the words. She was gripping her purse so tightly her knuckles were white. "There was...was more but mostly I remember that then you were...on top of me. And I was...I was saying, was begging you to...to...to...And you did and it felt so...so..."

"So we made love?" Josh asked gently, interrupting her halting words.

She nodded, grateful to him for summing it up so neatly. "Yes! God, I'm so sorry, Josh. I can only imagine what...what you must think of me now." She put a hand over her eyes, her purse still gripped tightly in the other. Tears of humiliation were wetting her hot cheeks and she was actually shaking with shame. Could this stupid wish get any worse?

"Hey, come on, now, Phil. It was just a dream." Josh pried her hand away from her eyes and lifted her chin. "Seriously, don't cry," he said softly.

"I can't... I can't believe I told you that."

"Hey." He tried to smile. "Did it upset you that much to have one X-rated dream about me?"

"No." Phil bit her bottom lip, anxious to make him understand. "It didn't upset me to have it. But...but...you're my best friend, Josh, but there are some things we just...we don't talk about. You know what I mean."

He nodded and rubbed his chin, making a faint sandpapery sound as his fingers brushed over his five o'clock shadow. "Yeah, I know, Swann." He took a step forward and looked at her intently. "There's a lot that's unsaid between us," he said, his deep voice dangerously soft.

"There is," Phil agreed. She could feel a current of barely grounded electricity flowing between them. "I mean...I never...I would never want to make you feel uncomfortable. I don't want you to feel around me the way I feel around Dickson when he starts talking nasty and trying to cop a feel."

The tension abruptly lessened as Josh let out a surprised snort of laughter. "Is that what you think? Listen, Phil, believe me, you don't have to worry that you make me feel the way you feel about Dickhead. I promise you that."

Phil swiped at her eyes with a shaking hand. She was relieved that they had kept the invisible barriers between them intact—barely. "So you don't think I'm some kind of pervert?"

Josh laughed again. "Hardly. You can't help what you dream. I've had some pretty, uh, interesting dreams myself from time to time."

"About me? I mean, us?" Phil asked before she could stop herself. "No, wait, forget I asked that. I'm sorry."

"Apology accepted," Josh said with a grin. "Now, come on, get yourself together and let me take you out to lunch."

Phil took stock of herself. She was sweating and trembling and she still had tears on her cheeks and a lump in her throat. "I'm sorry, Josh. But I'm not in any shape to be seen in public. I don't want to go out to a restaurant right now."

"Who said anything about a restaurant?" He took her hand, twining her fingers through his, and led her through the parking lot to where his car, a blue Toyota Hybrid, was parked. "I'm talking about a picnic *al fresco*." He held up the other bag he had been carrying and Phil saw it was his lunch bag. "I was just going to lunch when I heard the office scuttlebutt and came out to give you your purse."

Phil tried to smile. "Are you sure you want to have lunch

with a mouthy bitch like me?"

He grinned. "Absolutely. So what do you say, Swann? I'm inviting you to lunch at Chez Bowman. It doesn't have much atmosphere but I promise you the ham and cheese sandwich is divine. Five star cuisine all the way."

"I say...yes." Phil grinned at him, feeling a deep relief flood through her. She had said the worst, most embarrassing things her mind could come up with and Josh hadn't been offended. He still wanted to be around her. After the way everyone else had reacted to her birthday wish, it was wonderful to know that at least one person in her life didn't want to ditch her for speaking her mind.

"Great." Josh opened the passenger side door and helped her into the car with a smile. "Let's go to lunch."

Chapter Fifteen

They drove to the park but it was too hot to sit outside in the Florida summer sun. Phil was already feeling wilted from her fifteen minutes in the hot parking garage and she had cried most of her makeup off. So they parked in the shade of a large natural oak tree with streamers of Spanish Moss dripping down from its branches and ate in Josh's car. He kept the air on low and after a while, Phil began to feel more like herself.

"Okay, let's see what's on the menu today." Josh reached for his refrigerated lunch bag and unzipped it with a flourish. Besides the ham and cheese sandwich he had promised her, he had a bag of chips, a grape soda, and an apple. There were no plates, but he had several paper towels and Phil spread one primly over her lap as she ate her surprisingly tasty half a sandwich.

"You were right," she said, taking a potato chip from the bag that was open on his knee. "Five star cuisine. This sandwich is really good."

"It's the mustard that does it," Josh said modestly. "I buy it in a little gourmet shop around the corner from my apartment. Made with only the finest mustard seeds and dry white wine. Imported directly from France, I believe, because the name on the bottle is *French's*."

"Bowman!" Phil slapped him on the shoulder with her free hand. "You had me going for a minute there. And I suppose the 'little gourmet shop' around the corner from your apartment is a 7-Eleven?"

"It's a Shop Kwik, thank you very much. And I buy all my high-end groceries there." Josh grinned at her. "Thirsty?" He opened the bottle of grape soda and offered it to her.

"Thanks." Phil took a sip and smiled as the sweet fruity flavor filled her mouth. "You know, I haven't had grape soda since I was a little girl."

He grinned. "I drink it by the caseload. My one vice. Well, you know, besides the cloning farm I keep in my spare bedroom."

"Uh-huh. And what have you cloned so far?

"Well..." Josh took another drink of grape soda and handed her the bottle. "I started on mice and I've been working my way up the evolutionary ladder. Eventually I hope to clone myself so one of me can go to work and the other one can just goof off and have fun all day. Of course there *are* the obvious drawbacks to having a clone of yourself."

Phil raised an eyebrow. "Well, it would be the ultimate in identity theft."

"Huh-uh." Josh gave her a lopsided smile. "Nope, hadn't even considered that. Actually, I was thinking more about the inevitable fights with my clone over who gets to wear the special pair of jeans that make my ass look hot. You know, that kind of thing."

Phil had just taken a big mouthful of grape soda and she nearly sprayed it all over the interior of his car. She finally managed to swallow with a gasp. "Don't say that kind of thing when I have my mouth full!" she scolded. "I almost redecorated the inside of your car."

Josh grinned. "Well, you know, now that I think about it, Chez Bowman *is* kinda drab. We could maybe use a fresh coat of paint in here. Or grape soda, whichever you happen to have a mouthful of."

Phil laughed again, thinking that she couldn't remember having such a good time during a meal. Christian had taken her out to plenty of fancy restaurants in the past year, but all of those dinners had been dull affairs to impress new or potential clients. She couldn't remember laughing at a single one of them. In fact, she couldn't remember laughing with Christian at all in a very long time.

Thinking of her fiancé made her remember the fight they'd had that morning and her good mood evaporated like water spilled in the sun.

"Hey, Swann?"

She looked up to see that Josh was giving her his concerned look again. "What gives? We were having fun and then all of a sudden you got this look on your face like your puppy died."

"Oh, I'm sorry." Phil had finished her sandwich and she folded the paper towel nervously into fourths. "It's just that...this...this thinking out loud thing where I can't stop saying what's on my mind...it's kind of really put a crimp in my relationships."

"Trouble in paradise?" Josh raised one eyebrow but his deep voice remained neutral.

Phil shrugged. She'd always felt free to talk to Josh about everything—well, almost everything—to do with Christian, he wouldn't be her best friend otherwise. But sometimes she glossed over the worst aspects of her relationship with her fiancé because she got tired of defending him. She wanted to gloss over the fight they'd had this morning, too, but then the wish kicked in.

"I have...I want to go back to school—to law school." She looked up from her now tiny napkin square and saw Josh listening quietly as he finished the last of the soda. "And Christian and I had a deal that I would put him through first and then he would put me through. That way we wouldn't have to take so many loans. So he's been out of school for a while now—over a year—and I wanted to talk about going back. Well, first, I wanted to talk about finally getting married. I mean, we've been together five years now and it's getting ridiculous."

Josh cleared his throat. "So did you set a date?'

"No, that was what we were supposed to be talking about this morning. Christian has been dodging the issue forever and last night when I...when this whole speaking my mind thing started, I confronted him about it and he promised we'd talk over coffee."

"You don't drink coffee," Josh pointed out.

Phil shrugged. "No, but I make a pot for him every morning. Anyway, we started talking and some...things sort of came to light that, well, they really hurt me."

"He, uh, doesn't want to get married?" Josh was looking down at his hands so she couldn't read his expression.

"Well, no—actually, I don't know. He said we should save

up for a big wedding but I told him I was tired of waiting, you know? I even told him we could go to Vegas if he wanted to."

Josh looked up quickly. "You're not, are you? I mean..." He cleared his throat. "Are you really considering that?"

"I really don't know what's going on with the marriage issue right now. But as far as I'm concerned, it's secondary to my going back to school."

"Secondary?" Josh raised both eyebrows this time. "Wow, sounds serious."

"It is." Phil took a deep breath and let it out, wishing she could skip this part. It was so humiliating. But of course, the wish wouldn't let her stop. "We, uh, I brought up the idea of me quitting BB&D and going back to school. I've tried to tell Christian before what a hellhole it is. I mean, if it wasn't for you, I'd go crazy working there."

One corner of Josh's full mouth quirked up. "Thanks, Swann. Honestly, I kind of feel the same way about you."

"Really?" She reached out to squeeze his hand. "Thanks, Josh, that means a lot to me."

"Likewise." He nodded and entwined their fingers again so that they were holding hands loosely as they talked. "So go on, you told Christian you wanted to go back to school. What did he say?"

"He...he said that I ought to forget about it. That I should stay home and take care of the house, have a few babies, take some tennis lessons. You know, that kind of thing."

"He wants you to do the *Desperate Housewife* thing? Why?"

Phil nearly choked getting the words out. "He said...said that it would be a waste of money putting me through law school because I would be a lousy lawyer. Apparently I'd be...no good in a courtroom situation and I'd probably lose every case I tried."

"Hey." Josh put his free hand on her arm. "I hope those are his words, not yours."

Phil nodded. Her eyes were welling up again but she just let the tears come. "I...I turned down an acceptance to Stanford to put him through school. I've put my life on hold for him for the last four or five years, all because I thought he believed in me the way I believed in him. And now, to find out he has such a low opinion of me..." She swiped at her tears angrily with the folded paper towel. "But the worst thing is, he wasn't angry when he said it. I mean, we had been fighting but then he got very calm and said that he cared about me and didn't want me to get hurt by finding out the hard way that I just didn't have what...what it takes."

"Oh, Phil..." Josh squeezed her hand. "You know that's not true, right?"

"I...I feel like I don't know anything." Phil held onto his hand like a lifeline. "I mean, he says he cares about me, he kept reminding me of all the good times we've had together and then...then he drops this bomb. Crushes my dreams. And a part of me keeps thinking..." She choked back a sob. "Keeps thinking, what if he's right? What if I would make a rotten lawyer? What if everything I've wanted and waited and worked for is all wrong for me?"

Josh leaned closer to look into her eyes. Cupping her cheek, he brushed away a hot, salty tear with his thumb. "Come on, Phil, tell me you don't believe that."

"I d-don't know what to believe," she stuttered, unhappiness overcoming her at last. Josh released her hand and pulled her close, wrapping his arms around her and holding her, gently but very securely. The next thing she knew, Phil was sobbing against his chest. She hated herself for being so weak. But at the same time, it felt like a knot that had been inside her chest all day was finally loosening. Josh just stroked her shoulders and back, silently.

At last she felt her sobs taper off into sniffles. She struggled to sit up and Josh helped her, keeping an arm around her shoulders for support.

"Here." He handed her his paper towel and Phil shook off the sandwich crumbs and used it to blot her eyes and wipe her face. "Better now?" His melted chocolate eyes were filled with concern.

"Uh-huh." Phil nodded and took a deep breath. She looked down and saw that she had made a wet patch on the dark blue button down shirt he was wearing. "Wow, look at this." She plucked at the damp material apologetically. "I didn't mean to cry all over you. I'm really sorry, Josh, I just—"

"Don't be." He squeezed her shoulders gently. "I want to be here for you. Always. You can cry all over me any time. Anyway, it'll dry." He disengaged for a moment and reached down to unbutton the shirt, opening it so that the wet patch could air dry. The gap in the dark blue material showed a broad expanse of muscular chest that would have made Phil's mouth water if she wasn't still so miserable. *And still engaged,* she reminded herself. Were things with Christian really over?

"See? No harm done." Josh's voice broke into her mini-guilt session. He gave her a warm smile which she tried to return. "Now come here," he said and pulled her back against him.

"Thanks." Phil sighed and leaned her head against his shoulder. Somehow her right hand found its way inside his shirt to rest against the hard, warm wall of his chest and she felt the strong, slow, reassuring beat of his heart under her palm.

It occurred to Phil that she and Josh had never been very physical with each other until a few days ago. In fact, aside from a few quick hugs and the occasional shoulder rub, they had always kept a certain distance—similar to their silent agreement to avoid certain topics of conversation. But now it felt natural to be so close to him. It felt...safe somehow— soothing. Maybe because she instinctively knew she was in the arms of a man who would do anything for her, who believed in her more completely than she believed in herself. It was a good feeling.

"So this whole thing with Christian started because of the other thing—you saying everything you think?" Josh's voice sounded even more rumbly with her ear pressed against his chest.

"Uh-huh." Phil nodded, hearing the whisper of her hair coming loose from its tight bun against his blue cotton shirt.

"So, is this...an on-going problem? I mean..." He cleared his throat. "You said it was kind of like having Tourettes so do you...is it something you can control with medication, or...?"

Phil gave a sad little laugh and sat up to face him. "I wish I could explain it to you better—all I can say is it's something to do with my family. I guess you could call it a hereditary problem. And I'm trying to get it fixed but for now..." She shrugged. "I can't help it and it's making my life hell. You know I started out this morning by threatening my elderly neighbor?"

Josh raised an eyebrow at her and half laughed. "You're

kidding, right?"

"No." Phil shook her head. "See, she always steals my paper—well, Christian's morning paper. And he's in such a rotten mood in the morning if he doesn't get to read the sports section and have a cup of coffee. So she was making my life hard but I was always too, I don't know—nice? Afraid? Anyway, I could never make myself say anything. But this morning I told her she'd better not take it again. Oh, and I threatened to kick her dog. But only because it peed on my slippers," she added hastily. "While I was wearing them."

"Well, can't say I blame you there, Swann. Any dog that takes a leak on my loafers is pretty much gonna wind up in orbit."

Phil almost laughed. "Well, between that, and the fight with Christian, and all the trouble it caused in the office—it's been a real mess. Oh, and I yelled at the little blind pencil boy and stomped on his glasses."

"No kidding?"

"Uh-huh. Because, you know—he's not really blind or even visually impaired. But he's been guilting me into buy a pencil every day for three years. And today, well, I just got sick of it."

He laughed again and stroked a wisp of hair out of her eyes with his free hand. "Yeah, that kid's a real scam artist. I've seen him riding off on his bike when he thinks nobody's watching."

"See? Me too!" Phil exclaimed. "But I only got the nerve to do something about it today. And in a way...a sick way, I guess, it felt really...well, *good.*"

Josh frowned at her, the expression darkening his deep brown eyes. "Why shouldn't it feel good to stand up for yourself? Why should you just take what everybody dishes out without a word?"

"I know, but I said a lot of words I probably shouldn't have. Especially in that fight I had with Christian." Phil looked down at her right hand, still resting lightly against Josh's tan chest. "I, uh, criticized his bedroom technique. I guess that's the polite way to put it, anyway."

Josh winced. "Ouch. Well, I have to agree from a guy's point of view that hurts. But did he have it coming?"

"Well." Phil bit her lip, feeling embarrassed. "He's...been busy a lot. First with law school and then with the new job. I guess he doesn't quite...put as much effort into our love life as he used to." She coughed nervously, feeling the wish beginning to work. *Here we go again.* "He...we used to do things that we don't anymore. I guess he's too tired but...well...I miss some of those...things."

"Things?" Josh raised an eyebrow. "Could you be more specific, Swann? I guess I just have no imagination where these kinds of, uh, *things* are concerned."

Phil could tell he was just trying to lighten the mood. But his direct question had gotten her mind working and so her mouth started working, too.

"He used to take a lot longer getting me ready for...for sex," she said hesitantly. "He touched me...stroked me...asked me what I liked. And while we were...well, *during* I guess you could say, he always asked if I was enjoying myself." She sighed. "Now, well... He just kind of...does it."

"Damn." Josh made a face. "Um, it does sound like he's kind of a jerk in that area. Maybe he *did* deserve what you said."

"Maybe." She took her hand out of Josh's shirt, feeling guilty, and laced her fingers together. "Actually, I think that's one of the reasons I had that, uh, dream I told you about. Because it's been such a long time since...well, since Christian did some of the things you did to me. In my dream, I mean," she finished hastily, her cheeks getting warm again as her eyes flickered up to meet his.

"Uh-huh." Josh looked at her intently and there was something in his deep brown eyes, something Phil could have sworn she had never seen before. Or maybe it had always been there and she had just never noticed. "What..." Josh cleared his throat. "If you don't mind me asking, what *exactly* did we do in this dream of yours? I mean, since I was the star of the show, I'd kind of like to know how I, uh, performed." He laughed but it was clear that he was serious.

Phil bit her lower lip, feeling her heart begin to drum against her ribs. Before when she'd been forced to tell her best friend about her X-rated dream she had felt humiliated because she'd thought she was making him uncomfortable and she was afraid to go past the invisible line they had set for themselves. But now...now Josh was *asking* to hear exactly what had transpired in the dream. He wasn't offended or uneasy, just curious. And there was that something in his eyes. Something that compelled her to break the barriers she had kept between them for so long. This time Phil thought that even if her wish hadn't compelled her to tell him, she would have spoken anyway.

"Promise not to laugh?" She looked up at him shyly. They were still sitting very close in the car, with his arm around her shoulder. Phil could feel the heat from his big body radiating all along her left side and she could smell his cologne again—that warm, masculine aroma that seemed to do things to her insides. She wanted to touch the muscular tan chest she could see through the opening in his shirt again but she restrained herself.

"I promise." Josh's eyes seemed deep enough to drown in.

"Well..." Phil looked down at her hands, unable to meet the intensity of his gaze any longer. "Like I told you, it started with me sitting in a chair. I think I might have been at my desk at BB&D. And I was wearing a white silk blouse, just like this one." She nodded down at the shirt she had on. "But...but I wasn't wearing a bra under it."

"Oh, no?" She could feel his eyes traveling over her white shirt, probably picking out the outlines of the lacy white cups of the bra she had on that day.

"No," she whispered. "So I...I was sitting there and you came up behind me. You know like you do sometimes to surprise me and make me jump?" Josh did this at least once a week, sneaking up behind her and blowing in her ear or tickling her. Phil always scolded him but to be honest she kind of liked it.

"Uh-huh." Josh was nodding. "Go on, so did I tickle you?"

"No." Phil shook her head. "It was...the oddest thing. You just put your hands on my shoulders and whispered in my ear."

"What..." Josh cleared his throat. "What did I say?"

"You said, 'Don't move, Swann. I...I'm going to make you feel good.'" She looked down at her hands, feeling like her face must be as red as her lips.

"And did I?" Josh prompted in a low voice.

"Uh-huh." Phil nodded, still looking down at her hands. "You...you ran your hands down my shoulders and around under my arms until you were cupping my...my breasts." She looked up at her friend. "And here's the thing—it was so *real*. I mean, I could feel the silk of my blouse brushing against my...my nipples when you...when you pinched them. And then when you un-unbuttoned my blouse and cupped me again without the shirt in the way, your hands were so big...so warm on my bare breasts..."

She became aware that her breath was coming faster now and her heart was pounding double time. She couldn't tell how Josh felt about what she was telling him. He was sitting very still, giving her his complete attention as he always did.

"Josh?" she asked anxiously. "Am...am I going too far?"

His eyes were half-lidded in the soft gloom cast by the oak tree shading his car. "No, you're not going too far. But, uh, I thought you said there was more. More to the dream."

"There was." She took a deep breath and was surprised to find that she wanted to go on. "I, uh, I think I told you that the next thing I knew we were in bed together."

"Naked?" Josh's deep voice was slightly hoarse. The tension was back between them—the unseen current that she had felt when they first talked about the dream. How long had it been there, before today, with her ignoring it?

"Completely naked," she said softly. "We were...lying on our sides facing each other and you had your arms around me. I remember I felt so warm and safe."

"Mmm." He squeezed her shoulder gently and smiled. "I like that you feel safe with me in your dreams."

Phil smiled back and looked down at her hands. "I felt safe but I also felt so...so sensitive. Like every inch of my skin was alive the way it hasn't been in ages. You were touching me and holding me close so that our chests and...other things rubbed together. And you were stroking all over my back with your big, warm hands."

Josh gave a warm chuckle. "Uh, you seem to have a thing for my hands, Phil. In your dreams, anyway."

She smiled shyly at him and took his free hand in both of hers. "Well...I don't know, you have nice hands. Chris...I mean, other men I've known have really well-manicured hands, but they're too soft. I hate that. Now *your* hands are big and gentle and warm but they're a little bit rough, too—like you spend

117

some time working with them outside of work."

Josh grinned at her. "You got me, Swann. I'm a diesel mechanic on my off hours." He entwined his long fingers with hers and his expression turned serious again. "So far my dream self seems to be doing a pretty good job, if I do say so myself."

Phil laughed at him but she didn't let go of his hand. "Well, you were. We were kind of...rolling all over the bed, all pressed together and then you started...you were kissing me everywhere."

"Everywhere?" One side of Josh's mouth pulled up in a lazy grin. "Details, Swann. Where was 'everywhere'?"

She felt her breath catch in her throat and it was a minute before she could go on. "Like...like my breasts. You were...you kissed them and kissed my...my nipples too." She looked down at their entwined hands. "You sucked them."

"I was sucking your nipples?" His eyes darkened again. "How did that feel?" he asked softly.

Phil looked up at him. "Amazing," she said honestly. "It was...it was the most realistic dream I've ever had. I could feel your mouth on me—hot and wet and you were...it was so nice because you were taking your time, sucking each one until I was so turned on I couldn't stand it any more."

Josh seemed to catch his breath and he shifted in the seat beside her. "And what did you do when you couldn't stand it?" He was close now, close enough to kiss. Close enough that she could see each separate whisker on his strong jaw and the little crease at the corner of his mouth that turned into a lopsided smile when he was amused. But he wasn't amused now, Phil could tell by the serious look in his eyes and the set of his full lips.

"I..." Phil looked down at their hands again, unable to hold his gaze. She was gripping her friend's hand tightly but he didn't seem to mind. "I begged you to make love to me," she whispered.

She could feel his warm breath against the side of her neck when he whispered, "Did I?"

"Not...not yet. You said you wanted to see...wanted to know if I was really ready or not." She could feel the burn of embarrassment heating her cheeks again as she spoke. "I...I think I dreamed that because Chris...because my fiancé never bothers anymore. To find out if I really want to or..."

"I'm sorry, Phil. That sucks."

"It doesn't matter. I don't want to think about that right now." She looked up at Josh. "I think...I want to finish telling you about my dream. If you want to hear it, I mean."

"I do." He smiled at her. "I very much want to hear it, actually. So tell me..." He drew her a little closer with his arm, his fingers stroking her shoulder gently. "How did I, uh, make sure you were ready?"

"Well, first you touched me." Phil's heart rate had picked up again and she could scarcely believe she was telling him this part. "You...you spread my legs open and stroked me very...very gently. It felt..." She shook her head. "It felt so good—like I could actually feel your fingers touching me. And then you..." She trailed off, then took his index and middle fingers in her palm, gripping them tightly.

"I put my fingers inside you?" Josh guessed softly. Phil nodded, feeling her cheeks flame. Josh's voice dropped even lower as he leaned forward to whisper in her ear. "*Deep* inside you, Phil?"

The gentle rumble of his voice made something inside her throb. Again she nodded, reliving the dream. "You...you did. It felt so *good*."

"Mm-hmm." He shifted in the seat again, the muscles of his flat stomach bunching behind her. "Can I ask you something, Phil? In your dream, when I touched you, were you turned on? Were you wet?"

Phil caught her breath and for a moment she was afraid she might start panting. "Yes," she murmured, daring to look up and meet his eyes. "I was. I think because...because I wanted you so badly. Wanted to feel you touching me."

It was Josh's turn to catch his breath and she saw that his eyes were deep pools of need. "Phil," he said softly, "Are you wet now, talking to me like this? Telling me about your dream?"

Phil bit her lip and pressed her thighs together tightly, feeling the undeniable moisture gathering there. God! Who knew simply *talking* could make her heart race and her breath come short? And talking to the man she had always thought was only a friend.

"I'm sorry." Josh seemed to feel he had crossed a line. "I

didn't...maybe I shouldn't have asked you that." His eyes were troubled.

"No." Phil wanted to let him know she wasn't offended. But he was right—they were moving fast out of the friend zone and were headed for dangerous territory. Territory she wasn't ready to explore just yet. Or maybe ever. "No, I just...maybe I should just stick to the dream," she said at last.

"All right." Josh murmured. "So I was touching you...getting you ready. And what happened next? Did we make love?"

"Not yet." She looked down again, feeling a small stab of panic in her heart. Now here was something she wished she could skip. But the wish was very thorough.

"What happened next?" He seemed paralyzed, waiting for her to go on.

"I don't...it's hard to say." Phil squeezed her eyes closed. What she was about to describe—the thing that had happened next in her dream—was something Christian had never cared for very much. In fact, he'd only tried it once or twice early in their relationship before giving it up for good. But it was something that Phil, much to her shame, secretly craved.

"Phil, open your eyes and look at me," Josh directed. His deep voice was almost stern.

She did as he said, and found herself falling into those brown depths again. "Listen to me," Josh said softly. "Whatever it was, it was only a dream. And I want to know what you dream about. I always have."

"All right." She took a deep, trembling breath and stared at a spot on the dashboard of Josh's car. "You...you started kissing your way down my body," she said, trying to get the words out quickly. "My breasts, my stomach, my hips. Until you were...until your mouth was where your fingers had been."

"Hmm." Josh's deep voice sounded intrigued. "Are you saying I went down on you, Phil?"

"Uh-huh." She dared to look up at him and saw that something she couldn't define in his eyes again. "How do you...I mean, I hope that doesn't, um, you know, turn you off or..."

"What?" He gave a low, warm chuckle that she could feel vibrating through her side where she was pressed against him. "Why would the idea of going down on you turn me off?"

She shrugged uncomfortably. "I don't know. Maybe because it was one of those *things* I was talking about earlier. Those things that I miss because I never, I mean, my fiancé and I never, uh, do them anymore."

"Phil..." Josh untangled his hand from her and reached up to cup her hot cheek. "I want to be completely honest with you but I don't want to offend you or make you uncomfortable."

"Go on." Phil let her eyes meet his again, and the intensity of her friend's gaze almost took her breath away. If hearing her X-rated dream didn't offend Josh, she didn't see how anything he would say would offend her.

"The idea of going down on you, of spreading you open and tasting you there—of putting my tongue inside you until you moan and beg me to do more, well..." Josh lowered his voice. "I have to say I find that...incredibly arousing. Incredibly hot." The warm brown eyes were full of an unspoken desire that made her bite her lip. He was so close...it would be so easy to reach up and cup his jaw and pull him down to her. She could almost feel the sandpapery scratch of his whiskers against her palm and the warm press of his full mouth covering hers...

"Oh." She couldn't let herself go on thinking like this. "I mean that's...I guess I just, I...thank you," she mumbled, not sure what she was saying. Josh actually *wanted* to do that to her! The idea made him hot—almost as hot as telling him about it was making her, Phil thought. She pressed her thighs together, trying to ignore the dampness she felt growing there.

"You're welcome," he said simply. Gently, he tilted her chin up so that their eyes met again. "Phil, you know we don't talk about these things and I think we both know why. But just once I want to say it out loud—I want you to know that I find you very desirable. I can't imagine any scenario you could dream up that I wouldn't want to act out with you."

The tension stretched between them like a warm thread of honey until Phil felt like she couldn't breathe. "I...I..." Blessedly, her mind was a blank. Josh seemed to realize that the atmosphere in the car was getting a little too intense because he pulled back a little and smiled at her.

"I guess what I'm trying to say is I wouldn't exactly kick you out of bed for eating crackers."

Phil gave a shaky laugh. It was so like Josh to let her know he found her attractive without making her feel uncomfortable about it. "I, uh, wouldn't kick you out of bed either," she said in a low voice, amazed that she was admitting such a thing to him.

"Uh-huh." He smiled at her. "Do you want to tell me what happened next?"

She nodded, relieved to finally tell the end of the X-rated dream. She'd never thought about her best friend in a sexual way before—had never *allowed* herself to think of him that way. He was always just sweet, funny Josh, the guy who cheered her up when she was down, the guy she could tell all her problems to and be sure to get an objective answer. But she had never thought of him as, well, as a man, Phil admitted to herself. He suddenly seemed so large, and so undeniably masculine sitting beside her in the close confines of his car with his warm, spicy scent filling her senses. It was both frightening and exhilarating to find the molten sensuality that lingered just beneath Josh's funny, sweet, nice guy exterior. Like seeing the hard muscular chest he kept hidden behind his adorably rumpled button-down work shirts.

"Phil," he murmured again, breaking into her thoughts. "Do you want to tell me the end of the dream?"

She looked up at him, her heart pounding. "I do. So, you were touching me...tasting me..." She almost couldn't make herself continue but Josh's low rumble of approval gave her strength to go on. "You...I think you finally said I was ready." She bent her head quickly but Josh stopped her, tilting her chin up so their eyes locked again.

"I want you to look at me while you tell me," he said softly. "All right?"

"I...okay." Phil bit her bottom lip and nodded, wondering how she would manage to get through the final intimate details while staring into his eyes.

"Go on," Josh prompted gently. His hand on her chin sent warm fire through Phil's veins.

"You were on top of me," she said, still holding his gaze. "And I was...was so turned on by that point, I was begging you to do it. Begging you to..."

"You were begging me to *fuck* you." Josh's deep voice was quiet but somehow his words resonated through her entire body like a shout. His eyes were hooded but she could see the heat smoldering in their depths.

"Yes," she whispered, still looking up at him. "That was...exactly what I want—*wanted*, I mean," she ended quickly.

"And did I?" he asked softly, stroking her cheek.

Phil nodded. "You did. When you...when you slid in...inside me it felt so...God, Josh, it was *so good.*"

"Mmm." He gave her a slow smile. "Was I all the way inside you, Phil? Was I *deep* inside you? Filling you up completely?" His eyes seemed to burn into her and she couldn't catch her breath. She could feel heat building between her thighs that couldn't be explained away by a dream, no matter how X-rated it was.

"Yes." Phil was surprised she was able to say anything at all. She was breathing in short pants and she swore she could feel her heartbeat in every part of her body at once. How could she get so turned on just talking this way with Josh? He hadn't even kissed her and despite his arm around her shoulder and his warm hand cupping her cheek, he wasn't touching her in any way that could be construed as sexual.

"You're blushing, Phil," he murmured. "Does it embarrass you to tell me this? Does it *excite* you?"

She nodded, her mouth dry. "B...both," she stammered.

"Tell me one more thing," he said softly. "Did you come? Did you come while we made love—while I *fucked* you, Phil?"

"Oh, God, *yes.* I came...came so *hard*, Josh. I..." She looked away, unable to stand the intensity of his gaze anymore. She was liable to jump Josh right here in his car.

"I think....I think maybe we should change the subject," she murmured, trying to get her breathing under control. She reached out to adjust the AC vent so that a stream of cool air was blowing across her heated face. "It's kind of hot in here, don't you think?"

"Sorry." Josh withdrew his hand from her cheek with obvious reluctance. "I shouldn't have said that. I guess I got carried away."

"It's okay," Phil assured him hurriedly. "I just...I think maybe we should head back. I don't think anyone will miss me at work, but I don't want you to get into trouble because of me."

He grinned. "No one will know. If I want to leave for a while,

I just put up a sign that says I'm testing the server and I shouldn't be disturbed. I don't do it much but it's invaluable when Dickhead Senior is being, well, a dick." He laughed and seemed to realize that they were getting back to their normal footing because he sat up straight and took his arm from around her shoulders.

Phil laughed too, relieved that things were getting back to normal. Josh was her best friend and that was the way things ought to stay. Anything else was just too complicated, especially considering that she was still engaged to a man she had been reasonably sure she loved for the last five years. She pushed the thought of Christian away with a twinge of guilt. She would think about her fiancé later.

"Are, uh, are you sure I didn't offend you though?" Josh asked, sounding a little anxious. He was buttoning his shirt, which was mostly dry now, hiding the delicious expanse of tan chest. Phil silently chastised herself for being disappointed. *He's your friend. Just a friend.*

"You know if you did I'd tell you. I wouldn't be able to help it."

He nodded. "Oh right, your thinking out loud thing."

"You know, talking about speaking your mind—about this problem I keep having," she said, not looking at him. "Yesterday, right before Alison came into the kitchen I got this...this feeling that you were trying to tell me something. Or maybe that you were trying to ask me something." She wasn't sure why she was bringing this up now, just when they were getting over the awkwardness of her dream. Maybe she wanted to see that look in his eyes again and couldn't admit it, even to herself.

"Uh-huh." Josh's voice sounded uncertain. "I...um..."

"Josh?" she said, looking up at him again. "You know you can tell me anything, right? I mean, I told you about my horrible, embarrassing dream. And we're best friends. What are friends for but telling deep dark secrets?"

"Friends... right." Josh gave a short, humorless laugh. He took a deep breath. "Well, actually, there was something I wanted to say to you. To ask you, I mean. But you have to promise not to laugh at me."

"Why would I laugh?" Phil felt her heart pound. *Had he*

dreamed about her, too?

"I, um..." Josh took a deep breath. "I wanted to say that...that I don't have a swim suit for that stupid office beach party on Thursday. And you know me and shopping. I was, uh, hoping you would come with me tomorrow to pick something out." He smiled. "'Cause without a woman's input, I might end up in one of those bright yellow Speedos that are so popular now. And you know how it is when two people at a party are wearing the same outfit? So damn awkward."

Phil stifled a giggle at the idea of her best friend in the same banana yellow Speedo that Dickson Junior had worn to last year's beach party. Certainly Josh had a better build for it. He was tall and athletic as opposed to Dickson's short, squat, and hairy. But still, there was something inherently ridiculous about a man in what Josh liked to call a banana hammock.

"Okay," she said, both relieved and a little disappointed that the tension that had developed in the car had suddenly blown away. "I need a new suit too. So if I even still *have* a job after my awful HR review tomorrow, I'll go shopping with you after work."

"It's a deal. Shake on it." Josh grinned at her and reached out a hand to seal the deal. But just at that moment, the muted strains of "Pachelbel's Canon" began drifting out of Phil's purse.

"Oh, wait a minute," she said, rummaging in the depths to find the phone. "I'm sorry, let me see who this is."

"Fine." Josh folded his arms over his chest and gave her a mock glare. "Just so you know though, I think people who talk on their cell phones in restaurants are the *worst*. In fact, Chez Bowman, we've been considering implementing a 'no phone' policy during dining hours."

Phil started to laugh, but the sound died on her lips when she saw Rory's number on her display. Her baby sister never called in the middle of the day when she knew Phil was at work unless there was a problem. She flipped open the phone quickly. "Hello?"

"You have to come." Rory sounded breathless. "I mean, I know you're at work, but please, Phil. I've been trying to get Cass on her cell but it's turned off. I think she's doing a session in her studio and I don't have a car to go get her."

"Of course I'll come, but what is it?" Phil felt her heart rate pick up again at the panic in her youngest sister's voice.

"It's Nana," Rory said. "And this time I think it's serious. Please, Phil, come *now.*"

Chapter Sixteen

"We have to go." Phil clicked her phone closed and looked at Josh.

"What's wrong? Did something happen?" He was already putting the car in gear but he threw her a worried glance as he backed out.

"It's my grandmother—my nana. She's...gotten into some trouble." Phil really couldn't explain it any better than that and besides, she didn't know the details. Rory had been so upset—gabbling something about Nana and her potion and Phil could only imagine what a mess their grandmother had gotten herself into this time.

"Trouble?" Josh frowned. "Is she in the hospital?"

"That's not the kind of trouble my nana usually gets herself into," Phil said grimly. "Look, Josh, I'm sorry but could you just take me back to my car? I've got to get straight over to Nana's house and pick up my little sister. Then we have to head over to my other sister's studio and pry her away from her art long enough to rescue my nana from whatever scrape she's gotten herself into now."

"Okay, but let's not waste time going to get your car." Josh braked at the park's exit sign. "Which way to your nana's house?"

"Oh, Josh, I couldn't possibly ask you to—"

"Forget about that. You need to think of your grandmother. Now which way to her house?"

Phil pointed helplessly, knowing she shouldn't get her best friend involved in her crazy family's problems. But she didn't want to waste precious time in getting to Nana. This kind of thing would never be an issue with Christian, of course. Since he and Cass hated each other like poison, he never wanted to have anything to do with her family. Phil had split her last four Christmases between their apartment and her nana's house since he and Cass fought like cats and dogs the minute he walked in the door of the big lavender mansion.

She wondered what Josh would think of her outspoken sisters and her eccentric nana. And what they would think of him.

By the time they got to the large lavender Victorian house at the top of States Street, Phil was trying to think how she could explain if things got crazy. But the sight of Rory's white, worried face drove every other thought in her mind away. She fumbled with the unfamiliar controls on Josh's car and finally got the window to roll down.

"Get in," she told her sister. "Hurry up."

"Nana's got herself in trouble over at Peaceful Beach this time. Who's this?" Rory asked, climbing into the back seat of the Hybrid and giving Josh the once over.

"This is—"

"Wait a minute, I recognize him now!" Rory leaned up between the front seats and offered Josh a wide grin. "This is the hot guy from all your office pictures. The one you're always talking about."

"This is my best friend, Josh," Phil said, feeling her cheeks burn. "And Josh, this is my youngest sister, Rory. She's got a big mouth."

"Nice to meet you." Josh grinned and reached around to stick out his hand. Rory pumped it enthusiastically.

"You're even hotter in person," she said, smiling at him. "And Phil is right—you have really nice hands for a guy."

"Well...thank you." Josh grinned and raised an eyebrow at her. "So does she, uh, really talk about me that much?"

"Oh, yeah," Rory started. "Everything is always, 'Josh said this' and "Josh did that' and—"

"Rory do you think you could stop embarrassing me long enough for me to give Josh directions to Cass's studio?" Phil interrupted her. To Josh she said, "Take a left and keep going until you reach Bender Boulevard. Go all the way down and it's the fourth building on the left. The one with the rooster in the window."

Rory gave her a surprised look. "Wow. Cass said you were different after your birthday wish but I can't believe how different. You never would have told me to shut up before."

"What birthday wish?" Josh frowned and Phil and Rory exchanged stunned glances. Phil had already been surprised that the FG's magic let her explain as much as she had about her botched birthday wish to her best friend. But she had never expected him to be able to hear her discuss it with one of her sisters. Josh shouldn't even have been able to hear their words, let alone understand them.

"You heard that?" Rory asked, leaning forward to see Josh's eyes in the rearview mirror. "I mean, it didn't sound like a bee or a fly buzzing or make you want to talk about something else entirely?"

Josh gave her a puzzled glance. "Uh, why would it sound like a fly buzzing?"

"Maybe because Rory wants to be a veterinarian," Phil interjected hurriedly. "So, uh—she does excellent animal impersonations. Show him, Rory—do a bird." Obediently her little sister opened her mouth and let out a warble.

Josh frowned. "No offense, Phil, but what the hell does that have to do with a birthday wish?"

Phil and Rory exchanged worried glances again. "Uh, it's a...uh... tradition in our family that you have to make a wish on your birthday," she explained haltingly. "Rory is just teasing me about mine."

"Oh." He laughed. "You must have wished to be more assertive, huh? With your whole speaking your mind thing?"

Phil and Rory exchanged looks for the third time and Phil shrugged slightly. She had told Josh about her problem in the most roundabout way possible but the magic should have kept him from connecting that with her birthday wish.

Rory cupped a hand over her lips and mouthed, *"Does he have fairy blood?"*

Phil shook her head. She knew she would have felt the familiar prickle in her fingertips when she touched her best friend if that was the case. There was no doubt that he made her tingle, (lately anyway) but in a completely non-magical way. Had she ruined everything today, despite Josh's assurances?

Before she could explore the idea any further, Josh was pulling up in front of a restaurant that had a statue of a golden rooster as big as a Dalmatian in the window. Across the plate glass window in cursive script were the words, *El Gallo de Oro.*

"Here we are." Josh eyed the large golden rooster doubtfully. "Boy, you weren't kidding about the rooster."

"Of course not." Phil was already unbuckling her seatbelt.

"It's a Cuban restaurant," Rory told him, sliding out of the back seat. "Best *ropa vieja* in town. You should try it. Cass's studio is in the back."

"We won't be a minute," Phil told him. She and Rory hurried into the tiny restaurant which was filled with old men speaking Spanish and playing chess over thick china cups of *café con leche.* At every table was a different rooster statue although none were as eye-catching as the Dalmatian-sized rooster in the front window. Today she barely smelled the spicy aroma of the deep fried *empanadas,* she was in such a hurry to get to the back where her sister's studio was located.

The plain wooden door at the far end of the back hallway led to what had used to be a large storage room. Cass, who was addicted to the restaurant's strong, sweet *café con leche* had gotten the bright idea to rent it as a studio and the owners, an elderly Cuban couple, had been agreeable. Why she couldn't just take one of the empty rooms in the large lavender mansion on State Street was beyond Phil. But for some reason her sister preferred to rent a studio space when she could have had it for free. Go figure.

There was a hand-lettered sign tacked to the door which read *Art in progress—Do Not Disturb!* in Cass's elaborate script. From behind the panel of wood, a female voice that sounded like her sister was talking.

"Shh!" Rory put a finger to her lips even though Phil hadn't said anything. "Listen—you can hear what she's saying."

Phil put her ear to the door and heard her sister say, "Oh, God—that's perfect! Just the right spot. Now if we can just get into a different position...like this..."

Rory's emerald green eyes widened as she looked up at Phil. "What do you think is going on in there, anyway?" she whispered, nodding at the door.

"I have no idea and we don't have time to find out," Phil

said. She knew the old Phil would have knocked timidly and hoped that her sister wouldn't yell at her too much for disturbing her concentration. But she wasn't that woman any more and their nana was in trouble. She turned the knob and pushed her way into the small studio.

She was greeted with the disturbing sight of her sister kneeling before a gorgeous man with thick sable brown hair and a lush, pouty mouth that looked just made for kissing. He was reclining on a ratty old sofa that had obviously been salvaged from the dump. The sofa was draped in a dark red velvet throw that looked wonderful against his tan skin. And there was a lot of skin to see because he was completely naked.

"Oh my God!" Phil muttered. She grabbed for Rory and slapped a hand over her baby sister's eyes. "Don't look," she commanded.

"Too late." Rory's voice sounded smug. "I saw it—*all* of it." As usual her voice carried and both Cass and the naked man looked up.

"What the hell? You promised no one else would see me!" The man jumped up, wrapping the red velvet throw around his waist in outraged modesty.

"Wait. Wait!" Cass implored as he began to gather his clothes—a crumpled pair of jeans and a T-shirt—in one hand while the other still clutched at the throw. "I can explain," she told the man. "These are my sisters."

"A private sitting—that's what you said." He sounded mortally offended. "That's the only reason I let you sketch me nude."

"But it *is* a private session. I mean, I didn't plan this. Wait!" Cass begged, but it was too late. The gorgeous muscular mostly naked man threw one offended look over his shoulder and headed for the door. On the way out, he ran headlong into Josh, who was just coming in.

"Whoa—Hey, man. Sorry." Josh stepped aside as the man, still wearing only the red velvet drape, exited the studio. From the general commotion that followed his exit, Phil could only assume that the old men had finally looked up from their chess games and *café con leche*.

"What the hell do you think you're doing?" Cass stormed, throwing down the large sketch pad she'd been holding and putting her hands on her hips. "Do you have any idea how long it took me to get him to pose nude? For months I've been coaxing him a little at a time. First his shirt...then his jeans...I just got him to take off his underwear fifteen minutes ago and you have to come in and ruin it!"

"So *this* is why you don't want to set up a studio in Nana's house." Rory grinned at her. "Nana would have kittens if she knew you were playing artistic strip poker with naked men."

"It's a study of form and texture," Cass muttered sulkily. "But he has such *nice* form and texture. And now he'll never strip for me again."

"Well, maybe if you get a few singles and buy him a set of pasties..." Josh trailed off when Cass didn't laugh. "Hey, I'm sorry. I'm supposed to be waiting in the car."

"Who is this joker, anyway?" Cass turned to Phil, still frowning. "And why did you come bursting in here and interrupt my session?"

Phil opened her mouth but Rory beat her to it.

"This is Josh. You know—*the* Josh?" she gushed to her sister. "Isn't he hot?"

Cass looked at him critically. "I'd have to see him naked to be sure."

"Hey, hey, hey." Phil stepped in front of her friend protectively. "He's *my* best friend."

"Meaning nobody gets to see him naked but *you*?" Rory wiggled her eyebrows comically.

"That's not what I meant and you know it." Phil felt her cheeks start to burn. "Rory, you *know* I'm engaged."

"To a complete ass," Cass said frankly. She stepped forward, extending a hand to Josh. "Nice to finally meet you. Any male friend of Phil's who's not her asshole fiancé is a friend of mine."

"Uh...okay. Nice to meet you too." Josh pumped her hand firmly and smiled.

"All right, enough with the introductions," Phil snapped. "I'm sorry we interrupted your Playgirl posing session but Nana's in trouble again so we need you, Cass."

"Again?" Cass frowned and headed for the door. "Why didn't you just say so? Where did she go this time?"

"Peaceful Beach," Rory said as they all piled out of the studio and Cass locked it behind them.

"Peaceful Beach? What's she doing at a retirement community?" Cass demanded.

Rory shrugged. "I don't know, Cass. Maybe she went there because you told her to find a man her own age this time."

Phil rounded on her younger sister. "You *told* her to go looking for a man? Have you lost your mind, encouraging her like that?"

"Well, it's better than her hitting on boy scouts!" Cass snapped.

"But not as good as keeping her from hitting on anyone at all," Phil pointed out acidly.

Cass frowned. "You know, Phil, I really hope you can get the fairy godmother to reverse this last wish. I thought it was a good idea at first but I think I liked you better when you were 'meek as a sheep' as Rory puts it."

"Fairy godmother?" Josh frowned and looked at the three of them. "What are you guys talking about?"

Cass's violet eyes widened and she looked at Phil for an explanation. Phil could only shrug uncertainly. Once again, her best friend had heard something that should have been completely unintelligible to non-fairy ears. What was going on?

Josh was still frowning at her as they left the little Cuban restaurant and Phil struggled to manufacture an explanation. "Cass is just kidding. She likes to joke a lot," she said lamely. "Come on, we have to get to Peaceful Beach." But as they piled into Josh's blue Hybrid, she couldn't help wondering if there was more to her best friend than met the eye.

Chapter Seventeen

Peaceful Beach labeled itself as an "Adult Community for Active Seniors" and it was almost like a town unto itself. There was a swimming pool, a shuffle board court, and a huge rec room in the assisted living area where the residents could play bingo or watch the big screen TV on movie night. It was the kind of place that Phil couldn't ever imagine her nana living in. Mainly because, despite her age, Nana's fairy blood kept her spry and she looked and acted much younger than she was. She didn't belong at Peaceful Beach any more than she had belonged at the Eagle Scout bowl-a-thon.

Phil was anxious to park and go looking for her grandmother but the long winding road that led from the front gates to the main facilities was a one way lane. Just as Josh was pulling through the gates, a purple and pink golf cart with long pink fringe hanging from its canopy pulled out in front of him. An old couple with gray hair was sitting in the cart; the man was driving and woman was moving her hands in excited gestures as she talked. Her excitement didn't seem to affect her companion in any way, though—or at least, it didn't affect his driving. The cart crawled along at a sedate fifteen miles per hour making sure they were stuck driving at a parade pace instead an Indy 500 clip, which would have suited Phil's frayed nerves a lot better.

"What's the deal with the stupid golf cart?" she demanded, unable to help speaking her mind. "Don't those things go any faster? And why is it all decorated in pink and purple fringe like that? It's bizarre."

Rory piped up from the back seat. "That's how they get around here since so many of the residents have had their licenses taken away. They all drive golf carts all over the place. We studied it in my Psych of Aging class."

"I guess they like to customize their carts the way we customize our cars," Josh said with a grin. "You know—pimp my cart."

"Nana hasn't called again and you know she would if things got really hairy," Rory pointed out. "Be patient, Phil. Maybe someday it'll be you driving around on a pimped-out golf cart. Look at that old couple—aren't they cute? Can't you see you and Christian on a cart like that fifty years from now?"

"I don't know," Phil said honestly. She bit her lip and looked out the window at the couple in the cart ahead of them.

Rory frowned. "What do you mean, you don't know?" she demanded. "You're always talking about how you want to grow old with the man you love and gushy stuff like that. Cass says you're worse than me half the time and you know I'm a hopeless romantic."

Phil didn't want to go into this right now, but the wish kicked in and she had to speak her mind. "I mean I don't know how I feel about Christian right now," she said, looking straight ahead at the old couple on the golf cart so she didn't have to see her sisters' faces as she spoke. "He's been so distant this whole past year. And, well...we had a fight this morning and he said some things that really hurt me."

"Things? What things?" Cass demanded from the back seat. "Maybe things that made you come to your senses and decide to leave his boring ass?"

"I don't want to talk about it right now," Phil said truthfully. She glanced over her shoulder at Cass and Rory who were looking at her eagerly. "It's just...when he said what he said, I don't think he was trying to hurt me. But it hurt just the same."

"What hurt? What did he say?" Rory was practically bouncing up and down in her seat.

Phil opened her mouth but at that moment the pink-and-purple golf cart turned off into a side road and the way ahead was clear. "Punch it!" Phil leaned forward as though she could make the car go faster with the force of her will.

Josh gave her an amused glance. "Okay, but do we know where we're going once we get there?"

Phil looked back at Rory. "Did Nana say where she was when she called?"

Rory shrugged. "She just said she was at Peaceful Beach in the rec room and that things were getting, uh, a little out of hand."

"Crap, Nana would probably say the same thing about a nuclear meltdown," Cass pointed out, frowning. She looked about as impatient as Phil felt, her black eyebrows pulled down in a scowl.

They were pulling into a large parking area now and Phil could see a series of buildings, some of them public areas and some apartments, all crowding a well landscaped area crisscrossed with clean, even sidewalks. "Look at this," she said, gesturing towards the maze of buildings and walkways. "How are we going to find out which one is the rec room?"

"I have an idea." Cass rolled down her window. "I'm thinking we'll be able to follow our noses."

Phil rolled down her window as well and put her head out, taking a deep breath of the humid Florida air. She withdrew when she caught whiff of something that smelled like burning hair and rotten eggs. "Ugh! Is that Nana's potion?"

Rory rolled down her own window and took a sniff. "Yup, that smells like the latest batch all right. She spent all night in the kitchen making it. I tried to get her to stop but you know Nana. She's so stubborn when she decides she wants something."

Josh had rolled down his window as well and he took a deep whiff of the unmistakable miasma floating on the breeze as he parked the car. "Wow." He got a strange look on his face as he turned toward Phil. "That smells *terrible*. And yet..." He took another deep breath and frowned. "And yet, I kinda like it. Is that weird?"

Cass looked grim. "She must have perfected it."

"Well she couldn't get much *farther* from perfection," Phil pointed out, thinking of the debacle at the bowling alley. "Come on, we'd better go get her."

They left the car and followed their noses to a low gray building that had ramps instead of steps, for easy wheelchair access. But long before they reached the door, they could hear the commotion going on inside.

"Hurry!" Phil reached for her sisters' hands, feeling the tingle of power, and dragged them toward the entrance. "Who knows what she'd gotten herself into now!"

They hit the door running with Phil in the lead. But it opened onto a scene of such confusion that for a moment they all just stood there, stunned. The room had been set up for a bingo game, with rows of long, thin tables covered with paper cards and piles of dried kidney beans to use as markers. At the front of the room a smaller table held a large plastic bingo ball filled with numbered ping pong balls. It was the kind that turns with a crank until one of the ping pong balls pops out the spout. But aside from one elderly woman who was quietly nibbling her pile of dried beans, no one was sitting at the tables. No one was working the bingo ball or calling numbers and no one was marking their cards.

Instead, everyone was at the front of the room in a teeming mass, not a single one of them under the age of seventy-five. They weren't standing around talking as the Eagle Scouts had been the night before in Splitsville, either. Instead, arms were waving and people were shouting. As she watched, Phil saw one elderly man brandish his cane at another man who looked even older.

"She's mine, I tell you! I saw her first!" he yelled, whopping his neighbor with the wooden cane. "You get away from her, Smithers!"

"She's my angel!" the other man yelled in a hoarse, cracked voice. "She doesn't want anything to do with you, Bernstein!" As Phil watched in horror, he raised his walker and used it like a lion tamer uses a chair, fending off further strikes with the cane and trying to push the other man to the ground. The entire room reeked of the horrible potion and the shouting was so loud Phil was tempted to drop her sisters' hands and put her fingers in her ears.

In the middle of the mêlée, Nana was standing her ground with a man who looked to be at least ninety gripping her hand tightly. Today she wore a hot pink pantsuit and a pleased expression on her plump, pretty face. She was actually *enjoying* herself, Phil thought dismally as the battle royal continued. Nana always had liked causing a scene.

"Now, now, gentlemen, there's no need to fight over me." Nana's silvery voice rang out over the confusion. "I'm sure we can work this out in a civilized manner. Maybe I can go out for a date with each one of you on a different night."

"You're not dating Harold!" screeched a woman who, if possible, looked even older than the man who was holding Nana's hand in a death grip. She had fluffy white hair with a pale blue tint and she was wearing an old fashioned pair of horn-rimmed glasses. "He's my husband, you hussy! And if you think you can bring your painted, perfumed self over here and break up a marriage that has lasted for sixty-five years then you've got another think coming!"

"She's got my Benjy too!" shouted another little old lady whose salt and pepper hair was twisted into a scanty bun at the back of her neck. She pointed to a man who appeared to be in his eighties standing on Nana's other side, trying to nibble on her ear with his false teeth. "Fifty-five years together and he never cheated on me once. Now just look at him!"

"Wow," Josh muttered and Phil turned to see him staring wide-eyed at the scene in front of them. "Is that, uh, your grandmother in the pink pantsuit?" he asked, giving Phil a sidelong glance.

Phil felt her cheeks begin to heat. *He was totally appalled, just like Christian had been.* "I'm afraid so. Nana, um, loves being the center of attention. You just wait here—we'll go get her." There was a new outcry and she saw that one of the little old ladies—the one with the horn-rimmed glasses—had tried to slap Nana and missed. Instead, her wrinkled hand connected with her friend's cheek. The second lady's false teeth flew out of her mouth at the impact and skittered across the floor reminding Phil of a pair of those wacky wind-up walking teeth you see in joke shops.

"Help!" yelled the senior citizen who had been de-toothed. "My theeth! Thombody get my theeth!"

"Oh my God, what a *mess*," Cass muttered. "Come on, Phil. We'd better get in there before somebody breaks a hip."

They waded into the crowd of Peaceful Beach residents, dodging canes and walkers until they reached their grandmother. Nana was watching breathlessly as the action unfolded around her, no doubt feeling like the star of a movie featuring very old actors.

"Nana!" Phil shouted. "Nana, come away from here.

Somebody's going to get hurt!"

"Oh, but it's so exciting!" Nana smiled, her plump cheeks a girlish pink. "And I hate to disappoint my new beaus."

"Nana, these men are spoken for." Cass nodded at the angry little old ladies who were trying to get through the crowd to rescue their husbands from her grandmother's evil clutches. "Besides, they're too old for you."

"But you told me to find someone my own age!" their grandmother protested, pointing at Cass. "And besides, they're very charming."

"Charming or not, we have to get you out of here," Phil said, fending off a cane with her elbow.

"Yeah, Nana, come on!" Rory insinuated herself between her grandmother and the man who was trying to nibble her ear. Slowly the three sisters formed a half circle around their grandmother, just as they had the night before.

"Well, if I must..." Nana looked disappointed but at least she seemed willing to come away from the senior citizen riot she'd caused. However, it didn't look like the seniors were ready to let her go. Phil looked around in dismay at the sea of wrinkled, angry faces.

"It's the potion, same as last time," she shouted to her sisters. "Rory, do you still have that breath spray?"

"Sorry, Phil. We used it all up last night."

"Crap." Cass looked around, frowning. "Well, what the hell are we going to do? They won't let us through—the men all want to hump Nana's leg and the women all want to kick her ass."

"Young lady, watch your language." Nana sounded shocked.

"We need a distraction," Phil yelled. "Something to take their minds off Nana. They're not going to let us go as long as they're all fixated on her." Someone stamped down hard on her foot with the rubber tip of a cane and tears of pain sprang to her eyes. What a ridiculous way this would be to die, she thought. Mauled to death by senior citizens.

Suddenly a deep voice boomed above the roar of the angry elderly crowd. "I—nineteen," it shouted and several of the seniors turned to see where it was coming from. "B—forty-four," the voice continued loudly. "Come on, folks—back to your seats. You're missing the numbers. N—twelve."

More and more heads were turning to see where the voice was coming from, Phil's among them. She was surprised to see Josh standing by the big plastic bingo ball, cranking the handle and grabbing the plastic ping pong balls as they came out the spout.

"O—fifteen," he yelled. "I'd get back to your seats, folks. The grand prize is on the line—two free tickets to the Golden Apple Dinner Theater's production of *My Fair Lady*." He caught Phil's eye across the room and winked at her when she mouthed *Thank you!*

There were excited mumbles from the seniors in the crowd and some of them began drifting back to the long tables with their paper cards and piles of dried kidney beans. Now that Phil and her sisters were between their grandmother and her admirers, the elderly men seemed to lose some of their interest. One by one they allowed their wives to drag them away, the little old ladies shooting poison glances at Nana.

"I—twenty-nine. G—fifty." Josh kept shouting numbers until most of the crowd had dissipated and Phil and her sisters were able to lead their grandmother out of the Peaceful Beach rec hall. Phil had never felt so relieved in her life as when the door closed behind them and she could get a breath of fresh air.

"My, my—that was certainly exciting." Nana's cheeks were still flushed and her green eyes were dancing with excitement.

"It wasn't exciting, it was *dangerous*," Phil snapped. "You started a riot and some of those people were really old, Nana. What if all the stress you just caused gave someone a heart attack?"

"Oh..." Nana pressed one hand to her plump bosom. "I didn't think about that," she said, her smile beginning to fade.

Never in her life had Phil spoken harshly to her grandmother, but now she couldn't help saying exactly what was on her mind.

"Well maybe it's time you *do* start thinking before you do something like this," she scolded, voicing a thought she'd often had but had never been able to say out loud before her birthday wish. "Honestly, Nana, we have to come rescue you time and again from this kind of mess. Has it ever occurred to you that it's time for you to *grow up*?"

"I...I never..." Tears sprang into Nana's bright green eyes. "I had no idea you felt that way, Philomena. I'm so sorry I've become a burden to you in my old age."

"Look what you did!" Cass turned on Phil accusingly. "I can't believe you said that!"

"I can't believe you made Nana cry." Rory put an arm around her grandmother's shaking shoulders.

Phil felt horrible. "Nana," she said, patting her grandmother awkwardly on the back. "I'm so sorry—it's just my latest wish acting up again. I didn't mean to say all those things—they just slipped out."

"Well you need to try and keep anything else from slipping out," Cass said. "Nana knows what she did is wrong. In fact, I'll bet she's willing to promise to give up using witchcraft altogether now, aren't you, Nana?"

Their grandmother nodded her silver head, her eyes still streaming. "I will. If it bothers you girls that much, then of course I will. I'll give up my one dream of happiness—my dream of finding someone to love me in my old age when all of you are gone."

"Now, Nana, don't say that," Phil implored. "You're a very attractive woman. You don't need witchcraft and potions to find a man. And besides, just because we're grown up and moving out of the house doesn't mean we won't still come see you."

"You're a fine one to talk about that," Cass scoffed. "We almost never see you since you and Christian moved in together. When was the last time you came and had dinner with Rory and Nana and me?"

"She's right, Phil," Rory put in. "You're almost never at the house anymore. No wonder Nana feels abandoned."

"I can't help it," Phil said, looking from her accusing sisters to her crying grandmother. "And it's not all my fault." She pointed at Cass. "If you would only make an *effort* to get along with Christian, maybe he wouldn't refuse to let us come over for dinner."

"Listen to yourself," Cass scoffed. "*Let* you come over? Do you hear what a puppet you've become, Phil? Why do you always let him tell you what to do?"

"Well I don't anymore!" Phil exploded. "I *told* you—we had a huge fight this morning, right before I told off my neighbor and everyone in my office, including my boss. Could you cut me some slack here, Cass? I've been having a horrible day and I don't need all this family guilt crap on top of it!"

Her two sisters and her grandmother grew suddenly quiet as they stared at her in awe. Phil had never been a shouter. She supposed they were all used to her taking their criticism without a word. Part of her wished she could go back to being the quiet, meek one—the sweet girl who agreed with everyone and did as she was told and never made her grandmother cry...but part of her didn't. That part was glad that she could stand up to Cass now and defend herself and her motivations. Although she had to admit that staying away from her family just because Christian didn't like them was pretty indefensible.

"Well, dear." Her nana broke the silence and came forward to take her hand. "I don't know what that latest wish of yours was all about, but it certainly brought you out of your shell."

"Sure has." Rory was still looking at her wide-eyed. Cass was frowning but she didn't comment.

"In fact," Nana continued. "I feel like I need to get to know my oldest granddaughter all over again. What we need is a good old fashioned family dinner—all of us sitting around the table talking about our day and getting reconnected with each other. What do you say?"

"Well, I..." Of course, tonight was Christian's pre-Fourth of July office party. It was being held at one of the senior partners' mansions on Bayshore Boulevard, the most expensive neighborhood in South Tampa, and it was a black tie affair. Christian had been talking about it for months. He seemed to think it was absolutely essential to make a good impression, which probably included showing up with his fiancé on his arm, looking beautiful. Or as beautiful as you could be with weird sparkly sunshine hair, abnormally red lips, and eyes that changed color with the weather, Phil thought sourly.

"Please, Phil," Rory begged. "Nana's right—it's been ages since we were all together at dinner."

"We've missed you," Cass said grudgingly. "I know we get together for brunch once in a while but it's really not the same."

"Please say you'll come, my dear." Nana patted her hand. "It would mean so much to me. To all of us."

"Well, I want to but..." Phil bit her lip, thinking of how upset her fiancé would be if she blew off his important party to have dinner with her family. Then again, he hadn't come to a single one of *her* office parties. She'd even asked him if he could get a day off in order to go to the annual BB&D beach day and he'd refused without even seeming to think about it. Also, in her current wish-condition, she would *not* be an asset to Christian at any social event.

And then the new post-wish Phil got angry. Cass and Rory and Nana were right—she hadn't spent much time with them in ages, all because of Christian. Besides, she didn't feel like spending an entire evening posing as Christian's arm candy—in fact, she didn't feel like spending any time with him at all until they talked things out. The way she felt now, she would start another fight with him the minute she opened her mouth. It was better to take a night off from each other's company, she decided. Better for her and for their relationship.

"All right," she said, smiling at her nana. "Christian is having some kind of an office party tonight but I guess he'll live if I don't come with him. I'd love to have dinner with you guys tonight. I'll do it." She would simply explain to Christian that he would have to go without her. He would get over it.

"You'll do what?"

Phil turned to see Josh standing behind them, grinning and holding a plastic ping pong ball with I-17 printed on it in black letters.

"Oh, young man." Nana fluttered toward him, her tears and anxiety completely forgotten. "We were just talking about having dinner tonight at my house with all my lovely granddaughters. And, as my savior from that awful brouhaha in the bingo hall, of course you are invited."

"Oh, Nana," Phil said hastily. "Josh probably doesn't want to have dinner with a bunch of women sitting around the table making girl talk all night."

"Sure I do." Josh smiled at her and took her nana's hand. "I'd be delighted to accept your invitation, uh, ma'am. And as a matter of fact—" he grinned at Phil "—I love girl talk. I have three older sisters back home in California, you know. Sometimes I kind of miss it."

"Are you sure?" Phil asked. She knew her best friend was from the West coast and that he had three sisters, but she was surprised to hear that he really didn't mind spending his evening in the company of a bunch of women. Christian would have hated it.

"Sure, I'm sure." Josh grinned. "Uh, unless you don't want me to come?" He looked at her uncertainly. "I don't want to cut into your time with your family."

"Of course she wants you to come. We all do," Rory protested.

"She's right. We'd like to get to know you." Cass gave him a friendly smile and Nana reached up to pat his cheek.

"What did you say your name was again, young man? Josh?"

Josh smiled and nodded but his eyes were still fixed on Phil, as if he was asking her permission.

"If you really think you want to spend the evening with my crazy family..."

Josh laughed and looked at his watch. "Well, seeing as how I've already spent most of the afternoon with them, I don't think a few more hours will kill me."

"Wonderful!" Nana declared, tucking her arm into his. "Now let's see. I think I still have some charcoal briquettes for the grill. Young man, do you know how to barbeque?"

"Yes, ma'am, I do." Josh shot Phil a bemused glance and she returned it with a hesitant smile. It was wonderful how quickly her family seemed to be taking to her best friend but she wondered how Josh would feel after spending a whole evening with them. Even more, she wondered what she was going to tell Christian.

Chapter Eighteen

"Yes, I know it's important to you but spending time with my family is important to *me*." Phil hunched over her cell phone, standing on the large, wrap-around porch that encircled the lavender mansion on States Street. Christian was even angrier than she'd expected him to be and she was still getting used to being able to stand up for herself. This was turning out to be a difficult conversation.

"You've known about this for months, Phil." Christian's voice was impatient. "You know how important it is for me to go in there looking successful and make a good impression. How can I do that without you there to support me?"

She felt a lump rising in her throat. "What about when I need support, Christian? I asked you to come to my office beach party months ago when you would have had plenty of time to get the day off and you completely blew me off."

"We went over that already. We decided that my missing a productive day of work to make an appearance at your beach party wasn't a good use of my time. Remember?" Christian sounded frustrated.

"No, *we* didn't decide—*you* decided." She heard the quiver in her voice and tried to control it. "You said you didn't want to go and that was the end of it. Well now I'm telling you *I* don't want to go to your party either. You can go by yourself and tell everyone I'm sick."

"That is *not* acceptable." She could almost hear the frown in Christian's voice. "What's gotten into you, Phil? You used to be so easy going and now all of a sudden you're constantly emotional." His voice rose an octave. "My God, you're not pregnant, are you?"

"I don't see how I could be," Phil said acidly. "I can't even remember the last time we made love."

"C'mon, babe." Christian sounded uneasy now—uneasy but relieved. "You know I've just been tired from working these long hours. Now why don't you be a good girl and come on back to the apartment to change? If you leave now we can still make it in plenty of time for cocktails."

"Christian, I'm sorry." Phil made her voice as firm as she could. "But I said no and I meant it. It wouldn't do us any good to be together tonight anyway—we'd just fight the whole evening. I'm going to stay here and have a family dinner with my nana and my sisters." She didn't mention Josh and it gave her a little twinge of guilt to keep that piece of information from her fiancé. But it wasn't like they were running away together— they were just having dinner at her grandmother's house.

"I can't believe this!" He sounded genuinely bewildered. "What happened to my sweet little fiancé who never caused any trouble?"

"She's gone—for good, I hope," Phil told him. "And by causing trouble I suppose you mean standing up for myself and not jumping every time you say to?"

"You can call it what you want, Phil but you've changed and not for the better," her fiancé said darkly. "I was hoping that maybe you were just starting your cycle or something this morning but now...I don't know *what* the hell is wrong with you."

"Maybe it has something to do with the fact that you shot down my dream this morning—did you ever consider that?" she said, giving in to her anger. "Maybe it has to do with you wanting me to stay home and play *Leave it to Beaver* while you do the big macho corporate man thing."

"Christ," she heard Christian mutter. "Not this again! Look, Phil, you and I both know this isn't the time to discuss that issue."

"Well when is the time?" Phil demanded. She was squeezing the phone so tightly she could hear the plastic casing creak. "I've been waiting for over a year to talk about this and you give me fifteen minutes this morning. *Fifteen minutes* of your valuable time in which you tell me that I've been working for the last four years for nothing because you never intended to hold up your end of our bargain in the first place. Tell me, Christian, how am I supposed to feel about that?"

"You want to go to law school? You want to waste hundreds of thousands of dollars instead of having the easy life I offered you?" Christian exploded on the other end of the phone. "Fine. You can go to law school. We'll get married tomorrow if you want and you can apply to any school in the area. Will that make you happy?"

"I didn't give up a school in this area to be with you, Christian," she said quietly. "I gave up Stanford. And I did it because I loved you. I thought you loved me too."

Christian sighed deeply and she could almost see him massaging his temples with one hand, the way he always did when he was tense. "Babe, I never said I didn't love you. But you're making things damn hard on me here."

"How?" Phil demanded. "By asking you to live up to your end of the bargain? By asking you to believe in me the way I believed in you? Christian, you have no idea what kind of day I've had. I got into it with my boss this morning and now I have to go to a HR review tomorrow. I...I don't even know if I'll have a job when it's all said and done."

"You *what*?" Christian's voice was ragged. "Phil, I know you hate that job but we can't afford for you to stop working just yet. I mean that is the ultimate goal—to just have you stay home and take care of the house and kids whenever they come along—but we're not there yet."

"Whose goal is that?" Phil asked through numb lips. "Yours? Because it certainly isn't mine. Don't you even want to know what happened? Don't you want to hear my side of it?"

"Your side, your boss's side—it doesn't matter, Phil. What matters is you hold onto your job just a little while longer."

Phil felt like crying. "You really don't get it, do you Christian? You have no idea what he did to me—what he said. And you don't care, either."

"Babe, I don't know what you want from me and I don't have time for this right now." His voice was flat. "Now are you coming to the party or aren't you?"

"If I said yes, that I would come to your party tonight, would you consider coming to my office beach party the day after tomorrow?" she asked, already knowing the answer.

"I already said no to that Phil. You know my answer isn't going to change."

"Fine." Phil took a deep breath, trying to calm herself. "I'm not willing to change my answer either, Christian. But I think you should know that I feel like our relationship has hit a dead end and I...I don't know where to go from here. What you said to me today hurt and right now I don't know if I can forgive you for that."

"So *that's* what this is really all about." Christian took a deep breath and his voice was suddenly soft and coaxing. "Okay, I'm sorry if what I said hurt you, Philly-babe—I truly am. I was just trying to spare you pain on down the line. But please don't punish me like this. I need you by my side tonight. Come be with me. Please?"

His pleading tone almost melted her but Phil knew she had to be strong. This was no longer about her fiancé's office party—it had become a matter of principle. "I can't, Christian," she said, trying to push back the tears that threatened to choke her voice. "I just...I can't be with you tonight. I need some time to think. Some space. I feel like you and I are going in two separate directions."

"I'm going in the same direction I always was." Christian just sounded tired now. "You're the one who jumped the tracks, Phil. I don't know what the hell's wrong with you lately but I wish to God you'd get whatever it is resolved and get back to your normal self."

"I may resolve some of it," she said, thinking of her desire to get her fairy godmother to reverse the disastrous birthday wish. "But I'm not going to go back to being a doormat. I've put my life on hold long enough and I deserve to make some progress instead of always treading water."

"I don't know what to tell you, babe," Christian said. "I know we're going through a hard time right now—maybe the hardest we've ever had. Just...don't make any rash decisions, all right? Try and remember the good times and focus on that."

"I'm trying." Her voice was choked with tears. "But I can't live on the past, Christian. I need something concrete to carry me into the future."

"And I'll give it to you, Philly-babe," he said. "I swear I will, just not right now. I understand that you don't want to come with me to my office party but if I don't go now, I'm gonna be late. We'll talk about all this later—I promise. Okay?"

"Christian, I—" she began but he had already hung up. Phil stared at the phone in her hand for a moment, her gut churning with so many different emotions she couldn't name them all. *It's always later,* she thought. *Always, 'later, babe, I don't have time right now.'* The sun was setting and a soft breeze had sprung up, bringing the scent of her grandmother's garden to her. But Phil couldn't take pleasure in any of it. All she could think about was the past.

She remembered the first apartment she and Christian had shared together—so horribly hot in the summer and freezing cold in the short Tampa winter. The way they used to go to the Tampa Yankees games together—they were a Triple-A team but the seats were only five dollars apiece and she and Christian would share a hot dog and cheer no matter who was winning. On weekend nights they always went to the drive-in because it was cheaper than the movie theater. They watched cheesy horror movies and ate microwave popcorn they smuggled in. Phil remembered hiding her face in Christian's shoulder during the scary parts and feeling so safe, so loved... *When did that feeling melt away?* she wondered dismally. *It's not just my birthday wish that's changing things—I know it's not. When did I stop feeling like Christian and I were the center of each other's universes?*

She and her fiancé had history together, it was true. They had been through some hard years when he was going through law school and she had always believed if they could make it through that, they could make it through anything. But now she wasn't so sure.

"Swann?"

The familiar voice behind her made her turn quickly, still clutching the cell phone in her hand. Josh was standing there with a big grin on his face, wearing one of her nana's flowery aprons with the lace edged pockets. With his five o'clock shadow and the devil-may-care grin on his face, he looked like a pirate that had decided to try his hand in the kitchen.

"What do you think?" he asked, spreading his arms. "Your nana said she didn't want me to get my nice clothes all dirty while I barbecued. I hope you like balsamic glazed chicken by the way—it's my one and only gourmet meal and this is the first

149

time I've tried grilling it."

"Sounds delicious." Phil crossed her arms over her chest and tried to make her voice light. "I can't wait to try it."

"Hey." He stepped forward and touched her cheek with the tips of two fingers. "What are these for?"

"Oh." Phil took a step back and raised her own hand to her cheek. Her fingertips came away wet. "It's nothing." She tried to smile. "Just...nothing. Christian wasn't very happy about me staying at Nana's house for dinner tonight but he'll get over it. It made me think about the past. The way things used to be and...they way they are now." She sighed and lifted her chin— she wasn't going to let the fight with her fiancé spoil her evening. "So, I never got a chance to thank you for providing a distraction at Peaceful Beach. Starting the bingo game again was a stroke of genius."

"Well, you know. Mainly it was the dinner theater tickets that got them going—I'm going to have to buy a pair and send them over so whoever won the game won't be disappointed. I knew that would do it—my grandparents *love* that crap. They took me with them once to see a production of *Beauty and the Beast*." Josh laughed. "I was the only person in the room that was over ten and under sixty. All the other grandkids that came were little girls who couldn't wait to meet Belle after the show."

"What about you?" she asked. "Didn't *you* want to meet Belle?"

He rubbed his chin, making a sandpapery sound and pretended to consider. "Well, she *was* pretty hot but I was kind of afraid my grandma would make me wear one of the little sparkly 'birthday' tiaras all the other girls were wearing and you know I'm just not the tiara wearing type." He gestured to the apron. "This is about as girly as I get—sorry if that ruins your image of me as a domestic goddess."

She smiled. "So do they live around here—your grandparents, I mean? Did they retire to Florida?" Josh didn't talk about his family much but she sometimes got the feeling that she missed them a lot.

"Nope—still in California along with everyone else. I've been, uh, thinking about that a lot lately. I ought to move back there while Grandma and Grandpa are still alive so I can spend time with them. My sisters, too—I mean, they're all married now, having kids. Oughta get to know the nieces and nephews before it's too late to be the 'cool uncle.'"

Phil felt a strange, empty sensation in the pit of her stomach at the idea of her best friend moving so far away. "Why would you want to move all the way back there and leave me alone at BB&D?" she joked, trying to grin. "What would I do without you to bandage my paper cuts and give Dickson's hardware viruses?"

Josh laughed, his brown eyes twinkling. "Oh, man. That sounds wrong in so many ways—but maybe I just have a dirty mind." He stuck his hands in his pants pockets, looking completely at ease despite the flowered apron that hung to his knees. "Speaking of having a dirty mind," he said, lowering his voice. "Your nana wears the worst perfume I've ever smelled. But she's really sweet and...I found her kind of attractive. Is that weird?" He looked so upset about it that Phil had to laugh.

"It should be, but it's not. Not in my family, anyway." She tried to think of how to explain things to him without sounding like a lunatic. "It's that awful, uh, *perfume* that makes her so attractive. It's kind of a...well, I guess it's like a pheromone spray and I think it works on just about anything male—that's what caused all the confusion at Peaceful Beach. So it's not your fault if you think she's kind of a hottie."

"Oh, good." He put a hand over his heart and rolled his eyes in relief. "And here I thought I was developing an Oedipus complex. Or at the very least, an interest in older women."

Phil slapped his arm lightly. "Don't let Nana hear you say that. She's on the prowl for a boyfriend and she'd snap you up quick if she knew you were single."

"Well, you'll just have to tell her my heart's already taken." Josh smiled at her but his deep brown eyes were serious. Phil felt her stomach do a flip-flop.

"So Nana put you right to work, huh?" she said, trying for a quick subject change. "She doesn't waste much time."

He nodded. "Yeah, and your sisters sent me out here to ask you to come in and help in the kitchen. Well, that wasn't *exactly* how they put it, but..."

Phil laughed and wiped at her eyes again. "Knowing Cass she probably told you to tell me to get my lazy ass in the kitchen and pitch in."

151

Josh broke into a grin and ran a hand through his hair. In the last light of the setting sun it had reddish highlights. Phil wondered how she had never seen them before. She suddenly wanted to reach up and touch it—touch *him*. But the wish didn't extend to physical action and she was able to restrain herself.

"Yeah, well, something like that," Josh said. "Now if you'll excuse me, I have to get back to the grill and watch the chicken. An outfit like this demands perfection, as I'm sure you'll agree."

She laughed again. "Uh-huh. I can see that. If only you'd had it on earlier when you were serving me my sandwich at Chez Bowman."

"Oh, this is too fancy for Chez Bowman," Josh protested as they walked around the porch to the kitchen door. "This is haute couture. I couldn't possibly wear it anywhere but your nana's backyard. Or, you know, the presidential inauguration—whichever. It's that special."

"It's special all right." Phil was still laughing when he gave her a mock salute and went back to his post by the barbeque pit. She decided to have a good night tonight no matter what.

Chapter Nineteen

Her determination wavered almost at once. When she pushed open the kitchen door, the horrendous burnt hair and rotten eggs smell nearly knocked her over. Cass was doing dishes and Rory appeared to be looking for something in the dark oak cabinets that covered the far wall of the large eat-in kitchen.

"Ugh!" Phil put a hand to her nose. "Is that Nana's potion?"

"Sure is." Cass nodded at the stove where a large sauce pan filled to the brim with brownish green gunk was sitting. "And you're elected to get rid of it."

"Why me?" Phil protested, crossing her arms.

"Because we did it last time." Rory pulled a box of rice pilaf mix out of the cabinet and studied the directions.

"And just because you don't live here anymore doesn't mean you're absolved of all the family responsibilities," Cass added. "Come on, Phil, just dump it and come back and make the salad. You know we can't eat with it in the house."

"Fine," Phil muttered. Taking a careful hold of the saucepan's handle, she carried it out the door, holding it as far away from herself as possible. She would have to dump it somewhere in the yard, she decided, and probably bury it, as well.

She didn't want to answer awkward questions about Nana's cooking skills so she took the long way around the porch, avoiding Josh and the barbeque pit. Along one side of the house Nana had planted a flower and vegetable garden. A long length of green garden hose coiled like a snake in the grass and her trowel and gloves lay discarded on the small ornamental bench to one side of the rose bushes. Phil made use of both, digging a hole in the middle of the zinnias with the trowel and pulling on the gloves to complete the operation of disposing of the noxious potion.

She was just putting the finishing touched on her own private toxic waste dump when she heard an excited *yipyipyip* and looked up. Nana's yard was separated by a chain link fence from the nearest neighbor, an elderly gentleman named Mister Clausen who bred toy poodles. He usually had anywhere from ten to twenty animals on the premises, depending on their breeding cycles, so Phil wasn't completely surprised to see six or seven little bundles of fluff with beady black eyes staring back at her from across the fence. Three or four of them— probably the males—were sniffing the air and pawing at the fence excitedly.

"No, guys—this isn't for you," Phil told the eager poodles. Maybe she should have found a better place to bury the potion. Then again, the flower garden *was* separated from the neighbor's yard by a fence. For good measure she piled more dirt on the spot where the potion was buried and packed it down with the flat of the trowel. There.

"H'lo, Philomena. Long time no see, as I believe they say these days."

Phil looked up to see Mister Clausen himself smiling down at her from across the chain link fence. He had kindly blue eyes surrounded by a net of wrinkles and a comical shock of hair as white as his poodles' coats.

"Oh, hello, Mister Clausen." Phil tried to smile. "Yes, in the past few years I haven't gotten over here as much as I'd like to. Not since I moved in with my fiancé, actually." She hoped he wasn't able to smell the potion she'd just buried. She didn't think she could handle it if Nana's kindly old neighbor climbed the fence and started humping her leg. "You seem to have a good batch of puppies this time," she said, indicating the fluffy, yipping poodles.

"Oh my lands yes, three litters at once, don't ya know. I reckon if I let 'em all out at the same time my back yard would be so full of landmines ya couldn't see the grass." He hooked a thumb over his shoulder at his lawn, already liberally dotted with poodle droppings.

"Looks like your lawn is already more brown than green," she said before she could stop herself. "Those poodles are just little fluffy white crapping machines, aren't they?" Oh God, she had done it again—said the first thing that came to mind. Phil wanted to sink into the ground with embarrassment but luckily, Mister Clausen just laughed.

"You about hit the nail on the head there, young lady," he chortled, nodding his head until his fluff of white hair waved in the breeze like an oversized dandelion.

Phil decided she had better go before she said something more offensive. She made sure the saucepan was out of sight behind the zinnias. "Well, I better get going. I think that about does it for gardening today." She put the gloves and trowel back on the bench where she had found them and dusted her hands together as though she'd just done a hard day's work.

"Ya know, Philomena," Mister Clausen said, still giving her that genial smile. "When I saw you out here I thought you looked like you could use a little refreshment. So I brought you this." He reached over the waist high chain link fence and held something out to her. Phil walked closer, expecting a big glass of water or lemonade. Instead, she saw a familiar, but dreaded, sight—an éclair. It sat on the small china plate looking limp and withered. On the top of its cracked chocolate glaze sat a small curly clump of white poodle hair, like a bizarre garnish.

"Went down to the market day before yesterday and it looked so good I just had to have it," Mister Clausen continued. "But don't ya know, my diabetes is actin' up just now so I can't eat it. And when I saw you out here, somethin' told me you'd want it."

Phil hated éclairs anyway and this one had certainly seen better days. She made herself walk forward to take the plate, struggling to hold her tongue.

"Thank you. It looks horrible," she blurted, before she could stop herself. "Horribly good, I mean," she amended. "But I...I shouldn't eat it all by myself. I should take it inside and share it with Cass and Rory."

"Well, that's fine then." Mister Clausen winked at her. "You just tell that pretty little grandma of yours she can bring me back the plate whenever she's a mind to. I'll see ya later." He nodded at her and called the toy poodles which bounced around his legs like animated cotton balls as he ambled back to his house.

Phil waited until the screen door had banged shut behind him and then grabbed the trowel and dug a new hole in the dirt, right beside the buried potion. She tipped the withered éclair into its grave and covered it decently, shivering in disgust as she did so. Thank goodness Mister Clausen hadn't insisted that she take a bite. If he had, Phil honestly thought she might have been sick, right there in the zinnias.

She washed the sauce pan out with the garden hose (no way was she taking it back into the kitchen still coated in gunk) and walked back the way she had come. Cass and Rory had all the windows and the door wide open and the kitchen smelled almost normal again.

"There." Phil dumped the pan and Mister Clausen's éclair plate into the soapy water where Cass was washing dishes. "Mission accomplished. But don't think that familial guilt is going to get me to do any of your other disgusting chores. Dumping that potion was bad enough to pay for missing the last four Thanksgivings *and* only spending half days on Christmas," she said, washing her hands to get the last of the potion off them.

Her sisters exchanged a look. "Mouthy, isn't she?" Cass asked Rory with a grin. "So when are you gonna get the FG to reverse that wish, Phil?"

Phil dried her hands and began digging in Nana's ancient avocado green refrigerator for salad fixings. "I don't know, but it has to be soon. I've already told everyone in my office off and earned myself an HR review for tomorrow. If I don't get her to change it by tonight I'll just shoot off my mouth all over again at the review and get myself fired."

"Oh, no!" Rory put a hand to her mouth. "That's terrible, Phil."

"That's not the worst, either." Phil pulled out a head of lettuce, a cucumber, and some tomatoes. As she fixed the salad, she told her sisters about her fight with Mrs. Tessenbacker over the paper, her confrontation with the little blind pencil boy and her coworkers, and her argument with Christian.

"What?" Cass banged the pot she was scrubbing against

the side of the sink. "Are you telling me that dirty rat bastard never intended to put you through law school in the first place?"

"He didn't say that exactly." Phil concentrated on dicing a cucumber. "He said...he said it would be a waste of money because...I wouldn't be a good attorney." She tried to swallow the lump in her throat. "But it wasn't so much what he said—it was the way he said it."

"What—did he yell and scream at you?" Cass asked.

"No, he got really quiet. And he said that he was just trying to save me the pain of finding out...finding out that I don't have what it takes."

"What? Phil, that is *so* not true," Rory objected. "You'd make a great civil rights attorney—you're so smart. That's just an excuse because he doesn't want to spend the money."

"Money he *owes* you," Cass added indignantly. "You ought to sue him, Phil. Isn't that breach of contract or something? Come on, you're the one who wants to be a lawyer—help me out here."

"Cass is right—you *should*." Rory agreed, stirring the rice pilaf so vigorously half of it landed on the stove top.

"It's not a matter of suing him, you guys." Phil finished with the cucumber and grabbed a tomato. "In fact, just now on the phone he told me to apply to any law school I wanted and name the date for the wedding." She sighed. "He just sounded so...angry when he said it. Like I was inconveniencing him, asking him to do what he'd promised. And then he got distracted again and promised that we would talk later. But that's what he always says."

"I never liked him." Cass scrubbed viciously at a frying pan. She looked so mad Phil thought she would scrub a hole right through it. "He's a controlling asshole, Phil. I say cut him loose."

"Yeah, but you've been saying that for the last four or five years," Phil pointed out. "You two never got along—it's one reason I haven't been over here as much as I'd like to."

"So dump him and find somebody who *does* get along with the family," Rory said. "What about Josh? He's funny and sweet and you told us he's an IT guy so you know he's smart."

"And he doesn't freak out if something a little weird

happens. Like today at that retirement ranch, he was really cool, even when all those senior citizens were climbing all over Nana," Cass pointed out.

"Josh is my best friend," Phil said, slicing steadily. "And I don't care how well he dealt with the Peaceful Beach situation— I still don't want you guys freaking him out. So let's not discuss family business at the table, all right?"

"Oh, right." Rory nodded. "Because he can hear it."

"Yeah, Phil, what gives?" Cass frowned and rinsed another pot. "How come he can hear us when we talk about the FG's magic? Most non-fairies just hear buzzing or it completely escapes their attention and they start talking about something else. I didn't feel a tingle when I shook his hand so I know he doesn't have fairy blood."

"I'm as surprised as you," Phil admitted. "But that's even more reason to watch our mouths. No mention of magic at dinner, okay?"

Rory shrugged. "Sure, I guess."

Cass frowned. "I still say he could handle it."

"Well what if he couldn't?" Phil demanded. "I like him a lot. I don't want you guys scaring him off the way you did Christian. He makes a big deal about not getting along with Cass but I'm pretty sure that's not the only reason he refuses to come over here any more."

"Like that time Nana wanted to make mock turtle soup but she couldn't figure out what a mock turtle was?" Cass said, her violet eyes dancing with mischief.

"Oh, right! So she tried to conjure one up," Rory added, beginning to grin. "But she got the recipe wrong and doubled it or something and the entire house was full of those tiny little turtles the size of your palm, crawling everywhere?"

"And Christian was sitting at the table when it happened and suddenly there was a...a turtle right on top of...of his head," Phil gasped, beginning to laugh along with her sisters.

"And it...it...it *crapped* right in his hair." Cass was laughing so hard, her pale face was flushed red. "And he started yelling and shouting and throwing turtles everywhere..."

"And there was turtle crap running down his cheek..." Rory was laughing so hard she was crying. "And he kept...kept on saying, 'What the hell *is* all this?' And...and Nana came out and

158

said, 'Christian, language *please*. It's only mock turtle soup and it will pass.'" She imitated their grandmother's prim tone of voice so well that Phil laughed until her stomach hurt.

"God, what a mess." Cass blotted her eyes on the hem of her black T-shirt. "It took *days* to get rid of them all. For about a week afterwards I was still finding them at the bottom of my closet and swimming in the bathtub."

"I took a bunch of them to the pet store and sold them. Kept me in fun money for a month." Rory sounded smug.

"As I recall, that was the last family dinner Christian ever came to," Phil said, sobering up. "He's never admitted it but I think part of the reason he doesn't want to come over is that he's afraid something weird might happen at any time."

"Well, it might," Cass agreed. "You never can tell with this family. And that's the point, Phil. You need to find someone who can deal with the weirdness."

"Look." Phil put down the knife she'd been using to chop tomatoes with a *thunk*. "You two act like I'm auditioning new fiancés just because Christian and I had a fight or two. But we've been together too long just to throw it all away. We've had a lot of good times—we're just going through a rough patch right now." Deep down she knew she wasn't really being honest with her sisters—or herself for that matter. But she just didn't feel like facing the truth—not after the horrendous day she'd had. "I'm telling you once and for all," she said, pointing at Cass and Rory warningly with one finger. "Josh is just my friend and that's *all* he is."

"No, he's also a hell of a good chef." Josh walked into the kitchen, still wearing Nana's frilly apron and carrying a platter of delicious looking grilled chicken breasts. "Dinner is served." He presented Phil with the platter, making a low, comical bow but when he straightened up, she could see the hurt in his deep brown eyes.

"Josh, I'm so sorry. I didn't mean—"

"Hey, it's all right." He grinned at her, making light of the situation. "You're perfectly right—we are just friends. And it's not like I was about to declare my undying love or anything, Swann. Unless it's my love of this beautiful apron." He turned to Cass and Rory, modeling the apron with a smile. "What do you think, ladies? Could your nana be persuaded to part with this fabulous piece of clothing? 'Cause I have to tell you, I'm thinking it's just the thing to wear next casual Friday at the office. I'll be the envy of the entire IT department."

Phil watched her two sisters laughing while Josh clowned around but she had seen the expression on his face before he masked it. More than any other thing she had said since her birthday wish had come true, she wished she could take her last statement back. The last thing she'd ever want to do was hurt Josh. She felt tears rising to her eyes and choked them back down with an effort. She *had* to get this stupid birthday wish reversed so that every damn thing that entered her head didn't come flying out of her mouth.

Inwardly she resolved that she wouldn't go to bed that night before contacting her fairy godmother.

Chapter Twenty

"Fairy Godmother come for my need is dire! *Fairy Godmother come for my need is dire!*" Phil yanked on her earlobe for what felt like the nine millionth time and shouted the words into the cool, dark interior of her car. She was parked outside her apartment, in the same spot she'd been for the last hour.

Dinner at Nana's house had run long, mostly because Josh had kept everybody talking. He had asked each of her sisters and her grandmother to relate their most fascinating and embarrassing 'Phil stories,' despite Phil's vigorous protests. One story had led to many until her friend knew far more about her than Phil had ever wanted him to.

Cass and Rory had kept their word and only related non-magical incidents, like the time she'd stuffed her bra for school pictures in seventh grade and the tissue could be seen sticking out of the neck of her shirt in the photo. Or the time she'd tried to dye her hated sunshine blond hair red and it had turned out bright pink instead. "Bright pink and sparkly," Rory had explained with a giggle. "Cause Phil's hair always sparkles no matter what she does to it."

"I've noticed." Josh had said softly, smiling at her. "Not that it's easy to see—she keeps it up all the time in that roll at the back of her neck. I keep telling her she should go with a new look—like maybe the Princess Leah cinnamon buns on the sides of the head thing. Now *that's* sexy."

"Sexy," Cass scoffed. "Phil wouldn't know sexy if it bit her on the ass."

"Language, Cass," Nana admonished.

Josh had said, "Oh, I don't know about that." His warm

smile across the table had made Phil blush and drop her eyes, remembering the X-rated dream and the discussion they'd had earlier.

But on the whole, it had been one of the most enjoyable nights Phil could ever remember having with her family. Her nana couldn't be prevented from telling magical stories, of course, but Josh just smiled and nodded politely. Phil got the impression that he thought her grandmother was sweet but a little eccentric, which was basically the truth.

At the end of the night, Nana had kissed Josh on the cheek and invited him back any time. Phil was glad that her best friend was such a big hit with her family but she couldn't help wishing that her fiancé could be as well. But, she acknowledged to herself, it was probably too late for that. If Christian hadn't warmed up to her sisters and Nana by now, he probably never would. It was a shame because being with them at dinner that night reminded her how much she missed her family and she wished she could spend more time with them.

Josh had given her a ride back to the BB&D parking lot where her blue VW bug was still parked. Phil had half expected him to bring up their earlier conversation again or even try to kiss her. The look was back in his eyes—the look she couldn't define—and he was quiet for a long time after he pulled into the empty spot by her bug. Her heart was pounding and she was wondering what to do if he leaned in. But in the end he only wished her luck on the HR review and reminded her of her promise to go swimsuit shopping with him after work. He waited to see that her car started and followed her part of the way home to make sure she was okay. And that was it.

Phil felt empty somehow—unsatisfied. As though now that they had chosen to go past the invisible line they had set for themselves, she wanted more from her friend. *Not that I could have it anyway,* Phil reminded herself. After all, no matter how attractive she found Josh (and she had to admit she was finding him pretty damn attractive lately) she was still engaged.

Now she was sitting in front of the apartment complex she and Christian had moved into earlier that year, yanking on her earlobe and trying to get her fairy godmother's attention. She was determined not to go back up to the apartment until she had her birthday wish reversed. Fighting with Christian, shouting at her boss and telling off her coworkers and neighbors was one thing, but she had also made Nana cry and hurt her best friend's feelings. Enough was enough. And there was no way she could do her HR review tomorrow if she was still like this.

Taking a deep breath, Phil yanked on her earlobe and shouted at the top of her lungs, *"Fairy Godmother come, for my need is dire!"*

"All right, all *right*. I was getting ready for my yearly vacation to Patagonia but no, you couldn't wait. You had to call me *now*. So for heaven's sake, whatever are you caterwauling about?" There was a puff of pink, choking smoke and her fairy godmother was suddenly sitting in the passenger side seat of the VW bug looking bored. "And why do you keep summoning me to this miserable, smelly little vehicle?" She passed one anorexicly thin hand over her coifed blond hair.

"I called you because my birthday wish is screwing up my life—again," Phil snapped. "I'm fighting with my fiancé, I'm about to lose my job, and I hurt some people who are very close to me because I can't stop saying what I think."

"Well, that *is* what you wished for," her fairy godmother sniffed. *"I wish I could really speak my mind,"* she parroted in an exact imitation of Phil's own voice. "I didn't think it was a particularly intelligent wish myself. But then, I don't make up these wishes, I just grant them." She waved her silver wand to illustrate her point and Phil had to slap at the sparks it dripped onto the VW's seat.

"I just wanted to be able to stand up for myself," she protested angrily. "I didn't mean that I wanted every single thought in my head to come straight out of my mouth."

"Well then, you should have worded your request more carefully," her fairy godmother snapped back. "And now I suppose you want me to fix it."

Phil's mouth got the better of her. "Damn right I want you to fix it! You need to reverse this wish right now—before *my* life is completely ruined by *your* incompetence." She regretted her hasty words as soon as she said them. As inept and irritating as her fairy godmother was, there was no point in antagonizing her. But with the wish controlling her mouth, there no helping it.

"Well!" The FG fanned her mother of pearl wings in

agitation, causing a small hurricane inside the bug that whipped the loose strands of Phil's hair into her eyes. "Of all the horrid, disgusting, ungrateful—"

"Look, I'm sorry," Phil said. "But I can't help what I say! Your magic seems to have removed all the filters between my brain and my mouth. Please just reverse the wish. *Please*?"

"All right." Her fairy godmother lifted her chin and a strange glitter came into her silvery eyes. "Granted," she said in a very unpleasant voice. "Your wish is hereby *reversed*. Now don't bother me again!" Phil felt the all-over Pop Rocks in Diet Coke tingling sensation of a granted wish. Then the FG vanished with another puff of pink smoke and a nasty laugh leaving nothing behind her but the odor of burnt rose petals lingering in the air.

Granted. Her wish had been granted. Phil breathed a cautious sigh of relief, then decided she'd better test it out first. Closing her eyes, she thought of what she really thought of her fairy godmother which included some of the filthiest four letter words she knew and waited to start shouting her thoughts out. But no, to her intense relief, her lips stayed shut. She opened her eyes. She was cured. But wait—did that mean that she was back to having a lamb-like temperament too?

Phil closed her eyes again and remembered her last argument with Christian. Should she have dropped her dinner plans with Nana and her sisters and Josh to go to her fiancé's party? Did she have an overwhelming urge to go apologize for ruining his night? She frowned, feeling upset all over again. Hell no. And no to giving up law school, too. And no to putting off the wedding... Well, maybe that could wait for a little while. She and Christian needed to do some serious talking before they walked down the aisle. But at least she didn't feel the need to apologize for everything she'd said and try to smooth things over.

And in the mean time, it looked like she was cured of her foot-in-mouth disease. *And* she had retained the ability to think for herself. Great!

Phil fairly skipped up the stairs to her apartment. She knew what she would find when she opened the door. Christian would be sitting up waiting for her, no doubt worried that she had been out so long after midnight. They would sit on the couch and talk late into the night, the way they had when they were first dating. Phil would explain quietly, and with tact, all of her concerns and her fiancé would listen to her—really *listen*, she was sure. Then they would come to an agreement about the future and she would find out all their fights about her going to law school had been based on a big misunderstanding. Probably he had been trying to offer her what he thought was a better life than the one she had planned for herself and he had just expressed himself badly. After all, Christian was a man and men were always saying the wrong thing, weren't they? And after the last day and a half she certainly knew how *that* felt.

She unlocked the front door, ready to fall into her fiancé's arms. But he wasn't there. He wasn't sitting in the living room waiting for her and he wasn't making pot after pot of coffee worrying about her, either. When Phil found him, he was snoring on his side of the bed.

"Christian?" She patted him lightly on the arm. "Christian, I'm home. I'm sorry dinner ran late."

"Hmph." He rolled over in his sleep and exhaled in her face. Phil jerked back—his breath was thick with Scotch fumes. Well, so much for the idea of him worrying about her, she thought sourly.

She sighed and went in the bathroom to catch a quick shower before bed. Well, at least she was back to normal now. They could talk things out in the morning.

Chapter Twenty-One

But in the morning when she rolled over, Christian's side of the bed was cold. Phil fumbled around until she found a note on his pillow. *Early meeting at the office. See you tonight. Christian.*

She read the note twice before crumpling it into a ball and throwing it across the room. Now that her thinking out loud problem was cured, she wanted to sit down and talk to her fiancé like rational adults. Her feelings for him had changed significantly in the past several months and that scared her. She wanted to know that he was scared too. She wanted reassurance that things were going to be all right. She wanted to hear Christian say he loved her so she could remind herself that she still loved him too. Was that so much to ask?

Phil got up and was halfway to the front door to get the paper by force of habit when she stopped in her tracks. Christian wasn't here so why should she fetch his paper? Let Mrs. Tessenbacker have it for once. But no...if she did that, all the ground she'd won yesterday would be lost. Better get it after all.

Sighing, Phil opened the door and looked out. Sure enough, the paper was there, unmolested by either Mrs. Tessenbacker's sticky fingers or her nasty little dog's urine. All was right in the world. Phil was just reaching out to take it when she heard a slight creaking. Looking up, she saw Mrs. Tessenbacker's beady little eye staring at her through the crack of the door.

"Good morning, Mrs. Tessenbacker," she said, relieved that she felt no need to express any of the thoughts she was currently having about her cheap, thieving neighbor out loud.

Mrs. Tessenbacker made a noise like *hrmph* and started to

shut her door. But then, to Phil's surprise, she opened it instead and came out into the hall. Doodle-bug danced out behind her yipping and growling at her feet. She stood out in front of Phil's front door and put her hands on her broad hips.

"Cheap, she calls me," she said loudly, frowning at Phil. "And says my little Doodle-bug smells!"

"Please, Mrs. Tessenbacker, keep it down!" Phil looked up and down the hall at the other apartment doors to see if anyone was coming out to see what the racket was about.

"But you don't understand what my life was like," her elderly neighbor continued loudly. "I came up during the Depression. Never enough food, my father couldn't keep a job, so if there was anything to take, we took it."

"Um...okay." Phil crossed her arms over her chest, hoping Mrs. Tessenbacker's personal version of *The Grapes of Wrath* wouldn't take too long. "I'm sorry you had a hard childhood. But I really don't see how that has to do with you taking my paper instead of buying your own."

"We took it!" Mrs. Tessenbacker insisted loudly, as though Phil hadn't spoken at all. "And that's why I still take things. Your paper, fruit at the grocery store, aspirin at the drugstore..."

"Um...Are you trying to tell me you're a...a shoplifter?" Phil stared at her blankly. Why in the world would her neighbor tell her such a thing?

Mrs. Tessenbacker's tiny, beady eyes grew wide and she shook her head vigorously. She had a miserable look on her face and yet she seemed compelled to keep talking.

"I can't help myself," she went on. "I just get such a thrill when I take something that belongs to someone else and put it in my pocketbook. It's like a little trophy, reminding me I can take anything I want and no one will know."

Phil looked at her neighbor, at a loss for words. Apparently Mrs. Tessenbacker wasn't just a shoplifter—she was a kleptomaniac. Phil made a mental note never to invite her in for coffee or tea.

"I, uh, have to get ready for work," she said, before Mrs. Tessenbacker could reveal any other embarrassing personal details. She was inching back into her apartment when Mrs. Tessenbacker let loose again.

"I'm an old lady!" she bugled and at her feet, Doodle-bug began to howl. "Nobody ever suspects an old lady. I take what I want when I want it and nobody can stop me!"

"Goodbye Mrs. Tessenbacker." Phil shut the door hastily and stood with her back to it. Had her elderly neighbor finally cracked? Why else would she stand in the hallway and shout out her darkest secrets for everybody to hear? Phil wondered for a moment if she should call someone...but who? Social Services? The local mental institution? The police? She supposed she could alert them that a not-so-dangerous criminal was living in her apartment building and had given a full confession.

Phil sighed. She should just get dressed and go to the dreaded HR review. Well, at least she didn't have to worry about embarrassing herself. Poor Mrs. Tessenbacker. Maybe after she had her morning meds she'd be feeling more like herself. As she got ready for work, Phil wondered if that was really such a good thing.

She got to the BB&D parking lot just as a lot of other people were pulling up and it took every bit of nerve she possessed to get out of the car. At least Alison hadn't parked in her space this time, she noted as she pulled in. There was John Nash from accounting, Terri Sanchez from billing, and Hector who worked in the mail room. They all gave her sidelong glances as she locked the bug's door and started her long walk to the elevator. Phil was sure that by now everyone in the entire law firm had heard about her rampage the day before and must be wondering the same thing she was wondering—if she was going to get fired or not. But she kept her chin high and kept on walking—or she would have, anyway, if she hadn't seen the little blind pencil boy.

He was standing in his usual place by one of the concrete pillars, jingling his pencil cup as always, a wide, appealing grin on his face. He hadn't seen Phil yet and she stopped short and stared at him. Well, the kid had guts, she had to give him that. Still, it irked her that he would have the nerve to come back here after she had exposed him the day before. He had a new, expensive-looking pair of sunglasses on his face and she wondered what brand they were—Foster Grants?

She thought about confronting him, but then she thought better of it. The management of BB&D were already aware of the scene she'd had with the little blind pencil boy the day before and she really didn't need to make another one. As much as it burned her up to see him brazenly taking advantage of people, Phil decided to keep her head down and keep moving.

She saw the pencil boy flinch when he recognized her. God, how could she have ever bought his act? Phil was dimly aware that other people were watching her as she passed him. *They're waiting to see if I'll do it again. Waiting to see if I'm crazy. Vultures.*

Phil was doubly glad that her birthday wish had been reversed now. The uncharitable things she was thinking about her coworkers were definitely not anything she wanted to say aloud. The pencil boy had something to say, though. As she passed him, he yelled,

"All right! I'm not blind!"

Phil stopped in her tracks, startled, and turned to face him. She saw John and Terri and Hector do the same.

"I'm not! I'm not blind! There's nothing wrong with my eyes. I'm not even nearsighted!" the pencil boy repeated in a loud voice, looking wildly at Phil. "But this is the best paying gig I've ever had. I can make over a hundred dollars a day this way and I don't have to work at no fucking hamburger shack to do it—all I have to do it look sad and pathetic."

Phil couldn't think of a thing to say. Terri, who was a tall thin woman with a knife blade of a nose, came back to stand in front of him.

"What are you saying?" she asked, frowning. "I've been buying two or three pencils a week from you for years. *And* I gave you fifty dollars at Christmas. Are you telling me you're not sight impaired at all?"

"No, I'm not." The pencil boy looked so upset Phil was almost tempted to feel sorry for him. What was going on here?

John and Hector had wandered back as well and were staring at the pencil boy. "What the hell?" John, who was built like a linebacker was frowning like a thundercloud.

"Yeah—why are you telling us this?" Hector demanded.

"I...I don't know." The pencil boy dropped his cup with a clatter and pencils and change went rolling all over the concrete. The look on his face almost reminded Phil of herself the day before, when she'd been forced to say everything she thought out loud.

"Hey, what—?" Terri began but the pencil boy broke and ran, dodging around concrete barriers and leaping over parking bumps in a display that proved he had been telling the truth.

"Hey, look at him go!" John shouted, pointing as the boy hopped on his bike and sped away. "Damn it! He's about as blind as *I* am. And I've been buying those fucking pencils of his for years now."

"Me too!" Hector looked almost as upset as John and Terri. Phil fled past them to the elevator, her heart pounding hard against her ribs. A terrible feeling was growing in her chest. First Mrs. Tessenbacker had shouted out something she would no doubt have rather kept hidden, and now the pencil boy had outed himself, too. Both of them were acting exactly as she had been the day before when she couldn't stop saying what was on her mind. It was almost as though they were being *forced* to reveal their private thoughts when Phil came near them.

It couldn't be! Phil jabbed the *close door* button on the elevator, thankful that her coworkers were still too busy discussing the con artist pencil boy to join her in the elevator.

Closing her eyes tightly, she tried to think. Her fairy godmother had reversed her birthday wish so that she no longer had to tell everyone she saw exactly what she was thinking and how she felt about them. So why were the people around her suddenly having the same problem she'd had?

Phil pressed her fingers to her temples, thinking frantically as the elevator climbed higher. She remembered the unpleasant glint in her fairy godmother's eye and the nasty tone of her laughter. What exactly had she said to Phil before she disappeared? *"Your wish is hereby reversed!"* That was it, that was the word she had been searching for—reversed!

Her fairy godmother had screwed her again—this time on purpose because she was pissed off at Phil for speaking her mind. Instead of *Phil* feeling the overwhelming need to spew her innermost thoughts and feelings at the people around her, now *they*, whoever she was in physical proximity to, would feel the exact same urge. Everyone around her was going to be compelled to speak their minds.

"Oh, God," Phil moaned. What a nightmare! She knew the vindictive FG had known exactly what Phil wanted when she asked to have the wish reversed. All Phil had been asking was to be able to keep her thoughts about other people inside her head instead of saying them out loud. But the fairy godmother had used the ambiguous wording to literally reverse the wish and make Phil's life even more difficult.

Phil wanted to kick herself. She should have spelled things out to the letter instead of leaving such a gaping hole for the magic to do as it pleased. Now she was stuck in an office full of people she had told off, cussed out, and in the case of Davis Miles, sexually harassed the day before. People who would feel compelled to say exactly what they thought of her right to her face. Oh God, it was going to be worse than high school.

Phil was about to press the down button and get the hell out of Dodge when the elevator dinged and the doors opened on her floor. She dared to stick her head out and saw Josh passing by, a worried look on his usually calm face. Oh no—what if he felt compelled to say something awful to her or admit some horrible secret she really didn't want to know? Phil started to shrink back inside the elevator but it was too late—her best friend had already seen her.

"Swann!" He smiled at her but it was a distracted, worried smile that made her forget her own problems. For as long as she'd known him, Josh had been an easy going, almost unflappable guy. So the anxious look on his face must mean something was wrong—really wrong.

"Josh, what is it?" She caught his hand and pulled him around to face her. "What's wrong?"

"It's that obvious?" He ran his free hand through his rumpled hair and tried to laugh. He was wearing a deep maroon shirt with the top two buttons unbuttoned and his black tie was askew as always.

"To me it is." Phil realized she was still holding his hand and let it go reluctantly. "So what happened?"

"Oh," He blew out a breath. "It's the server. Of all times for it to actually go down! I've been on it since I came in at seven this morning and I still can't find the problem." He lowered his voice. "The senior Dickhead has been chewing my ass like bubble gum. I feel like I'm gonna start pulling out my hair by the roots until I'm as bald as he is."

"Don't do it." Phil tried to smile at him, wanting to cheer

him up the same way he always cheered her up when she had problems. "I like your hair just the way it is. And you'd look awful at the beach party—a chrome dome in a Speedo."

Josh chuckled but then his face fell. "Damn—the beach party. I forgot all about our plan to go shop for suits. I'm sorry, Swann, but if something doesn't give, I don't know if I can make it."

Phil felt her heart sink a little. In the back of her mind, she'd been thinking that no matter how horrible the HR review turned out to be, at least she still had Josh's company to look forward to afterwards. But she didn't want him to feel worse when he was already so stressed out.

"Well, I probably won't need a suit anyway." She shrugged. "I mean, I'm pretty sure I'll be fired, and they'll rescind my invite to beach day."

"Shit." Josh ran both hands through his hair this time which made him look almost wild. "I'm so sorry, Phil. I completely forgot. Look, no matter what happens just remember you have at least one person on your side. If they kick you out, I'll walk too."

"Hey, no, you don't have to do that." She was a little taken aback at his offer, even more so because she knew Josh didn't go back on his word. If he said he'd quit his job if BB&D fired her, he meant it.

"Hell." Josh gave a shaky laugh and yanked at his tie. "If I don't get the damn computer system working again, it'll be a moot point because they'll hand me my walking papers and we can leave together."

"Oh, Josh, I'm so sorry." Phil wanted to pull him into her arms and just hold him close, wanted to comfort him the way he had comforted her the day before in his car. But she was well aware that they were in a public hallway and anything they did would be grist for the office rumor mill. So instead she reached out and squeezed his arm, trying to put all her sympathy and compassion into the small gesture.

He smiled. "It's all right, Swann. Anyway, I thought *I* was the one who was supposed to be comforting *you*."

Phil smiled back, relieved to see the easing of tension around his brown eyes. "Comfort is a two way street, you know. You certainly gave me enough of it yesterday. I owe you some."

"You don't owe me anything," Josh said, suddenly serious. He took a step closer to her. "The pleasure of comforting you, of holding you in my arms, was all mine."

"Wow, Josh. That's... beautiful. Thank you." Phil was a little taken aback by his intense statement until she remembered her reversed wish. *Well, if this is the worst thing he has to say to me, it's no sweat,* she thought.

Judging by the look on his face, Josh was surprised at his words, as well. "Okay, enough mooshy stuff." He jammed his hands deep in his pockets and leaned one shoulder against the pale pink wall. "You have to go to your HR review and I have to go back and slay the flaming server dragon or die trying. So here goes—quick pep talk. You first."

"Um..." Phil thought fast. This was a game they sometimes played on the phone when one of them was having a crappy day but was too busy to stop for a full fledged "bitch session" as Josh called it. "You can handle this, Bowman," she said, looking him in the eye like a basketball coach with a star player during the Final Four. "You're the smartest guy I know and if anyone can find out what's going on with the server it's you. You're going to go back there and look at things from a fresh angle and find out what's wrong. Then you're going to...to...to fix the *shit* out of it and get done in time to come bathing suit shopping with me anyway. And...and see me buy the first bikini I've had since I was twelve." She put her hands on her hips and smiled. "There—how's that?"

Josh laughed—the same deep sound she'd grown to love because it warmed her from the inside out. "Fix the *shit* out of it?" His melted chocolate eyes twinkled. "Damn, Swann! And are you telling me I get to see you in a teeny-weeny yellow polka-dot bikini if I succeed in my quest?"

"Well..." Phil felt herself blushing. "I was trying to motivate you. But when you put it that way it doesn't sound very motivating, I guess."

"Oh, no, it's motivating." Josh was serious again. "I've known you for years but all I ever get to see you in is your office clothes. Well, except for last year's beach day, but you wore shorts and a T-shirt to that. Hardly Playboy material. Not that I haven't imagined you in much more revealing outfits, of course." He seemed to catch himself and looked confused. "Uh..." He dug his hands deeper into his pockets. "God, Phil,

I'm sorry. That was...well, I don't know where that came from."

"I do. I mean, um... I just..." Phil shrugged but inside she couldn't help feeling a little tingle. So Josh actually imagined her in different outfits? In *sexy* outfits? She knew it was wrong to feel secretly pleased about what he had revealed under the power of her fairy godmother's screwed up magic, but she couldn't help it. After all, it had been so long since Christian showed any interest in her that way. It felt good to be noticed—good to be wanted.

"Phil, really, I..."

She realized that Josh was still looking abashed, no doubt thinking that he had offended her.

"Look, don't worry about it." Phil glanced at her watch and saw that it was getting late. "I need to get to my desk. So come on—pep talk. Give it to me quick."

"Okay, okay." Josh cleared his throat and squared his shoulders. "You're sweet and wonderful and way too smart to be working here," he said. "And you've got more class in your little finger that everybody else in the rest of this whole damn place put together. You're gonna get out of here and go to law school so no matter what happens in there, I want you to remember that. I also want you to remember that...that, uh..." His eyes suddenly darkened and Phil caught a glimpse of that certain something she'd seen in them the day before when they had let their barriers slip by mutual agreement. "Remember that you're beautiful," Josh went on softly. "You're so beautiful it hurts me to look at you. But I couldn't stop looking even if it meant I'd go blind. Remember that, Phil."

"Oh...uh..." She knew it was just her wish making him talk like that but still, it wasn't the way their pep talks usually went. Josh usually ended by reminding her not to let the man get her down and giving her a slap on the back. There was no denying, though, that it gave her a thrill to hear that he thought she was beautiful. With her weird hair, too red lips, and changeable eyes (even though people without fae or fairy blood didn't notice them) Phil had always felt kind of like an ugly duckling. It was nice to hear that someone considered her a swan.

"I'm sorry." Josh took his hands out of his pockets to rub his temples. "I didn't mean...I mean I did, but." He sighed and ran a hand through his hair. "Look, just remember you're in the right and Dickhead Junior is in the wrong. And if he lays a hand on you again, I'll punch his lights out. Okay?"

"Wow—thanks." Phil grinned at him. "That's the best offer I've had all day." She glanced at her watch again. "Okay, now I really need to get going."

"Right—pep talk over." Josh still looked confused, but now he was distracted again too, no doubt thinking about the problems ahead of him.

"See you later. And good luck." Phil turned for her cubicle.

"Right. Go get 'em, tiger. And call me when it's over." He sketched her a quick salute and was gone around the corner back to the tech department. Phil sighed and headed for her cubicle, as well. It was time to face the music and she had a feeling she wasn't going to like what she had to hear.

Chapter Twenty-Two

"Ms. Swann? The head of HR will see you now." Mrs. Bloom, Herbert Dickson's ancient secretary seemed to impart the words with a tolling, bell-like doom. Or maybe that was just Phil's nerves acting up. It was almost noon and she'd been waiting for the better part of an hour in the HR director's outer office, wondering when the review was going to start. She felt like a kid called to the principal's office and made to wait for a paddling.

The only bright spot in her day was that she hadn't had to hear any more wild outbursts. She'd spent most of the early morning working quietly at her desk while her coworkers avoided her like the plague. As long as they didn't get too close and Phil didn't interact with them, the wish didn't make them blurt out their thoughts and feelings. It was a relief not to have any confrontations after two days straight of nothing else. So Phil stayed at her cubicle until she was called to HR.

Now she stood on shaky legs, ready to answer to the charges against her, trying to remind herself that she was no longer a doormat or a dishrag. She was an intelligent woman who spoke up for herself and didn't take crap from anybody. Someday she was going to be a civil rights attorney and that was how she was going to conduct herself now. As though this was a trial and she was acting in her own defense. Right. Phil took a deep breath. Mostly she just wished like hell this whole experience was over.

"Good morning, Ms. Swann. Please, be seated." Herbert Dickson's office was almost as posh as her boss's even though he was the only Dickson in the family who wasn't an attorney. He was a tall, cadaverously thin man who looked like a funeral director. In fact, he was almost the exact physical opposite of his cousin and Phil's boss, Atwood Dickson, who was seated to his left at the far end of a semicircle of chairs that were arranged around the imposing mahogany desk. Phil wondered why there were so many chairs in the office. Had a meeting just broken up? Trying not to look at her boss, who was giving her a leering grin, she walked quickly to the far side of the semicircle and sat on the end chair, as far from him as possible.

Keeping her eyes on the head of HR, she folded her hands on her lap to stop their trembling. "Mister Dickson," she said, addressing Herbert, not Atwood. "Before we start this review, I'd like to say that I know I made some...well, some very imprudent statements yesterday. But I'd like it to go on record as saying that I feel many of them were justified and I was severely provoked."

"Severely provoked? What the hell—" Atwood began angrily.

"Atwood, pleased." Herbert raised a hand to keep his cousin quiet. "Ms. Swann," he said, giving her a cold look. "We are not nearly ready to begin yet. When your statement is called for I will let you know. Now." He cleared his throat with a high, whiny cough as Atwood gave her an evil look. "It was brought to my attention yesterday that there were several staff complaints against you, Ms. Swann, not only from your superior, Mister Atwood Dickson, but from several coworkers, as well."

"I can explain—" Phil began, although she had no idea how in the world she could. What was she going to say? *I'm sorry I was so rude yesterday but I was under a magic spell and I couldn't help myself.* Oh yeah, that was going to go down *reeeeal* well if the FG's magic even let them understand her, which she doubted. But she didn't get a chance to try. Herbert Dickson held up his long thin hand again, cutting her off in mid-sentence.

"Please, Ms. Swann. As I indicated earlier, when I want a statement from you, I will ask for it."

Phil subsided into a miserable silence, twisting her fingers in her lap. Herbert Dickson might just as well hand her the pink slip now. There was no way she was getting out of here with her job, or the letter of recommendation Dickson Senior had promised her. No way in hell. And how was getting fired going to look on her law school applications? *Like a big, fat black mark,* Phil thought morosely. *No legitimate school is going to want me if I get fired like this.*

"As I was saying," Herbert Dickson continued, breaking her train of thought. "There have been several complaints about you. In the past if such a situation was brought to my attention, I would have interviewed all the participants separately and come to my own conclusion. However, in light of the recent sensitivity training we've all undergone I felt it would be more appropriate for us to have a group session. That is, I want all of the injured parties in one room together. In that way, the people you hurt and insulted can express their feelings to you, Ms. Swann, and perhaps you can explain to them what motivated your behavior in the first place."

Phil's mouth went dry as she realized what he was saying. All of them? She was going to be forced to confront *all* of the people she'd insulted yesterday *at the same time?* She wanted to get out of her chair and bolt from the room, but her coworkers were already filing in.

Kelli was first, her lips pressed into a thin, white line as her eyes flickered to Phil and then away again. Next came Davis Miles, looking very uncomfortable. If Phil had had to guess, she would bet that he wasn't there of his own free will. Probably upper management had forced him to attend this travesty. Last came Alison, slinking close behind Miles with an amused half-smile on her face. She seemed eager to see Phil get what was coming to her. *At least Caroline Sanders isn't here,* Phil thought dismally, wondering what color eyebrows her elderly coworker was wearing today.

They ranged themselves around the semicircle with Miles sitting closest to Phil, Alison on the other side of him, and Kelli beside her. Phil tried not to look at any of them as the head of HR got up and shut the heavy office door, trapping her in the room.

"Now." He settled back at his desk and rubbed his long hands together with a dry, papery sound. "Let's get started, shall we? Who would like to air a grievance first?"

"I will." Kelli raised her hand as though she were in school and knew the answer to the teacher's question.

"Yes, you may begin." The HR director nodded at her and drew a pen and paper forward to take notes.

"Okay, right. So Philomena came in here yesterday

practically an hour late and when I told her how late she was, she jumped all over me. And then when I tried to make small talk with her, she yelled at me and told me to shut up!" Kelli's eyes brimmed with easy tears. "I mean, I don't know what got into her! We've been friends for all these years and suddenly she just turned on me like... like some kind of rabid dog or something, I don't know. And—"

"Enough." Herbert Dickson held up a hand. "Ms. Swann," he said, turning to Phil. "Have you anything to say in your defense? Or perhaps an apology you'd like to make?"

Phil looked between the head of HR and her annoying cubicle mate and was filled with a rush of helpless rage. No doubt they expected her to do one of two things—one, she would knuckle under as she always had and mutter an abject apology she really didn't mean. Or two—she would have another outburst the way she had yesterday and tell them all to shut up and go to hell. That would give them grounds for firing her at once which was no doubt what Herbert Dickson wanted. After all, disgruntled employees who are fired for acts against other employees don't have the strongest case in court should they decide to sue. If Phil yelled sexual harassment, they could always point at her file and say that she was a problem employee who had been called on the carpet for abusing and harassing others. It was a catch 22. Damned if she did, damned if she didn't.

"Ms. Swann? We're waiting." Herbert Dickson sounded annoyed and Phil realized she'd paused too long before giving an answer. She took a deep breath and decided not to meet either one of their expectations.

"Firstly, let me say that we are coworkers, Kelli," she said, facing her tight-lipped cubicle mate. "But as far as I am concerned, we have never been friends. Every work day for as long as I can remember, I have had to put up with your chatter about your personal life while I was trying to meet the goals and expectations set by my superiors. Yesterday I was, as you say, late, and I wasn't feeling myself. When you started in with the inane details of your life for what felt like the five millionth time, I just lost it. I realize I shouldn't have told you to shut up but then again, you shouldn't have been talking to me about personal business when I was trying to work."

Phil sat back in her chair and released a trembling breath

as she watched Kelli's jaw drop. There. Professional and to the point. She didn't scream and she didn't apologize. Well, not much anyway. She could almost hear Josh's voice inside her head, cheering her on. *Suck on that Dickhead!*

"Well. I'm afraid that's a rather unfortunate way to put things." Herbert Dickson's mouth was pursed as though he'd been sucking something sour. "But if we may move on—"

"Wait! I'm not ready to move on." Kelli sounded genuinely angry. She glared at Phil from her side of the semicircle and Phil did her best to return the look coolly.

"Really now, I—" Herbert Dickson began.

"You said we'd get a chance to say what we felt," Kelli pouted. "Well I'm not done yet." She crossed her arms over her chest and directed her statements to Phil. "It seems to me that if you had a problem with me you could've told me instead of waiting until you went crazy, exploding all over me that way. And honestly, I don't know why I talk so much. Maybe because when I'm talking, I can't hear myself thinking. Because I think a lot. About some very scary things."

"Well, I think that's—" the HR director began again, but Kelli was on a roll.

"I think about death and dying and how it's going to be when I get old and dried up and nasty looking and I know I'm gonna die real soon," she continued. "And I know everybody thinks about things like that, but I think about worse things, too."

Phil raised an eyebrow at her. "Worse than dying?"

"Yeah." Kelli's bottom lip quivered. "I think of all the things I'm afraid of. Like cockroaches—what if one crawled in my ear while I was asleep at night? I would just die—I couldn't live through something like that, I know I couldn't. And what about spiders? Poisonous ones like black widows and brown recluses? I read about a man who got bitten by a brown recluse and the venom or poison or whatever you call it ate up his entire left leg and they had to amputate. What if something like that happened to me? How could I stand it?"

"Now, we really must—" Herbert Dickson tried for the third time.

"And what about clowns? How scary are they?" Kelli's bottom lip was trembling now. "I used to dream when I was a kid that a killer clown lived in my closet. And I was so sure that he would come out one night, his face all white from the greasepaint and his big rubbery lips all red with blood, holding a machete and calling my name. *Kelli...Kel—*"

"Please! That is enough!" thundered the director of HR. "Kelli, will you please *shut up!*" The moment the words left his lips, he looked as though he wanted to pull them back, but of course it was too late. There was a muted gasp from the others in the room, but no one said anything.

Phil cleared her throat as her coworker sank back into her chair in sulky silence. "Mister Dickson, maybe you can see my point now," she said quietly.

The director of HR glared at her. "You will kindly keep your comments to yourself until I ask for them, Ms. Swann," he said icily. "At any rate, now that Kelli has had her say—"

"I was just getting started," Kelli muttered, but Herbert Dickson went on as though he hadn't heard her.

"Now that Kelli has had her say," he continued, "I think someone else might like to say how they felt when you abused them."

Phil opened her mouth to object to the word "abused" when Alison raised her hand.

"I'll say how I felt, Mister Dickson," she said, giving him a big-eyed look that was guaranteed to melt any man on the planet.

"Very well." He smiled at her. "We'll continue with you, Alison. Now I believe that Ms. Swann, er...criticized your wardrobe choices."

"She called me a slut," Alison said, glaring at Phil. "And I resent that because..." She paused, her mouth working but nothing coming out.

"Because...?" Herbert Dickson prompted.

"Because..." Alison had a strange look on her face—a look that might have been terror. "Because I *am* a slut," she said at last, all in one breath. "But that's only because my father never loved me. He...he...he abandoned me and my mother when I was only five and ever since I've been looking for a man who'll love me the way he should've." Her eyes widened. "Oh my God, that's what my therapist says anyway. That I confuse sex and love and that I use sex as a weapon. But..." She shook her head. "But why am I saying this?"

"I, er...don't exactly know. But if you're quite finished—" the HR director said.

"He says that I sleep with men in power to try and get back at my father. And that I make them buy me expensive gifts to punish him for never caring about me. Like the Mercedes that Atwood bought me." Alison slapped a hand over her mouth and Phil had the pleasure of seeing her smug boss look distinctly uncomfortable.

"Now, Alison, you know I never—" he began.

"People, people!" Herbert Dickson pounded on his desk. "Let us get back to the subject at hand. Now I think Alison is quite finished. So we need to move on to, uh... Counselor Miles." He cleared his throat and looked expectantly at Davis Miles. "Davis, isn't it true that yesterday in the break room, Ms. Swann propositioned and sexually harassed you?"

"I...I...yes, in a way." Miles shrugged unhappily. "But...but what she said was actually mild compared with what Alison does," he continued, getting red in the face. "I mean, Alison is *constantly* in my personal space and hanging all over me. Once I walked into my office to find her leaning over my desk with her skirt pulled up. She...she begged me to spank her and she called me Daddy!"

"People, please!" The director of HR was staring at them helplessly.

"What?" Alison shrieked. "Davis, how dare you say that?"

"I'm saying it because it happened. And because I'm *sick* of it. Why don't you leave me alone, Alison? What do you want from me?"

"What do you think I want from you?" she snarled. "You're the hottest attorney in the office and you're bound to make partner in the next five years. I want you to marry me and take me away from all this. My therapist says I'm projecting my dreams of a perfect man on you and that I should give it up but I don't want to. I want to be *rescued*, damn it!"

"Well find someone else to rescue you!" Davis Miles roared. "I don't want to be your white knight! I have no interest in you at all because *I'm gay!*"

There was sudden and complete silence in the office and then everyone started talking at once. Herbert Dickson pounded on his desk with both fists. "Stop it! Everyone just *stop talking!*" When everyone had quieted down, he stood up and leaned over his desk, glaring at all of them like naughty school children. "People," he said, breathing heavily. "May I remind you what we are here for? Please keep your remarks relevant to the matter at hand. Now if we may continue..."

"I'll go next." Atwood Dickson stood up with a swagger. Clearly he wanted to have his say and get out of the room.

"Atwood, please, I really don't think—" Herbert Dickson began, but Phil's boss ignored him.

"I had a yearly review with Philomena—Ms. Swann— yesterday in my office. I told her I had received some very troubling reports and offered her several options—"

"You mean when you offered to give me a clean report if I slept with you?" Phil demanded.

Her boss's face got beet red. "I never...I never..." He stuttered and stammered but the wish was working overtime in the enclosed space of the office and he couldn't finish the lie.

"Ms. Swann, may I remind you that I will ask for your comments when I want them?" Herbert Dickson asked, glowering at her.

"And may I remind *you*, Mister Dickson, that this is supposed to be a HR review, not a character assassination," Phil retorted, fisting her hands in her lap. Her heart was thudding against her ribs but she was damned if she'd sit still and listen to her repulsive boss put his own spin on things. "For literally years I have put up with all kinds of disgusting behavior from Atwood Dickson and yesterday I got sick of it! He's constantly making lewd remarks to me and trying to touch me in inappropriate ways and when he practically threatened to fire me yesterday if I didn't go to bed with him, I—"

Her boss's face had been getting redder and redder until he looked ready to explode. "Well, it's not like I would have actually screwed you, you little bitch!" he exploded. "After all, I haven't had an erection with a real woman for the last *six months.*"

"What?" Herbert Dickson was as surprised as the rest of the people in the room, Phil included, to hear this little fact. But judging from the look on his face, none of them was as shocked as Atwood was to be telling it.

"That's right," he blustered, unable to stop. "I'm impotent

when it comes to having sex with a real live woman. The only way I can come is if I'm jerking off to the computer."

"Atwood, I really think you'd better stop," Herbert Dickson commanded, in vain.

"Because...because..." Atwood Dickson's face was now brick red and Phil wondered if he was going to have a stroke. "Because I'm addicted to hentai. *Furry* hentai."

"Huh?" Phil, Miles, Alison, and Herbert Dickson said in unison.

"Furry hentai?" Kelli grimaced. "I know what he's talking about. It's these little Japanese cartoon porn thingies—they look like animals only with human faces and ...other parts." She shivered. "They scare the crap out of me."

"Eww, Atwood." Alison made a face. "Is that what those little things were? I always wondered why you wanted to look at the computer all the time instead of me. I mean, if I say so, I look a *lot* better naked than some hairy animal."

"*That's* certainly a matter of opinion," Davis Miles muttered.

"How dare you? I have never..."

Phil wrapped her arms around her waist as her coworkers went off to the races again. She wasn't sure if she ought to feel glad or upset. She settled for being quiet.

"People! People!" Herbert Dickson roared. He had to bang on his desk for almost five minutes before the talk subsided this time. At last, all eyes were fixed on him in sullen silence.

"May I remind you..." The director of HR was breathing hard and looking very red in the face himself. "May I remind you that this is *not* the place to air your dirty laundry. And speaking of laundry, may I further state that I...I...'" His face worked as though he was fighting to find the right words to continue—or as though he was trying not to continue at all. "I— I am currently wearing *women's underwear*."

Phil's mouth fell open as another breathless silence descended on the room. But the head of HR wasn't done yet.

"A nice black lace bra and panty set." His narrow face grew pale as he talked. "It makes me feel so sexy to know I have it on under my suit and none of you knows about it..."

"Well, we know about it now!" Kelli yelled. "And we know

Davis is gay, and that Alison is a slut—well, we already knew that—but now we know she has an Electra complex too, and where her Mercedes came from. And we know Atwood likes to look at furry cartoons having sex and you're a cross-dresser... And I thought being afraid of *clowns* was bad."

"Enough!" Herbert Dickson gasped. His formerly red face was now so white Phil thought he looked like a ghost. "I...I don't know what's going on here," he almost moaned. "But this...this review session is adjourned."

"What about me?" Phil stood up. "Am I free to go and resume my duties *without* further harassment?"

"Yes, yes...just go. Hell, take the rest of the day off—just get out of here!" The Director of HR looked like he was going to be sick.

With a last backward glance at her squabbling coworkers, Phil opened the heavy wooden door and fled the HR director's office. Her review had not gone as planned.

Chapter Twenty-Three

Just as she was gathering her things to leave the office, her phone rang. Phil almost didn't answer it but then she saw the tech department's extension lit up.

"Hello?" She picked up and hunched over the phone, anxious to avoid any further confrontations with passing coworkers.

"Swann?" Josh's deep voice was filled with concern. "How did it go?"

"Oh, I..." Phil wished she could tell her best friend all about the crazed scene in the HR review, but how could she possibly explain it? "It went better than I thought," she finally said. "I still have a job, anyway. In fact, I get the rest of the day off."

"Huh, same as yesterday." She could hear the smile in his voice. "Sounds like you plan to make a habit of working half days, there Swann. Some people get all the breaks."

"Yeah—some break. You should have seen it in there—it was a zoo. But hey, how about you? How's the server problem?" Phil felt guilty. In the confusion of the HR review, she had almost forgotten about her friend's predicament.

"Well as a matter of fact, you may be talking to one of the most brilliant men in the country—nay, dare I say it? The entire world."

"You fixed the shit out of it, huh?"

"I fixed the shit out of it. It turned out to be a really simple error and I just didn't see it at first because I was looking for something big so..." Josh rattled on in technical jargon that went over her head, and Phil listened, a little smile tugging at the corners of her mouth. It was wonderful to hear Josh in high spirits again, wonderful to share his triumph and have him share hers.

"I'm so happy for you," she said, when he came to the end. "I mean, I have *no* idea what you just told me but it all sounds wonderful."

"Wonderful? Hell yeah, it's wonderful." Josh sounded like he was grinning. "*And* it means we're back on for our original plans—we can go suit shopping together. In fact, why don't we both make it a half day and go now? Now that everything's fixed, no one will miss me and to be honest, I really need to get out of here."

"Oh, um..." Phil wasn't sure that being alone with her best friend was a good idea. She had just seen the devastating power of her reverse wish in action not ten minutes before. What she really *needed* was to go home and start yanking on her earlobe to get her fairy godmother's attention again.

"Hey, you promised me if I made good on the server that I'd get to see you in a polka-dot bikini, or something equally embarrassing," Josh protested. "You chickening out on me, Swann?" He started making clucking noises on the other end of the phone that made her laugh.

"No, I'm not chickening out." Suddenly Phil decided she didn't care. She'd had a horrible morning and she deserved some time off with her friend. There would be time to contact the fairy godmother later. *The wish was working when I saw him in the hall this morning,* she reminded herself. *And the worst thing he said to me was that I was beautiful and he liked holding me in his arms. So how bad can it be?*

"So you'll go?" Josh sounded hopeful. "'Cause I don't mind telling you, I *really* want to get out of here for today."

"Not only will I go," Phil promised recklessly. "I'll try on the teeny-weeniest, polka-dotted-est bikini we can find. How's that?"

Josh took a deep breath on the other end of the phone. "That's a deal. Look, I just have a few more things to finish up here and then I can go. You want to wait or you want to meet me at the mall?"

"Meet you in the food court at Citrus Park," Phil said without hesitation. No way was she hanging around BB&D for a second longer. "I'll get us both a smoothie. No lunch until after shopping though. You can't try on bathing suits on a full stomach."

"I bow to your superior wisdom, oh goddess of fashion," Josh said dryly. "Make mine a peanut butter banana one. I have a feeling I'm going to need my strength."

"Great. See you there." Phil hung up the phone and made her escape.

Citrus Park was a nice, middle of the road mall that was swanky enough to have a Saks but still down to earth enough to have a huge Old Navy outlet in it as well. It was only five minutes from BB&D and Phil had spent many a lunch hour there window shopping with her best friend. Josh was the perfect shopping companion because he didn't start whining about going home to watch the game five minutes after they walked into the mall. He also didn't mind giving his opinion on something she wanted to buy instead of just saying, "I don't know—they all look the same! Are you almost done?" which was the answer she most often got from Christian.

The only time Josh had ever refused her was when Phil had tried to get him to have a pedicure with her. "No, Swann," he'd told her firmly. "I'm your *best* friend but not your *girl* friend. I'm not going to get my toenails painted Tahitian pink so we can go shoe shopping together and squeal over adorable sandals. A man has to know when to draw a line in the sand and my line is right here, in front of the Pretty Pedi Day Spa." Phil had laughed so hard smoothie almost came out of her nose, and relented on the pedicure.

At the entrance of the food court a man was handing out bite-sized samples of éclair. Phil took one happily and tossed it in the nearest trash can. She felt light and happy and free, despite the fact that her birthday wish still wasn't right. She'd gotten through the dreaded HR review without a scratch, *and* she'd just gotten rid of her daily éclair with no problem at all. Yes, life was good.

She had just finished ordering one peanut butter banana smoothie and one raspberry swirl, her favorite, when she felt a tap on her shoulder and turned to see her best friend grinning at her.

"Josh! That was fast." She smiled. "Here, just let me..." She reached in her purse for some money but he put up a hand.

"I've got it." He pulled some bills out of his wallet and handed them to the pimply-faced college student across the counter. "You don't have to do that," Phil protested. "I wanted it to be my treat."

"Don't worry about it." A smiled tugged at the corners of his full mouth. "And if you want to treat me, just keep your promise and try on the teeniest bikini you can find. I'm *really* looking forward to seeing you with next to no clothes on. I mean, uh...wow, that wasn't very cool." His ears went pink with embarrassment. "Sorry, Phil—open mouth, insert foot, I guess. I really didn't mean to..." He looked puzzled and Phil realized he was probably trying to figure out why he'd said something so inappropriate out loud. It was her wish at work again but she was determined not to let it ruin the rest of her day.

"No big. Actually, *I'm* looking forward to seeing *you* in your skivvies too," she said lightly, defusing the situation. "But if I would've known you were going to be so close behind me I wouldn't waited for you in the BB&D parking lot."

"Couldn't get out of that place quick enough." He made a shrugging motion with his broad shoulders, as though throwing off some invisible weight. "Yeesh—I thought Dickhead Senior was gonna blow a blood vessel. If I didn't pop one first, that was."

"Well, it's over now." Phil took a sip of her smoothie and smiled at him. "And you don't have to see him again until...well, until tomorrow. But at least you'll get to see him in a swimsuit. I know that's going to improve your morale."

"You know it." Josh took a sip of his own smoothie and threw an arm around her shoulder companionably. "Speaking of which, oh fashion guru, where are we going to start looking for the perfect suit?"

Phil put her arm around his waist and smiled up at him. "Maybe RipTide. Last time Cass and I were here they had plenty of nice looking suits that didn't cost an arm and a leg."

"RipTide it is. Lead the way." They ambled away from the food court at a leisurely pace, sipping their smoothies. This time of the day there were almost no customers at the mall. Citrus Park had an open design with skylights overhead so that they walked through patches of slanting sunlight in comfortable silence with the ubiquitous mall Muzak playing in the background.

Phil was glad that the wish to speak her mind was no longer in effect because she would have had to tell her friend how nice it felt to be close to him, to feel his arm around her shoulders and smell his warm, spicy scent. In fact, it surprised her a little how much she liked being close to Josh when she had never thought about it much before her birthday. Thoughts of Christian and whether or not they were still engaged threatened to intrude, but she resolutely put them out of her mind and decided to enjoy herself.

"Well, here we are," Josh said, breaking the silence and interrupting Phil's guilty thoughts.

"Uh-huh." She threw her mostly empty cup in the trash and Josh did the same. "Well, let's see what we can find."

RipTide was a long, narrow shop decorated with surfboards, hula skirts, and Hawaiian shirts. There was a counter near the front of the shop where a lone attendant, a teenage girl with a bored expression and a pair of earbuds plugged into her heavily pierced ears, stood. The iPod Nano she had on was turned up so loud that Phil could actually hear the Shins playing from three feet away.

"Hi," she said, nodding at the girl, who was currently bent forward drawing something in a notebook. The girl kept drawing.

"I don't think she can hear you," Josh said. "Hi!" he shouted.

"Huh?" The girl looked in surprise. "Oh, hi, welcome to RipTide," she greeted them mechanically. "Men's suits on the left, women's on the right and dressing rooms in the far back. All the rooms are unlocked so you can help yourselves. If you need anything you'll have to come up here and ask me. I'm the only one here so I can't leave the front." She went back to her drawing.

"Guess we're on our own," Josh said, wandering away from the counter, toward the women's section of the store. "Let's look for those bikinis."

"Uh-uh." Phil grabbed his hand and steered him back to the men's section. "Let's get you a suit first. It'll probably take a lot less time because I'm really picky and you..."

"And I am *not*," Josh finished for her. "Okay then, do your worst. Just don't put me in anything with lime green stripes. Those clash with my pretty pink nipples."

Phil laughed and slapped him lightly on the arm. "Come on, you. I think I see something that's about your size."

After ten minutes, they wound up in the dressing room with four or five pairs of trunks that were Josh's size, none of them with lime green stripes. Phil sent him into one of the stalls with instructions to come out so he could see himself in the three-way mirror at the end of the row. "Try on the black ones first," she told him. "And be sure to take off your socks and shoes while you try them on. You can never tell what a bathing suit is going to look like when you have socks and shoes on with it."

"Yes, Mom." Josh grinned and disappeared. In less than two minutes he was back out, sans socks and shoes and without his shirt, too. "What do you think?" He looked down critically. "It may be a little loose in the waist. I don't want them to fall off the minute I dive under a wave."

What did she think? Phil looked her best friend up and down. Josh looked...there was no other word for it—*hot*. She always saw him in his office clothes, which usually consisted of a button down oxford shirt and dress pants, and even at the last beach day he'd been wearing a T-shirt with his trunks. She'd caught a glimpse of his chest when he opened his shirt the day before but it hadn't quite prepared her for what she was seeing now.

Scanning his broad shoulders and chest, which were hard with muscle, and looking at his ripped abdomen, Phil felt her mouth go dry. The black swim trunks hung gracefully around his narrow hips and flat stomach and ended just above his knees and muscular calves. There was a little patch of curly brown hair just between the flat copper disks of his nipples and his well developed biceps bunched as he twisted this way and that, looking in the three way mirror.

He looks amazing. She caught a glimpse of herself in the mirror behind him and realized that her mouth was open and she had a hungry expression on her face, like a dog that sees a bone it wants to chew. She closed her mouth abruptly.

"Well?" Josh looked at her and Phil realized that she had been standing there staring at him for the last thirty seconds without saying a word.

"I, uh...I like it," she managed. "I like it a *lot*." She hoped Josh didn't know that she was talking about more than the swim suit.

"Yeah, but do you think they'll fall off?" he asked, still frowning. "I mean, I really doubt we're going to a nude beach tomorrow so that would be a bad scene."

Phil didn't think so but she didn't want to make him uncomfortable by ogling his body too openly. "They might." She came forward casually and put her hand on his waist, as though she was just testing to see how loose the fabric was. Without thinking about it, she let her fingers slide upwards and around to the front until she could feel his rock hard abdominals bunching beneath her fingertips. A little trail of light brown hair led from his belly button down into the black trunks. His skin was like warm satin under her palm and she felt a shiver run through him at her touch.

"Phil?" He raised an eyebrow at her. "That..." He took a deep breath. "That feels really good. The way you're touching me, I mean."

"I, uh..." Phil snatched her hand away, embarrassed. "I guess I can get you the next size down," she babbled, trying to pretend she hadn't just been stroking her best friend's rock hard stomach. What was wrong with her lately, anyway? Just because they had relaxed their unwritten rules didn't mean she should start acting on any impulse that came along. "But, uh, this suit looks really good on you. If the next size down fits, I don't think you should bother with the others."

"Is that all?" He looked at her intently and took her hand, which was still tingling from the warm touch of his skin. "Is that all you want to say to me, Phil?"

"I..." Phil looked up at him, her heart thumping against her ribs. *There's a lot between us that's unsaid,* Josh's words from the day before rang in her ears. But should she start saying it now? *No,* Phil told herself, trying to be firm. *No, I can't do this right now. I can't go there with Josh when I have unfinished business with someone else. It wouldn't be fair to him or Christian.*

"Phil?" Josh pulled her closer so that her breasts were almost brushing against the hard planes of his chest.

"No," Phil finally managed to get out. "I mean...that's...that's all. All I wanted to say, I mean."

"Okay." Josh sighed and released her. "So let's go get the other size and pick out a few suits for you."

Phil felt a quiver of apprehension in her belly but she tried not to show it. "Okay, but just so you know, I've never thought of myself as much of a bikini model." She tried to laugh, to ease the tension that had grown almost tangible between them. How was she going to get through this?

"Well, you are now." Josh grabbed her hand, leaving his clothes in the dressing room, and pulled her back out into the store.

Chapter Twenty-Four

"No...no..." Phil shook her head in disgust. "I don't like any of these on the rack—are you having any luck?"

"Some." Josh was standing in the far corner looking at something on the ground. "Come look at these."

Phil went over to see what was so fascinating and was delighted to see a whole box full of unpacked merchandize sitting in the corner of the store. No doubt Miss iPod was supposed to be stocking them but the girl was still hunched over the counter at the front of the store. Phil recognized the look on her face—it was the same look Cass got when she was painting or sculpting in her studio. Nothing short of an earthquake would get the girl's attention at this point.

"Hey, some of these are pretty good," she murmured as she dug through the box looking for her size. They came back to the dressing room with a wide assortment, some of them modest and some, well, not so modest, Phil thought, eyeing the bright red bikini Josh was holding. It appeared to consist of three quarter-sized triangles made of open-weave mesh and a bewildering array of strings.

"I hope you're going to try that one on yourself," she said, nodding at the tiny red suit. "Because you're not getting me into it."

Josh laughed. "See, you read my mind. This one is just for me and I'm not sharing." He hung the suit along with several others he'd picked out for her on the hook inside the dressing room. "Try on what you want, Phil," he said, his eyes dancing. "Some of these are serious choices but some of them are just double-dog-dare you suits."

194

Phil raised an eyebrow. "Excuse me? Double-dog-dare you?"

Josh laughed. "Yup. I double-dog-dare you. You should only try them on if you're feeling brave."

Phil laughed at him. "I'm afraid you're going to be disappointed, Josh. I'm a coward when it comes to that kind of thing."

He shrugged his broad, bare shoulders and she couldn't help admiring the play of muscles over his chest and abdomen. His skin was a warm, even natural tan that made her want to touch him again. Sternly, she repressed the impulse. "Suit yourself," he said. "Ha—get it? *Suit* yourself?"

"You're impossible. I'm going to try some of these on. Remember—no peeking!"

Josh held up two fingers in a salute. "Scout's honor, ma'am. I'll wait right here to offer my opinion. Try the polka dotted one first."

Phil shut the dressing stall door and dug through the pile of hangers until she found the one he was talking about. It was a fairly modest, Brazilian cut bikini that was sky blue with tiny white polka dots all over it. Feeling self-conscious, she stripped off her work clothes and pulled on the suit.

The top fit perfectly, which made her wonder if Josh somehow knew her cup size or if he had just made a lucky guess. When she had the bottoms on, Phil looked at herself anxiously in the mirror inside the room. She'd never loved her body, but she never hated it either. Her personal opinion was that she was a little too big in the bust and hips and her stomach wasn't as flat as she would have liked, but what woman's was? She was very glad that Cass's pre-birthday gift to her had been a leg and bikini wax so that she was smooth and very bare in the sky blue suit. Actually, it was kind of sexy, she decided. Josh had good taste.

"All right, try not to laugh." She came out of the dressing room, self-consciously adjusting the bra cups to make sure everything was covered. What Josh had said earlier was true— he had almost never seen her in anything but office clothes and she wasn't sure what he would think.

The minute she stepped out of the dressing room, Josh took in a breath. Then he let out a long, low wolf whistle.

"Damn, Phil—you look gorgeous. I knew that suit was going to work on you. It's the exact color of your eyes when it's sunny outside and there aren't any clouds."

Phil stopped in her tracks. He was doing it again—noticing things he shouldn't have been able to notice. Magical things that hid themselves from non-fairy eyes. Most people, if asked to describe her eyes, would have said they were a blue-gray color. No one without fairy or fae blood in their veins should have been able to see that they were constantly shifting depending on the exact shade of the sky outside.

"How..." She frowned at him. "What do you mean about my eyes?"

"What I said." Josh nodded at the suit. "It's sky blue—like your eyes when it's sunny and there aren't any clouds. But if a storm comes up, they get kind of blue gray. And when the sun sets, they're a deep, deep blue that's almost black. Am I right?"

"Yes." Phil wrapped her arms around her waist and leaned back against the door of the stall weakly. "But how did you know that? You're not...nobody's supposed to notice that about my eyes. Everybody just kind of thinks they're a bluish-gray. So how did you notice?"

"I don't know." Josh shrugged, his broad shoulders rolling again. "I just did. I noticed things about you from the minute I saw you crying in the storage closet because Dickhead Junior was being a prick. There's something different about you, Phil— something special. I can't put my finger on it but I don't have to. It's just you."

"Oh," Phil said faintly. She wondered again if her best friend had fairy blood. But no—if he had a single drop she would have felt it when she touched him. Was it possible for a non-fairy to notice things her fairy godmother's magic should have hidden from his eyes just because he was close to her? Just because he, well, *liked* her? It didn't seem right because if that was the case, wouldn't Christian have noticed and mentioned her changeable eyes, her sparkly hair, her naturally rose red lips at some point in the five years they'd been together?

"Hey." She looked up to see Josh looking at her with concern. "Did I say something wrong?" he asked softly. "I didn't mean to hurt your feelings. I just meant that the suit looks really nice on you. And that, well, I think you have beautiful eyes, no matter what color they are."

"Thanks, Josh." She squeezed his arm, noticing the rock hard muscle again in passing. Why had she never noticed those arms before? Probably because he was always wearing long sleeved shirts to work. "That's really sweet of you. But maybe I should try on another suit."

"Uh-huh. Go ahead." He shot her a mocking smile. "Maybe it's time for a double-dog-dare you suit."

Phil laughed. "In your dreams, mister."

"You are," Josh said unexpectedly, his eyes growing dark and serious again. "In my dreams, I mean." He took a step towards her and reached out to cup her cheek. "That dream you had about me? That was nothing, Phil. I dream about you like that all the time. I dream of touching you...holding you...kissing you."

"Oh." Phil felt her cheeks grow hot as his gentle touch sent a shiver through her body. She was very aware of how very close they were standing and how few clothes they had on. She wanted to ask Josh the details of his dream but she was afraid to. Afraid that she would want to hear more—or do more. So instead she said, "I'll, uh...I better try on another suit," and retreated into the dressing stall.

Once inside she leaned against the wall with a hand to her chest. She could feel her heart drumming under her fingers. *Have to get control of myself,* she thought. *He's only saying those things because he can't help it—it's just my stupid wish working on him again.* Blindly she reached for the next suit on the rack and started pulling it on.

"Hey, Phil?" Josh's deep voice was muffled. "You okay in there? I, uh, don't know why I said that about the dream thing. I hope I didn't offend you."

"No, no, I'm fine," Phil called, hurrying to adjust the straps of the new suit. They were clear plastic and so sheer the peach slices they held in place over her breasts and sex seemed almost to float on her creamy skin. With a start, Phil realized this was one of Josh's "double-dog-dare" suits.

"You've decided to stay in there all night, haven't you?" Josh sounded mournful now and she got the idea he was only half joking. He really thought that he'd pissed her off by saying too much.

"No, honestly, I'm not. And the idea of spending the night in the RipTide dressing room doesn't do anything for me." Phil gave herself a final glance in the long rectangular mirror and took a deep breath. The slices of sheer peach material just covered her nipples, leaving the outer and inner curves of her breasts exposed. And as for the bottom, if she hadn't just had a bikini wax...well, she was glad she'd had one.

"I, uh, think I grabbed one of your dare suits by mistake," she said, stepping out of the stall, feeling very exposed. She didn't like to call attention to herself, which was one reason she wore her hair up all the time. And as for wearing anything revealing—well, she didn't. Phil didn't even think she had any underwear this tiny. "Well," she asked nervously. "What do you think?"

"What do I think? *Damn*, Phil." Josh was staring at her with an unmistakable heat in his eyes. "That's just...God, you're gorgeous. And that suit is amazing. I've always wondered what your breasts looked like and this is...wait." One corner of his mouth went down. "Did I just say that out loud?"

"Uh-huh." Phil resisted the urge to cover her breasts with her arms. It wasn't that she didn't like the feeling of Josh staring at her, it was that she liked it *too* much. She couldn't remember the last time Christian had looked at her that way.

"God, Phil, I'm so sorry." Josh took a step back and put a hand to his head, as though he was checking himself for fever. "I keep saying the most outrageous things today and I don't know why."

"I do." Phil sighed, deciding she'd better come clean. "Remember that thing I had where everything I thought came right out my mouth?"

"Yeah, but what does that have to do with me wanting to cup your breasts and see how that silky material feels over your hard nipples?" Josh winced and a muscle in his jaw clenched. "Damn it! There I go *again*."

"Um." Phil could feel herself blushing all over and yet, it still felt good to know that Josh wanted to touch her. She put a hand on his arm. "It's the same thing I had yesterday only now it's reversed. So you can't help saying what you think when you're around me. And knowing that, I promise not to get offended no matter what you say, okay?"

"But...but how can that be?" Josh pinched the bridge of his nose between his finger and thumb and frowned, his brown eyes troubled. "I mean, how can a condition you had yesterday be affecting me today?"

Phil sighed. "I wish I could explain but I can't, Josh," she said. "It's...it has to do with my family again. It's tied in with the reason my eyes change colors and the way weird things happen around me. I'm really sorry. If you want to call it a day and go home I completely understand. I wouldn't blame you for wanting to get away from me under the circumstances."

"Get away from you? Are you kidding?" Josh put his hands on her shoulders and pulled her closer so that he was looking down into her face. "Phil," he said huskily. "I don't care what weird things happen around you, nothing could make me want to put distance between us. In fact, all I can think of right now is kissing you, touching you, I..." He stopped and took a step back helplessly.

"Josh, it's...it's okay," Phil tried to reassure him. Tension twisted like a wire in her stomach and her heart was pounding so loudly she was sure he could hear it. *What if he really tries to kiss me?* Her hands itched to reach up and cup his square jaw, to feel the bristly prickle of his five o'clock shadow against her palms and pull him down to her—but she knew she shouldn't. "Look," she said, trying to get back to normal. "Let me just try on a few more suits and you tell me what you think. And I promise, I *promise* that I won't be offended no matter what you say. Because I know how it feels not to be able to help saying what you think—okay?"

Josh gave a shaky laugh. "Okay, it's just...I don't want to come off like Dickhead Junior trying to cop a feel. I've been saying some pretty suggestive things lately and I just...I mean, it's not like me."

Phil felt herself melting inside. "Of course it's not, Josh. That's one reason I...I care about you so much. One reason I love being around you. Because you always go out of your way to make me feel comfortable. And you don't have to worry—I don't feel offended or harassed when you tell me what you think. In fact I feel kind of...flattered." She felt her cheeks burning but she didn't look away from him.

"Well…if you're sure." Josh was still looking at her uncertainly.

"Of course I'm sure." Impulsively, she reached up and gave him a hug. Josh reacted at once, putting his arms around her and pulling her close until her breasts were pressed against the broad planes of his bare chest. Phil stiffened at first, then relaxed and let herself melt against him. It felt so good, so *right* to be in his arms and the little peach bikini she had on almost made her feel like she was hugging him nude. It was a delicious, naughty feeling that made her heart race even faster.

"God, you feel good in my arms," Josh murmured, stroking her nearly bare back with his big, warm hands. "And your skin feels so soft and smooth." His breath was hot against the side of her neck and suddenly Phil felt his mouth, warm and wet against the tender skin of her throat. Josh was planting gentle, open-mouthed kisses along her sensitive flesh, sending a shiver of desire straight to her throbbing sex.

"Josh, I…" She pushed back from him, almost frightened by how hot his kisses were making her. *I can't…I shouldn't…*she thought wildly. Her breath was coming short and it was hard to remember why she shouldn't keep going. But if she did this, she would be slamming the door on Christian—she couldn't cheat on him and pretend it didn't happen, and she knew he would never forgive her. Was she ready to move on? Was she ready to let go of the picture she'd had of her life for so long— the man she was sure she'd grow old with? That brought things back in focus. She pushed on Josh's chest again.

"Sorry, I'm sorry." He let her go and took a step backwards, raking his hand through his hair. "You're just so gorgeous, Phil and I wanted to feel you pressed against me in that hot little suit. God, the feel of your soft, ripe breasts and your nipples rubbing against my chest is so…" He scowled, the muscle in his jaw jumping. "Damn, this thinking out loud thing is really inconvenient."

Phil laughed shakily. "Tell me about it. Look I'm just going to…I'll try on one more suit, okay?"

"Uh-huh. But take your hair down too. I love to see it loose around your shoulders and…" Josh clamped his mouth shut, putting his hand over his eyes.

"Okay." Phil slipped back into the dressing stall once more

and tried to control her breathing. The barriers were coming down faster than she could build them up again. And Josh looked so damn good in those black swim trunks. *This is Josh,* she reminded herself. *Not some stud muffin male stripper.* But that only made her wonder what he would look like *without* the trunks. She couldn't take her mind off the way the big muscles in his abdomen and chest bunched under his tan skin when he moved, the way his biceps flexed, the way his arms felt like warm, flexible steel when he wrapped them around her. It seemed like all she could smell was his spicy, masculine scent, all she could see was the look of need in his dark eyes, all she could feel were his big, knowing hands all over her body...

Have to stop thinking like this! She had to take control of the situation *now*. And yet...and yet...it felt so nice, so *wonderful* to be admired and told she was beautiful.

Phil closed her eyes and let herself remember the last time she'd tried to get Christian interested in more than just a quickie, which was all she'd been after the night before her birthday after she drank too much champagne. That was because she knew it was useless to try for anything more. It wasn't that she and her fiancé didn't have a good sex life—well, they *used* to have a good sex life, anyway. But since he'd started his new job, it had fallen off considerably. Phil had decided to try and revive it by seducing him.

She'd bought herself a little white lace negligee from Frederick's of Hollywood and draped herself over the couch so that she would be the first thing he saw when he came home. She'd waited for over an hour, jumping every time she heard something outside the door, her heart pounding. It was by far the most daring thing she'd ever done and she was sure it would rekindle the spark that had been missing from their relationship lately.

But after all that anticipation, the reality had been a big disappointment. Christian had come in the door with an armful of paperwork and hadn't even glanced in her direction until Phil called his name. And then he'd given her a tired smile and said, "Not tonight, huh, babe? I mean, I'd love to but I have a big case to prepare for and not enough time to get ready. You understand, don't you?"

Yes, Phil had understood. She had understood that for whatever reason, her fiancé had lost interest in their love life.

She hadn't had that warm, tingly feeling of knowing that a man found her attractive in months—or was it longer? So was it really so surprising that having Josh look at her and tell her he liked what he saw excited her? Phil thought not. In fact, she wanted more. Craved it.

You shouldn't be doing this, Phil! She pushed the disapproving little voice out of her head and instead of grabbing one of the more modest swim suits, she took a deep breath and reached for the tiny, mesh, fire engine red bikini and put it on, trying not to think about what she was doing. She was only trying on a bikini, so what was the big deal—right?

When the suit was tied in place, she stared at herself in the mirror for a moment, biting her lower lip and trying to get the nerve to walk out of the stall. The mesh was an open weave design which clearly showed her nipples and the slit of her sex. She felt like a sex kitten in this outfit—only one thing was missing.

Phil reached up and unclipped the tight bun of hair at the back of her neck, letting the long mass fall down around her shoulders. It shimmered even in the dim light of the dressing room and when she looked in the mirror again, she saw an entirely different woman. A curvy woman with sky blue eyes and lustrous silky hair like pale gold stared back at her. The woman had a naughty little smile tugging at the corners of her mouth and she was wearing a see-through barely there bikini that showed off all her assets. God—could she really go out dressed like this? What if someone else happened to come in the dressing room?

"Phil? You okay in there?"

"Uh, yeah. I'm fine." Still biting her lip, Phil opened the door and looked out. "I, uh, put on the ultimate double-dog-dare suit but I don't want to come out of the stall in it. You come in and tell me what you think—okay?"

"Sure." Josh crowded into the dressing stall with her, even though it was barely large enough for two people, especially if one of them was as large as him. When they were both inside with the door closed, he seemed to fill the tiny space.

"Well?" Phil held her breath while he looked at her, his eyes widening. She could feel her nipples getting hard from being so exposed in the open-weave mesh and she wondered if Josh noticed. "What do you think?" she asked at last.

"I think...I think..." He frowned.

"It's okay, Josh." She touched him lightly on the shoulder and was surprised to feel how tense his body was. "You can say it, I won't be offended."

"God." He shook his head. "I'm sorry, I can't help it. I think I want to pull off that skimpy little top and suck your sweet pink nipples until you scream."

"Oh!" Phil bit her bottom lip again, feeling a warm, sexual flush rising from between her breasts to heat her throat and cheeks. "I...do you really? What else do you want to do?" They weren't doing anything, she told herself. Just like the other day when she was telling him her X-rated dream, they were only *talking.* Surely there was no harm in that. She hadn't passed the point of no return.

Josh gave her a level stare, his brown eyes burning with need. "Do you really want to know? Do you want to know what I'd like to do to you if I could, Phil?" he growled. She understood what he was really saying—that she shouldn't push him or the invisible boundaries they had put between them might crumble. But Phil wanted to push. Wanted to hear what he had to say— to feel his hungry gaze devour her like a flame.

She nodded greedily, her mouth too dry to speak. Here was a side of Josh she had never seen before their lunch together in the car. He was always so sweet and funny that she sometimes forgot he was a guy. Now he seemed so big, so *male* looming over her in the tiny dressing cubicle.

"Phil," he murmured in a low, intense voice. "I want to push you up against the wall and pull down those tiny little bikini bottoms and touch your hot, wet pussy, just like I did in your dream. Ever since you told me about that I haven't been able to stop thinking about it." The muscle in his jaw jumped under the dark stubble on his cheeks as he leaned closer, blocking her in.

"Oh, I..." Phil felt like she was drowning. "What...what else?"

Josh took a deep breath, his muscular chest expanding, and she knew he was no longer even trying to fight the urge to speak his mind. "I want to get on my knees in front of you and spread open your thighs and go down on you, Phil. I want to taste your sweet juices and put my tongue inside you. I want to lick your clit until you come all over my face. Just like in your dream."

"It...it was only a dream," she almost whispered, hearing her heart thud in her ears.

"I know." Josh stepped closer to her and reached out to brush his fingers over her hot cheek. "But I want to make it a reality."

"We...we shouldn't," Phil whispered, but she didn't know when she'd been so hot. She could feel the slippery wetness between her thighs and her nipples felt hard enough to cut glass.

"I know," Josh murmured. "I know we can't, but I want to. I want *you*."

"I...I want you, too." Phil couldn't believe she was saying it, couldn't believe she was finally admitting it. But once the words were out, she found she had no desire to call them back.

"You're driving me crazy." Josh's deep voice was ragged.

"Show me," Phil whispered, daring to reach up and touch his bristly cheek with her palm. "Show me what you mean—how you want to touch me."

"I'll show you." Josh pulled her around so that they were facing the mirror and he was standing behind her. For a moment, Phil admired the picture they made, the wide-eyed blond woman and the tall man with dark piercing eyes looming over her possessively. With a start, she realized that his shoulders were almost twice as broad as hers. How had she managed to be around him for so many years without letting herself notice how attractive he was? How had she maintained the barriers between them for so long?

Then Josh drove every other thought out of her head by reaching around to cup her breasts in his large hands.

"Like this," he murmured in her ear as Phil gasped at the contact. She could feel the sensitive tips of her nipples rubbing against the palms of his hands through the open weave of her top and she knew Josh could too. She was still watching in the mirror as the large man with intense brown eyes started untying the tiny red mesh bikini strings from around her neck.

Phil bit back a moan as he pulled it down, baring her breasts completely as they both watched in the mirror. Never had she dreamed of doing anything like this in a public place, and never had she dreamed of doing it with Josh. And yet, the wet heat between her thighs attested to the fact that it was the single most erotic experience of her life. And she was having it right here and now in the dressing room of RipTide with her best friend.

"More?" Josh growled in her ear as he rolled her tight nipples between his finger tips. "Do you want me to show you how I want to suck them, Phil?"

Breathlessly she nodded and he moved back at once, sitting on the triangular bench in the corner of the dressing cubicle and pulling her with him. Phil gasped as his hands encircled her waist and positioned her between his spread thighs. He held her eyes for a long intense moment before dipping his head to take her right nipple into his mouth, sucking hard at first, then lapping at the sensitive bud until she thought she might scream.

I shouldn't be doing this! Phil moaned inside her head, and yet she couldn't make herself stop. Josh was working on her other nipple now, nipping gently with his teeth and sending showers of sparks from her sensitive tips to the hot, swollen flesh of her sex. Phil couldn't believe she was standing in a dressing room letting her best friend suck her nipples but she couldn't ever remember feeling so incredibly aroused—so ready for more.

At last Josh looked up, his brown eyes dilated with need. "Your skin tastes exactly like I'd always imagined it would," he told her in a hoarse voice. "Salty and a little sweet and completely delicious. God, Phil, I want to touch you so badly I can't stand it."

Phil closed her eyes. This was pretty intense but it wasn't something they couldn't come back from. But if she gave Josh permission to touch her, to taste her...she didn't know if she would ever be able to look him in the eye again. And yet she wanted what she'd had in her dream, the dream that Josh was making a reality.

"I...I want you to show me more," she said softly. "I...I don't want to stop."

"I don't either." He stood again and pulled her back into their former position with him behind her and both of them facing the mirror. "You want me to show you?" His deep voice was a rumble she could feel through her entire body as his chest pressed against her back.

Phil looked at the topless girl in the mirror, the girl whose nipples were red and hard from being sucked and licked. She nodded.

"I'll show you, then." Josh murmured in her ear, his breath hot against her neck.

Phil expected him to pull down the bottom of her suit and bare her completely. But instead, he reached around her with his left hand, his fingers splayed possessively over the curve of her hip and cupped her breasts with his right.

"Watch while I touch you, Phil," he breathed in her ear. "I want you to watch while I spread you open and stroke your hot little pussy."

Phil moaned out loud as she watched his large hand slip down into the tiny red bikini panties to cup her slippery mound. She had never dreamed that funny, sweet Josh could be so kinky! Making her watch while he touched her was turning her on like nothing ever had before.

"Is this all right? Do you like this?" Josh murmured in her ear. His hand felt warm and gentle as he cupped her and she knew that he didn't want to scare her.

"You know I like it," she whispered, laying her head back against his shoulder. "I...I can't help but like it. It feels so *good*."

"It's about to feel even better." He gave her a hot, gentle kiss on the side of her neck and pulled her closer. "I want you to untie the bikini strings and spread your legs for me, Phil. Then I want you to watch while I touch you, while I put my fingers inside you. *Deep* inside you."

Phil felt her breath catch in her throat but she felt helpless to disobey his orders. With trembling fingers, she reached down and untied the tiny red strings, letting the red mesh bikini bottoms fall to the floor of the dressing cubicle.

"That's good," Josh encouraged her softly. "Now spread your legs for me so you can watch me touch you. Open yourself up and don't be afraid."

"I...all right." Phil parted her legs, mesmerized by the sight of the naked girl in the mirror doing the same thing. Josh's big hand still cupped her but as she watched, he spread his fingers, opening her so that the slippery pink center of her sex was exposed.

"God, you're beautiful," he murmured, stroking one long finger slowly up and down the tight bundle of nerves at her center. Phil bit her lip at the intensely pleasurable sensation the gentle motion caused.

"I...I am?" she managed to gasp, her eyes still riveted to the performance going on in the mirror.

"You're perfect," Josh assured her. "I've always thought so. Look at how hot you are, Phil, with your soft little pussy all spread open and your sweet little clit so sensitive and swollen." He brushed his fingertips lightly along the tiny pink bud making her moan and press back against him. "You have no idea how often I've thought about doing this," he whispered. "How often I wanted to take you in my arms and touch you everywhere. To pleasure you, make love to you, make you *mine*. I've wanted you for years, Phil."

"I..." Phil gasped again as his fingers slipped over her swollen folds. "I think I always knew that. But I just...couldn't let myself see it."

"Well you can see it now because I'm showing you—telling you." Josh kissed the side of her neck again. "God, you feel good in my arms. I want to touch you everywhere." His deep voice dropped to a lower octave and he murmured in her ear, "Are you ready to feel my fingers inside you? Ready to spread yourself open and let me press deep inside your hot little pussy?"

Phil nodded, almost panting with need. She was so used to being with a man who couldn't find her clitoris with a flashlight and a map that it was amazing to see that her best friend was apparently an expert in female anatomy. To be honest, she was pretty sure Christian had stopped trying long ago. But now Josh was stroking her in just the right way, building the pleasure between her legs until she felt like she was going to explode.

"Please," she whispered, spreading her legs even farther. "Please, I need..."

"I know what you need. Relax, Phil, and I'll give it to you." He kissed the side of her neck again, nipping and sucking and licking possessively, sending helpless shivers of need down her spine. "I want to make you feel good," he whispered, just as he had in her dream.

Phil moaned as she watched two of his long, strong fingers slide into her, filling her in a way that made her bite her lip to keep from crying out. Her eyes flickered up to Josh's, meeting his gaze in the mirror and she saw the same something she'd seen the day before in his car. That look in his eyes that said he wanted her in every possible way.

"Does that feel good?" Josh whispered as he slid his fingers in and out of her wet sex. "Is that what you need, Phil?"

"Oh, God...Oh, Josh...I...Oh!" Phil squeezed her eyes shut, unable to watch any more. It was too much. She was so hot, so close. If he would touch her just a little bit more she knew she was about to go off like a rocket on the fourth of July...

Suddenly he stopped and she felt him pulling away from her. With a little cry, Phil opened her eyes and turned her head to look at him. Was he sorry they had gone this far? Somewhere in the back of her brain, Phil was pretty sure she was going to be very sorry at some point, but she still didn't want to stop. She wanted to feel Josh's hands on her, she wanted him to make her come.

"Please, Josh," she whispered, looking up into his eyes. "Please, I was so...so close. I just..."

"I want to taste you." His voice was low and intense and his eyes were dark with need.

"Wh...what?" Phil stuttered, uncertain of what she'd heard. Had he really just said...

"I want to taste you, Phil. Right here, right now, I want to get down on my knees in front of you, spread you open and eat your pussy until you come all over my face."

Once more, Phil felt like she was drowning, like she couldn't get enough air. The hot, erotic words spoken in his quiet, intense voice were almost enough to make her come right there. But Josh was still looking at her, as though for permission. Somewhere in the back of her head Phil heard a little voice reminding her that she was engaged and that Josh was her best friend. How could their friendship ever be the same if she let him do this to her? If she let him kiss and lick and taste her wet sex until he made her come?

Yes, it was a bad idea all the way around. Phil opened her

mouth to say, "no" and heard, "Yes, oh, God, yes," come out instead. How had that happened? She was sure she'd meant to say no and yet she still didn't want to stop.

In a flash, Josh was kneeling in front of her on the thin carpet of the dressing room floor and she could feel his hot breath against her inner thighs. "Relax," he murmured, stroking her sides gently and playing a soft kiss on her right hipbone. "I want you to just relax and let me in, Phil. Can you do that?"

Mutely, Phil nodded. She couldn't believe she was in this position. She'd been best friends with Josh for years but never had she imagined herself naked in a public dressing room about to let him go down on her. And yet...there was something right about it somehow, something so white hot and intensely sexual that it was like her body was telling her what to do, that this was right. As Josh stroked her thighs gently with his large, warm hands, she allowed her legs to part and watched breathlessly as he leaned forward to place a soft, tender kiss at the apex of her sex.

"That's right, Phil, open up. Let me taste you," Josh murmured softly. He bent forward again and again she felt his mouth against her. This time he was kissing her more deeply— kissing her sex the same way he might kiss her mouth, gently, tenderly, and with an intense passion that took her breath away. She moaned as his tongue slipped over her wet folds, stroking along the sensitive side of her clit. "God, Phil." He looked up after a long moment and licked his lips. "You taste so damn good," he murmured, cupping her hip in his palm. "So absolutely delicious. I could eat you all day and all night long."

Phil caught her breath. "Please, Josh..." she murmured, reaching out to run a hand through his hair. "Please, I need..."

"I know what you need," he told her again. "And I want to give it to you. I want to make you come." He leaned forward again and Phil moaned with breathless pleasure as he spread her gently with his fingers and licked a warm, wet trail from the bottom of her sex to the top of her slit. God, she had never had anyone do this with such enthusiasm, with such obvious pleasure. Christian had tried going down on her once or twice when they first got together and she remembered vividly how much he'd disliked it, barely daring to plant a few, hesitant kisses over the outside of her sex before giving up. Now Josh was spreading her open and licking her like a little kid with his favorite flavor of ice cream. He was more than tasting her—he was devouring her from the inside out. There was no question that he derived pleasure from tasting her and pleasuring her. No doubt that he was enjoying pushing her higher and higher, trying to make her come.

Phil gasped as he pressed her back against the wooden wall of the stall. She had to steady herself by grabbing his broad shoulders or she would have fallen—the pleasure he was giving her was too intense to bear and it made her legs feel weak and wobbly. She cried out as he sucked her clit into his mouth and began tracing the sensitive bud with his tongue, curving around and around in patterns of pleasure that made her moan and thrust up to meet him shamelessly. God, what was happening to her? She had never been the type to give herself to a man so wantonly, to open herself and let him do anything he wanted to do. But then, her fiancé had never been the type to demand that of her. It was clear that Josh wanted nothing less than her complete surrender as he pressed forward, lapping and sucking and nuzzling.

Once more Phil felt herself trembling on the edge of orgasm—and not just any orgasm, either. This was going to be a ten on the Richter scale or a class five hurricane or a monster Tsunami or however you wanted to put it. But just as she was just about to tip over the edge, Josh stopped again.

"Josh, please!" Phil felt like she might start crying from sheer frustration. "I was close—so *close*. Please, make me come. *Please*. I can't stand it!"

"God, I dreamed of hearing you beg like this," he murmured, looking up at her. "I just need to get a little more leverage. Need to put my tongue inside your hot little pussy and taste you deeper—more. Here, I'll show you." He lifted her left leg so that all her weigh was braced on her right and positioned her thigh over his broad shoulder.

Phil gasped as she felt the new position spread her even farther, opening her completely to Josh's seeking mouth. The stubble of his five o'clock shadow scratched against her tender inner thighs, making her moan with sensation. And then he was bending forward again, using the new leverage he'd gained to enter her with his tongue and press deep inside her until she thought she was going to explode.

"Oh, God...Josh...*Josh!*" Phil buried her hands in his hair and pressed forward, giving herself utterly, holding nothing back as he pressed his tongue deeply into her open sex. She had never felt this hot before, this needy. She had never been with a man who wanted to make her come the way he wanted his next breath. Josh was driving her, pushing harder and harder, closer and closer to the point of no return. Phil knew their relationship would never be the same after this but she had almost stopped caring. All she could think about was the way he was pressing inside her, tasting her center as though he was reaching for her heart with each eager thrust of his tongue. She was close...so *close...*

He shifted positions again and she felt him slide up and suck her clit into his hot mouth once more. He lashed her with his tongue and at the same time two long, strong fingers entered her, thrusting deep to press hard against the end of her channel. Phil felt herself tipping over the edge at last, her hips bucking as she rode his face and sobbed his name aloud, not caring if anyone else could hear her, only needing to express the intense pleasure she was feeling.

The orgasm rolled over her like a blinding wave of light and as she squeezed her eyes tightly shut, she actually saw fireworks. Showers of sparks exploding behind her eyelids as she gave in to the release Josh's talented mouth and fingers had teased from her. Phil threw back her head and moaned, her breath hitching in her chest as she felt hot prickles of moisture behind her closed eyelids. It was too good, too much, the most intense sexual experience she had ever had in her life

"So good," she heard herself murmur. "God, Josh, I've never felt that way. Never come that hard. Not even...not even when I touch myself." She blushed, wondering what had made her make such an intimate confession but Josh didn't seem bothered at all.

"Mmm." He looked up at her, his eyes half-hooded with desire. "Now that's something I'd like to see. Maybe another time."

Another time? Sure, why not? Since it looks like you've decided to go ahead and cheat on Christian even though you know how wrong it is. Now that you've started, why not keep it up?

The nasty little voice in her head cut its way through her

pleasure-soaked brain as her orgasm ebbed, leaving her shaking and breathless, her back still pressed hard against the wooden side of the changing stall and her hands still buried in Josh's thick hair.

Phil closed her eyes. *What am I turning into?* She was engaged to one man and yet she'd just had oral sex in a public dressing room with another. It was exactly the same kind of slutty behavior she'd always deplored in Alison. And yet, here she was, leading her best friend on and cheating on her fiancé at the same time.

It's all my fairy godmother's fault, Phil tried to tell herself. *If only she hadn't reversed the wish so that Josh was compelled to speak his mind and tell me exactly what he wanted to do to me, I wouldn't have been tempted to let him do it.* But she knew she had done what she did because she wanted to, even though she was screwing up her life by going with her impulses. Before her latest disastrous birthday wish she had never been impulsive or reckless. Cass used to tease her and say she was as cautious as an old lady. And now here she was, screwing up not only her own life, but Josh's as well.

"Phil? Phil, are you okay?"

She opened her eyes to see Josh's face filled with worry. His full lips were wet and shiny with her juices, reminding her all over again of the extremely inappropriate behavior they'd just engaged in. "You're crying," he said, softly, and the concern in his eyes was more than she could bear.

"I...uh..." She struggled to disengage herself, feeling suddenly vulnerable and exposed. I just..."

Josh eased her leg off his shoulder and stood, still watching her anxiously. Phil felt shaky and uncertain and horribly naked. Josh still had on the black swim trunks but she had nothing at all to cover herself. The red mesh bikini lay in a crumpled ball on the dressing room floor, staring up at her accusingly.

"Oh, God..." She took a step and almost fell—would have fallen if he hadn't reached out and caught her under the arm and then pulled her close to his chest.

"Phil," he murmured. "Phil, I'm so sorry. I shouldn't have done that. I should have known you'd regret it."

"I just...it's just that..." She bit her lip, trying to explain. "I can't...I shouldn't be doing this, Josh. My...I'm still engaged to Christian and I'm so afraid this is going to ruin our friendship."

"It won't," he murmured into her hair. "I swear it won't. I won't let it."

"Well what are we supposed to do?" Phil looked up at him, swiping angrily at the tears that were blurring her vision. "Are we just going to pretend this never happened? Go back to being office buddies who cheer each other up and give each other pep talks when my boss or yours acts up?"

"No." Josh shook his head firmly. "No, I don't want that either. I want to be *more* than that, Phil."

"I...I don't understand." But as she looked up into his face which was full of tenderness and need, she was terribly afraid that she *did* understand.

"Phil..." He sighed. "I don't want to go back to being just friends and I don't want to be friends with benefits either. This...what I feel for you goes so far beyond the physical. This is a way to express it, but not the only way."

"Oh, no." The tears streaming down her face now. "Don't, Josh. Please, please don't."

"I can't help it." He shook his head, his deep brown eyes reflecting a need so great it tore at her heart. "I know this isn't what you want to hear right now but I can't help saying it. Phil..." He lifted her chin gently and cupped her cheek so she couldn't avoid his gaze. "I'm in love with you."

Chapter Twenty-Five

Phil caught her breath, trying to think. She could see in her best friend's eyes what he wanted her to say—that she loved him, too. That she was ready and willing to change everything in her life to be with him. But she wasn't ready—and she wasn't even sure she was willing, despite the intense experience they had just shared. Even though things with Christian had been awful this last year, they'd had rough patches before. They had always pulled through and things had been better than ever. If she ran into the arms of another man every time they had a fight, how could she hope to have the kind of marriage she wanted? The kind of marriage her new outspoken self knew she deserved?

Good, bad and ugly, things with Christian were *real*—this interlude with Josh felt like a fantasy. And she couldn't forget that most of what had happened was the result of her stupid wish. Where would they be if she hadn't asked the fairy godmother to make her speak her mind? Friends forever. How could Phil trust something that might be a simple side effect of an ill-conceived wish?

She wasn't sure what she felt except that she was scared. Scared of ruining her life and the lives of the people she loved. Scared of losing everything she knew to chase a daydream that might pop like one of her nana's enchanted soap bubbles that played snatches of sweet melody and smelled like flowers when they burst.

"Josh, I'm so sorry." She tried to pull away but he held her a moment longer, searching her eyes. Searching for something he didn't find. At last he let her go, the muscle on the side of his jaw clenching.

"I've loved you from the moment I found you crying in the supply closet, you know," he said in a low voice, stooping to pick up the discarded swimsuits scattered on the floor. "And when I found out you were engaged—well, I think a little part of me died. But I couldn't stop hoping that one day things would work out. I hung around BB&D even though everyone in my family was telling me I was being stupid, that I should just give it up and come home to California."

"Josh, I—" Phil was pulling on her business clothes hurriedly and trying to talk at the same time. But he didn't let her finish.

"That's what I was really trying to tell you the other day when Alison walked in," he said, hanging the red bikini on its hanger with slow, deliberate motions. "Phil, I have a job interview back in Sacramento, where I'm from. The pay is twice what I make at BB&D and it's right by my family."

"Oh." Phil sank suddenly onto the little triangular wooden bench, her blouse half buttoned and only one shoe on. All the strength had run out of her legs and it felt like her stomach had dropped, like it does when you go down the first really steep hill on a roller coaster. "When...when do you fly out?" she managed to ask, trying to sound nonchalant and failing miserably.

"Tomorrow night, after the beach party." Josh shrugged, his broad shoulders rolling with the motion. "I, uh, agreed to take the interview because I didn't think there was any future for me here. I mean, before your birthday, I never thought that you had anything but friendly feelings for me. Well," he corrected himself, "I thought there was *something* there. Some attraction. But I never thought you'd let yourself acknowledge it. Then, when you told me about your dream, and let me know that things weren't exactly going great with Christian lately, well, I started to hope."

"Oh, Josh." Phil felt like she was going to start crying all over again. "I just...I don't know how to feel or what to say. I can't believe we just did...what we did. You know I'm not the kind of person to let myself get carried away with my emotions and make hasty decisions..."

"I know it's not fair to ask you." He sighed and scrubbed a hand over his face. "I should have told you how I felt earlier but I just...didn't want to screw up our friendship."

She let a jagged laugh escape her. "But of course what we just did won't screw it up at all."

He looked stricken. "I'm sorry, Phil. There was no way I should have done...what I did. I just..." He reached forward to brush a sheaf of hair out of her eyes. "You're so exciting and beautiful and vibrant," he said softly. "I've loved you for so long...wanted you for so long. I think I just...wanted to show you how I felt."

Phil felt immediately guilty. "No, it's not all your fault. I encouraged you. I...I wanted it too." Just the memory of his big hands on her, of his hot mouth exploring her, tasting her, was enough to send a shivering rush of desire down her spine. Phil suppressed the emotion ruthlessly. She was mostly dressed now and she slipped into her other shoe and stood up. "It's just...Josh, I've been with Christian for the last five years of my life. He...up until today he was the only man I've ever been with. We're having a rough time right now but we've had hard times before and come through them. I just don't know if I can throw everything I have with him away in the heat of the moment."

"You just did." Josh's voice was harsh now and his eyes were hard. He crossed his arms over his chest, the muscles in his arms tightening into solid knots of tension. "I know exactly how long you've been with him, Phil—it's almost exactly how long I've been waiting for you. But you know what? I can't wait forever. I'll be honest with you—everything I own is packed. If the job interview's a go—and I think it will be—then I won't come back for my stuff. I'm just going to have it shipped to me. Because coming back here and seeing you, knowing I can't have you, is just too damn painful."

"What do you want me to do? What do you want me to say?" Phil had been trying to put her hair back into its usual tight bun but now she held out her hands in supplication, her hair hanging loose around her face.

His eyes softened from the hard brown stone they had become to the warm melted chocolate she knew so well. "Just say you'll think about it," he said. "I wouldn't ask if I thought I'd be breaking up your perfect, happy relationship—hell, that's one reason I stopped myself from telling you how I felt for so long. But judging from some of the things you've been telling me lately, I don't think you've been happy for quite a while. Because I don't think your fiancé, Christian, puts your happiness first." He took one of her hands in both of his and planted a warm, gentle kiss on her palm. "And, Phil, I *would*. If we were together, your happiness would always come first with me. You know that."

Phil felt her heart starting to race again at his gentle touch. Yes, it was true—for as long as they'd been friends, Josh had always been thoughtful and kind and gone out of his way to make sure she was happy and comfortable. For a moment she let herself imagine what it might be like, living with a man that always put her first. A man that cared more about her than himself or his career. A man—

"...think the pink one is totally you. And it matches that little flip skirt you bought at Shopahaulic," a high, female voice was saying outside the dressing room.

"You don't think it's gonna make me look flat? Because there's like *no* support. And I—" a second female voice replied.

"No, no, don't worry about that. You're going to be in the pool for most of the party. You don't need support. They float— remember?" Both voices broke into high pitched, girlish giggles as they passed by the dressing stall where Phil was currently holding her breath.

I have to get out of here! But if she and Josh left at the same time, the girls who had just entered the dressing room would know what they had been doing. Phil had always hated calling attention to herself and this was the worst scenario she could imagine. Well, maybe leaving the bathroom of an airplane at the same time would have been more obvious, but just barely. If she walked out of here with Josh in tow she might as well be wearing a big neon sign on her forehead that read *I just got some in a public dressing room!*

She pulled Josh down and whispered in his ear. "I'll leave first. You wait five minutes before you go."

"Wait." He took both her hands and spoke carefully, in a low voice. "You'll think about what I said? Because my plane leaves tomorrow evening at six. I'm sorry to do this to you, Phil, but—"

"I'll think about it," Phil promised him, feeling desperate but trying to cover it. "But I...I need time, Josh. Please!"

"All right." He released her hands and folded his arms over his bare chest. "I guess I'll see you at the beach party tomorrow?"

"Yes. Yes, we can talk about it then." Phil nodded and slipped out of the stall, straightening her skirt and trying not to look like a woman who had just had the best and most confusing sexual experience of her life.

As she was attempting to exit the store inconspicuously, the iPod girl at the front counter finally looked up. "Find anything that was, uh, *good* for you?" she asked.

Phil felt her face heat in a blush. "Look, I didn't mean to," she babbled, clutching her purse. "I mean, it's not like me to do a thing like that. He's my best friend and I guess I've been attracted to him for a long time, only I couldn't let myself admit it because I'm engaged. But seeing him in those swim trunks—I mean, did you look at him? He looks *incredible.* So then when I tried on that last bikini I guess I just lost it. And I *know* you're not supposed to do that kind of thing in a public place like a dressing room but he was making me so hot the way he..." She shook her head. "Not that it's his fault. If anything it's *my* fault. And I'm sorry if we made a lot of noise. I guess I was screaming pretty loud there but you have to know I didn't mean to—I just couldn't help it! I mean, I should have stopped him instead of encouraging him. But you're a woman too—you can understand, right?"

She ran out of breath at last and realized that the girl was looking at her like she was crazy.

"Uh, lady," she said, eyes wide. "I was just, uh, making a reference to the fact that you and your *friend* were digging in the box of new merchandise which you are *not* supposed to do."

"Oh," Phil said in a small voice, feeling utterly mortified.

"Yeah." The girl frowned, making the piercings in her eyebrows bunch up. "I had no idea you and stud-boy were getting kinky in the dressing room. Until you *told* me. TMI, okay?"

"Oh, no." Phil felt like she might start crying again. "You're not...you wouldn't call the police, would you?"

The girl made a face. "Yeah, right. And have to fill out a freaking incident report form? As long as you're not shoplifting, I really don't give a shit." She looked thoughtful and Phil could feel her reversed wish beginning to work. "Actually, I don't care too much about shoplifting either," the girl admitted. "My shift is over at five and I'm out of here. So you could be wearing half the size twelve rack under your skirt and I couldn't care less. It's no skin off my ass."

"I'm not a size twelve," Phil said indignantly, forgetting to be embarrassed for a second.

"Oh, no? With those hips?" Miss iPod eyed her critically. "Listen, *chica*, I hope you at least stole stuff that will fit you."

"I didn't steal *anything!*" Phil nearly yelled.

"Like I care." The girl arched her pierced eyebrow in a look of ultimate boredom. "But do yourself a favor—next time you're in the mood for dressing room sex, go check out Flirtz. They have padding on their seats in there. It's *much* more comfortable."

Phil opened her mouth but nothing came out. Hunching her shoulders, she ran for the exit, feeling that she had to get out of the store soon or suffocate from humiliation.

She made it to her car and was halfway home again before she burst into tears. What the hell was she going to do?

Chapter Twenty-Six

She tried to convince herself she could play it cool, but by the time she got home Phil was resigned. There was no way she could hide it from Christian. She sat on the couch, twisting her hands together, her stomach tied in knots. She knew women—plenty of women—who would have written what she had done with Josh off as a one-time fling and kept it to themselves. But Phil was learning a lot about herself—including the inconvenient little fact that she had never really learned to lie. Being a doormat meant she had always gone along with whatever other people said, and there had been no need.

There was also the fact that she just plain felt it was wrong to cheat on her fiancé. She had felt guilty just wondering what Davis Miles looked like with his clothes off. And now she'd gotten to second base (or was it third? Sporting analogies always confused her.) with her best friend in a public dressing room. It was so tacky, so slutty, so...so damn hot! Phil felt her breath coming in little pants every time she let herself remember what it had been like—Josh down on his knees in front of her, spreading her open, kissing her, licking her, telling her he wanted her to come all over his face...

Okay, enough of that! Phil gave herself a mental rap on the knuckles. Just because Josh stirred her in ways that Christian hadn't in years was no reason to throw away five long years of mutual history and trust. A trust that she had now broken. But who knew, she thought, her mind going down the same path again, that her funny, kind, sweet best friend had such a hot animal side to him? Who knew he wanted to push her up against the wall and feast on her, to suck and lick and tongue her until she screamed her submission? Wait, there she went again. It was time to get serious here and think about what she was going to tell her fiancé.

It was past eight when she finally heard his key in the lock and Phil sat up straighter, dreading what was ahead. She had rehearsed very carefully what she was going to say but when the door swung open and she saw her fiancé standing there with the hand-tooled leather briefcase she had bought him for his last birthday, all the words left her.

"Christian?" she asked through numb lips and he turned to face her, a distracted look on his face.

"Hey, babe," he said absently, turning to shut the door behind him. "What're you doing sittin' in the dark all by yourself?"

"Oh, is it dark?" Phil had been so distracted that she hadn't noticed twilight falling outside.

"Sure is." Christian reached over to snap on the lamp, bathing the living room in a soft glow.

"I...I was waiting for you." Phil had taken a shower and changed into sweatpants and a T-shirt—comfort clothes—but now she wished she was back in her severely conservative office wear. She thought it might have been easier to talk to her fiancé about what had happened in a businesslike manner if she was dressed in business clothes.

Christian sighed. "Philly-babe, I know I promised you we'd talk but I had a long day in court and I'm beat."

Phil was tempted to send him straight to bed and table the whole discussion. But she wasn't a coward. "I'm sorry you're tired but I *do* need to talk to you," she said, twisting her fingers. Her mouth was suddenly so dry she could barely get the words out. "About...about infidelity."

"Oh, hell!" Christian exploded. "I knew it! I knew you'd find out. Did you have me followed?"

"Wh...what?" Phil quavered. "Are...are you saying... What are you saying, Christian?"

He threw his briefcase across the room and started pacing in front of the couch. "You want a full confession? Fine, I'll give you one. Her name is Jacqueline and we've been seeing each other for almost a year—for as long as I've been at my job with the firm, in fact. She's one of the finest litigators we have— smart, funny, sexy as hell. I..." He stopped and shook his head like a dog trying to get rid of a flea. "I don't even know why I'm telling you this."

Phil knew—it was her reverse wish still at work. Christian was just speaking his mind. And what was on his mind was another woman—one he'd apparently been seeing for almost a year.

"I...I..." Phil didn't know what to say. Her mind was a blank, but that didn't stop her mouth from asking questions. "Do you love her?" she managed to get out. "You want to leave me for her, is that it? Is that why you've been putting off the talk about getting married and putting me through law school?"

"Not exactly." Christian sat on the couch beside her and sighed. "She's got a husband and kids so we agreed it would be too messy for her to get a divorce. Besides, that doesn't go over well at the firm—they like to present the image of happy families and couples to the clients, not a bunch of bitter divorcees. That's why I was upset when you didn't come with me to the party. Didn't look good. Image is everything."

"Apparently not *everything*," Phil muttered. "So if you'd rather be with her but you can't, you'd just as soon stay with me—is that it? Is that why you haven't already called it quits?"

He sighed. "Come on, babe, I'm not a complete jerk. I'm still willing going to go ahead with the marriage and put you through law school like I promised if you insist on it, even though I still think it's a waste of your time and my money. I owe you that much."

"You owe me a lot more than that." Phil felt like someone had dipped her heart in liquid nitrogen and the slightest tap might shatter it into a thousand pieces. "Were you ever going to stop seeing her?"

"I already have." Christian looked sober. "I mean, it was her idea, not mine. She's doing some kind of therapy with her husband and she wants to go back on the straight and narrow. She told me last night at that damn party. Christ." He furrowed his brow. "I can't believe I'm telling you all this."

Phil couldn't believe it either. Despite his waning interest in their sex life and their relationship in general over the past year, she had never once imagined that Christian might be cheating on her. Suddenly what she'd done with Josh in the RipTide dressing room didn't seem quite so bad. It wasn't good but it wasn't as horrible as, say, conducting an illicit affair with a married woman for an entire year.

"This is why you don't want me any more," she said in a low, trembling voice. "This is why you haven't wanted sex other than a quickie or two in months, isn't it?"

"Look, babe." Christian was up again, pacing. "I know this comes as a shock and I'm really damn sorry you had to find out like this. But like I said, it's all over and it's not like I'm in love with Jackie or anything. It was just a fling—hell every man has a fling now and then."

"A year is a hell of a long fling," Phil pointed out. "But...so, you don't love her?" Mentally she was flipping through images of women who worked with Christian that she had met at one or the other of his interminably long and boring parties or dinners. If she remembered correctly, Jacqueline was a tall, stick-thin woman in her late thirties with nut brown hair and exotic amber eyes.

"I thought I did for a long time but...no. No, I'm sure I don't. She was just a passing thing. Hell, I'm so sorry, Phil." Christian stopped pacing and stood in front of her with his hands shoved deep in his pockets. He used to remind her of a remorseful little boy caught with his hand in the cookie jar when he stood like that. This time the image wasn't quite so endearing.

"So...so how do you feel about me?" Phil asked, wishing her voice wouldn't shake so much.

"How do I...?" Christian shrugged, a small frown on his handsomely shaped mouth. "Hell, I don't know. You're just Phil—*my* Phil. My rock. You're always there for me no matter what. We stick together through thick and thin, right? This is just a little bump in the road, babe. We'll get through it together."

"A little bump in the road? And I'm just *Phil?*" She stared at him in disbelief. "I notice that you didn't say you love me, Christian."

"Ah, hell. I'd be lying if I said I was madly in love with you, babe. I mean we're past that stage, you know? But I care enough to say I'm sorry and to do right by you. That's why I think we need to put this behind us and get on with our lives. After all, neither one of us can afford this place on our own yet.

And I'm going to need a steady, dependable wife to stick by me when my career really takes off. I guess what it comes down to is, I trust you, Phil."

Phil felt a throbbing in her temples. Was that all she was to him? Steady and dependable? Suddenly she wanted to hurt him—to hurt him as badly as he had hurt her.

"Well maybe you shouldn't be quite so trusting. What if I told you that I...I had an affair too?" She looked up at him defiantly and felt a quick stab of triumph at the look of disbelief on his handsome face.

"What? Who with? How long has this been going on?" Christian was in full lawyer mode, shooting questions at her like bullets. Phil did her best to remain composed.

"With Josh, my best friend at BB&D. And it only happened today. I'm not proud of it. I...I wanted to tell you about it and ask you forgiveness. But now...it looks like I've got a lot more to forgive than you have."

"Josh? You mean that tall computer geek we met that time in the mall?" Christian surprised her by laughing. "Oh, hell, for a minute I was worried."

"Well maybe you *should* be worried." Phil glared at him. "Unlike you, Josh is actually in love with me. He thinks I'm exciting, not just 'dependable'."

"Yeah, I'm sure he said that." Christian waved a hand at her dismissively. "But, frankly, Phil, I'm relieved. I mean, it was bound to happen sometime. That guy's been sniffin' around your panties for the last three or four years. And the way we've been fighting lately...no, can't say I'm surprised. But you say it only happened the one time?"

"Well...yes..."

"And you used protection?" Christian frowned, looking more like a stern father than an angry, jealous lover.

"We...we didn't actually..." Phil trailed off.

"You didn't even have sex?" Christian raised an eyebrow at her.

Phil couldn't believe he wasn't more upset. She felt sick—sick at Christian's admission of guilt and sicker at the idea that he only thought of her as *dependable*. That he was no longer in love with her and only wanted to stay with her for convenience. So they could make the freaking rent and look like a happy couple to his appearance-conscious firm.

"I...it was...he...not actual *intercourse,*" she stuttered, feeling like an idiot. "But...but there was definite intimate physical contact," she added, trying not to think about Josh's hot mouth on her and the way she'd buried her fingers in his hair and begged for more.

Her fiancé tilted his head philosophically. "Well, then let's call it even. These things happen—bumps in the road, like I said. And look, if you want, I'll even agree to some counseling sessions like Jackie and her husband are doing. Though God knows when I'll fit them in." He ran a hand through his hair and let out a harassed sigh. It was like he had done something minor—forgotten it was his turn to take out the trash—and now he was prepared to take it out for a whole month to make up for it. *When did he turn into such a bastard? Or was I just too blind to see it before?*

"I have to know one more thing," Phil said tightly. "All that stuff you said about not wanting to put me through law school because I don't have what it takes—was that true? Is that what you really feel about me?"

Christian opened his mouth and it looked like he wanted to say something but Phil's wish was in effect and he couldn't lie. "I think you'd do very well in law school and you'd probably even make a pretty good attorney," he said, and then looked shocked at what was coming out of his mouth.

"Uh-huh." Phil nodded. "So why did you feed me that line about trying to spare my feelings and save me pain?"

"I just wanted a wife who was there for me. Someone supportive to come home to after a hard day at the office and..." Christian shook his head, trying vainly to keep his jaw from working and the words from pouring out. "I didn't want to spend the money. I know I promised you I'd put you through school after you put me through but in the back of my mind I always figured I could get you to forget about that and settle down. That way I knew I'd get through school without having to take loans and you'd be dependent on me so I could pretty much do what I wanted."

"Why you...I can't believe..." He had been playing her for a fool for years. He had never once intended to live up to his side of their bargain. Phil was finally sure of at least one thing—she was done with Christian for once and for all.

She stood up with her keys in her hand. The old Phil might have cried, but ultimately she would have forgiven her cheating fiancé and agreed to forgo law school in order to salvage their relationship. But Phil wasn't that person anymore. She headed for the door.

"Wait a minute." Christian stepped in front of her. "Where do you think you're going?"

"I'm leaving you." Phil gave him a level glare. "I should have done it a long time ago."

"Now, hold on, babe," he protested. "I told you we can work this out. Think about all the good times we've had. Remember our first apartment—how hot it was? Or the Christmas we only had ten dollars to spend on gifts?"

"So we went to the dollar store and you got me a glass bunny and I got you a bottle of designer imposters cologne," Phil recited. "Yes, Christian, I remember all of that. But it doesn't change the fact that I'm leaving you. I told you I can't live on the past anymore—that I needed something for the future. Well now I'm going to make my own future. Without you."

Christian dropped the soothing tone of voice. "Where do you think you're going anyway? Gonna run back to computer boy?"

"I...I don't know." Phil crossed her arms over her chest. "For right now I'll probably just go back to Nana's house. I need time to think."

Christian threw up his hands. "Fine. Good luck being able to sort yourself out with your sisters yapping and your grandma going nuts—I'll be surprised if you can hear yourself think, let alone come to any kind of a decision."

Phil tightened her grip on her keys. "You know, Josh *likes* my family. He had dinner with us last night at Nana's and they like him too."

"What?" For the first time Christian looked genuinely angry. "So you blew off my important office party to show off your boyfriend to your crazy family?"

"It wasn't like that." Phil was strangely gratified to have finally gotten a reaction other than mild amusement from him. But his next words shattered that.

"Dammit, Phil, I really could have used you there at that party last night," he said, frowning. "It was damn inconsiderate of you to miss for something stupid like that. It didn't look right, me being there without you."

"It didn't *look* right?" Phil felt like she was screaming but the words came out in a hoarse whisper. "Is that all you care about, Christian? Appearances? You and I are over and you've been lying to me for years but all you care about is that I show up at the right place at the right time on your arm?"

"Philly-babe, be fair." He sighed. "I never said that. Now come on, put down your keys and let's go to bed. I've got a long day tomorrow."

"I'm not going to bed with you ever again. And I am *not* your 'Philly-babe.' Not anymore." Phil pushed past him to the front door of the apartment.

"Fine," he called after her. "You'll feel different after a night at that mental institution your family calls a house. I'll call you when you've had time to calm down."

Phil didn't answer, mainly because she couldn't think of anything mean enough to say. For the second time that night she was left wondering—what the hell was she going to do?

Chapter Twenty-Seven

"Wow, you look like *shit*." Cass clapped her hand over her mouth. "God, Phil, I don't know what got into me. I didn't mean to say that."

"Don't worry about it. It's my new wish, or rather, my old one, reversed. Now instead of speaking my mind, the people around me have to speak theirs." Phil pushed past her into the large kitchen. Someone had a pot heating on the stove, but thankfully the brown liquid bubbling gently inside it looked and smelled a lot more like hot chocolate than another one of her nana's potions.

"Wait...what?" Cass shut the kitchen door and turned to stare at her. "You're kidding, right? Not even the FG could be so stupid."

"She did it on purpose. At least, I'm pretty sure she did." Phil sank down at the table and put her head in her hands. "So I've been hearing people's secret thoughts and darkest secrets all day long. It's been horrible."

"Oh, Phil, I'm sorry." Cass wasn't usually the affectionate type but she came around the table and gave Phil a quick hug. "That sucks."

"You have *no* idea." Phil tugged at the hair scrunchy holding her hair in a bun at the nape of her neck. "I got to hear how one coworker is afraid of killer clowns and how another has a massive Electra complex." She ticked them off on her fingers as she went. "The lady across the hall that always steals my paper is a kleptomaniac. The cutest guy in my office is gay. The old lady that runs the filing department matches her eyebrows to the color of her underwear. My boss is addicted to Internet porn—and not just any porn—really skuzzy, bizarre porn."

"There are different levels of Internet porn?" Cass raised a coal black eyebrow at her.

Phil shivered. "Trust me on this. But that's not even the best part. The head of the BB&D human resources department likes to wear women's underwear under his suit. Josh is in love with me and has been for years and Christian is cheating on me. Which is why I'm here."

"Whoa." Cass sank down at the table beside her. "Back up, Phil. You totally lost me on those last two."

Phil sighed and ran both hands through her loosened hair. "What—you mean my best friend being madly in love with me or my fiancé cheating?"

"He cheated on you? With who? I knew he was a rat bastard." Cass glowered and Phil fervently hoped her sister wasn't going to say, 'I told you so.'

"With a woman at work. Another attorney who in his words is 'smart and funny and sexy as hell.' Whereas *I* am just dependable old Phil who's willing to put up with anything."

"You're not, are you? Willing to put up with it?" Cass demanded.

Phil spread her hands. "Here I am. I left him."

"Good for you!" Cass thumped her on the back. "I'm proud of you, Phil. There's no way you ought to stay with that cheating asshole."

"Well, it's not like I didn't cheat on him too. With Josh. In the mall. In the dressing room at RipTide" She put her head in her hands.

"You *what?* Details—I need *details.*" Cass pounded on the table with one hand just as the cocoa on the stove boiled over with a hiss. She got up hurriedly to rescue the pot. "So tell," she went on, pouring the hot chocolate into two mugs and bringing them back to the table.

Phil sighed. "All you need to know is that we did things...*intimate* things. Things I've never done with Christian. Oh, God." She bit her lip, trying to rid herself of the hot image of her best friend on the floor in front of her, kissing and tasting her.

"You're getting red. It must have been good." Cass pushed

the mug of hot cocoa towards her. "Come on, fess up."

"All right, it *was* pretty damn spectacular. But, it left me so *confused.*"

"What's to be confused about? In a nutshell—you cheated on Christian but he cheated on you first. They guy you cheated with just happens to be tall, dark and handsome—and he's madly in love with you. So you leave Christian to be with Josh. The end."

"No that's *not* the end!" Phil put down the mug of scalding cocoa and buried her head in her hands again. "When did my life turn into such a freaking soap opera?"

"The minute you were born," Cass said. "Seriously, Phil, belonging to this family practically *guarantees* you a daily allotment of drama. It's amazing you've managed to live as normal a life as you have for as long as you have. But face it— the weirdness finally caught up with you. Why don't you admit Christian is an asshole and own up to the fact that you want to be with Josh?"

"I don't want to just leave one guy for another!" Phil protested. "I don't want to be like Alison from my office, just roaming from man to man like a lion preying on antelopes in the Serengeti!"

"Oh, that's the slut girl at your work?" Cass was familiar with Phil's coworkers from many sisterly bitch sessions.

Phil nodded. "The one with the Electra complex."

"Uh, yeah. Well, listen Phil—news flash. There's a big difference between being the office slut and staying with one man for practically your whole life and then finding out he's an asshole and dumping him for a guy who actually cares about you. That doesn't exactly qualify you as a man eater, ya know?" Cass took another careful sip of cocoa. "So why don't you just admit you want to be with Josh and get on with your life?"

"Because it's *not that simple.*" Phil slapped her hand on the table, sloshing hot chocolate over its smooth wood surface. "I've only had feelings for Josh for the last two or three days. How do I know that I wouldn't just be getting together with him on the rebound?"

"Look, Phil." Cass sounded like she was nearly out of patience. "You've only had feelings for him *that you let yourself acknowledge* for two or three days. But I saw you two together last night. There's a spark there I never saw between you and Christian. Let me ask you something, how do you feel when you're around Christian? Or how did you feel *before* you knew he was cheating?"

Phil wiped up her spilled cocoa with a napkin, keeping her eyes on her task. "Well, anxious, I guess. Worried, nervous, ignored, slighted, dull, unimportant..." She looked up. "I guess I could go on but I don't want to."

"Uh-huh." Cass didn't look surprised. "And how do you feel around Josh?"

Phil shrugged. "I don't know. Happy. Safe. Respected. Funny, smart, good at what I do, intelligent, stimulated, sexy..." She trailed off, surprised at the number of words that came to mind when she thought of her best friend.

"Are you beginning to see a pattern emerging here?"

"Well, yes. But that still doesn't mean I ought to jump feet first into a new relationship. Except..."

"Except what?" Cass took another sip of cocoa, watching Phil over the rim of the mug.

"Except I have to give Josh an answer by tomorrow or he's leaving for California and never coming back."

"Come again?" Cass asked. Phil explained about the job interview in Sacramento. "Okay, Phil, now I agree with you. Your life really *is* a damn soap opera."

"See?" Phil spread her hands. "So what am I supposed to do?"

"Get in the car tonight, drive to Josh's apartment and jump his bones," her sister said. "No, wait." She held up a hand as Phil started to protest. "First take a shower and put on my little red silk nighty—*then* drive over and jump his bones. It's much more effective for seductions than those grungy old sweats you have on."

"That's not exactly helpful, Cass." Phil crossed her arms over her chest.

"Well, hell, Phil—what do you want me to do?" her sister exploded. "You sit here whining to me that the guy who was never right for you is history and the perfect guy, the one who loves you, the one who can't take his eyes off you whenever you're in the same room together, wants a relationship. And yet you say you don't know what to do! I wish *I* could have such cut

231

and dried problems."

Phil recoiled from her sister's outburst. "Well, I'm so sorry I inconvenienced you by telling you about my life. I won't bother you any further." She started to take her mug to the sink.

"Wait, Phil, I'm sorry." Cass put a hand on her arm and sighed. "You know I didn't mean to say that. I don't know what got into me."

"I do." Phil sank back down in her seat. "It's my stupid reversed wish."

"Oh, right. Well, before you deal with either Christian or Josh, I'd say you need to get that taken care of first. What a mess."

"You don't know the half of it," Phil mumbled. "But I'm sorry if I was getting on your nerves."

"You weren't," Cass assured her. "It's just...I've got problems of my own right now."

Phil gave her a small smile. "Those problems wouldn't have anything to do with a certain reluctant male model that we scared off in your studio the other day, would they?"

Cass blushed. "Leave Brandon out of this. He's...well, I'll deal with him later. But you know, Phil, you're not the only one with wish issues. My social life is in the toilet and my art...well, I have artist's block or something. I have this huge showing coming up at the ICU gallery but nothing is coming out right lately. And worst of all, my twenty-third birthday is coming up next month and with the FG already pissed off, I don't know how I'll make a wish that won't backfire."

"Why not wish to become un-blocked then? You're always saying how art is the most important part of your life."

"Hello? Which is *exactly* why I don't want our fairy godmother to have anything to do with it!" Cass exclaimed. "It's about the only part of my life she *hasn't* managed to screw up in some way or other. And I don't need her to start now. She might make it so all I could paint was cute kitty cats and fuzzy bunnies."

"As opposed to hot male nudes, like *Brandon*?" Phil tried to hide her smirk and couldn't. Her sister slapped her lightly on the arm.

"Ahem. Speaking of hot male nudes, Miss 'Did It In The RipTide Dressing Room,' I almost forgot—Josh brought you something. He said he didn't think it was a good idea for him to show up at your apartment so he wanted me to make sure you got it."

"What? When? Why didn't you say so before?" Phil jumped out of her chair.

"Simmer down—between you telling me about your klepto neighbor, your cross-dressing boss, and your cheating fiancé, it kinda slipped my mind."

"It's the head of HR that's a cross dresser," Phil corrected absently. "My *boss* is addicted to Japanese Internet porn. The skuzzy kind."

"Oh, right. Well, anyway." Cass got up and returned with the signature hot pink and aqua blue RipTide plastic bag and dropped it in her lap. "There. Satisfied?"

Phil looked down at the bag with something like dread growing in the pit of her stomach. What would she find when she opened the bag? Would it be the pale peach bikini that had seemed to float so indecently on her body? Or, even worse, the fire engine red mesh suit that showed everything? Had Josh bought it for her to remind her of what they had done?

"Well, go on—open it," Cass said impatiently.

With trembling fingers, Phil untied the drawstrings and opened the bag, peering into its depths. There was a piece of paper on top of the folded fabric and when she moved it aside, she breathed a sigh of relief.

Neither pale peach or fire engine red greeted her gaze. Lying in a demure pile was the sky blue polka-dotted bikini that Josh had found for her. The first one she had tried on. She drew it and the paper out of the bag, a big silly grin spreading across her face from ear to ear. Somehow if Josh had bought her one of the other bikinis she'd tried on, it would have been almost as bad as having him deliver her magical wish-induced éclair.

"What does the note say? And what are you smiling about?" Cass demanded. Wordlessly, Phil handed her the note.

Hope you'll wear this tomorrow so I can see how well it matches the color of your eyes. Josh.

Cass read it aloud and frowned. "Matches the color of your eyes?"

"When it's sunny and there aren't any clouds, Josh said my eyes are this exact color of sky blue." Phil nodded at the bikini.

"But..." Cass looked from her to the bikini and back again. "I don't understand. How does he know that? He's non-fairy—he shouldn't notice that your eye color changes with the sky."

"I know. But he does. You saw for yourself last night—he notices and hears all kinds of things."

"Notices what, my darlings?" The kitchen door opened with a flourish and their nana, wearing a fuchsia silk sundress and an enormous straw brimmed hat strode regally in. The fact that it was full dark outside didn't seem to deter her at all but Phil knew Nana would have worn a parka to the beach or Bermuda shorts to the Arctic Circle if it suited her. Wearing a sundress out when there was no sun was nothing.

"Phil's new boyfr—ah, *friend* notices things he shouldn't be able to without fairy blood," Cass said, wincing and rubbing her shin under the table where Phil had kicked it. "He noticed that her eyes change to match the sky."

"He can also hear us talk when we mention our fairy godmother," Phil added. "*And* he noticed that I hate éclairs. Something that completely slipped Christian's attention, by the way." She frowned, remembering the night of her birthday and the incident at the Italian restaurant.

"He noticed your éclairs?" Cass raised an eyebrow and Phil nodded.

"He got me a cheesecake for my birthday because he said he knew I hated éclairs."

"Damn." Cass was obviously stumped.

"Language, Cassandra." Nana shook a finger at her and frowned reprovingly. But she had a distracted look on her plump face and Phil wondered if she'd heard anything she and Cass had been saying.

"Nana," she asked, "Are you all right?"

"It's nothing, Philomena, just that I appear to have stepped in an unmentionable substance." Nana grimaced and examined the bottom of her dainty satin fuchsia mule.

"Stepped in dog shit again, Nana?" Cass asked.

"Cassandra!" Nana sighed, as though giving the language issue up as a lost cause. "Well, as a matter of fact, I did. I was out gardening and those nasty little poodles of Mister Clausen's had nearly dug a hole right under the fence between his yard and mine." She said it as though there was nothing strange about gardening at ten o'clock at night.

Phil felt her heart give a thump, remembering the potion she had buried among the zinnias. "Oh, uh, did any of them get through?"

"They did *not*," Nana said with satisfaction. "I filled their nasty little hole right in—it took me nearly an hour. I dare say I'll have to have a talk with Mister Clausen about it. In fact, I'd go over there tonight if it wasn't so late and if I didn't smell so." She wrinkled her nose delicately. "Really, I must shower."

Cass sniffed the air. "There *is* a funny odor in here but I don't think it's dog shit. Sorry, Nana, dog crap."

"Dog *excrement* might be a more lady-like thing to say," Nana huffed

Cass sniffed the air around their grandmother again and fixed her with a stern stare. "Have you been dabbling in the Craft again?"

Nana lifted her chin. "Certainly not. I gave my word not to and a fairy's word is her bond as you well know, Cassandra."

Phil jumped to her grandmother's defense. "Leave her alone, Cass. I'm sure she's telling the truth." She didn't want to admit to burying the last batch of potion in such a foolish spot and was immensely relived that their grandmother had filled in the hole dug by Mister Clausen's poodles. The last thing she needed after the day she'd had was more drama.

"You know, girls." Nana's full lower lip was trembling and her bright green eyes were abruptly about to overflow. "I understand that I've caused you some trouble this week, but it's only because I'm afraid to be all alone when all of you are gone. Oh, I *do* wish your grandfather was still alive! I miss him so much sometimes."

"Oh, Nana." Phil and Cass got up simultaneously to give their grandmother a hug.

"There, there, now. I'm just being a silly old woman." Their Nana patted Phil affectionately on the cheek and smiled at Cass. "You mustn't mind me. I must go and shower. You can always tell a true lady by her bewitching scent but right now I positively *reek*."

"Goodnight, Nana," Phil and Cass chorused and with a final pat to their cheeks, their grandmother swept out of the room.

"Well..." Cass yawned. "I think I need to turn in, too. It's late and I have to present at least two of the pieces for my show at the ICU tomorrow. Did you decide what you're going to do? Please don't be an idiot about this, Phil. Just tell Josh you care."

"I'll think about it." Phil wrapped her arms around herself and sighed. She wanted to be sure she was doing the right thing—not just going along with someone else as she had been doing her whole life. She knew Josh loved her, but how did she feel about him? The encounter in the RipTide dressing room still made her blush, but as Josh himself had admitted, there had to be more than just the physical element.

She thought of all the times she'd cried on his shoulder, all the times he'd made her laugh and given her pep talks, all the sweet, considerate little things he did for her on a daily basis. She felt warm just thinking about it—the way he always remembered her birthday, the way he knew she hated éclairs. There was definitely something there but she wanted to be fair to her best friend—was it enough to ask him to stay for? Or was she still in shock from her abrupt break-up with Christian? Everything was moving so damn fast Phil felt like she was stuck on the Tilt-a-Whirl at the amusement park and couldn't get off. If only she had a day or a week or a month to think things through!

Doubtless Christian would be calling her soon to ask when she was coming back. She still had to pack up her things and get out of the apartment she'd shared with him. Besides, Phil thought, if she *did* decide to start something with Josh in the future, she didn't want to base a relationship on something either one of them was magically compelled to say. She wanted a fairy godmother-free bond with her best friend and right now, that was impossible.

No, Phil decided, she was just going to be honest with her friend. *I'll tell him I care about him deeply but I need a little while to sort things out,* she told herself. She felt sure if she gave him hope, he would give her time. Time to get away from Christian, get over him, get on with her life. Time to find her feet again before she went jumping back into the deep end of the love pool. And time to get out from under this damn wish.

"Hello, Phil? Cass surprised her by snapping her fingers in front of her face. "Are you okay? You kinda zoned out on me there."

"Fine, I'm fine." Phil grabbed the cocoa mugs and put them in the sink. "Just tired and wondering how I'm going to get this wish fixed," she said, hoping her sister wouldn't keep harping on her romantic entanglements. "I mean, the FG was so nasty about it last time. I bet she won't show up again for a month no matter hard I yank my earlobe and scream."

"Oh, and you've got to go to that beach party tomorrow, don't you?" Cass gave her a sympathetic look. "Wow, no matter how good you look in that bikini Josh bought you, I wouldn't want to go out on a public beach and hear what everyone thinks of your body."

"Thanks for the vote of confidence, Cass," Phil said dryly. She picked up the RipTide bag, tucked it under her arm and sighed. "You're right, though. I don't need anyone telling me I look indecent or else saying out loud that they want to get into my polka-dotted panties. But I just don't think I'll be able to get the fairy godmother to show in time to change it."

Cass looked grim. "Oh, we'll make her show, all right. Wait until breakfast tomorrow. You and I and Rory are all going to summon her at once and you know we're stronger when we're all together—she'll *have* to come."

Phil frowned doubtfully. "Yes, but forcing her to show up won't exactly put her in a good mood when it comes to fixing this wish."

Her sister waved that minor detail away. "Just be sure you word your request very specifically this time. Don't leave her any loopholes to work with. We'll get it fixed so everybody can keep their opinions to themselves and you can stroll on the sand with your honey-bunny in peace. I promise."

"But what about you? Your wish is coming up in less than a month," Phil reminded her.

Cass looked slightly discomfited but then she frowned. "Well you know, maybe it's time to let her know we're tired of putting up with her crap. She's probably already pissed off so pushing her a little more won't matter. Anyway, you let *me* worry about me and *you* worry about getting that wish fixed so you can get with Josh."

"You're so brave." Phil smiled and gave her sister a quick hug. "We'll think of something airtight so that the FG can't screw you no matter how much she tries." She grinned. "Maybe you can wish that all Brandon's pants are permanently see-through? For the artistic potential."

"Uh-huh. Right. Good night, Phil." Cass went to bed, leaving Phil to run water in the cocoa mugs and contemplate exactly how she would word her wish.

Chapter Twenty-Eight

"Fairy godmother, come for our need is dire!" Phil, Cass, and Rory all yanked on their earlobes and shouted the words simultaneously for the second time. They were sitting around the large kitchen table, concentrating hard. But Phil was beginning to think this wasn't going to work. She was already wearing the sky blue polka-dotted bikini and she had left her hair down because she knew Josh liked it that way. She was still wondering what she was going to tell her best friend. Just thinking about it made her stomach feel like a hundred butterflies had taken flight and were currently doing nosedives and barrel rolls inside it.

"D'you think this is gonna take much longer?" Rory yawned hugely. "I need to get dressed and get going. Doctor Robinson hates it when we're late to work." Doctor Robinson was the head veterinarian at the animal clinic and kennel she was working for that summer.

"Don't get your panties in a knot," Cass snapped. "I have a big day too—I'm trying to get my show together for the ICU down on North Hanna. But Phil needs to get this wish reversed before she goes to the beach."

"Wish I could go to the beach," Rory mumbled around her cornflakes. "Phil, you look really good in that suit but I think the top is too small. I've always wished I had boobs as big as yours." She choked on her mouthful of cereal. "Oh my God! I didn't mean to say that out loud. Why did I...?"

"Because the FG screwed Phil the last time she asked for a redo." Cass nodded and added sugar to her own breakfast—a huge mug of black coffee. She always claimed the thought of food before noon made her retch. "So now instead of telling everyone what she's thinking, everyone else had to tell her. I'm sure you can understand why she needs our help."

"Yeah." Rory's eyes widened. "Wow, that has to be rough, Phil—I'm really sorry."

"And that's not the worst of it either," Cass continued. "She just found out last night that slime-ball Christian has been cheating on her for the last year."

"Oh my God." Rory frowned sympathetically. "Phil, that bites! But you know, I never liked him. Please tell me you dumped him when you found out."

"She handed him his walking papers all right," Cass said approvingly. "Sayonara, shithead."

"Could you guys please stop talking about me like I'm not here?" Phil sighed. It didn't take magic to tell how her sisters felt about her ex-fiancé. She ought to feel heart-broken and devastated about her break-up with Christian but strangely all she felt when she thought about it was...lighter. Like a big rock had been rolled off her chest. *Even if I've been screwing everything else in my life up, at least I did one thing right,* she told herself firmly.

"Sorry, Phil," Rory said. "We didn't mean to rub it in."

"That's okay, hon." Phil pinched the bridge of her nose to push back the headache that wanted to start behind her eyes. "And I know you two have a busy day planned. Maybe we should just let it go. After all, I survived yesterday so I can probably manage a while longer." But the thought of seeing her coworkers again and hearing more of their awkward secrets made her cringe.

"Nothing doing." Cass slapped the table with her palm. "We're sitting right here until the FG comes and fixes this screw up. We've taken her crap for long enough. Now once more, all together on three. One, two...three!"

"Fairy godmother come, for our need is dire!" all three sisters shouted, yanking their lobes like crazy. Nothing happened.

"All right, that's it." Phil shook her head. "I really don't think—"

Suddenly there was an audible *pop* and the room filled with pale pink smoke and the odor of burnt flower petals. Phil blinked and saw their fairy godmother floating in the middle of kitchen, her mother-of-pearl wings a blur of agitation. She was dressed in a pale pink tailored pantsuit and her silver wand was spitting sparks all over their nana's linoleum floor.

"What is it now?" the FG snarled. "Did I or did I not tell you that I was preparing for my yearly vacation in Patagonia? When will you get it through your thick, half-breed skulls that I have better things to do than tend to your every tiresome whim?"

"If you'd get it right the first time we wouldn't have to keep calling you back," Cass snapped at her.

Phil shot her sister a worried glance and shook her head slightly. She was every bit as pissed off with the FG as her sister but Cass's birthday wish was coming up next and fairies were notorious for holding grudges. However, her wish was still at work on her sisters and Cass apparently couldn't resist adding one more zinger.

"You have to be the most incompetent fairy godmother in history," she told the FG. "The Fairy Counsel ought to revoke your license for sheer idiocy."

"Why, you little—" The FG's face was turning red and to make matters worse, Rory chimed in.

"I've never liked you ever since you turned me into a dog," she said, pointing her cereal spoon at the FG accusingly. "You knew perfectly well that wasn't what I wanted when I wished to be able to speak to animals. Would it kill you to put a little effort into your magic once in a while?"

"You little ingrates!" The FG was hissing with rage and her wand was spitting enough sparks to set the house on fire. "I have never, in all my years as a practicing fairy—"

"Please, Fairy Godmother, they're just reacting to my wish," Phil said desperately. "They can't help what they're saying!"

"Well they'd better help it or I'll turn the lot of you into the slimy little toads you are." Their fairy godmother raised her wand threateningly.

"You wouldn't dare." Cass's voice had a hard edge to it as she glared at the FG. "The Fairy Council would have your wand if they heard of such an abuse of power. And I for one—"

Things were deteriorating rapidly. "I just need one more redo, Fairy Godmother," Phil said, interrupting Cass's rant. "My wish still isn't right. It's been causing me a lot of problems. And I do mean a *lot*."

The FG scowled and crossed her arms over her bony chest. "Fine but let it be understood that this is the *last time*. I'm going to Patagonia for a month and I'll be *completely* unavailable—I don't care if you yank your pretty little earlobes 'till they bleed."

"All right." Phil took a deep breath to calm herself. It wouldn't do any good to antagonize their fairy godmother further.

"And hurry *up*." The FG tapped her foot in mid-air, her thin aristocratic face still pale with anger.

"I don't want people around me to feel the need to speak their minds—by which I meant to shout out their innermost thoughts and feelings—anymore," Phil began carefully, trying to get the wording just right. She'd been up half the night rehearsing what she was going to say. "And *I* don't want to feel compelled to speak my mind and tell everyone around me exactly how I feel either," she continued.

"Right. If anything she needs the exact opposite," Rory put in.

"Rory, *please*." Phil shot her a glare. "I'm wishing here." But it was too late. There was a wicked gleam in their fairy godmother's silver eyes and her wand was already in action.

"The exact opposite it shall be!" she declared and Phil felt the tingling all over, the Pop Rocks in Diet Coke sensation that signaled a granted wish.

"Wait!" she yelled. "Fairy Godmother, I—"

"Don't bother me again!" There was another puff of acrid pink smoke and the FG was gone, leaving Phil with a sinking feeling in the pit of her stomach.

"Rory, why did you do that?" Cass turned on their youngest sister.

"I was just trying to agree with Phil!" Rory protested. "I'm sorry—I'm still half asleep."

"But the exact opposite? What does that even mean? And more importantly, what has the FG done to Phil now?" Cass turned to her, a worried expression in her violet eyes. "Phil, how do you feel? Do you have the urge to blurt out everything you're thinking again?"

Phil took a deep breath and thought about it but no, she didn't. If she had, she would have yelled at her youngest sister for shooting off her mouth in the middle of her wish. She wasn't sure what Rory's interference had done to her latest wish fix, but at least she wasn't right back where she'd started.

"Okay, then." Cass sighed. "I don't feel the need to say what I'm thinking either. Rory?"

Rory shook her head mutely, still looking miserable.

"Good." Cass looked closely at Phil. "Well, maybe she got it right this time."

"I'm sure she did," Phil said, even though she was still harboring serious doubts. But she couldn't hold her sisters up forever and the FG had made it abundantly clear she wasn't coming back a fourth time no matter what.

"Good, well..." Cass got up, drained her coffee mug, and put it in the sink. "Time to go. Have a good time on the beach, Phil. And remember—tell Josh exactly how you feel and everything will be fine."

Chapter Twenty-Nine

Starfish Cove, the private beach where the BB&D Third of July beach party was being held this year, was located across the bay off of Interstate 60, otherwise known as the Courtney Campbell. The Courtney Campbell was a long, winding road lined with palm trees on either side and had only two lanes, one coming and one going.

Normally Phil hated to take the Courtney Campbell anywhere because there was always some idiot in a hurry who wanted to pass when there was clearly no room to do so. But today the sun was shining, there wasn't a cloud in the sky, and traffic was light. She was on her way to tell her best friend that she wanted to be more than his friend—in time, that was, she reminded herself. They were going to have to take things slow for a while. Over and over she rehearsed exactly what she was going to say to Josh.

Josh, I've been thinking about what you told me yesterday about how you feel and I think I might feel the same way. But I need some time. I just broke up with Christian and I—

Phil was jerked out of her anxious contemplation of how Josh would react to her news by a blaring horn and the sight of a huge black pickup truck barreling down on her.

"What the..." she gasped, slamming on her brakes. The idiot in the pick-up was trying to pass an elderly couple in a large, slow moving Town Car and he had gone into Phil's lane to do it. It was exactly why she hated driving on 60. The truck was headed right at her and there was nowhere to go—the sandy shoulder of the road led directly down into the green waters of the Bay. Phil saw her entire life flashing in front of her eyes, reflected in the huge truck's chrome bumper. Just when she was regretting spending so much of it with Christian, the truck swerved back into place behind the Town Car.

Heart thundering in her ears, Phil took in a gasping breath. As the idiot in the pick-up blew past her, she laid on the horn and opened her mouth to tell him what she thought of him and his driving skills. "Have a nice day!" she heard herself shouting, shaking her fist at the man behind the wheel. "I think you're an excellent driver!"

She stared in bewilderment as the truck passed her. What she'd meant to say was that he was an idiot and the worst driver on the road or something along those lines. She could still taste the fear, sour and electric, at the back of her throat and her heart was galloping. She could have died back there! And a near death experience was enough to leave anyone tongue tied, wasn't it? Surely it didn't have anything to do with her wish...did it?

Phil tried to put the doubt to the back of her mind but she felt a niggling apprehension as she drove on towards Starfish Cove. Well, she reminded herself as the wind whipped through her hair, whatever happened, the most important thing was to let Josh knew how she felt. Nothing else mattered.

Starfish Cove was a quiet beach with spotless white sand edged by tall feathery bushes Phil didn't know the name of. She was fairly sure that her nana would have known since she loved to garden and made a mental note to ask her. The bushes provided some privacy and formed little nooks along the beach where covered picnic tables and outdoor barbeque grilles had been erected. It was perfect for a gathering the size of BB&D's, Phil admitted grudgingly. The last office beach party had been located at a noisy public beach.

She parked in the sandy parking lot and got out, the scent of cooking hot dogs wafting through the air. Her stomach fluttered as she adjusted her bikini top self-consciously, grabbed her big straw beach bag, and headed toward the beach. She was hoping like crazy that Josh would already be there but she wasn't too surprised that his Hybrid wasn't in the parking lot yet—her best friend had never been on time for anything in his life that Phil knew of. Instead, the first person she saw was Kelli. She was wearing a bright yellow one piece suit with an electric blue towel wrapped around her narrow hips.

"Hi, Kelli." Phil waved, determined to treat her coworker in a professional and adult fashion despite the debacle in the HR review the day before.

Kelli scrunched her nose and frowned. For a minute, Phil didn't think she was going to answer. But then her talkative nature seemed to reassert itself and she greeted her grudgingly. "Hi, Philomena. How are you?"

"Fine, thanks. How's the party so far?" Phil asked, feeling that things were going remarkably well all things considered.

"It's all right. You know, I wasn't going to talk to you today. Not after what you said about me talking too much in that HR thing, anyway. But I'm not the kind of person to hold a grudge."

Of course she wasn't, not when there was a chance she could get someone to listen to her yap. Phil was profoundly glad she didn't feel compelled to say that out loud, though, and since she was going to be working with Kelli for the foreseeable future, she decided it was better to smooth things over.

"You know, Kelli, what I said in the HR review didn't really come out the way I planned," she began. "What I really meant to say was..." *that we should limit our non-business conversation while we're at work.* To her surprise, what came out of Phil's mouth was, "we don't have enough hours in the day to catch up with each other."

"What?" Kelli frowned. "That's like, so *not* what you said it in the meeting."

"I...I...know but..." Phil frowned. She was giving Kelli the wrong idea and if she didn't get things straight her coworker would begin talking her ear off again.

"I mean, I thought you said you thought I talked too much?"

"I did say that and..." *sometimes you do talk too much, especially when I'm trying to work.* "And I was wrong. You don't talk too much at all. I really enjoy your conversation, especially when I'm working." Phil was horrified.

"Really?" Kelli was staring at her.

"I...I..." Phil shook her head violently, trying to make the words come out right. "What I meant to say was..." *I hate the way you're always talking about yourself and the trivial details of your life when I'm trying to work! Your constant yapping drives me insane!* "I love to hear all your fascinating little stories while we're at work. They really brighten my day."

"Well, isn't that *sweet*. Come on, the party's over here." Kelli linked her arm through Phil's, drawing her through the large feathery bushes and onto the expanse of white sugar-fine sand. "I guess you were just having a bad couple of days. Probably that time of the month—I know *I* turn into a total bitch when my aunt Gazelda comes to town."

"Aunt...Gazelda?" Phil asked hesitantly.

"Oh." Kelli gave a high pitched giggle that drilled through Phil's head. "That's what we used to call it when we got our periods. I have six sisters, you know, and we used to get into all kinds of trouble! The stories I could tell..." She gave Phil a sharp look. "But I don't want to bore you."

Phil felt strongly that hearing Kelli tell about her six sisters would be the most boring thing imaginable but when she opened her mouth to say so (in a tactful way, of course) what came out was, "Oh, no please! It sounds fascinating."

"Well, then. There was this one time..." Kelli dragged her down the beach towards the BB&D party while Phil tried to figure out what was going on. This had to be due to her birthday wish and her fairy godmother's maliciously lazy magic again. Would she now be forced to lie to everyone she met? Or was it simply that she was going to have to keep saying nice things she didn't mean? It would probably tickle the FG's funny bone (if she had one) to make Phil unable to say anything but insincere compliments after the way they had lambasted her yesterday morning.

"...so glad I can talk to you because, you know, Mister Dickson has expressly forbidden anyone who wasn't actually at the review to talk about it. On pain of losing our jobs—can you imagine?"

At least Kelli's prattle drew Phil's attentions from her own problems. Apparently they had moved from her coworker's childhood and back to the disastrous HR review.

"Did he really say that?" she asked weakly, glad that her words came out as she intended.

Her coworker nodded emphatically. "Oh, yes! In fact, I—oh, wait. Don't talk about it now. Hello, Alison!" she cooed as their coworker came strutting down the beach. She was draped over the arm of Greg Hansford, who was generally acknowledged to be the second most eligible bachelor at BB&D. He was smiling broadly, apparently unaware that he had replaced Davis Miles in Alison's affections only by virtue of his sexual orientation.

"Howdy, ya'll." He grinned, showing big white teeth like tombstones. He was from the Dallas/Fort Worth area and he always reminded Phil of the Westerns her nana had made them watch when she and her sisters were younger.

"Uh, howdy," she said, trying to smile. "How are you, Alison?"

"I'm just fine; don't you worry about me." Alison gave them a catty smile and pressed closer to Greg, rubbing her breasts against his arm. She was wearing a pink bikini so tiny it might as well have not been there at all. Phil had been of the opinion that she would never see a smaller or more revealing bikini than the red mesh one she'd tried on for Josh at RipTide the day before, but Alison's outfit left it in the dust.

Alison seemed to read her mind. "How do you like my suit, Philo*mena*?" she asked, giving Phil an arch look. "Greg here just loves it, don't you, Greggy?" She pressed her breasts against his arm again and Greg's chest puffed up with pride.

"Sure do, kitten." He gave Alison a wide grin and his eyes took a leisurely visual tour of her skimpy attire. "I think it's right pretty."

Greggy? Kitten? Phil felt like she might be sick. She would have liked to tell Alison *exactly* what she thought of her little pink bikini, but when she opened her mouth what came out instead was, "I think it's lovely, Alison. Very tasteful."

"Really?" Allison gave her a surprised look as Phil struggled inwardly. Then it hit her—the way her wish was screwed up. Rory's off-hand statement about Phil needing the exact opposite of her first wish had given their fairy godmother another loophole and now Phil was stuck saying the exact opposite of what she felt.

Phil went weak in the knees. How could she go through the next month or however long it took the FG to get back from Patagonia saying the exact opposite of what she was feeling?

"Philomena?" Kelli was nudging her. "Alison asked you a question."

"I'm sorry, what?" Phil looked up from her dazed contemplation of the sand around her flip-flops.

"I said, do you really like my suit or are you just saying

that?" Alison demanded, her eyes narrowed.

I think that is the single sluttiest suit I have ever seen. You ought to have more respect for yourself than to wear that in public. Not to mention the fact that it's disgusting the way you're hanging all over Greg Hansford just because you couldn't get Davis Miles, Phil thought. But what came out of her mouth was, "It's such a flattering suit, Alison, and it's wonderful that you have the body to wear it out on a public beach. And you and Greg make a great couple, too."

"Oh, you *do*," Kelli hastened to agree. "How long have you been together?"

Alison's mouth dropped into a round "O" of surprise but Greg Hansford just grinned. "Well since you ask, we just kinda hooked up today. Didn't we, kitten?"

"Um, yes." Alison seemed to remember that she was supposed to be charming Hansford's trunks off because she brightened her smile. "Yes, we did, Greggy-weggy. These office beach parties are so much fun because you get to see what everyone has on under their suits." She stroked Hansford's arm suggestively. "Turns out Greg here was hiding some pretty impressive muscles."

Phil eyed her coworker's rather flabby midsection. *I wouldn't quit my day job to enter the Mister Universe contest if I were you, Greggy-weggy,* she thought. But... "You certainly do look good in those swim trunks," she heard herself saying helplessly. "Maybe you should take some time off work and enter some kind of bodybuilding competition."

Greg Hansford's chest puffed up even farther. "Well, now, maybe I'll just do that one of these days. What do you think of Philomena's idea, kitten?"

"I think I need to take you farther down the beach where I can admire your muscles all by myself," she said. "Come on, Greggy." She must have thought Phil had designs on her latest catch because she shot her a dirty look before tugging Hansford back up the beach.

"Bye, Alison, see you later." Kelli waved happily with the hand that wasn't clutching Phil's arm. "Whew," she muttered under her breath as Alison and her latest prey made their way across the sand. "I thought you two were going to go at it hammer and tongs, Philomena! And, Omigod, if you had, I *so* would have been right there with you. Alison is such a bitch! And after what she said in that review yesterday..."

So they were back to the earlier subject of conversation. "Hmm." Phil nodded. She could see why both Dicksons would want to keep their nasty little secrets to themselves. "So you haven't told anyone?"

"Not a word. But I've been *dying* to talk about it. I mean, can you believe everything that came out? The cross-dressing and the porn, not to mention the fact that Davis Miles is g—" She shut up abruptly and when Phil looked up, she understood why.

They had finally reached the site of the main party and BB&D employees were milling around barbeque grills where some hotdogs and hamburgers were roasting. Standing in front of one of the grills with a pair of tongs in one hand and lite beer in the other was Davis Miles. And directly beside him with one arm around his waist was a handsome man with blondish brown hair and pale blue eyes. The hand on Miles's waist was very definitely more than friendly and as Phil watched, the man leaned forward and nuzzled against the lawyer's neck, making Miles blush.

"Stop that, Jonathan, we're in public," he yelped, but there was no real anger in his tone.

"It's a private beach and besides, you weren't complaining last night," the other man murmured, so low that Phil barely caught the words.

"Well, I didn't think... Oh, hello." Miles looked up and caught Phil's eye, giving her a friendly smile. "Hang on," he told the man. "I just need to say a word to my coworker here."

He approached Phil, and Kelli made a quick excuse and melted into the crowd. Phil got the distinct feeling that she thought gayness might be catching.

"Mister Miles," she said, hoping her mouth would behave. "How are you?" There, that had come out okay, she thought with relief. Maybe she'd be okay if she just stuck to questions instead of opinions.

"Ms. Swann...Phil, I just wanted you to know that I don't care if you talk about what I said in the HR review yesterday. I know there was a memo that went out saying any discussion would lead to instant termination but I don't feel that way. In fact I'm really glad what came out...well, came out." Miles grinned and gestured to the man still standing by the barbeque. "Meet Jonathan, my partner for the last five years."

"Hello." Phil nodded at the other man. Jonathan waved back and gave her a broad smile.

Miles cleared his throat. "I, uh, don't know what you did in there yesterday or even if it was you, but I never could have brought him here today if it hadn't happened. I'm very grateful that I was outted."

Phil was at a loss for words which was probably a good thing. "Uh, you don't say?" she murmured at last.

"Yes, he does." Jonathan came forward and put an arm around Miles's neck. "And just for the record," he said, winking at Phil. "He *does* look pretty spectacular naked."

Oh God—Phil had almost managed to forget the indecent remark she'd made when her birthday wish was first granted. *I didn't mean I really wanted to see him naked!* she wanted to protest. *It's not like my biggest fantasy or anything.* But she said, "I meant everything I said, you know. I really want to see Mister Miles completely buck naked—I fantasize about it all the time."

"Oh, er, really." Davis Miles was looking uncomfortable but Jonathan seemed to find Phil's statement hilarious.

"You and me both, girlfriend," he chuckled, patting Miles on the bottom. "You ought to see him when he does a strip tease for me. He starts out just wearing one of those crisp, sexy business suits and when he gets down to his hot little g-string—"

"Jonathan, that's enough," Miles said sharply. "These are my coworkers, not a group of our friends on Margarita Tuesdays at Benji's."

But Jonathan was on a roll. "Oh, and you should *see* him on Margarita Tuesdays, too. Get a few girly drinks into Davey here and he'll do anything. And I do mean *anything.*"

Phil was spared from making another embarrassing comment by a voice behind her.

"Ahem. Philomena, I need to speak to you. In private, please.'

Phil turned to see her boss Atwood Dickson Junior standing behind her looking uncomfortable. Predictably, he was wearing a bright orange Speedo that left little to the imagination. The vast, hairy slab of his belly overhung the garishly colored swimsuit and he appeared to have even more black, curly hair on his shoulders this year than he had the year before.

"Hi," she said. "Wow, that's a great swimsuit. It doesn't make me sick to my stomach at all to see all your body hair."

Dickson gave her a confused look, as though he was uncertain if he had been insulted or not. Jonathan stifled a giggle behind his hand. Davis Miles nudged his boyfriend sharply.

"Ahem. Well then." Dickson frowned. "As I was saying, I need to speak to you."

Phil nodded, afraid of what would happen if she opened her mouth. She allowed Dickson to lead the way around the main party and back toward one of the secluded little coves the high, feathery bushes made all along the beach. As she followed him, Phil tried not to notice how the hair on his back looked like a furry black jacket.

When they were alone, Dickson turned to her. "Philomena, I wanted to speak to you about the review yesterday."

"Oh?" Phil asked carefully.

"Yes. You left too early to hear the end of it or get the memo but it's very important to certain, ahem, *parties* that what was said in that room remains there."

Phil tried to hide her grimace. Like she *wanted* to discuss her boss's nasty furry porn habit with anyone she knew! *He's probably addicted to that kind of pornography because he's so hairy himself!*

"Do you understand?" Dickson demanded.

Phil wanted to simply nod, but her mouth opened its own accord and she said, "No, I don't understand. Besides, I want to discuss your addiction to Internet porn with everyone I know. I guess the fact that you're practically wearing a fur coat made out of hair doesn't have anything at all to do with your weird fetish."

"Why...I...You..." Dickson's face began to turn red. He took a menacing step towards Phil.

I'm sorry! she wanted to say. *I didn't mean anything I said just now. And I shouldn't have said that I'd rather sleep with a goat than you the other day either.*

"I'm *not* sorry for anything I said," she shouted, unable to help herself. "And I meant it when I said I'd rather have sex with a diseased billy goat than you."

"You little...I'll have you fired for that! You'll never work in this town again!" Dickson was looming over her.

"Mister Dickson, I...I..." Phil shook her head frantically, but her boss was not to be appeased.

"I don't know what's gotten into you this week, but I've had about enough of it!" he roared, clamping one meaty hand around her upper arm and pinching hard. "I don't want to hear any more of your lip, you little bitch!"

"Mister Dickson, please!" Phil slapped at him with the straw beach bag she was still clutching in one hand but there was no getting away from his punishing grip. Loose sand got into her flip-flops and she floundered helplessly.

"Now, you listen to me, *sweetheart,*" he growled, yanking her forward so that they were nose to nose. Phil noticed distractedly that his coffee breath was worse than ever. Who drank coffee on the beach? "You're going to apologize for all the bullshit you've been spouting and you're going to swear to take everything you heard at that HR review to your grave or so help me God, I'll—"

"Or you'll what? Ask your daddy to make you partner sooner because the paralegals have been talking behind your back?"

Phil looked up to see Josh standing at the edge of the bushes that hid them from view. He was wearing the black swim trunks and his arms were crossed over his bare muscular chest. There was a frown on his face and his dark brown eyes held a dangerous glint which Phil had never seen there before.

"What do *you* want?" Dickson snarled. "Philomena and I are having a little talk here. So *leave.*"

"I don't think so." Josh's voice was deceptively mild but Phil could see the muscles in his chest and upper arms bunching with tension. She was surprised that her boss wasn't a little more frightened at the sight of Josh looming over him like a thundercloud about to explode. His jaw was clenched and so were his fists. But apparently Dickson was so used to being in charge, he didn't see the danger.

"Josh," she said desperately, shaking her head. She didn't want to be the reason Josh lost his job and the testosterone was suddenly so thick she could have cut it with a knife. Violence was imminent.

"Let her go," Josh said softly, still looking at her boss. "I won't say it again, Dickson."

Dickson took a deep, growling breath that jiggled his hair belly and glared up at Josh. "And *I* won't say *this* again— Philomena and I are having an important discussion and until we reach an understanding, she's not going anywhere. So just turn around and leave, Bowman, or you can kiss your job goodbye."

"Then I guess you can consider this my two weeks' notice." Josh took a step forward, his brown eyes narrowed with rage. He moved so quickly his fist was a blur and Phil didn't even see the punch until it landed right in Dickson's face. Her boss didn't see it either because he didn't even try to duck. The next thing Phil knew, Dickson was down on the sand holding his streaming nose with both hands and yelping like a kicked dog.

"Come on." Josh grabbed her hand and pulled her away.

Chapter Thirty

"Oh my God, Josh! What did you...? Why did you...?" Phil looked up at her best friend in shock.

"He had it coming," Josh said shortly, shaking out his hand as though his knuckles hurt. "Hardheaded son of a bitch—I think he broke my hand." He gave a short, barking laugh.

Phil looked at him anxiously. "Josh, I just don't... Why did you do that? Your job—"

"Screw the job." He frowned at her, the muscle in his strong jaw still jumping. "You don't know how often I've wanted to punch that asshole, Phil. That was for every time he ever pinched you or touched you or made a nasty remark. For every time he made you cry."

"Oh, Josh..." Right there under the deep blue sky and the hot Florida sun, Phil felt her heart melting like a Popsicle. All her doubts seemed to fade away. How many times had she tried to tell Christian what she went through at work, only to be put off because he was too busy or too tired to hear it? Josh not only listened—he cared enough to do something about it. True, what he had done was macho and over the top and would probably get him fired, but just the fact that he didn't care if he lost his job as long as he got vengeance for her made her feel even warmer.

Phil put her arms around his neck and hugged him hard. Did she love him? Hell yes! Did she want him in her life as more than a friend? Most definitely. She still wanted to take things slow but she was sure Josh would understand that when she explained how she felt.

Josh pulled her close and wrapped her tight in his arms.

He nuzzled his face against the side of her neck and Phil felt a shiver of pleasure run through her at the intimate contact. The hard, muscular wall of his chest felt wonderful pressed against her body and the scent of his skin, warm and spicy, filled her senses.

"I love your hair this way," he murmured in her ear. "And I'm glad you wore the suit." He pulled back a little to look her up and down and then glanced at the pale blue expanse above them. "And I was right—it is the exact color of your eyes when the sky is clear."

Phil still didn't understand how he could notice such things but she didn't care either. All that mattered was that she had realized her true feelings for her friend before it was too late. Before he got on the plane for California and she never saw him again. Just the thought made her apprehensive and a new worry entered her head. If he lost his job here for punching out Dickson, the job in California was going to look twice as attractive.

"Josh?" she asked, looking up at him uncertainly. "Are you still going on that job interview?"

He shrugged, his broad shoulders rolling. "Well, I probably should seeing that I'm pretty sure my talents won't be needed at BB&D any more. But..." He looked down at her hopefully. "Can you give me a reason to stay? I mean, I know it's not fair to ask while you're still with Christian..."

Phil shook her head mutely, afraid her words would come out wrong.

"So you're *not* with him anymore?" Josh's face showed a cautious optimism

"I..." Phil shook her head again, emphatically, and clamped her lips shut.

"Phil that's...God!" he pulled her close again and she shivered when she felt his warm breath against the skin of her throat. "Does this mean you think we could be more than friends?" Josh murmured in her ear. He stroked her hair and pressed a slow, hot kiss to the side of her throat, just the way he had in the RipTide dressing room the day before. "*Much* more than friends?"

Yes! Yes, I want you in my life as much more than a friend. She opened her mouth and said, "No. I'm sorry, Josh, but I just

can't see you in my life as anything more than a good friend."
Oh, God—now what?

Josh pulled away. "Phil, are you sure? I mean... Maybe I'm
coming on too strong. I just...I know you're probably going to
want to take some time if you just got out of a relationship and
this is moving kind of fast but I can't help it...I love you."

*I love you too! I want this as much as you do! I think I've
always loved you; I just couldn't let myself admit it while
Christian was in the way.*

"I'm sorry, Josh," her traitorous mouth said instead. "But I
don't love you. I don't think I ever had those feelings for you."

Josh was pale beneath his tan. He gave a shaky laugh and
ran both hands through his thick brown hair. "Okay, well,
that's..." He shrugged. "I guess that's it then. I'm uh, sorry I
misinterpreted your feelings."

Phil wanted to die. She wanted a hole to open up right
there on the beach and swallow her up. Why was her fairy
godmother such a bitch? She was losing the sweetest, kindest,
best man she had ever known all because of a bit of magic gone
wrong. Surely there must be a way around it!

"Wait, I..." She dropped her beach bag, grabbed Josh's
hand and pulled him towards the wet, packed sand closer to
the water.

"Phil, look, I really..."

"Wait. Look." Phil found what she was looking for—a long
thin piece of driftwood lying on the wet sand. She grabbed it
and began writing in straggling letters along the surf. *Josh, I am
so not in lo...* Crap! Phil looked at what she'd written and kicked
sand over it. She moved down the beach, the sun beating on
her head like a hammer and her heart pounding in her chest as
she tried again. *I don't love y...* was as far as she got this time.
Dammit! The stupid wish wouldn't even let her *write* what she
really felt.

"Phil, look. I get the picture—you don't feel like I do. But
you don't have to write it out. I can take a hint—I'll go."

No! Don't go! "Yes, I guess you'd better leave," Phil heard
herself saying.

Josh muttered something that sounded like, "Sorry." The
set of his broad shoulders was stiff and angry but Phil thought
she saw the glitter of tears in his warm brown eyes as he

turned. She'd driven away not only her best friend but also very possibly the love of her life.

Standing in the wet sand watching him walk away from her, Phil felt her eyes filling with tears. She wanted to run after him, to stop him from going, but what good would it do? She would only hurt him more because she couldn't help what came out of her mouth. The more she wanted him, the more she loved him, the more her words would drive him away.

She could imagine life with Josh so clearly—waking up with him in the morning, falling asleep with him at night, being held in his arms, laughing with him, loving him. And all of that was going straight down the drain because of her rotten, stupid birthday wish! *It's a damn good thing that skinny bitch is in Patagonia*, she thought savagely. *If I could get my fingers around her scrawny throat...*

The tinny strains of "Pachelbel's Canon" from inside the large straw beach bag cut into her thoughts. Josh was walking fast, already past the area where the BB&D party was being held and there was nothing she could do or say to stop him. Feeling a leaden sense of defeat, Phil wandered back up the sand to where her beach bag was lying on its side and fished for her cell phone.

"Hello?" she said dully, watching as Josh headed for the parking lot, disappearing from her life forever.

"Phil? Are you there? Listen, we have a major crisis over here."

"Cass? Is that you?" Phil could barely hear her younger sister over the chaos on Cass's end of the phone. "What's going on?"

"How fast can you get here?" Cass demanded. "No, never mind that—just come back to the house and hurry."

"Is it Nana? Did she mix another potion?" Phil demanded, panicking. She wiped the tears away from her eyes and stood up straighter.

"She swears she didn't but all hell is breaking lose anyway. Down—get down! I mean it!" This last didn't seem to be directed at Phil. "Look, Phil, just *come*," she snapped, and the phone went dead.

Chapter Thirty-One

The broad double doors to the huge lavender house stood wide open and a scene of unbelievable chaos greeted Phil's arrival.

Nana was standing on the cushions of the brown leather couch that had been in the living room for as long as Phil could remember. Only she wasn't really standing—she was dancing and holding a broom in her hands. She was beating at what looked liked nineteen or twenty yipping white animals that were trying to jump on the couch to get to her. They were such a blur of motion and activity that it took Phil a moment to realize they were miniature poodles—Mister Clausen hadn't been kidding when he said he'd had a big batch of them. And every male animal he owned was apparently hot for her grandmother.

"Get away from me! Oh, you naughty animals! Stop it—*stop it*, I say!" she cried, flailing wildly at the crazed poodles. Every once in a while one of them would make it up onto the couch and start vigorously humping one of Nana's calves until she swept it off the cushions again with broom.

As Phil watched, stunned, Cass rushed past her with a writhing poodle under each arm. "Well, don't just stand there!" she shouted. "Grab some poodles and chuck 'em outside." She ran to the front door and threw the poodles out, slapping it closed before they could get back in.

"I've got some!" Rory stumbled past them still dressed in the smock she wore at the veterinary clinic. Her arms were full of yapping poodles but as she threw her shoulder against the door and tossed them out of the house, the two that Cass had evicted moments before scampered back inside and resumed their frenzied vigil around the couch.

"Oh, *no*," Cass groaned. "This is never going to work! Don't keep letting them in, Rory!"

"I was *trying* to throw them out!" Rory looked close to tears and Phil wondered how long they had been trying to rid the house of lovesick poodles. She opened her mouth to ask but was interrupted by a pounding on the front door.

In a daze, she opened it, letting in the two dogs Rory had thrown out and coming face to face with a very angry Mister Clausen. Quickly she stepped outside and shut the door behind her, muffling the sounds of poodle panic.

"Yes, Mister Clausen?" she said, smiling helpfully.

"Philomena Swann, I want a word with you. I certainly do!" he exploded. His faded blue eyes were narrowed and his face was so red the shock of cotton white hair that always stuck up from the top of his head looked like it was pasted on a wrinkled beet. He held up a withered, dirt covered object that appeared to be oozing some kind of yellow gunk from one end. "What do you think this is?"

Phil looked at it in confusion. "I don't know. What *is* it?"

"It's the nice éclair I gave you t'other day as a little refreshment. And what do you do with it? Do you eat it? No!" Mister Clausen shoved the decimated pastry in her face and Phil saw that many tiny bites had been taken out of it. But her nose told her everything she needed to know—the eye watering whiff of Nana's last love potion came from the wizened éclair. "Instead you bury it in the dirt where my prize winning poodles can get at it."

"I...I..." Phil didn't know what to say but suddenly the reason for the poodles' crazy affection for her nana became clear.

"D'ya happen ta know what happens when a dog eats chocolate? Even a little bit like the frostin' on this here éclair?" Mister Clausen demanded.

As if to answer his question, the door flew open again and Cass stuck her head out. "Phil, get in here quick!" she gasped. "They're shitting everywhere!"

"What?" Phil turned from the enraged Mister Clausen to her desperate sister.

"Cass is right." Rory appeared beside her sister, sweating and pushing her bedraggled red hair out of her eyes. "It's worse than the time we had an outbreak of distemper at the kennel!"

"Wait just a gol durn minute! Have you got some of my dogs in there?" Mister Clausen pushed past Phil and between Cass and Rory to get into the house, despite their efforts to stop him. Phil followed their neighbor; the situation inside had gotten dramatically worse.

"Oh, you naughty...nasty...Oh!" Nana was still beating the poodles back but now she was holding the broom with one hand and her nose with the other. The poodles appeared to be as enthusiastic in their courtship as ever but some of their white curly coats were not quite as white as they had been. Phil stared in dismay at the minefield Nana's highly polished hardwood floor had become. Then the stench hit her and she gagged.

"Holy cats!" Mister Clausen shouted over the yapping. "What the hell is goin' on in here? What have ya done to my dogs?"

"Mister Clausen, wait a minute. It's not what it looks like," Cass began.

"No, really it's not!" Rory added. "And we promise that—" But she stopped abruptly. "Mister Clausen? Are you okay?"

Mister Clausen looked at the remains of the éclair, which he still held in one hand and then brought it to his nose and took a deep sniff. Phil could see where this was going, but she didn't know how to stop it.

"Let him smell it!" she shouted to Cass, who was closest to the old man. "Let him smell it as much as he wants and I'm sure he won't get the hots for Nana at all!" Of course she was trying to say, *Don't let him smell it or he'll get the hots for Nana!* But the wish wouldn't let her. Cass only stared at her, uncomprehending.

"Let him smell what? Why would he have the hots for Nana?" she demanded.

Phil realized she would have to take matters into her own hands. Pushing past her sisters she tried to knock the potion-impregnated éclair out of Mister Clausen's arthritic fingers. But it was too late.

Mister Clausen's hand clenched and éclair oozed out of his fist. His gaze was already fixed on Nana.

"Minerva!" He growled Nana's name in a hoarse voice,

staggering toward the couch as though being towed by an invisible rope. "Have I ever told you how lovely you are? Your lips like autumn strawberries. Your ears, the tenderest cauliflower. Such a sexy lady!"

"Oh no!" Rory wailed as Mister Clausen reached the couch, kicking his beloved poodles aside and stepping in dog crap to get to their grandmother. "Now *he's* nuts for Nana too!"

"No shit, Sherlock," Cass muttered in disgust. Then she looked at the bottom of her black army boot. "Well, actually, there's plenty of shit but—"

"This is wonderful," Phil yelled, no longer caring if what she said made any sense at all. "This isn't at all what I was trying to warn you about!"

"What do you mean you tried to warn us?" Cass snapped. "You just kept shouting something about letting him smell something."

Rory frowned. "Yeah, Phil. What were you talking about? Smell what?"

Phil tried to think of a way to explain, but frustration overwhelmed her. "This is the best day of my life!" she stormed. "First I tell my best friend and the love of my life how I really feel about him, so there's no chance he's going to fly to California and I'll never see him again. And then I come home to find this lovely, peaceful scene of domestic tranquility which isn't even a little bit crazy."

"Sheesh, Phil, you don't have to be so sarcastic," Cass muttered. "We're sorry we had to interrupt your love connection with Josh but at least you got to tell him how you feel."

"That's just it—I *did* get to tell him how I feel. And I *didn't* tell him the exact opposite and drive him out of my life forever at all!" Phil yelled.

"Oh my God—the exact opposite!" Rory's face went chalk white. "What I said to the FG. Oh, Phil, I'm so sorry! Please tell me you didn't—"

"Mister Clausen—I'm surprised you're suggesting such a thing! I assure you that I am not now, nor will I ever be, interested in wearing a dog collar and being your 'bitch'." Their grandmother's sharp voice cut through the conversation and Phil turned to see Nana aim a well-timed swat of the broom at her elderly neighbor instead of his dogs.

"Now then, darlin', you don't mean that," he protested, ducking with surprising agility and trying to get close enough to nibble on her ear. "Let me just show you the collar. It's the prettiest little thing—just made for a dainty little gal like you."

"We've got to get him off her before he starts humping her leg—or worse," Cass said darkly.

"Well what are we supposed to do?" Rory wailed. "Call the police and tell them that Nana's neighbor and about twenty of his dogs are trying to assault her all at once?"

"You know we can't involve the police!" Cass's violet eyes flashed. "How could we possibly explain this mess? Hell, I don't even understand what caused all this in the first place." She glared at Phil. "Do you?"

Phil looked at the remains of the éclair, still smeared all over Mister Clausen's hand. "It probably doesn't have anything to do with the poodles getting into the éclair I buried next to the potion in the garden," she said.

"Why bring it up if it doesn't have anything to do with it?" Cass demanded.

"No, don't you get it? She's saying it *does* have something to do with it," Rory said. "It's what I said to the FG—it screwed up her wish and she's saying the opposite of everything she thinks."

"Phil, is that right?" Cass turned toward her, frowning.

"No." Phil said, nodding her head frantically.

"Wait—so you're saying you buried an éclair right by the potion where the dogs could get to it?"

"No," Phil said, nodding again.

"Well, I'm sure she didn't mean to," Rory defended her.

"Mister Clausen, I must insist that you keep your distance!" their grandmother's shriek made Phil look up again. Mister Clausen was trying to steal a kiss and Nana wasn't having any of it. She was trying to keep him at arm's length, but he was more determined than his poodles.

"Just one little kiss, Minerva, darlin'," he wheedled, dodging the broom Nana was poking at him like a martial arts expert. "I never realized what a sexy little lady you are."

"That's it." Cass started to march forward through the forest of yapping, crapping poodles, a grim look on her face. But

Phil had an idea.

"Wait!" She put a hand on Cass' arm to stop her, still eyeing the éclair smeared on Mister Clausen's hand. "We can't lead them all out onto the porch and spray them down with the hose," she said, hoping her sisters would understand her opposite speak. "There's no way it would help to get rid of the remains of the potion that's on the éclair Mister Clausen isn't holding."

"Okay, wait a minute..." Cass seemed to have the hang of it now. "You're saying we have Nana make a mad dash for the door, leading the poodles and Mister Clausen outside, then spray them all with the hose to get rid of the potion?"

"No!" Phil exclaimed, nodding emphatically.

"Actually that's a really good idea," Rory said.

"Probably the best we're going to get anyway," Cass muttered. "Okay, Phil, you go man the hose since nothing you say makes sense. Be ready to spray the minute I yell go."

"What do you want me to do?" Rory asked.

Cass turned to her. "Grab Nana's hand and help her off the couch. You pull her out the door while I keep Mister Clausen and those crazy dogs off her. Lead her outside so Phil can blast them with then hose when they follow. Everybody got it? Okay—go!"

Phil ran outside. It was a good thing she was still wearing the sky blue polka-dotted bikini, she thought, as she went for the hose. She turned on the water and pulled the long coiled length with its spray attachment around to the front steps, ready to let loose on the pack of potion drenched dogs plus one elderly man.

"Ready?" Cass shouted.

"No!" Phil yelled back, her finger tightening on the trigger.

"Okay then, we're coming out."

There was a scuffling sound and Phil could hear Nana protesting, then she and Rory came running out of the house, hand in hand, followed closely by Cass with the broom in her hands. Behind Cass, trying to get around the broom, was Mister Clausen. The nineteen or twenty now-more-brown-than-white miniature poodles were hot on his heels.

Phil waited until Nana, Rory, and Cass were past and then

opened fire at Mister Clausen. She only caught him a glancing blow but she sprayed the poodles pretty well. Then the whole bizarre parade was around the corner of the house and she had to wait for them to go all the way around the porch and come back to the front again.

On the next go round, she managed to spray Mister Clausen in the face but he only sputtered and kept right on after Nana. Her grandmother was running quite nimbly despite her age, Phil noted, and it wasn't long before they were around the corner again.

Around and around they went, Nana, Rory, and Cass, followed by a bellowing Mister Clausen and the yapping poodles, all of them getting progressively wetter. By the fifth circuit, some of the poodles were beginning to lose interest and were straggling down onto the front lawn to shake out their sodden fur. But there was no stopping Mister Clausen. Phil couldn't help but wonder if he had already had an interest in her grandmother that the potion had exacerbated. She kept trying to aim for the soggy remains of the éclair in his hand but he was moving too fast for her to hit it.

"Mister...Clausen...please!" Nana huffed as they made what had to be the tenth circuit of the house. "I...just...can't..."

"Minerva...I...want..." But what Mister Clausen wanted wasn't to be revealed. Just as Phil was preparing to spray him again, his foot skidded in a puddle of water and he went down on the porch with a flat slapping sound that made Phil wince.

"He's down! He's down!" Rory skidded to a halt, looking over her shoulder.

"Quick!" Cass was breathing almost as hard as their grandmother. "Get Nana inside. Phil and I will deal with him."

Phil threw down the hose as Cass ran to see if Mister Clausen was all right. Luckily for him one of the poodles had wound up between his head and the hard wooden porch, so he wasn't out cold, just mildly dazed.

"Are they all right?" Phil gasped. But as she watched, the poodle who had acted as a cushion shook itself and yipped once before trotting down the steps to join its brothers on the lawn. Mister Clausen was muttering something, the remains of the éclair still clutched tight in his hand.

"What was that Mister Clausen?" Cass asked.

"Such a...sexy...lady," Mister Clausen moaned, and fainted dead away.

Chapter Thirty-Two

Rory rounded up the poodles and put them in Mister Clausen's backyard while Cass called 911 and rode with their neighbor to the ER. Phil stayed to help Nana clean up the considerable mess in the living room, thankful that the house on States Street had hardwood floors instead of carpet. By the time it was all said and done and she and her sisters and grandmother were all gathered back in the living room—which smelled strongly of Lysol—the time was nearing four o'clock.

"Oh, God, I ache all over," Rory moaned from her spot on the brown leather recliner. "And I *hate* poodles. I don't care if I am going to be a vet—I'm going to be a vet that sees any animal but poodles."

Cass gave a weary laugh. "I've heard of specializing in a certain kind of animal but never of excluding one." She and Phil were collapsed on either side of their grandmother, on the wide brown leather sofa which Phil and Nana had cleaned within an inch of its leathery life.

"I don't think it's a good idea. If Rory hates poodles, she should deal with them all day long," Phil said.

"What's that, dear?" Nana frowned at her.

"Don't pay any attention to Phil, Nana." Cass made a shooing motion with her hand. "The FG screwed her again so that now she has to say the opposite of everything she means."

"She's wrong, I don't," Phil agreed, nodding. She had been luckier than her sisters, having gotten a shower after the ordeal. Of course, there was nothing for her to put on afterwards but Cass's little red nighty since neither Rory or Nana's clothes would fit and everything else Cass owned was in the wash.

Phil didn't even care about the fact that she was lounging around in lingerie—she was just so glad to be clean. But now that all the excitement with Nana and Mister Clausen and the poodles was over, she felt her heart growing heavy. Josh was probably on his way to the airport by now.

"It's all my fault." Rory looked like she might cry. "It was something stupid I said when Phil was trying to get her wish fixed. And now because of me she's made Josh think she doesn't like him."

"I don't more than like him," Phil said sadly. "In fact, I think I don't *love* him."

"You love him? Oh, Phil—I could just *kick* myself." Rory's green eyes brimmed with tears.

"Oh, Rory." Phil sighed. "I don't forgive you. It was all your fault."

"This is...very confusing to say the least, my dears." Nana looked from Rory to Cass to Phil. "So Christian is...how do you girls say it now...out of the picture?"

"He sure is." Cass answered for her. "He'd been cheating on her for over a year! He admitted it to Phil last night."

"Oh my!" Nana put a plump hand to her bosom. "Well then, you're better off without him, Philomena. But what about that nice young man we had to dinner the other night? That Josh? Are you saying you ran him off, too?"

"She didn't mean to, Nana," Rory said miserably. "But she couldn't help it. He must have asked her if she had any feelings for him and she had to say 'no' because of the wish."

"That's exactly what didn't happen," Phil said nodding. "You shouldn't have seen the look on his face. I...I don't think he was crying when he left." She felt like she might cry herself, especially hearing the foolishness coming out of her own mouth. The idea of trying to make herself understood until the wish could be reversed was daunting but it wasn't nearly as depressing as the idea of losing Josh.

"Did he say anything about the swimsuit matching your eyes when it's sunny and there aren't any clouds again?" Cass asked.

Phil nodded, too wretched to speak.

"Wait a minute, he noticed that your eyes change?" Rory frowned. "How can he do that? I mean, I knew he could hear when we were talking about the FG but he *really* shouldn't be able to see your eye color."

"He can, though," Cass assured her. "He even noticed she hates éclairs."

"Wait, my dears." There was an excited sparkle in Nana's pale green eyes. "Are you saying that this young man, this Josh, notices things that should be invisible to non-fairy eyes though he has not a drop of fairy or fae blood in his veins?"

Phil nodded and Cass said, "That's what we were trying to tell you last night, Nana. But you were too distracted by the dogshi…uh, excrement on your shoe to pay attention."

"Oh, my dear, if only I had known!" Nana was almost breathless with excitement. "Although I *did* have a feeling from the moment I saw him…"

"Have an idea about what?" Phil demanded, glad to hear at least one sentence come out of her mouth ungarbled.

"Well, my dear, don't you see?" Nana's cheeks were flushed.

"See what?" Cass and Rory asked together.

"That this man is perfect for Philomena. He's her Prince Charming, I suppose you could say. *That* is how he is able to notice things about her that he shouldn't."

"What?" Now all the girls were talking at once. Their nana was usually so flighty it was hard to get two words of sense out of her, but every once in a while she let drop some startling nugget that shocked them all. Phil often thought it was inconvenient that their only sources of information about the fairy part of their heritage were a whimsical grandmother and a sullen fairy godmother.

"Think about it, girls." Nana laughed. "What force in the universe is stronger than magic? *All* kinds of magic?"

"Uh…" Phil had never considered that there might be a force stronger than her fairy godmother's badly wielded wand. If she had, she would have been out looking for it instead of begging like a pathetic pauper to have her wishes reversed for years.

Apparently Cass was thinking along the same lines. "You mean there's a way to undo all the crap our fairy godmother puts us through without dragging her back here and begging for a redo? Nana, why didn't you tell us before? *Years* before?"

"Silly girls, I am not speaking of Lucinda's wish granting, although I will allow that it sometimes leaves much to be desired." Nana sniffed. She was the only person Phil knew who used the FG's first name.

"Then what are you talking about?" Rory asked.

"Love." Nana patted Phil's cheek, a little smile playing around the corners of her mouth. "Love is stronger than magic. Love is why your friend—and I liked him very much by the way, Philomena dear—notices things he shouldn't be able to. To Josh, nothing about you is to be taken lightly. He notices you because he *loves* you."

"Are you serious?" Phil put a hand to her chest. She remembered thinking the same thing—or something like it—in the dressing room of RipTide, but it had seemed crazy at the time.

"Nana, are you just blowing smoke up our skirts?" Cass arched an eyebrow skeptically.

"Why ever would I do that, Cassandra? And where would I get the smoke? Cigarettes are such a vulgar habit," Nana said disapprovingly. "But to answer Philomena's question, yes, my dear, I am in deadly earnest. How do you think I met and married your grandfather? He noticed me—the real me. In my youth, you see, my hair was as blond as Philomena's with the most beautiful lavender tint. Now I know girls these days dye their hair any shade of pink or purple or green that suits them but it wasn't so when I was younger—not a bit," Nana said. "On the day when your grandfather bought me a silver necklace with an amethyst charm to match my hair, I knew he was the one even though he had not a drop of pure fairy or fae blood in his veins."

"Oh, Nana—that's so romantic." Rory smiled at her and even Cass was grinning.

"Nana, you scamp," she teased. "You never told us that before."

"You never asked." Nana patted her silvery hair primly. "Of course it didn't sit well with my father at all. He was a full-blooded fairy and he'd gone to a great deal of trouble to arrange for me to marry a man who was the same. He didn't want the family magic getting any more diluted than it already was, you see." She lifted her chin. "But I defied him and ran away with your grandfather on a night when the moon was full.

"I still remember that magical tingle the first time he took me in his arms and kissed me and I knew that I loved him with my whole heart..." She shook her head. "But there's no sense in mourning for my past—not when we have your future to look after." She gave Phil penetrating look. "Philomena, dear, if you've found a man who loves you—really loves you enough to notice all the little fairy peculiarities about you, then you ought to hang onto him."

"But, Nana, it's too late," Cass objected. "He's supposed to be flying out to California tonight and he told Phil he wasn't going to come back if they couldn't be together." She looked at Phil. "What time did you say his plane was leaving?"

Phil felt like she might cry. "Not six," she managed to say.

Rory looked at the clock. "It's past four thirty. He's probably already at the airport what with all the baggage checks and things they make you do now."

Phil felt a small stirring of hope deep down at the bottom of her heart. Josh was never on time for anything and she certainly couldn't see him getting to the airport two hours early. Chances were, he was still in his apartment in New Tampa getting the last of his things together. But then, what good would it do even if he wasn't at the airport yet? Even if she could get to his apartment in time to stop him, nothing she could say would keep him from going. In fact, whatever she said would probably make him want to leave faster!

"There is always hope, especially where true love is concerned," Nana said, cutting into her dreary thoughts. "Now, Philomena, this is serious. I want you to go find that boy and tell him how you feel."

"But she *can't*, Nana—that's what drove him away in the first place," Rory protested.

"Yeah, what is she supposed to do? Tell him how much she *doesn't* love him?" Cass said. Then she frowned thoughtfully. "But I guess one of us could go with her and explain to him. Usually the magic keeps you from talking about it to non-fairies but if he can hear and notice all that other stuff..."

"No!" Nana's voice was more stern than Phil could ever remember hearing it. "This curse—for it *is* a curse and a wish no longer, my dears—has been laid on Philomena and Philomena alone. And she alone must break it. No other may help her and no other may guide her except her heart."

"But...but I..." Phil shook her head, unable to express her doubts and fears.

"Philomena, you must go *right now*," Nana insisted. There was a steely glint in her eyes that Phil had never seen there before. "You must not waste your one chance at true love. Do you think it was easy for me to defy my father and leave in the dead of night to be with your grandfather? To leave the Realm of the Fae and come to the mortal world? It most certainly was not! But I did it and my darling, I have never regretted it for an instant." She nodded regally at Phil. "Go now and do not come back until you have found him."

"Nana's right—you should go to him, Phil," Rory said.

"Yeah, there's no harm in trying," Cass chimed in.

"Uh..." Phil bit her lip. "But what am I supposed to say?" she asked in despair, even as Cass jumped up and started pulling her to her feet.

"Say what is in your heart, my dear." Nana smiled serenely. "And remember that words are not the only means of revealing your emotions. Sometimes in this world, you have to make your own magic."

Rory and Cass were pushing her out the door. Before she knew it, Phil found herself on the still damp front porch barefoot and wearing only Cass's flimsy red baby-doll nighty.

"But...But...what about what I'm wearing?" She gestured helplessly at the tiny red lace outfit that was scarcely more decent than some of the double-dog-dare-you bikinis Josh had picked out for her the day before.

"So much the better," Cass said. "Remember what Nana said—words aren't the only way to express yourself. Use the international language."

"I think she means *body* language," Rory put in, grinning. She shoved the keys to Phil's car into one hand and her beach bag into the other. "Here, just in case you need your cell phone or something. Go get 'em."

"But...But..." Phil felt close to panic. She was fairly certain her grandmother hadn't meant her advice the way Cass was interpreting it. But her sisters were unstoppable. Even as Phil turned to protest some more, they shut the door in her face and she heard the click of the lock.

It looked like she was on her own.

Chapter Thirty-Three

As Phil headed for the car wearing nothing but the tiny nighty all she could think about was the angry set of Josh's shoulders and the tears in his true brown eyes. She almost turned back, but remembered her grandmother's words. Josh loved her—really *loved* her in a way Christian never had. In fact, he was perfect for her, according to Nana. But how could she let him know that?

Her fairy godmother's malicious magic was standing between her and the man she loved. If this was a fairy tale she'd be the princess in the tower, waiting to be rescued or the fair maiden under a spell, waiting for love's first kiss to awaken her.

Phil squared her shoulders and lifted her chin. *This is no fairy tale and I'm not helpless princess!* she told herself. *And I'll be damned if I'll sit around and wait for someone to rescue me. Nana's right—it's up to me to break this curse and get Josh back.* She felt a surge of determination and glanced down at her watch. Crap! It was almost four forty-five—she had to go now.

Phil ran to her car, not caring that the gravel driveway was sharp and pointy under her bare feet. She slipped into the driver's seat, keyed the ignition, and gunned the engine. Normally she was a very careful when she drove—what Cass called a 'granny driver'—but as she barreled out of Nana's driveway, she would have put any NASCAR driver to shame

Every light seemed to be red and every car in front of her seemed to creep but Phil finally found herself parked outside Josh's apartment building. He had a second story apartment, just a little one bedroom mostly taken up with bachelor clutter and technical equipment. She pulled up in front of the wide tan building and looked for his car. Oh, thank God—his Hybrid was still there!

Phil was about to jump out of her bug when she saw Josh on the second story landing, arguing with someone. It was a man she had never seen before—he had a huge bushy black mustache and was carrying a large tray in one hand. Her best friend was wearing a pair of jeans and a tight black T-shirt that clung to his muscular chest in a way that made her mouth water. He was carrying a suitcase and a laptop bag. Oh God, if he was taking his computer, he really was serious.

Normally Phil would have been reluctant to go out in front of God and everybody dressed in a nighty which barely reached the tops of her thighs. But desperate times called for desperate measures. Gathering her courage, she hopped out of the car and, clutching her large beach bag in front of her as a shield, she marched up the steps.

Josh was so distracted arguing with the man with the mustache and tray that he didn't see her right away.

"No, I'm telling you I didn't order those," he said, his voice annoyed. "I'm leaving to catch a plane—why the hell would I order something like that?"

"It say right here!" the man insisted in heavily accented English. "Deliver to twenty-one B. So I deliver to twenty-one B. You live twenty-one B so you pay. You pay *now*."

"No! I'm not paying for those. I'm not...Phil?" Josh broke off his argument to stare at her wide-eyed.

Phil gave him a little wave and kept her mouth shut, not knowing what she could say to keep him from going to the airport.

"Phil, what are you doing here...er, dressed like that?" There was a faint spark of hope shining in his deep brown eyes and Phil was so afraid of extinguishing that spark she actually bit her tongue.

"Josh," she ventured at last and then didn't dare to say anything else.

As she and Josh looked at each other, the man with the tray was eyeing her up and down. His mustache twitched with disapproval.

"You pay!" he said again, shaking his fist at Josh. "You can afford hooker lady, you can afford to pay for what you order!"

"What? She's not a hooker!" Josh protested, quick to jump

to her defense. "And for the last time, I didn't order those."

Phil dragged her eyes from her best friend to see that the man with the mustache was holding a bakery tray with a clear plastic lid like one you might get on a fruit or lunch meat arrangement at the local deli. But instead of fruit or cold cuts, the tray held no less than two dozen plump chocolate éclairs, all oozing yellowish custard. She felt her stomach turn over, but they couldn't stand here arguing all night.

"How much?" she asked the delivery man.

"You pay, hooker lady?" He raised a bushy eyebrow at her.

"I told you, she's *not* a hooker," Josh said insistently.

"How much?" Phil asked again, digging in her beach bag and praying she had enough cash.

"Forty dollar," the delivery man pronounced with relish.

Phil winced. No doubt about it, her fairy godmother's malignant magic was at work again. But of all the years her éclair wish had been in effect, she'd never had to actually *pay* for the loathsome pastries before. Especially not forty dollars worth.

"Phil, this guy is a con artist—you don't have to pay for those," Josh protested even as she shoved the cash at the delivery man and took the tray from him.

The man frowned under his mustache at the crumpled twenty and two tens she had given him. "No tip?"

"No, no tip! Now get out of here," Josh growled. The man ambled off, muttering something under his breath that sounded like, "cheap hooker lady", but by the time Josh turned to yell that she wasn't a hooker again, he was gone.

"I don't understand why you did that," Josh muttered, glaring at the tray of éclairs. "I thought you hated those things."

"Do you have a place I can set them?" Phil asked, trying to ask questions to avoid saying things she didn't mean.

"Sure, I guess. But I was about to turn my key in to the front office."

"Please?" Phil gave him a desperate look.

"Well...all right. But I'm already late." Even as he spoke he was unlocking the front door to let her in.

Phil stepped inside and felt a chill run down her spine. Josh had a furnished apartment so the battered couch and coffee table were still where she remembered them, but there were dozens of cardboard boxes standing around the apartment, stacked and labeled and ready to be shipped. For the first time it hit her—Josh *really* was going. That was, unless she could stop him.

"Uh, excuse the mess." Josh made a path through the boxes so she could put the tray down on the counter separating the living room from the tiny kitchenette. "I have a moving company coming in tomorrow to ship the rest of this stuff back home."

Back home. Phil felt panic rising in her throat. "Josh," she said dropping her beach bag and stepping close to him. "You have to go. You and I would never make a good couple."

The spark of hope she'd seen in his eyes died abruptly and he sighed. "I know that, Phil. You told me on the beach. Hell, you wrote it out for me."

"Wait!" She clutched at his arm, feeling like a fool. "Please...you're not the only man in the world for me! If you leave now I know I won't regret it for the rest of my life."

"What?" Josh was giving her a quizzical look. "Phil," he asked carefully. "Are you, uh, on something? Because you've been acting kind of weird all day." He glanced at his watch. "And I really need to go if I'm going to make my plane."

Phil was so frustrated she could scream. He was leaving! He was walking out of her life and there was nothing she could do about it! Then her eyes happened to fall on the tray of oozing éclairs and she had a sudden inspiration.

"Josh," she said, still hanging on to his sleeve. "Did you see Alison's bikini today?"

He shrugged. "Uh, yeah. I guess so. Pretty tacky, huh?"

"No," Phil said. "It was the most tasteful outfit I have ever seen."

"What?" Josh frowned at her, looking more confused than ever. Phil plowed ahead.

"And you know Mister Dickson, my boss?" she continued, looking at him earnestly.

"Of course I know him. He's—"

"He's the *best* boss I've *ever had,*" Phil said clearly.

Josh let out a short laugh. "Now I *know* you're on

277

something. What have you been smoking?"

"Josh, listen!" she insisted, pointing at the tray of éclairs. "Do you know how I feel about éclairs?"

"You hate them," he said immediately.

"No, I love them," Phil insisted. "I *love* éclairs. But listen..." She put both her hands on his shoulders and looked up to meet his gaze. "I don't love you, Josh." She put her heart into the words, feeling her eyes fill with unshed tears. If only he would understand! "I don't love you," she repeated softly. "Oh, Josh, I don't love you *so much.*"

"Wait...you don't...you..." Josh frowned in obvious confusion. "You don't love me, but you do love éclairs," he said slowly. "You think Alison's suit was tasteful and Dickhead Junior is the best boss you've ever had..." He frowned and then his eyes cleared. "Wait a minute, Phil. Is this something like the problem you were having where you had to say everything you thought? And then later, where *I* had to say everything *I* thought?"

"No! No!" she agreed eagerly, nodding.

"Phil..." He scrubbed a hand over his jaw, making the familiar sandpaper sound. "This is going to sound really stupid, but are you under some kind of a...I don't know, some kind of a spell or something? Like in a fairy tale?"

"No!" She nodded enthusiastically.

"Well..." Josh grinned at her uncertainly. "In every fairy tale I ever read as a kid, there was only one way to break the evil spell." He cupped her cheek in one large palm and pulled her close. "I've been waiting to do this from the first minute I saw you."

He leaned forward and took her mouth in a kiss that set her on fire. Phil reached up to bury her hands in his hair and kissed him back, giving in to the desire that had been burning in her for days.

Josh was gentle at first, barely caressing her lips with his own, but when she responded so eagerly, he kissed harder, wrapping his arms around her and demanding entrance to her mouth.

Phil opened for him willingly, giving in to the sweet, devouring kiss with her whole being. God, this was what she had been needing for so long! She no longer cared about taking things slowly or waiting a decent interval after her breakup with Christian to start a new relationship with Josh. All she could think of was how much she wanted him—how much she *needed* him. That and the warm tingling sensation racing through every nerve in her body.

Wait a minute—tingling sensation? Phil opened her eyes and pulled back from the kiss. Josh released her at once.

"Sorry, I didn't mean to—" he began, but Phil shushed him with a shake of her head. The moment she broke contact with him, the familiar tingling sensation disappeared. Experimenting, she reached up and brushed her lips against his, and was rewarded with an electric prickle that reminded her of...where had she felt that before?

Suddenly, her nana's voice echoed in her head. *"I remember that magical tingle I felt the first time he took me in his arms and kissed me and I knew I loved him with my whole heart."* That was it, Phil realized. The place she'd felt the magic tingle before was when a wish was granted. But it only happened when she and Josh were kissing. And the more intense the kiss...the more intense the tingle.

The wish that had become a curse—could they actually break it this way? There was only one way to find out. Phil reached up and pulled Josh down for another kiss. God, his mouth tasted good, like the cinnamon candy he liked so much, and his arms around her felt like warm steel. She could feel the strength and urgency in his grip, his need for her in the way he stroked her hair and back and pulled her close against him. And the way he kissed her—like he wanted to *devour* her. Christian had never kissed her like that.

"God, Phil!" It was Josh that broke the kiss this time, breaking the magical tingle as well. He was almost panting as he looked down at her, his brown eyes dark with desire. "I don't know where we're going with this but if you want to stop, we need to put on the brakes pretty soon here. I've wanted you for years and seeing you in this tiny little outfit isn't doing a damn thing for my self-control." He nodded at the lacy red nighty and Phil felt herself blushing with pleasure and desire. Suddenly she knew what she needed to do to finish breaking the curse— kissing wasn't enough. It wasn't nearly enough.

"I want you to stop now," she whispered in his ear. "And I don't want you to fuck me, Josh. I don't want you to fuck me all night long."

He drew in a breath and looked down at her, his eyes blazing. "Phil, I've never been the kind of guy who thinks no means yes but in this case..." He leaned down and picked her up in his arms. "I think I'm going to have to make an exception."

Phil wrapped her arms around his neck and nuzzled her face against the side of his strong throat, breathing in his warm, spicy fragrance. "No, Josh," she murmured, pressing herself against him. "Oh, God, *no.*"

"All right then." He passed through the towers of boxes stacked in the living room and headed straight for the bedroom at the back of the apartment. Phil shivered when he kicked open the door to reveal a queen sized bed. The mattress had been stripped bare in preparation for his move, but she didn't care. At this point she wouldn't have cared if he chose to take her right up against the wall or on the bare floor—she just *wanted* him.

Josh laid her down gently and stroked her hair. "You know, I waited until the last minute to leave. I was hoping you'd come."

"Oh, Josh." She reached up to cup his cheek, feeling the scratch of his stubble against her palm. "Please," she whispered, wanting to feel his mouth on her again. "Please, I..."

"I know," he whispered. "Me too. But let me just hold you for a minute. I've waited so long to have you, I want this to last."

Phil tugged at his T-shirt. "You should put your clothes on."

He chuffed out a laugh and sat up to pull the shirt over his head, revealing the broad expanse of his tan, muscular chest. "You know, I could almost get used to this. But I think I liked it better when you had to tell me everything you were thinking. That dream..." He shook his head. "It has to be the hottest thing I've ever heard." He lay back down beside her wearing only his jeans and gathered her close in his arms. "Never thought I'd get to make it a reality," he murmured against her neck.

"Mmm." Phil arched her back, practically purring with the pleasure of being wrapped in his strong arms. His chest was a warm, solid wall of muscle pressed against her barely covered breasts and it seemed like she just couldn't get close enough to satisfy herself. She thought about all the times Josh had hugged her or put an arm around her when she was in need of comfort. How many years had she ignored the attraction she felt for him because of the unspoken barrier between them? How many times had she pretended to herself that she felt nothing but friendship for Josh because she was blindly determined to stick with Christian no matter how bad things got? But she was free of those obstacles now and her path to Josh was clear. She was finally getting her wish—to be close to him, to be caressed all over by those big, warm gentle hands—and it was a hell of a lot better than any wish the FG had ever granted for her.

Josh nuzzled her neck again, planting a hot kiss against the vulnerable side of her throat. Phil moaned softly as another warm, magical tingle ran through her. Oh yes, this was exactly what she wanted—exactly what she *needed.*

"God, Phil, you're so soft and warm," he said in a voice that was slightly hoarse. "And this little piece of nothing you have on is driving me crazy." He pulled at the red string that tied the top of the baby doll nighty together and Phil moaned as the bow parted and the two sides fell away from her naked breasts. "Beautiful," Josh murmured before leaning down to take one of her nipples in his mouth. He sucked hard and then nipped her very gently, making Phil gasp and arch her back as a bolt of pleasure/pain shot down her spine to the damp V between her legs. She had on the tiny red lace bikini panties that went with the nighty and she wondered how long it would take for Josh to strip them away.

But Josh seemed intent on taking his time. He sucked and lapped her nipples until they were both as red and hard as cinnamon drops. Phil moaned as she felt the warm magical tingle growing between Josh and herself, like an electrical current that increased with every touch, every taste. She felt her breath catch in her throat as Josh stroked her sides and cupped her breasts. He was so gentle, so infinitely tender. It was as if she was the most precious thing he had ever touched and he didn't want to damage her.

"Josh," she moaned, pulling him closer, "Please...please no...don't suck me...my nipples any more."

He laughed softly. "I must be some kind of a pervert but hearing you beg me not to do things while I do them is making me so damn hot." He leaned down and sucked one of her nipples hard for a moment, then looked up at her again as she moaned. "You're so beautiful, Phil. I just want to touch you and kiss you everywhere." His brown eyes were full of emotion and the intensity of his gaze made Phil feel desired and cherished at the same time. It was a strange and wonderful mixture of emotions that she had never experienced before. She looked back at him, wishing she could really express how she felt and then she had an idea.

"Josh," she murmured, stoking her hand through his hair. "Please...please don't kiss me lower. Further down, I mean. Please?"

"Mmm." The sound came out almost as a growl and Josh smiled at her. "So you don't want me to kiss you here?" he asked, and planted a soft kiss just below her breasts. Phil felt the warm magical tingle and groaned.

"N...no," she whispered breathlessly. "Please, not lower. Don't kiss me lower..."

"Like here?" Josh murmured and his mouth traveled further down her body until he was licking a warm, wet trail around the cup of her naval.

"Oh, no...please," Phil gasped as the pleasurable sensation sent shock waves down her spine. She could feel herself getting wetter and hotter by the moment and she wondered how long Josh would draw this torture out.

"What about here?" Josh asked, and moved down her body until he was planting soft, hot kisses right above the low slung border of the tiny red lace panties which barely covered her mound. "Or here?" he asked in a low voice, placing his lips directly on the little scrap of red lace that was all that separated him from her wet sex.

Phil felt her breath catch in her throat as she remembered the last time his mouth had been in contact with that particular part of her anatomy. God, the memory of his fingers inside her, of his mouth on her was too much to resist.

"Please," she whispered, barely able to get the words out, "Please, Josh, don't kiss me there. Don't...don't..."

"Don't go down on you?" he asked in a low, dangerous voice. "Don't pull off your panties and spread you open so I can taste your hot little pussy? Is that what you're asking?"

Somehow, Phil managed to nod. "Please Josh, oh, God,

please...please don't do that to me," she begged softly. She was panting now and it seemed hard to get a deep breath because of the way her heart was racing.

"God, Phil, you're making me crazy," he growled, hooking his fingers into the thin side bands of the panties and pulling. They came off too quickly and one side snapped, making Phil gasp. She was going to owe Cass a whole new lingerie set—not that she cared at this point. She just wanted to feel Josh's mouth on her, to feel him exploring her with his tongue, kissing her, licking her...

She didn't have to wait long. Before she knew it, Josh had pulled her to the edge of the mattress and positioned himself between her legs. Phil bit her lip to keep back a moan at the delicious sensation of his warm hands spreading her thighs even wider so he could get to her.

"You're so beautiful," he told her again. "I love the way you look, love to breathe in your scent. I love that I can take my time with you and make you moan—I want to taste every bit of you. Want to eat your creamy pussy until you scream." He planted a soft kiss on her inner thigh and looked up at her, a devilish glint in his eyes. "Is that what you want, Phil? Tell me— I want to hear you say it. All of it."

"Oh..." Phil moaned. She was trembling with need and it felt like her heart was beating in every part of her body at once. She was sure she couldn't take this, but she knew what her lover wanted to hear. "No," she whispered, reaching down to stroke her hand through his hair. "No, Josh. Please don't...don't go down on me. *Please* don't make me scream."

"But I want to," he almost whispered, still smiling at her. "I want to do this..." He kissed the slit of her swollen sex, making Phil gasp. "And this..." He spread her open with his thumbs, exposing her completely, and placed a soft, sucking kiss over the aching bud of her clit, making her jump and groan. "And this," he murmured. Lowering his head, he licked a hot, wet trail from the bottom of her sex to the top.

Phil cried out, unable to help herself, unable to care about how she sounded. All she could think about was his mouth on her, his tongue exploring her and the magical tingle that built with every delicious movement as he kissed and licked and sucked her.

Josh looked up for a moment, his brown eyes drowning deep and his full mouth wet with her juices. "That's right," he told her in a hoarse voice. "Give it up for me, Phil. I love those soft little noises you make when you get hot. I love to hear you let it all go." Then he cupped her hips in his hands and pulled her even closer, cradling her pelvis as though it was a bowl of water and he was a man dying of thirst.

She gasped and arched her back, offering herself completely. When he had done this before in the RipTide dressing room, she had been standing up and it was impossible to be as open as she was now. But lying on the bed with Josh positioned between her legs, Phil realized she had never felt so vulnerable and yet so safe at the same time. It felt so good—so right. Josh had meant it when he said he wanted to take his time; he was exploring her thoroughly with his tongue, lapping her throbbing clit one moment and pressing his tongue deep inside her the next.

Phil cried out as he sucked the aching bud of her clit into his mouth and began to draw slow patterns across it with the tip of his talented tongue. Where had he learned to do that? And why had she known him for so many years before she found out his hidden talents? When she thought of all the time she had wasted with Christian...but she didn't want to think about that now. She just wanted to revel in the delicious feeling of being utterly and lovingly devoured as the tingling built inside her in a slow and steady arc.

"No more," she managed to gasp. "Please, Josh, no more!" Her begging seemed to make him redouble his efforts and before she knew it, Phil had both hands buried in his thick hair and she was pressing her pelvis up to meet him with complete abandon. She felt wild, shameless, and hotter than she could ever remember being in her life. This was Josh, she reminded herself, sweet, funny, sensitive Josh who could always make her laugh or talk her out of a bad mood. But there was another side of him, a hot, masculine, animal side that wanted to explore her, wanted to touch her in a way she had never been touched, to own her in a way she had never been owned.

Phil reveled in the sensation of being opened and tasted and owned but when Josh entered her with two long, fingers, she knew she wanted more—needed more. His fingers and mouth felt so good, but she needed more to reach the peak. She needed Josh inside her.

"Please," she gasped, tugging at his hair. "Please, Josh, I...don't want...don't need..." She shook her head as he looked up at her, his eyes heavy lidded with desire.

"What is it you don't need, Phil?" he growled softly. "Tell me, baby. Let me know."

The soft endearment almost as much as the intense look in his eyes made Phil's breath catch in her throat. "You," she almost whispered. "Inside me, Josh. Please, I don't need..."

"All right." Then he was on the bed beside her, cupping her cheek in his palm and sharing a sweet, hot kiss. Phil hummed in delight as he fed her the taste of herself. Finally they broke apart panting. She felt like she was going to explode if she didn't have him.

Phil stroked one hand down his warm, broad chest until she was tugging at the belt loops in the front of his jeans. "Don't take these off," she told him. "Don't take them off, *right now.*"

He grinned. "Pushy, aren't you? I think I like that." He slipped off the jeans and the shorts beneath and Phil was able to see for herself exactly how much he did in fact like it. She had seen most of him when they were trying on swimsuits, but this was the first time she'd ever seen him completely nude and she liked what she saw—all of it. His thick shaft was high and tight, close to his stomach, and it looked achingly hard. It was also quite a bit larger than what she was used to but really, she only had Christian's to compare it with.

"Can I...?" Phil raised her eyebrows at him in question and Josh nodded.

"Sure, help yourself," he said with a nervous laugh. "I just..." But his words trailed off when Phil closed her fingers around the hard, thick length of his shaft, delighting in the silky feel of his skin and the hot pulse of his desire in her palm. She felt the tingling between them spike higher at the intimate contact and smiled at the look on his face.

"God, Phil!" Josh groaned low in his throat, a sound of almost painful bliss. He half closed his eyes and tilted his head back as though overcome by pleasure. "Your soft little hand feels so good but you can't...you have to stop or this will be over before we get started. You have no idea how long I've wanted you, how long I've dreamed of this moment. I can't hold out if you keep touching me like that."

Reluctantly Phil released him. She would have liked to taste him as he had tasted her, but she sensed that Josh was too much on edge for that. Besides, there would be plenty of other opportunities for exploration—the rest of her life if she had anything to say about it. Just the thought of that, of having Josh in her heart and her life and her bed forever gave her a rush of emotion and she knew she couldn't wait any longer. She needed him now.

"Josh," she said softly, lying down on the bed and opening her legs. "*Please.*"

"Hang on just a minute." He fumbled in his discarded jeans and she saw that he had a small foil packet in one hand. How like Josh to be so considerate, she thought, not even making her ask if he had protection. And then everything else was driven out of her mind as he lay down beside her and pulled her into his arms.

"I want to hold you like this for a minute," he murmured. "All naked and soft and warm pressed against me. I love the way you feel in my arms." He kissed her again and she felt the magical tingle climb to new heights with anticipation. But Phil hadn't had sex in a very long time, months actually, now that she stopped to consider it, and she needed Josh inside her so badly her entire body ached.

"Please," she whispered urgently. "Please, Josh—I don't want you *so much.*"

"I want you too, Phil," he said, looking into her eyes. "I just didn't want to take things too fast."

Phil shook her head, trying to indicate that he couldn't possible do that, and then nuzzled under his chin, kissing his neck and nipping at the strong cords of his throat. She had never been very sexually aggressive before but she was a different woman than she had been—was it only three days before? Phil didn't know and didn't care, but she did know she liked the soft growl she got in response to her actions.

"All right then." Josh rolled her over suddenly, pinning her to the mattress with her arms above her head. "If that's the way you want it, that's the way I'll give it to you," he said. "Is that what you need, Phil? You need me to fuck you hard?"

"Oh, God, Josh, *no*," she moaned. "Please don't...don't fuck me hard...so hard and deep."

"God, Phil, you're driving me *insane*," he growled, pulling her closer. She shivered with anticipation as he pressed between her legs and she felt the head of his shaft slip over her sensitive clit. And then he was entering her, stretching her tender flesh deliciously wide, pressing deep and hard just as he had promised until he reached her center.

"Oh!" Phil arched her back, her arms still pinned helplessly above her head as she felt him bottom out inside her. The familiar tingling grew to a new pitch until she could feel every nerve ending in her body prickling. This was what she needed, she felt instinctively. She needed Josh inside her, deep and hard and fast, filling her with himself in order to reach the elusive peak.

"You're so *tight*." Josh held still, concern clouding his eyes as he leaned over her. "You okay, Phil? I'm not hurting you, am I?"

It was so like her best friend to make sure she was all right even though he had to be dying to move, dying to take her. At any rate, she knew she was dying to feel him move inside her. It was true that she felt full and stretched open. But it was immensely pleasurable. She shook her head firmly to let him know she was all right and to prove it, she thrust up with her pelvis, grinding against him in a way that could leave no doubt about exactly how she felt.

Josh groaned low in his throat and pulled back until he was almost out of her before plunging in again. Phil gasped and tilted her pelvis to meet him, feeling warm prickling sensations shoot up her spine as he thrust into her, giving her everything he had.

She could feel the pleasure building inside her, cresting higher with every thrust. She was already so close, brought almost to the edge by the way he had tasted her and pressed his fingers and tongue inside her. Phil knew it wouldn't take long for her to come and when she did, she was going to come so *hard*.

"Josh...*Josh!*" She was moaning his name out loud now, unable to help herself, unable to stop and not caring a bit. She wrapped her legs around his lean, muscular hips and urged him on. She could feel herself getting closer and closer to a complete meltdown and she wanted it—she worked for it, moving her hips in time with his.

"*Phil.*" Josh groaned her name even as he released her hands and pulled her closer. "God...love you so much," he told her as he pressed deeply into her body. "Come for me, baby. Want to hear you come—*feel* you coming all around me."

It was as though his words triggered something deep inside her. Phil felt the tingling sensation build to a climax of overwhelming proportions, washing over her in wave after wave of pleasure as she cried out beneath him. Josh moaned and pressed deeply into her, pulsing inside her as he allowed her orgasm to trigger his own.

"Josh," she gasped as the brilliant sensations burst inside her. "Oh no...no...n...*Yes!*" As the word left her lips, she felt something explode deep within and she was suddenly shivering with the familiar Pop Rocks in Diet Coke sensation of a wish granted. Or, in this case, she realized, a curse lifted.

It was Josh that had done this for her. His love, his willingness to listen to her and stick by her. It was his need for her that awakened her need for him. Without him she might never have been free. Without him she would still be stuck in a miserable failing relationship wondering why her life sucked and feeling powerless to change it. Tears rose to her eyes and poured down her cheeks in a warm wet flood at both her realization and her release.

"Phil?" Josh's voice sounded almost panicked. "Phil, oh, God—did I hurt you?"

Poor Josh, he must think I cry every time I have sex. She did her best to wipe at the tears smearing her cheeks.

"I'm sorry," she managed to say. "It's just...just that I love you. I love you *so much.*"

"Oh, no!" Josh looked crushed. "God, Phil, please don't say that. I'm so sorry, I just..." His brown eyes filled with remorse.

She realized that he must still think she was saying the opposite of everything she felt. "No, no!" She reached up to cup his cheek in her hand and looked at him earnestly. "No, Josh— you cured me. You broke the curse. I can say what I want now—what I really feel."

"Honestly?" He looked at her hopefully. "You really can?"

Phil nodded. "I really can."

He narrowed his eyes. "What did you think of Alison's suit?"

"Tacky," Phil said promptly.

"Dickhead Junior?"

"He's a bastard—and he's addicted to some kind of weird Japanese Internet porn," Phil added as an afterthought.

"Hmm." Josh raised an eyebrow but refused to be deterred. "This is the big one, Phil. How do you feel about éclairs?"

"I hate, loathe, and despise them," Phil told him. Then she pulled him closer and gave him a hungry kiss on the mouth. "But *you* I can't live without. All right?"

Josh gave a shaky laugh, the corners of his eyes crinkling with relief. "Whew. I was worried there for a minute." He bent his head and nuzzled her cheek. "I guess that I've wanted you for so long, it's just hard to believe I've really got you."

"You've got me all right," Phil told him. "And there's no getting rid of me now, Bowman." She sighed contentedly. "I'm so *glad* the curse is broken."

"Ya know, Swann, in every fairy tale I ever read, it only takes a kiss to break the evil spell."

Phil laughed and pulled him closer. "Well these are modern times, so it takes a little more. Sometimes you have to stop sitting around wishing for things and make your own magic."

"Mmm." Josh nuzzled her neck, lapping at the sensitive skin of her throat until she shivered. "Speaking of magic, I wouldn't mind making a little more of it with you right now."

Phil grinned at him. "Well, what are you waiting for? I wouldn't mind either."

Josh kissed her ravenously before pulling back to look into her eyes. "Your wish," he said, "is my command."

Epilogue

"So BB&D didn't fire you?" Cass eyed her older sister with surprise. Phil was lounging on the brown leather sofa beside Rory, looking happier than Cass could ever remember seeing her. Phil was wearing a breezy pale pink sundress and her long blond hair was loose around her shoulders instead of up in a tight knot at the back of her head. She wasn't wearing neutral lipstick either, just some gloss on her rose red lips to highlight their color. Her eyes were the deep dusky blue that meant twilight must be falling outside.

"Nope, they didn't fire us—we left. And as a matter of fact after Josh and I put in our notice they offered us generous severance packages, too." Phil smiled and twirled a piece of her sparkly hair between her fingers. "*And* I got that letter of recommendation that Dickson Senior promised me. It makes me sound like one of the greatest undiscovered legal minds of our time. Not that I'm complaining."

"What? But I thought Josh punched your boss!" Rory was looking at her oldest sister with wide eyes.

"He did. But he punched Dickson while he was in the act of assault and battery—on me."

"Wow." Cass couldn't help giving her sister a look of admiration. "Spoken like a true lawyer. So you told them you'd sue and they forked over the severance?"

"Well, it didn't hurt that I knew some very, let's say *embarrassing* details about some of their senior employees." Phil grinned and flipped her hair over one shoulder. "Some details they wanted to keep strictly confidential."

"Damn, Phil, what's gotten into you?" Cass demanded. In

the week since her sister's birthday wish, Phil had changed from a mousy, uncertain girl to a happy, confident woman. She knew some of that had to do with Phil finally getting together with Josh but she thought it also had to do with the fact that she had broken the fairy godmother's magical hold over her. Never again would Phil have to accept a birthday wish, because the FG's magic no longer worked on her. In fact, she didn't even get her daily éclair anymore, which made her blissfully happy. *Too bad she couldn't have fixed it so Rory and I don't have to take our birthday wishes anymore too,* Cass thought with a touch of envy.

"That is *so* romantic," Rory sighed, cupping her chin in one hand. "To think that Josh punched him to save you. I wish *I* could find a knight in shining armor like that."

"Watch your mouth, Rory—you know better than to throw around the 'w' word like that," Cass admonished.

"I don't know what you're so upset about." Rory looked sulky. "After all, *you're* the one whose birthday is coming up next. Have you even thought of a wish? Do you want to have a strategy session?"

"Not right now, Rory. I've been so busy trying to get this show together down at the ICU gallery that I haven't had time to think about what to wear, let alone what to wish for." Cass looked at Phil. "Speaking of dreams come true and wishes granted, where is Mister 'Knight in Shining Armor', anyway?"

"In the kitchen helping Nana. Everything has to be perfect for *Arturo* and she asked him to make his specialty—balsamic glazed chicken. "

Cass frowned. "Who is this 'Arturo' and how did she meet him? Are we sure there's no witchcraft involved here?"

"She said she found him on an online dating service." Rory shrugged. "According to Nana, he's hot."

"Hot?" Cass snorted. "Are you serious? Between the boy scouts and the senior citizens Nana wouldn't know hot if it bit her on the ass."

Rory shrugged. "That's what she said."

"You know," Phil said thoughtfully. "I kind of thought maybe she and Mister Clausen might get together after all that mess with the potion and the poodles. I mean they *are* about the same age."

"Nothing doing." Cass shook her head. "She told me he was a dirty old man and she didn't want to have anything to do with him or his nasty dogs. I just didn't know she was looking for a man online. Now I don't know *what* to expect."

Phil smiled. "I wouldn't worry about it too much—Nana has pretty good taste in men. She loves Josh to death and he thinks she's great. Even after she accidentally conjured his favorite pair of jeans full of fish."

"She *what?*" Rory asked.

Phil smiled. "Well, he had broken the zipper and he was asking her if she knew how to fix it. But when he said zipper for some reason Nana thought he asked for a *kipper*—you know those weird smoked fish they eat for breakfast in England?" Cass and Rory nodded. "Only in typical Nana fashion, she didn't just get one—she got like, I don't know, a whole *bathtub* full. But all in Josh's jeans. *And* they were still alive." Phil laughed. "You should have seen the look on his face! Luckily he wasn't wearing them at the time."

"But wasn't he mad?" Cass was so used to Phil's dour ex-fiancé's temper that it was hard to get used to her current flame's easygoing ways.

"Nope." Phil grinned. "He just laughed after he got over the shock. We were cleaning up fish for hours, though—those suckers are slippery!"

"Wow," Rory murmured. "I can't believe he didn't even get a little bit upset. That's wonderful, Phil."

"Well it's certainly an improvement over Mister 'Stick up his Ass' Christian," Cass acknowledged. "Speaking of which, has he accepted that you two are broken up yet?"

Phil sighed. "I think so but it took a while. At first he kept calling me and demanding that I forget all this 'breaking up foolishness' and come back to him. But I think I made myself pretty clear when Josh and I went to pick up my things yesterday."

"Ooo, what happened?" Rory asked excitedly.

"Well, I went during business hours hoping to find him out of the apartment so I could get my stuff in peace but he was there anyway—almost like he'd been waiting for me." Phil frowned. "He started in right away with the same old song and dance, 'Oh, Philly-babe, how can you want to leave after all we've been through together?'" Phil did a surprisingly good imitation of her ex that made them all snort with laughter.

"Did Josh punch him?" Rory wanted to know, still giggling.

"Of course not—did he?" Cass couldn't imagine Phil's even-tempered boyfriend punching anyone but he'd done once it before and if anyone deserved a knuckle sandwich, in her opinion, it was Christian.

"Well, he *tried* to stay out of it as much as he could. Besides, I can stand up for myself, you know." Phil lifted her chin. "I told Christian that I deserved to be with someone who really loved and valued me, someone who believed in my abilities and cared enough to be faithful to me. And then I asked him if he knew what color my eyes were."

"Oh, that's *good*. What did he say?" Cass was getting as excited as Rory now. She couldn't help it—she had never been able to stand Phil's ex and it was great to hear that he had gotten what was coming to him.

Phil shrugged. "He stuttered and stumbled around and but in the end he really didn't know. So then I asked Josh, 'honey, what color are my eyes?' and he said, 'what color is the sky?'" She grinned. "Then Christian looked at us like we were both insane and said he was washing his hands of me and he hoped I'd be happy going to law school where I clearly didn't belong. *Then* Josh punched him."

"Oh my God! Did he bleed?" Rory was on the edge of her seat.

"Don't be so bloodthirsty, Rory," Cass scolded. She looked at Phil. "Well—did he?"

Phil smiled. "Let's just say I don't think I'll hear anymore about how we *have* to get back together. I think Josh's punch finally got it through his thick head that we're finished."

"I'm glad to hear that but *damn*—he had a lot of nerve." Cass frowned. "You should have told him you and Josh are already making plans for the wedding—really rubbed it in."

Phil blushed prettily. "Well, it's not like we're getting married tomorrow. We haven't even set a date or gotten the ring yet."

"Where are you going to live?" Rory asked. "You're not leaving us, are you?"

Phil shrugged. "Even if I do, it won't be for good. I'm looking into different law schools right now so wherever I get accepted, that's where we'll go, at least until I finish school. Josh can get a job anywhere and he said he'll come with me wherever it is."

"That is so—" Rory started.

"We know—*romantic*," Cass finished for her, shaking her head. She was glad that Phil's situation had worked out so well but she thought that Rory needed to take off her rose-colored glasses. "Honestly, Rory," she told her younger sister. "You need to get your head out of the clouds and realize that life isn't all peaches and cream and trouser trout."

"Hey—it was kippers Nana put in Josh's pants, not trout!" Phil protested. She winked. "Not to say that his trouser trout isn't pretty spectacular because it definitely is."

"Whatever." Cass rolled her eyes. "The point is—we're not living in a fairy tale here."

Rory grinned at her. "That doesn't mean we can't live happily ever after. Look at Phil."

"Phil is the exception and not the rule," Cass grumped. "At least in this family." She knew she sounded like a world class grouch but she couldn't help it. Her own life was tied up in knots. Brandon still refused to pose for her and she was supposed to be getting a show together in one of the most prestigious galleries in town but she was in a real slump with her art. Not that she would make a wish about *that*—her art was about the only part of her life the fairy godmother hadn't screwed up and she didn't intend to let her start now. But then, what *was* she going to make a wish about? Her birthday was in less than a month and Cass just knew the FG was going to hold a grudge. How could she make a request the malicious fairy couldn't screw up on purpose to get revenge? Just thinking about it made her head hurt.

"Well I just..." Phil began and then the front doorbell rang.

"I'll get it." Rory hopped up and ran to the door. She opened it to reveal a tall man who looked to be somewhere in his forties with blue-black hair and piercing gray eyes.

"Excuse me, ladies," he said in delightfully accented English. "But I am here for Minerva. Is she available?"

"Wow." Rory stood back from the door, her jaw hanging open. "*You're* Arturo?"

"I am he." The tall man stepped inside and made an

abbreviated bow. "And you must be her lovely granddaughters that she so often speaks of. But tell me, where is my silver-haired beauty?"

"Oh, Arturo, is that you?" Nana swept into the room, a smile on her plump face. She was wearing a mint green silk tea-length gown and her hair was up in an elaborate new style.

"Minerva, my darling, you are too kind to invite me to your lovely home for dinner." Arturo made a sweeping bow and kissed her hand.

"Oh, my! You're very welcome," Nana fluttered. "Why don't you go on ahead into the dining room and I'll be there directly to fix us some drinks?" She pointed the way but before Arturo followed, Josh came into the room. He and Arturo shook hands briefly and then he said,

"Dinner is served. Better get it while it's hot."

"Mmm, sounds delicious." Phil stood up and went to give him a kiss on the cheek.

"Not as delicious as you." He nibbled her neck.

"Get a room," Cass said, only half-joking.

"Well, why don't we all go in to dinner?" Nana was smiling broadly but as she was about to lead the way into the dining room Cass pulled her back.

"Hang on a minute Nana," she said and took a surreptitious sniff. But all she could smell was her grandmother's perfume—there wasn't even a whiff of potion.

"Yes, Cassandra, dear?" Nana raised an elegant silver eyebrow at her.

"What's going on with Arturo there?" Cass asked. "He seems, uh, tall dark and handsome and all that, but don't you think he's a little *young* for you, Nana?"

"I beg your pardon." Nana lifted her chin. "You are only as old as you feel, my dear. And at heart I'm still the sixteen-year-old waif with lavender hair who ran away with your grandfather."

"But...but..." Cass shook her head, bemused. "But how did you do it?" she asked at last. "I don't smell any potion."

"I didn't use any." Nana gave her a secretive smile and patted her cheek. "It's as I told your sister, my dear, sometimes you have to make your own magic. But I have a feeling that you're going to find that out for yourself very soon. Isn't your birthday coming up?"

About the Author

Evangeline Anderson is a registered MRI tech who would rather be writing. And yes, she is nerdy enough to have a bumper sticker that says "I'd rather be writing." Honk if you see her! She is thirty-something and lives in Florida with a husband, a son, and two cats. She had been writing erotic fiction for her own gratification for a number of years before it occurred to her to try and get paid for it. To her delight, she found that it was actually possible to get money for having a dirty mind and she has been writing paranormal and sci-fi erotica steadily ever since. To learn more about Evangeline Anderson, please visit www.evangelineanderson.com. Send an email to Evangeline at vangiekitty@aol.com or join her Yahoo! group to join in the fun with other readers as well as Evangeline!
http://groups.yahoo.com/group/evangelineandersonbookchat

True love is better than infatuation.

To Fat and Back
© *2008 Beverly Rae*

Carrie Flannagan dreams of Michael the Magnificent, the office hunk. He can have his pick of women, and his pick isn't Carrie, the office chubby. He's only got eyes for her best friend, Shiloh of the slender, smokin' hot body.

When Carrie accidentally-on-purpose breaks Michael's arm, a self-professed sorceress with a secret agenda of her own gives him a pill to magically heal the bones. That little pill also has an accidental-on-purpose side effect—one that makes him balloon to over three hundred pounds. To Carrie's surprise and delight, he turns to her for emotional comfort. But those new layers of fat on his body reveal a side of him that wasn't part of her fantasy.

Billy Whitman will put up with almost anything to be near to Carrie, even if she sees him only as a blend-into-the-background, dependable friend. Even if it means putting up with her fantasies about Michael, and being the clean-up man as Michael's life falls apart.

For now, he's willing to bide his time, hoping she will someday see the light—the light of love in his eyes.

Warning: Side effects of this title include, but are not limited to, the following: Snorting milk through your nose, laughing until your ribs hurt, drooling over handsome heroes, fanning uncontrollably during hot scenes and subsequent severe cravings for more of Beverly Rae's books. Do not read while driving or operating heavy machinery. May be consumed visually with friends (especially that special friend) or alone.

Available now in ebook and print from Samhain Publishing.

Enjoy the following excerpt from To Fat and Back...

"Ohmigod, ohmigod, ohmigod." Carrie rushed to Nate as others helped him stand up. Although obviously shaken, he didn't seem to have any major injuries as the others helped him along the hall toward the elevator.

Spinning away from Nate, Carrie leaned over the railing and stared at Michael's crumpled body on the landing below her. Already people rushed to him, offering him their help. *What have I done? Why in the world did I do such a horrendous thing? The authorities should lock me away forever. Ohmigod, I'm such a bad, bad person.*

Firm hands gripped her shoulders as she was jostled out of the way of the curious onlookers. "Carrie? Carrie, answer me. Are you all right?"

At first she thought she couldn't take her eyes off the prone Michael, as if God had already punished her by making her incapable of movement. But a hard shake, along with a body moving to block her view of her victim, broke her trance and she lifted her gaze to see Billy's concerned face searching hers. "W-what?"

He edged closer and tried again. "Carrie Bear, are you all right? You seemed almost comatose."

When she tried to shift position to see Michael again, he adjusted with her and kept her from looking. "Let me go. I have to get to him. I have to say I'm sorry. I have to—"

"No, Carrie. You don't. I won't let you."

He didn't understand. How could he? He had no way of knowing what an abominable monster she was. *She* hadn't known until a minute ago. "You don't understand, Billy. I have to. I'm the one—"

He brought his nose within a centimeter of hers, and whispered hard and low. "I understand. I do. I saw everything."

Why does he keep interrupting me? Wait! He saw me? Shame ripped through her and she couldn't look him in the eyes. "Ohmigod. Then you know what I did. You know how terrible I am."

"I know what happened because, yes, I saw it all. Michael

wasn't paying attention and he tripped over his own big feet. Or Nate's. Either way, it wasn't your fault."

She met his gaze and saw what he wasn't saying. He knew the truth, but wouldn't admit it. But why not? He wasn't the evil person who'd hurt Michael. They'd been friends for years, but would he cover for her? Should she let him?

A groan echoed up the stairs spurring Carrie into action as she pushed Billy away to see. Michael sat on a bench in the lobby, holding one arm next to his stomach. Yet it was the way he held his arm that tore at Carrie's heart. He—she—must've broken his arm. Although part of her didn't want to, the other half—the better half—of her propelled her body forward. She readied herself to face Michael and beg his forgiveness.

But what about the possible legal consequences? Would she go to jail? Was what she'd done called assault? Or worse, would a judge think she'd tried to murder Nate? Or Michael? Or both? She gulped even as the saliva in her mouth dried up and her shoulders slumped. She'd definitely lose her job. Yet no matter what punishment she'd have to face, she had to tell the truth. "I have to confess. I have to let everyone know I made him—them—fall." *Damn, even now all I can think about is Michael. What kind of pitiful person am I to forget about Nate?*

Billy took her arm and held her in one spot. "No. I refuse to let you confess. You don't deserve to be punished."

"But I did it. I hurt him—them—on purpose." She frowned and tried to remember. Had she really done it on purpose or had her subconscious taken over, anger at Nate dredging up the evil Carrie hiding within her? Michael had probably known about the bad joke, but had she wanted him to fall too? Could she plead temporary insanity? Still, the reason didn't matter. No matter what, she was to blame.

When Marla from accounting looked quizzically at them, Billy pivoted Carrie around to face him again and turned her away from the accountant. "Be quiet and listen to me."

"No, I have to explain. It's the right thing to do."

"Yeah, it is, but I won't let you. Sometimes doing what's right isn't what's right for you."

"Huh?" Why was he so determined to stop her? She gave him her meanest look and hoped it would do the trick. "You can't stop me."

But Billy's mean glare put hers to shame and had her glower scampering away like a dog with its tail between its legs. "Oh, yes, I can. I'll take the blame before I let you take it."

Her mouth dropped open and he reached over to close it for her. "Listen to me. You didn't do anything wrong, Carrie. Got it? And I won't let you say you did, either. I'd do anything for—" Billy clamped his mouth closed and nodded at the group of people surrounding Michael. "Who do you think they'll believe? You, the sweetest nicest girl in the whole damn company? Or me? The guy who's had argument after argument with Michael and who's always said Nate's an imbecile? Everyone will remember what happened in the boardroom not five minutes before they fell and they'll believe me when I tell them I did it."

She was torn, too confused to sort through all the thoughts jumbling in her mind. She studied the determination on his face and knew he'd take her punishment. Billy was ready to take the fall for her in an amazing demonstration of friendship. But how could she make yet another mistake by letting him cop to a crime she'd committed? What kind of friend was she? Could she find another way to tell everyone the truth and make them believe her?

"Carrie, trust me. No one has to know anything. Let Michael think he tripped. It is what he and Nate did, after all. They tripped. Why they tripped doesn't have to come out. I know it's wrong, but it's time you caught a break. Sorry, no pun intended. Besides, check him out. He's loving every minute of the attention."

She did as he said and watched as girl after girl fought their way to Michael's side. Michael, although obviously in pain, spoke to each woman in turn, flashing them his I'm-such-a-brave-guy-even-though-it-hurts-like-hell smile.

Shit. Even in pain the guy plays the ladies.

No magic for two weeks?
What's a fairy to do? Go to Vegas, of course!

Survival of the Fairest
© 2008 Jody Wallace

Princess Talista of the fairy clan Serendipity has been sent, like all young fairies, to a remote forest in humanspace for mandatory survival training. But headstrong Tali's got different ideas about where to spend two weeks without magic. What better place than Las Vegas to learn to live like humans, a *true* test of survival?

Tali might not blend, but she'd like to be shaken and stirred with stage magician Jake Story. Their attraction is instant and electric...and Tali senses there's more to Jake's show than flashy tricks.

Jake always knew he was different, even before he developed an unusual flair for hypnotism. He has no trouble mesmerizing the luscious Tali during act three, but the lights that appear around them when they kiss weren't part of the program.

When the authorities from Tali's homeland track the missing princess to Vegas, Jake and Tali end up on the run. In between magic experiments, evil gnomes and astonishing sex, Tali learns what it really means to be human—by falling in lust, followed closely by love.

But Tali's not human. And Jake doesn't believe in fairies. The truth will either bind them together—or tear the fairy realm apart.

Available now in ebook and print from Samhain Publishing.

hot
stuff

Discover Samhain!

GREAT
CHEAP
FUN

Discover eBooks!

THE FASTEST WAY TO GET THE HOTTEST NAMES

Get your favorite authors on your favorite reader, long before they're
out in print! Ebooks from Samhain go wherever you go, and work with
whatever you carry—Palm, PDF, Mobi, and more.

Samhain Publishing, Ltd.

WWW.SAMHAINPUBLISHING.COM

Breinigsville, PA USA
18 August 2009
222490BV00002B/4/P